AS THE ECHOES OF WAR REVERBERATE ACROSS A NATION, THE ROAD TO PEACE PROVES TO BE A BITTER AND BLOODY ONE....

GREELEY BROWN—His commitment to the Union cause has made him a hated figure to the rebels. Before this war is done, they've vowed to make him the honored guest . . . at a hanging party.

MIRIAM FRY—The one woman Greeley loves, she may be forced to repay his trust and sacrifice with the ultimate betrayal.

CAP FLETCHER—A rebel turned bushwhacker, he is the most feared man in the mountains of Tennessee, leaving his mark of violence in flesh and blood.

THATCHER BROWN—A New York newspaperman, he is about to experience the horrors of w~~ ~~~~~~ ~ Confederate prison.

AMY DEACO~~ ~~~~~~~~~~~~~~~~~~~~ spy are over. But she's de~~~~~~~~~~~~~~~~~~~~~~~~~ his war to the world . . . ev~~~~~~~~~~~~~~~~~~~~~~ the life of her unborn child.

BEN SCARLETT—For years he has fought his own war for emancipation . . . from whiskey. But now he may once again be losing the battle—and losing hope.

SALLY CLUNG—An aged mountain hermit, she's out to bring a dead man back to life and turn him into an avenging angel.

NANNY—A slave who sacrificed everything, including her own child, for freedom, she will now spend her new life in a desperate attempt to recover what she's lost.

Also by Cameron Judd

BOONE:
A Novel Based on the Life
and Times of Daniel Boone

CROCKETT OF TENNESSEE:
A Novel Based on the Life
and Times of David Crockett

PASSAGE TO NATCHEZ

The Mountain War Trilogy

THE SHADOW WARRIORS:
A Novel of Unionist Resistance
in Tennessee and North Carolina,
September 1860–January 1863

THE PHANTOM LEGION:
A Novel of Unionist Resistance
in Tennessee and North Carolina,
February 1863–December 1863

SEASON OF RECKONING:
A Novel of Unionist Resistance
in Tennessee and North Carolina,
January 1864–February 1866

Available from Bantam Books

Season of Reckoning

Book III in the Mountain War Trilogy

A Novel of Unionist Resistance
in Tennessee and North Carolina,
January 1864–February 1866

Cameron Judd

Bantam Books
New York • Toronto • London • Sydney • Auckland

To Matt

SEASON OF RECKONING

A Bantam Book/November 1997

ISBN 0–553–57390–X

Published simultaneously in the United States and Canada

Bantam Books are published by Bantam Books, a division of Bantam Doubleday Dell Publishing Group, Inc. Its trademark, consisting of the words "Bantam Books" and the portrayal of a rooster, is Registered in U.S. Patent and Trademark Office and in other countries. Marca Registrada. Bantam Books, 1540 Broadway, New York, New York 10036.

PRINTED IN THE UNITED STATES OF AMERICA

OPM   10   9   8   7   6   5   4   3   2   1

AN INTRODUCTORY NOTE . . .

During the grim days of the American Civil War, there was in the hills and mountains of western North Carolina and East Tennessee a large population of people, mostly rural and agrarian, who remained staunchly loyal to the Union while living within the bounds of the Confederacy. Some of these loyalists struggled, often vainly, to remain publicly neutral. Many others risked their freedom and even their lives to "stampede" through rebel-occupied territory and reach the Federal lines to volunteer service to the Union military. Others went underground or undercover within the Confederacy itself, acting as citizen insurgents, burning railroad bridges, fighting as irregulars, serving as Union spies, smugglers, bushwhackers, or "pilots" for those fleeing north for Union military service. Some smuggled both escaped slaves and fleeing loyalists along the Underground Railroad. For such "tories" the war experience was often not so much one of great battles between formal armies on vast battlefields, but gritty, brutal, underground warfare fought at their very doorsteps, often by men and women who never wore uniforms or held military commissions. These loyal hill people and mountaineers, isolated in the midst of a rebel-controlled region, saw the ugliest underbelly of the Civil

War. Many were deprived and abused, or conscripted into military service for a cause they opposed. Some were imprisoned for their political beliefs, some were murdered, and some were hanged under authority of the Confederacy.

Some endured and ultimately forgave. Others never did, and learned to dole out bitterness for bitterness, brutality for brutality.

Their story is seldom told. It is told here.

From far-off conquered cities
Comes a voice of stifled wail,
And the shrieks and moans of the homeless
Ring out like a dirge in the gale.

I've seen from the smoking village,
Our mothers and daughters fly;
I've seen where the little children
Sank down in the furrows to die.

In God's hand alone is vengeance!
But He strikes with the hands of men,
And His blight would wither our manhood,
If we smite not the smiter again.

—From S. Teackle Wallis
"The Guerrillas" (1864)

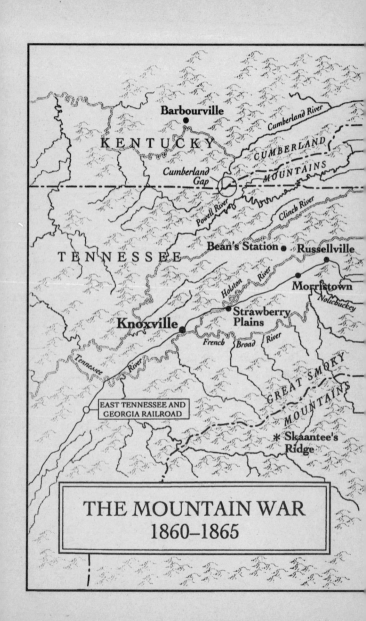

THE MOUNTAIN WAR
1860–1865

VIRGINIA

Clinch River

N. Fork Holston R.

Watauga

EAST TENNESSEE AND
VIRGINIA RAILROAD

River

Elizabethton

Lick Creek

Colter
✶

Jonesborough

Greeneville

River

Shelton Laurel Cr.

Warm Springs

Marshall

NORTH CAROLINA

Asheville

0   20   40

Scale of Miles

✶ fictional sites

Part I

MIRIAM

Chapter 1

January 1864, in the Carter County mountains,
East Tennessee

A wind colder than the glint of the intermittent moonlight howled down from the high ridges, stinging Greeley Brown's face and fingers, turning breath to ice that dangled from his whiskers. Squinting against darkness and cold, he gazed from the tree line across a mostly empty field that was once familiar but now foreign, and wondered why he bothered to pause here.

He wriggled the fingers of his left hand continually to keep them warm. A wound administered by a bushwhacker's saber some months ago had left his left arm and hand lacking much feeling, and he was ever aware of the danger of undetected frostbite. Those numb fingers could freeze to useless sticks before he knew it. Thus he kept them in motion, kept the warm blood pulsing.

Snowfall the night before had blanketed the gently sloping meadow that stretched before him, and disguised the blackened rubble of what had been a cabin in the midst of it . . . *his* cabin, lost back in '61 to rebels who had come to capture or kill him, but who had been forced to content themselves with merely burning him out. Anticipating the raiders, he hadn't been home when they came. Since that day, he had occupied nothing he considered a real home, only huts and shelters out in the laurel-tangled ridges. He lived in the high and lonesome places as one more of the legion of gaunt refugees who had been driven into isolation by war; human phantoms who haunted the mountains from Tennessee into the deep Carolina wilderness.

The moon, lost behind scudding clouds for the last two minutes, reemerged, bathing the field with light. Greeley stepped deeper into the tree's shadows—an instinctive move, avoiding the light, but for once unnecessary. He was sure he was alone. The biting cold, miserable as it was, provided the benefit of keeping rebels huddled near fires and shelters, not out scouting for underground Unionists, Confederate deserters, and conscription dodgers. At the moment, most of Longstreet's rebels here in the northeastern end of the state were in winter camps, trying to keep their bellies full and feet warm. Of course, it wasn't only Longstreet's regulars Greeley Brown had to worry about, but also the Home Guards and the irregulars; the civilian soldiers, bushwhackers, and mountain ruffians. Greeley hoped that tonight the weather was sufficiently cold to keep even them from ranging about.

Greeley pictured the rebels sitting in their huts or around their fires, complaining of the cold and lack of good provision. He thought: Let them suffer! Whatever the rebels endured, the loyal Union people of these mountains were enduring worse in this cursed war. Many a good Union man shivered this very night in poorly sheltered mountain camps, some in sight of homes to which they could not return for fear the rebels were watching. If the rebels agonized in this cold, let them recall that it wasn't the loyal Union folk of these mountains who had dragged the country into war. It wasn't they who had prodded and provoked Abe Lincoln into sending down his armies. It wasn't they who had turned the remote hills and mountain valleys of East Tennessee and western North Carolina into a hell where good men who dared to disagree with rebel sentiment were at risk of losing their lives.

Not all mountain Union men had been content to merely hide out. Many who had done so initially now enjoyed the relatively improved station of being regular Union soldiers. This was thanks in large part to Greeley Brown—which was the source of more pride than his social humility would let him admit. He had led many bands of Unionist "stampeders" out of these mountains and to the Union lines in Kentucky. Piloting Union recruits through hostile country was his calling, his duty, his service to his country, and the very reason he had been out roaming this night. He was fresh back from talking on the sneak to some who would be among his next stampeder band. Greeley's piloting work was an undercover enterprise from start to finish. His proficiency at it had led the Confederates to place a sizable reward on his head, and many rebels were eager to collect it. Greeley Brown had much reason to be a careful man.

Now, he hefted onto his left shoulder his lever-action Henry rifle, a highly accurate, sixteen-shot weapon that was a terror to rebels and a comfort to its owner, and stepped into the clearing. He reached the burned-out cabin, stopped, and sucked in a long, cold breath. Touching his eye, he dabbed away a tear before it could reach his beard and become one with the ice already clinging there. He hadn't expected this twinge of emotion. It wasn't as if his best days had been lived out here. Those days had been enjoyed elsewhere during a brief marriage to a wife who had died in childbirth. The child had died with her. A second woman whom he had later asked to marry him, whom he would have brought back to this very cabin, had refused him. So this cabin had never been more than a lonely bachelor's outpost, yet Greeley was struggling against tears and didn't know why.

Or maybe he did. This obliterated cabin symbolized what had happened to the world he'd known. So much was changed, ruined, destroyed, gone. Some war scars ran so deep that Greeley wondered how they could ever fade.

Greeley remained by the cabin rubble only a few minutes, then shook off the stiffening cold and began walking down toward the road, from there to continue his journey to his present home, if "home" was a word applicable to the latest of a continuing series of huts here and there through the Carter County mountains. He never dared stay in any one spot for long.

Nearly to the road, he stopped and turned toward the forest to his right. Movement, furtive and quick, back in the trees . . . The skin on the back of his neck and scalp grew tighter; his face was suddenly warm despite the icy wind. He heard the movement again. If it was human in origin, there was certainly more than one human generating it.

Fear struck like wind bursting through a shattered window. Had his instincts failed him? Was he not alone here after all? He hurried to the closest clump of trees and hid, waiting and listening. He heard only the whine of the wind and an occasional muffled thump of snow clumps blowing off trees to the ground. Then dogs emerged from the trees into the moonlight. A pack of skinny, cold curs. Greeley exhaled in relief, stepped out from hiding, and headed on down toward the road. The dogs barked at him, then stopped and wagged their tails, looking imploringly at him.

Greeley shooed them off. Cursed war. Even animals suffered more than usual since nature's two-legged creatures had started shooting at each other.

He went on to the road, crossed it, and reached a snowy path that threaded through the woods. The masking snow and darkness made the way hard, but he had traveled it many times and did not lose it. He would hike along it for two miles to reach his current dwelling, where he would struggle to get by until the designated day came for him to be off on the next stampeder run.

That run would not be exactly typical. All prior journeys had been to Kentucky. Now, for the first time, Greeley was going to lead a band to Knoxville, which had been taken by Burnside the prior year, and retained despite a strong effort by Longstreet to recapture the city.

A Knoxville journey ought to be an easier and shorter trip, but Greeley was nervous about it. He was accustomed to the Kentucky journeys, hazardous as they were, and didn't much like having to change. He was like most East Tennesseans: Conservative to the core, he preferred keeping things as they were unless there was a darned good reason to change them. It was one of the very traits that had made the great southern rebellion so unappealing to him from the outset.

Greeley awoke the next morning with a violent jump. He quickly left his blankets and reached for his rifle, breath coming in white gusts in the cold air of his little cabin hut, where the meager heat belched by the banked fire mostly went up the stick-and-mud chimney.

Clad in long underwear, he went to the door and slid back the little panel that covered a rifle hole drilled through the pine. Peering through, he grunted, set the rifle aside, and slid the locking bar from its hooks. Throwing open the door, he yelled out, "Corny, is that you?"

"Yes, it's me—you can see it's me!"

He sounded pretty worked up. "You are alone, ain't you, Corny?"

"Yes I'm alone. Lordy, Greeley, let me in there!"

Cornelius Shelton was a stocky piece of short-legged, bearded humanity descending the forested hill, toward the hut, in an obvious state of agitation. Corny's face was red with exertion, his breath steaming like bursts from a locomotive stack. A hearty mountaineer Greeley had known much of his adult life, Corny didn't get worked up without reason.

"Come in, Corny. What's wrong?"

Shelton ducked into the snow-shrouded cabin like a troll slipping under its bridge. "Greeley, there's trouble, some terrible, sorrowful trouble."

"What trouble?"

"Have you heard the name Fletcher lately?"

"No. Who's Fletcher?"

"A scoundrel. A murderer. He's the latest rebel devil to come in from Virginia, and he's got him a band of, I don't know, thirty or more with him, and he's got ties to the local Home Guards, though I don't know that they're what you'd call *official* ties. He and his men got good horses, good weapons. I don't know if he's regular military, but they say he's claiming he was sent to catch conscription dodgers and haul them in. But that ain't what he's doing."

Greeley rubbed the back of his stiff neck. "So what is he doing, then?"

"Plundering. Horse stealing. Insulting Union women in ways a decent man don't speak of. Burns a little cross-mark scar onto his saddle for every Union man he murders or whose house he sets ablaze. I hear he's burned at least two houses in Carter County so far, and a sight more in Johnson."

"So why haven't I heard of this fellow, if he's doing so much as that? And why'd you pick this morning to come tell me about him?"

"You ain't heard of him because he ain't been in this county long. He's been over in Johnson County. Now he's here, in Carter County. And Greeley . . . Tom Wilmoth and his younger boy, they've been hung. They're dead as they can be, and Fletcher done it."

Greeley's legs went weak and his empty stomach gave a sickening heave. "Dead."

"That's right. I found them myself, at sunrise, hanging in eye-shot of my house." Shelton's voice went tight and his eyes reddened. "I heard sounds in the woods last night, Greeley. Voices and maybe a yell, but I didn't do nothing. I closed up my shutters and sat by the door with my rifle, but that's all. I should have done something . . . but I didn't know. I thought maybe some of the Home Guard had come after me."

That was a reasonable fear. Greeley had warned Corny several times that he was spending too much time at home, making it easy for the Home Guard to find him if they decided to come looking. "You couldn't have done nothing but get your own self killed, Corny." Greeley was trembling all over. "Are they still hanging?"

"Yes. Lord help me, I didn't know what to do when I seen them. All I could think of was to come fetch you. It's ugly, Greeley. Them hanging there, right where my wife and children can see them by just looking out the window. I should have covered their faces at least, so my children wouldn't have to see."

"I wonder if Tom's wife knows."

"I doubt she does. Tom's been scouting lately, ain't been about his place much. He was probably caught in his camp."

Greeley ran his fingers through his hair. "How do you know it was this Fletcher who hung them?"

"By the cross. It's a . . . but you just come see, Greeley. You'll see what I'm talking about."

They moved swiftly on foot, treading silently through the snowy woods, keeping watch as they went.

Fletcher. Greeley repeated the name in his mind. *Fletcher.* Another rebel ruffian bent on violence toward Union folk. The last thing this county needed. He thought of Tom Wilmoth's wife, Florence, a fine, quiet, religious woman who cared nothing about the war, took no side in it, and who actually trembled at every mention of it. Poor Flory! How would she get by with Tom murdered? How would she stand losing a husband and a son?

Greeley wriggled his numb fingers against the cold and cursed the Confederacy. How was it that a rebel government and military force that seemed to have a shortage of every-thing, had such a seeming profusion of men ready to inflict every misery they could on the loyal Union people of the mountains? When Burnside had marched into Knoxville the prior September, with hordes of cheering Unionists lining the roads and trailing in his wake to welcome him, Greeley had hoped that better times had finally come to the highland loyal-ists. Instead everything had grown worse. Federal troops were concentrated at Knoxville and Chattanooga rather than in the loyal rural upper eastern counties. There was little significant Federal protection for the mountain loyalists. So these people bore the brunt of rebel anger. Stories of atrocities were spread-ing at an alarming pace, and Greeley had never seen more de-mand for his piloting services. It was growing ever more hazardous to be a Union man and remain in the mountains, and those who had held out this long, primarily because they feared leaving their families unguarded, were now beginning to take flight out of necessity.

How much more dangerous would the mountains be now, with this Fletcher fellow roaming about? And Greeley had heard of another Virginian leading a band of rebel avengers, one Captain R. C. Bozen. The prior autumn, yet another rebel military man, Colonel V. A. Witcher, Jr., had rampaged through the region, making his name infamous and bragging about the number of "Lincolnites" he killed. One of his more bloody escapades had drawn comparisons to a slaughter of loy-alists in North Carolina's mountainous "Bloody Madison County" back in January of '63.

"Will you tell Tom's wife what happened, Greeley?" Shel-ton asked. "I don't know that I've got the courage to do it."

Greeley despised the prospect of such a miserable duty, but said, "I'll tell her, if nobody else will." He had done that same task with other families this season. He hated it above all other things, except the cursed Confederacy itself.

Chapter 2

The hanging bodies were pale and pitiful. Greeley saw at a glance that the Wilmoths hadn't died swiftly. As in most mountain lynchings, death had come not with a merciful fast snap of the neck, but a slow, agonizing choking.

It was snowing hard, white streaks blurring the terrible sight. Greeley stared at the corpses swinging in the wind. Body heat had abandoned the dead forms hours before and now snow clung to their hair and shoulders.

"See the mark, Greeley?" Shelton asked in a quiet tone. "There on their faces. That's Fletcher's cross."

Greeley stepped closer, squinting. On the left cheek of each hanged victim was a cross-mark cut, sliced into their flesh by a sharp blade. Blood was crusted abundantly around the cuts, showing that they had been inflicted before death, while the hearts were still pumping blood.

"Why a cross, Corny? Is that some sort of wicked religious joke or something?"

"No. It's the Confederate cross, like on the Stars and Bars flag," Shelton replied. "Fletcher marks them he kills with the rebel sign."

Greeley stared at the ugly slashes. The snowfall began to

slow. He glanced toward Corny's nearby house and saw two of his children standing on the porch, watching. It was atrocious, children having to see something like this. "Let's cut them down, Corny."

Try as they would to make a dignified removal of the bodies, there was still something loathsome and ugly in how they thumped to the ground and lay in the snow with eyes partially open and glazed, mouths in a now permanent half-gape, tongues frozen to their teeth.

"What do we do with them now?" Shelton asked, folding his pocketknife closed.

"We have no good way to carry them, but I don't want to just leave them. You got a horse or anything?"

"No. I lost my last horse to thieves a month ago."

"We'll have to carry them ourselves, then." It was a dreadful prospect. "But we'll leave them before we reach sight of the Wilmoth house. Seeing us toting her dead husband and son in on our backs would be no way for Flory Wilmoth to find out what's happened."

"Us? So you want me to go with you?"

"Well, I sure can't carry both of them myself."

"I ain't going all the way to that house, Greeley. I couldn't bear it. I'll stay with the bodies while you go tell."

"If that's how it has to be, then so it will be. But blast you, Corny, I don't much appreciate it, you leaving the worst of this job to me. You think I want to have to bear this news alone?"

"I can't help it, Greeley. I'm weak that way, and I admit it."

Greeley looked at the dead. "So how old was this poor boy here?" he asked.

"Fifteen, I believe," Shelton replied.

"Fifteen." A mere boy of fifteen, dying so hard a death, and having his face cut on besides. It was obscene. Fifteen years old.

As Greeley labored along under the dead weight of Tom Wilmoth, he thought how hideous a parade this was, he and Shelton hauling the frozen bodies of dead men through the forest. They avoided the road, though it made for harder travel, for two reasons: The prospect of encountering some stray traveler while engaged in such a bizarre and ugly job was embarrassing, somehow, and both feared that Fletcher and his band might still be about.

Shelton and Greeley were exhausted when they reached the ridge beyond which stood the Wilmoth house. They dumped the bodies on the ground, too worn-out to care how roughly they did it this time, and stood huffing, looking at one another and then at the grim burden they had just cast off.

"See if you can lay them out to look as decent as you can, in case Flory or her other boy comes running here when I tell her," Greeley instructed when he had his wind back. "I want her first sight of them to be as easy on her as we can make it."

"I can't make them look good, not with their faces carved on."

"I know. Do the best you can." Greeley drew in a deep breath and said, "Well, I'll go on now. Think about me. I dread having to tell her."

"I will. You're a strong man to do this. Stronger than me."

Greeley made his way up the ridge. *Stronger than me.* No. Greeley knew he wasn't strong. He just did what had to be done, as much as he hated it.

Pausing at the ridgetop, he looked down on the tiny log house that had been home to Tom Wilmoth, his wife, and two sons. At one time there had been three other Wilmoth children, but one had died while still a baby, and the other two had drowned in the Doe River. The Wilmoths' situation reminded Greeley of his own tragic childhood days, when he had lost a father and several siblings, and seen his mother become a hateful, bitter woman because of her loss. The necessity of being mature had fallen early upon Greeley's shoulders; perhaps, he thought, that was why he was strong enough to do what he was doing right now, while Corny Shelton, who had enjoyed a happy and settled home as a boy, could not.

Greeley stared at the house a full two minutes, trying mentally to prepare the right words to break such sad news. But there were no right words. He sighed and started down the ridge, then stopped again, noting something odd.

No smoke spilled from the cabin's chimney. A snowy, cold day—and no smoke.

Greeley's breath came faster. His heart thumped loudly.

He headed down the slope on a run, reached the flat, then moved slowly toward the cabin, full of dread.

"Miz Wilmoth!" he called. "Flory Wilmoth, are you in there?"

The door opened slowly, and a woman he knew but at this moment scarcely recognized emerged. She was clad only in a thin, torn dress, and her bare and bony arms held a shotgun. She leveled it clumsily at Greeley.

"Flory, put that down! It's me, Greeley! Greeley Brown!" He lowered his Henry rifle into the snow and spread his arms, the right arm rising higher than the permanently injured left one. "See? It's just me. It's all right."

Florence Wilmoth let the shotgun sag and fall to her feet. She sobbed aloud, putting her hands to her face.

Greeley picked up his rifle and came forward. *Why is she crying? Does she already know?* Stepping onto the porch, he picked up her fallen shotgun as well and cradled both weapons in his left arm. He put a hand on her shoulder and peered at her.

"Flory, what's wrong?"

"Billy's dead!" she screeched. "My Billy, he's dead, and I don't know where Tom and Frank are!"

"Flory, let's step inside. It's cold out here."

"Billy's dead! He's dead!"

Billy . . . the eldest son. So Fletcher got him, too, Greeley thought. Florence Wilmoth was even more bereaved than he had known, and worse, than she yet knew herself.

"Let's step inside, Flory," he repeated. "Don't you have a fire today? It's cold. I'll build you a fire."

She nodded, weeping quietly. Greeley gently pushed her into the cabin and followed.

The fire had been dead since the night before. The one-room cabin was frigid. On one of the beds in the corner lay the graying form of Billy Wilmoth. His eyes were three-quarters closed. No steam rose from his nostrils or lips.

Florence Wilmoth stumbled to the bed and sat on the side of it. Tears streaming, she mumbled and muttered and stroked back the hair of her dead son. Greeley looked for signs of violence done to the boy and saw none, but the covers were pulled to his chest, so he couldn't know what might be hidden. He was sure this must have been Fletcher's work. Someone must have set him upon the Wilmoth men, and he had carried the task out with thoroughness, killing one here, two out in the mountains.

Greeley stood by the bed and rested his hand on the woman's shoulder. "How'd it happen, Flory?"

"Fever," she said, surprising him. "He's had the fever so bad. Days now. Last night he was so very sick . . . and then he stopped breathing. Just stopped. He's dead, Mr. Brown. My boy's dead."

So it *wasn't* Fletcher! Greeley began to tremble, his tongue growing thick in his drying mouth as he realized that now the news he brought would strike all the harder. Had Fletcher caused Billy Wilmoth's death, Florence Wilmoth might already have a strong suspicion that her husband and second son were dead, too. As it was, he would have to break it to her cold.

"Flory, why did you meet me at the door with that shotgun?" He asked the question mostly to delay having to deliver his news.

"Because there were men, riders, out there last night. I don't know who. They came by, I heard them stop, but no one came to the door. I heard them ride on."

It must have been Fletcher. Why he had chosen not to stop, Greeley couldn't guess. Maybe he already had Tom and Frank Wilmoth with him at the time, and Tom had successfully pleaded with him to leave his wife and ailing son alone. Maybe he had come intending to hang the Wilmoths in sight of their own house, and Tom, to spare his wife the shock, had been able to persuade Fletcher that this wasn't his house, and led the marauders to Corny's place instead. Who could know? It didn't matter now.

Greeley went to the fireplace, laid in kindling and firewood from the supply beside the hearth, and got a warming blaze going within minutes. He found it sad to picture poor, bereaved Florence Wilmoth passing the night in this dark place, so full of grief over her dead Billy that she hadn't even noticed the absence of light and heat.

He got the fire going to his satisfaction, then went back to the bed, pulling up a chair and sitting down beside her. She was still stroking Billy's hair, but for the moment, her tears were gone.

"Flory, I need you to look at me."

She did, and he found it hard to hold her gaze. "Flory, you've had a hard blow struck you with the death of your son here. And now I must give you news that'll strike you harder yet. God knows I hate to have to do it."

She didn't seem to comprehend. Struggling to get the words out, Greeley said, "Flory, Tom and Frank are gone."

She actually smiled a little. "I know they're gone, Mr. Brown. They've been scouting for a long time now. They come home when they can. Billy was scouting with them, too, until he took sick. Tom brought him home to his mama when he took sick."

"Flory, what I'm trying to tell you is . . . Tom and Frank are dead. I'm sorry."

She looked confused. "Dead?"

"Yes. I'm sorry. It was rebels, apparently some under a Virginia ruffian named Fletcher. They must have found them out scouting. They hung them from a tree. I'm sorry. I'm so very sorry."

She looked past him, staring at the fire, brows knitting into a frown. "Tom's dead? And Frank? No, no. You must be wrong, Mr. Brown."

"I ain't wrong, Flory. I wish I was, but I ain't. Corny Shelton found them this morning. They was hung over near his house."

She looked at Billy again and silently went back to stroking his hair.

"Do you understand what I've told you, Flory?"

"Yes. I'm alone now. My husband and my boys, they're all dead. All of them."

He had expected wails and tears, but there were none. Her calm manner was more unsettling to him than an emotional outburst would have been.

"Who did you say done it, Mr. Brown?"

"Corny Shelton believes it was a rebel captain out of Virginia, named Fletcher. He and his men have been in Johnson County, but now it appears he's come here."

"Fletcher. That's a pretty name, Fletcher. Tom and me thought about naming Billy that when he was born. But we didn't. We named him Billy."

Greeley didn't know what to say to that.

"Poor Billy," she said. "Poor Billy, and Tom, and Frank . . ."

"Flory, I've dreaded having to bring you this news. I know there's no comfort to give you. All I can do is remind you that there's plenty of others hereabouts who have had such losses since this cursed war began. They can give you help and such. They'll know how you'll feel." His words, well-intended, sounded hollow and worthless as soon as he said them.

"They're all in heaven now," she said. "They were all good Christians. My boys have been in church every Sunday since they was small, up until the war came and they had to stay hid out."

"Yes. There's no suffering or war for them now."

"I'm left alone," she said. "No one left for me. I wish I was in heaven, too, with them."

"I know. It's so hard to be left behind in such times."

"Where's their bodies, Mr. Brown?"

"Near by, over the ridge. Corny's with them. We carried them here. Corny and me will bury them for you, if you want. Maybe you'll want us to fetch a preacher and have a burying service over them."

She thought about it. Still that strange, disturbing calm. She continued to stroke Billy's hair all the while. She shook her head. "No. No need for a funeral. If you and Mr. Shelton will lay them away for me, that's all that will be needed."

"Are you sure? You want no scriptures nor prayers spoke over them?"

"I can read my own scripture and speak my own prayers." She looked at Greeley and smiled, startling him. "I'm glad there's heaven, Mr. Brown. It must be so much a finer place than this world. No wars, no fever, nobody dying, ever and ever."

"Yes. You want me to go fetch in the bodies now?"

She smiled again, as if he had just offered her a welcome cup of tea. "Yes, please. If you'll do that, I'll appreciate it so much."

"It's fine for me to leave you here alone just now, then? You want me to stay a bit longer?"

"No, no. You go on and fetch my men. Bring them home. I'll just sit here with Billy, and we'll talk about heaven."

He nodded, standing. He leaned her shotgun against the

wall beside the bed and picked up his own Henry rifle. "I'll go now. I do need to tell you before I do that this Fletcher, he put a mark with a knife onto their faces. It was a wicked and evil thing to do, but he done it, and I wanted you to know so you wouldn't be so shocked when you saw it."

"They were already dead when he did it?" For the first time since he broke the news, there was a touch of emotion in her voice, a pleading tone in her question.

"Yes," Greeley lied. "They were already dead." He'd be sure to wipe away the crusted blood from their faces before bringing them down to her, so she wouldn't see the truth.

"I'm glad of that," she said. "I'd have hated for them to have felt someone cut on them."

Greeley turned quickly, about to break down and cry. What a miserable world this was, what a wicked place! Right now he despised the entire human race for having brought such a foul thing as war into existence.

Greeley turned and headed for the door. She began to sing softly, words from an old mountain hymn: *I am a poor, way-faring stranger, while traveling through this world below, but there's no sickness, toil or danger, in that bright land to which I go . . .*

He bit his lip, hard. He swung the door open. . . . *And though the dark may gather 'round me, and though my way seems rough and steep, still beauteous fields lie just before me, where God's redeemed their vigils keep. . . .*

He closed the door and headed at a fast pace across the snowy yard and toward the ridge.

When he was halfway up the ridge, he heard the blast of her shotgun, loud despite the muffling of the cabin walls. He jerked in surprise, then realized he should not have been surprised at all. He should have seen it coming. He should have stayed with her, or at the very least taken the shotgun.

Greeley sank to his knees in the snow, leaning against his rifle and feeling the greatest sorrow rise within him.

When the burying was done, and while the terrible but familiar news of another tragedy spread from mountain community to mountain community, Greeley Brown remained hidden away in his own little cabin for three days, paralyzed by a deep, frightening depression, deeper even than that which tortured him after his wife and child had died.

In the depths of his depression he was also reflective. He thought back to the beginning of the war, remembering how some people, mostly rebels and mostly young, had actually looked forward to the conflict. Greeley had never looked forward to it. He had known it would bring suffering and sorrow and loss on all sides. But in his worst imaginings he had not anticipated a situation so terrible as what was becoming so familiar in these mountains.

He had figured it would be over by now. He had looked forward to a sweeping Federal invasion as far back as late '61. In that anticipation he had become one of the Unionist bridge burners who destroyed several key railroad spans to open the door to a Union insweep. That invasion hadn't come, diverted by the Federals themselves in a sudden change of strategy. Greeley and his fellow bridge burners had found themselves infamous and hunted, condemned in advance by Confederate proclamations that bridge burners would be hanged after a drumhead trial. Several men, unfortunate enough to be caught, had in fact died in just that way.

Greeley had been lucky. He had evaded the rebels so far, and this without ever stepping out of the Confederate boundaries except for those times he led stampeders to Federal territory. At the beginning, he had enjoyed the benefit of a partner when he led his stampeder runs, a young former store clerk named Sam Colter, descendant of a well-known pioneering family of Carolina and Tennessee. But he had lost Sam, lost him twice. The first time was when Sam had the misfortune of being captured and forcibly conscripted into the Confederate army. Sam had served the hated cause only briefly, then deserted with some fellow conscripts into the North Carolina mountains, where they became part of the command of a rather mad Unionist bushwhacker named Merriman Swaney. But Sam and Greeley had found each other again, and plans had been afoot for them to once more work together as pilots. Then, at the train station at Greeneville, Tennessee, in sight of the very oak from which two of the bridge burners of '61 had been hanged, Sam was stabbed by the young son of one of

Merriman Swaney's victims. The boy had recognized Sam as one of the bushwhacker band that had killed his father. Sam's wound proved fatal.

Greeley's grief over Sam's death had lingered for a long time, only recently beginning to fade. Now it was back in full strength, mixed with sorrow over the Wilmoth tragedy and a general, overwhelming weariness with a war that wouldn't seem to end.

Greeley realized he was a very tired man, tired of living as a refugee in his own mountains, of dodging Confederate Home Guards and rebel devils such as Witcher, Bozen, and Fletcher. He was tired even of his piloting work, important as it was.

For the first time, Greeley thought about giving it up. There was one more stampeder run already in the works, due to commence in two days. In the past he had always come back at the end of such runs and immediately rounded up another stampeder band. Maybe this time he wouldn't. No, maybe this time he'd move on, head north, find someplace to wait out the war. He'd done more than his share already. There were other pilots besides Greeley Brown. Let them continue the work. He had done all he could stand.

The prospect was enticing, but his conscience argued against it. There were other pilots, to be sure, but few possessed his skill or his record of success. Many Union people in these mountains saw him as a leader and source of hope. He had realized over time that he was, for some reason, an inspiration to the mountain Unionists. They looked to him as a protector, a giver of reassurance, and an encouragement not to give up no matter how terrible it all became.

But I want to give up. I want to be finished with all this. I want to lie down at night and not wait to hear the sound of Home Guards and night riders. I want to rest. Just to rest, that's all, where there isn't war. I want to. I must.

In a transition scarcely noticed, what had been a possibility suddenly became a certain intention in Greeley's mind: one more stampeder run. That much he could handle, but no more. One more run, and then would come the rest and the peace. One more run, and then for Greeley Brown the war would finally be over.

Chapter 3

On Buffalo Creek in Carter County

Corny Shelton strode up to Greeley and nodded his head. "All here and counted," he said.

"You sure?"

"Yep. Thirty, all ready to go."

"None of their women and children still lingering about?"

"No. They left when you told them."

"Good. Then let's get started."

Greeley shifted the haversack on his left shoulder until it felt comfortable, then slipped the strap of his Henry rifle over his right. As he strode up to the head of the quiet assembly of men, Greeley thought that if prior stampeder groups had needed him, this one time it was he who needed them more. During his struggle with depression, he had actually thought a time or two about doing what poor old Florence Wilmoth had done, putting a gun to his head and bringing an end to his career in the most final way. Two things more than any other had kept him from it: his promise to himself that this would be the last of his stampeder runs, and the fact that these men had cast their confidence on him. They were relying on him, and that reliance gave him the motivation to shake off his sorrow and go on.

But the self-destructive demon whispering of those dark days alone in his hut had frightened him deeply, and convinced him he was right in putting this piloting life behind. He hadn't realized how deeply the horrors of mountain war had touched him. He was secretly embarrassed to think that maybe he was becoming a weaker man, and irrationally feared that others would be able to look at him and somehow detect this. Pride wouldn't allow that. He'd pilot this stampeder run with more bravado than any before it. He'd let no one know that there would be no further such runs. He'd place these men with the Union forces, and then he'd vanish. *Vanish.* The word rang like a beautiful musical note in his mind. To vanish, to slip away, to put it all behind . . . paradise itself couldn't seem more enticing.

"Let's get moving," he said to the men closest to him, and began walking.

It was dark, about two in the morning. Visibility was poor. A break in the weather had fortunately melted the snow the day before, but the air was cold and getting colder, and Greeley feared more snow before they were through. They needed to make good time.

"Will we go on past Walter's house tonight?" asked Monty Hennegar, an old acquaintance of Greeley's who had wearied of hiding out in the hills and finally decided to cast his lot with the Union army.

"Probably not until morning. By the time we get there and get our breakfast, the night will probably be about gone. You sure he's got the provision to feed so many of us?"

"He says he does. He's managed to hide most of what he has from the armies. And he swears he'll take no money for what he feeds us, neither."

"I'll be sure to let him know how much I appreciate him. It's folks like him a pilot relies on."

"Walter's a good one, sure enough. I'm proud he's my brother."

Greeley stepped forward. The darkness was a challenge, forcing him to concentrate and to move more slowly than he would have liked. The men strung out in a long, almost single-file line behind him, each keeping on track by watching the man before. Most kept silent; a few carried on whispered conversations despite his commands for silence.

An hour passed, then two. By that point no one was conversing, and muscles were already growing sore. The cold was worse, but compensated for by the heat of their exertion.

They reached the Hennegar house a couple of hours before dawn and found Walter Hennegar awaiting them, along with an eager son of nineteen years, Walter Jr., who would join the stampeders. The elder Walter's haggard-looking wife and daughters, weary from cooking pan after pan of corn bread, nodded greetings to the big band of new arrivals, then set out to slice the corn bread into big hunks that were soaked down in sorghum molasses. The hungry men ate every bite offered and would have taken more if it had been available. Greeley spent his time resting his muscles, eating slowly to make it last, and mostly nodding and grunting as he listened to Walter Hennegar expound on the cruelties of rebels and his hope that before long the Confederacy would be fully driven down. Though the Federals had made some significant advances in past months, and some said the Confederacy now had virtually no chance of victory, Greeley refused to put much stock in Hennegar's kind of optimism. Any optimism he'd ever possessed had long since been worn away by the trials of his life. He'd believe the war was over only when the last rebel had laid down his rifle and the last Fletcher, Bozen, and Witcher had been driven from the hills.

A half hour before dawn the band set out again, enlarged by one with the addition of the younger Walter Hennegar. As the light rose, Greeley felt new apprehensions; most of his stampeder runs had taken place almost exclusively by night, but this time there would be much day travel, Greeley having calculated that any risk was offset by the advantage of speed. There were no guarantees, however, and he kept as close an eye as possible on the terrain all around, and was quick to move his men into hiding whenever he heard or saw something suspicious. Every alarm, however, proved false, and a sense of confidence began to grow. When Greeley led the group up a mountainside and shifted their travel route to the line of the mountaintop, every man felt assured that they were, for the moment, not in imminent danger. The mood grew downright cheerful, and Greeley heard much quiet banter and laughter in the long line behind him, and a renewal of conversations.

He knew it wouldn't last, and it didn't. As the men began to realize how hard their pilot intended to push them, as the midday sun rose above and then began edging down again with no stop made for rest or food, joviality gave way to grumpy weariness. Those who had to pause for the necessities of nature were terribly rushed to do so, their comrades moving on and threatening to leave them behind while they dealt with their private business.

Greeley's pushing of the men was not motivated by cruelty or indifference. Experience had taught him it was vital for each man to realize who was in authority here; otherwise carelessness and disobedience would grow, and danger with it. It was important as well to put as much distance behind them as quickly as possible to lessen the inevitable second thoughts and backward glances that would afflict some. The farther they traveled, the less practical it was for any to consider turning back.

About dark they came off the mountaintop and entered Greasy Cove. Carter County was now behind them. Here Greeley allowed them to stop and eat, warning them to limit how much they consumed. "We have more miles to go before sleeping, and you don't want a heavy gut," he said, eliciting groans and curses from the ravenous men.

They ate and went on, mile after mile, ridge after ridge, until they reached the Nolichucky River. Greeley traveled alone to the house of a Union man whose name and residence location had been given him by Walter Hennegar, and gained the man's agreement to ferry the stampeders over the river by canoe, a few at a time. This took much time, allowing for some needed rest. Once across the river and while waiting for the others to come, several stampeders fell asleep leaning or even standing against trees. When the last man was across, Greeley woke the sleepers and told them to start walking.

Their route brought them to the Flag Pond Road, a narrow, winding, climbing road seldom traveled by anything but mountain pedestrians and horsemen. The tangled laurel all around created a claustrophobic atmosphere. Trudging on, the stampeders at length reached the swollen, semifrozen Indian Creek.

"What now, Greeley?" Corny Shelton asked in a tired and despairing tone, as if he didn't already know the inevitable answer.

"What do you think? We cross."

"Right through the water, you mean?"

"That's right, unless you can jump a dang long way."

Grumbling, sore, hungry, and already bitterly cold, the men removed shoes and stockings and waded into the slushy water. Groans and protestations rose from almost every man as they waded across, concentrating hard on keeping their footing, because all could imagine how much greater the misery would be to plunge full-bodied into the water.

On the far side they dried their feet and legs as best they could, trembling and wretched to the last man. Greeley encouraged them to speed, urging and prodding like a hard-hearted schoolmaster.

"How much farther, you cursed slave driver?" one man asked.

"As far as I say," Greeley snapped back. But in a softer tone he added: "Just a mile or so. Then we'll build some fires and eat us a bite or two before we get some sleep."

That bit of encouraging news gave a spark of life to the sullen group. That final mile was pursued eagerly, and so Greeley stretched it into two before finally calling the halt and ordering fires built. The men dug out their provisions and ate, letting the flames bathe them in welcome heat.

Despite a coldness in the ground that the fires couldn't touch, the men slept well that night. Greeley, having mercy on them, took the first watch and made it a lengthy one. When he finally shook Corny Shelton awake to relieve him, he lay down and fell asleep at once, too tired to dream.

Morning broke in a cloudy, windswept winter sky. By eight, the stiff and sore stampeders were making their way over rugged terrain, crossing streams and ridges until Greeley paused, looked around, and recognized from landmarks he'd known since boyhood that they had passed from Tennessee into Madison County, North Carolina. Greeley would be more relaxed today, not as hard-driven as before. This was a county he'd known well all his life; there was hardly a ridge he hadn't hunted or a stream he hadn't trapped. Also, he knew that pushing hard was pointless: The sore feet and muscles of the men would not move as quickly today no matter how hard they tried.

The day's travel brought them to Shelton Laurel, a rugged, isolated mountain region whose name would ever be remembered because of the Unionists massacred there back in early '63, in brutal retaliation for a raid carried out against a Confederate salt depot in the town of Marshall. Most of those slaughtered, everyone said, had nothing to do with the salt raid. "Bloody Madison," folks called this county now.

At dark they came to the mountainside house of an uncle of Corny Shelton's, Corny being part of the extended Shelton family after whom this community had been named. The old widower, Branch Shelton, living with a thin, quiet old-maid daughter and a half-witted grown son who could make noises but not speak, was impoverished and had no food to offer such a large band, but he made them welcome and seemed pleased that they had stopped. As he talked about his Union loyalty and the suffering he and his people had seen, tears streamed down his face and his shoulders quaked. He would surely die, he declared, before he could see the rift torn open by this war brought back together again. Corny patted the old man's back and told him that the Union was on the rise and would drive the rebels out of the country as quick as it could be done. The rebels were on the decline, he assured the old man, the war as good as won. "The reckoning season is coming to the rebs, Uncle Branch. It's time now for them to start paying for what they've done to the good and loyal folks. And pay they will, I'm here to tell you." He patted the old fellow again, turned and winked at Greeley, and half whispered, "Uncle Branch cries easy. He's softhearted. I've seen him cry killing a hog for butchering."

Morning put the stampeders on the march again. By now their muscles had begun to toughen and weren't so sore, but feet were blistered raw throughout the group, arches were sagging and aching, toes were stubbed and burning from the cold. Greeley heard many a man declare himself "plumb crippled, can't take another step," but he told the complainers to take the step anyway, and they did, and the next and next one again, on and on. Greeley knew that if a rebel squad appeared around the bend, those supposedly crippled men would find their feet suddenly swift and light as swallows.

They reached one of Greeley's favorite landmarks in all the western North Carolina wilderness: a rugged, many-ledged and -faceted cliff, back some yards from the bank of the rushing French Broad. This cliff had been called Paint Rock as long as anyone could remember. Older than the name itself was the feature of the rock that had inspired it: colored markings on the cliff's rough face. Though the mysterious markings looked pretty much like faded splashes of paint, the Indians of Carolina declared there had been a time when images of birds, fish, animals, and people could be made out. Weathering and age had blurred the images, but even so, Greeley always felt his imagination stirred by the sight of the great painted rock, and he would wonder who had put the pictures there, and why.

There was no time for such reflection just now, however, nor even any light by which to see the markings. In the dark, Paint Rock was merely another North Carolina bluff. A narrow mountain road ran before the rock and parallel to the river, and linked to another road leading back into the hills and finally on to Greeneville in Tennessee, the town where Greeley's late piloting partner, Sam Colter, had put in time as a store clerk before the war. *Sam.* Greeley wondered how long it would be before each remembrance of him ceased to bring such pain.

Leaving Paint Rock, the stampeders struggled through the wild land and reached Meadow Creek Mountain. Dreadful as it was to be climbing another mountain by night, no one complained. They knew it would be pointless: Greeley had proven to them that whimpering among the men only made him push them harder.

They crossed the mountain and were partway down the far slope of it when Greeley called a halt. Thanks poured over him profusely; this leg of the journey had wearied the men more than any prior one. Soon fires blazed on the mountainside, worrying Greeley some because he feared they were potentially visible from far off, but he chose to let it go. The night was cold and snow was falling. The fires were needed, and on this cold night he doubted any rebels in the area would feel sufficient motivation to investigate the fires even if they did see them flickering off in the high distance.

The fires kept Greeley from getting much rest, however, because it fell to him to keep them stoked through the night. A couple of others tried to help, but kept falling asleep. Without complaint Greeley limited his own sleep to brief naps between fire-stoking sessions, and when morning came he was feeling very weary. But an hour past sunrise he was leading the trek down the mountain, moving with as much evident energy as before and challenging his better-rested followers to keep pace with him.

The base of the mountain was a goal deeply desired, because it marked the beginning of country not quite so rugged. From their campsite on the side of the mountain, they had looked out come sunrise over a great, broad valley, stretching for miles in a series of hills and smaller valleys, winding streams and rivers, until Bays Mountain jutted up from the valley floor, running southwest to northeast like the valley itself, giving way to the valley of the Holston beyond it, then the knobs and ranges that grew into the massive Clinch Mountain.

Greeley had crossed steep Clinch Mountain many a time on runs to Kentucky, but his new destination would spare him that ordeal this trip. Knoxville lay about eighty miles west of them, many small ridges and even more twisting waterways separating them from it, but no terrain nearly as rugged as what they had just passed through.

Greeley stopped the group at the mountain's base and said, "Men, I give you congratulations. You've now passed the worst of it. The land will roll easier from here on, and we should, too."

They did make better progress. Traveling at a hard pace for most of the day, they reached the French Broad River. Looking for a means of crossing, they came upon a small, homemade ferry, merely a wide raft bound to a rope stretched tight across the river. They were within sight of a house higher up the bank, and knew they were probably being watched, but decided to take their chances and cross anyway. The raft passed back and forth, back and forth, the rope keeping it from being washed off with the current, and every man made it over without incident, and with no sign from the house to indicate any observers there objected to what they were doing.

They aimed for the Big Pigeon River, but stopped before

they reached it to camp out the night. Walter Hennegar, Jr., made Greeley an offer he accepted with gratitude. That night Greeley slept without interruption while Walter saw to the fires and kept the hardest hours of watch.

Rising the next day, eating sparingly of a fast-dwindling food supply, the stampeders came to a series of ridges thick with ivy and laurel, so dense at places that they had to crawl through one at a time. It was exhausting, but after they came out they soon reached the Pigeon, and on its banks encountered a young boy who provided not only an offer of free crossing in his canoe, but also some unexpected and welcome news.

"I know you, Mr. Brown," the boy said, extending his hand to Greeley, who shook it with a certain anxiety. Was he so well known now that strangers recognized him? He had never seen this boy before. The boy's next words reassured him. "My uncle pointed his finger at you once when we was all visiting him and some other kin over in Carter County, and you was passing on the road, and he said, 'That there man is Greeley Brown, nephew, and you look at him good so you'll know him, for you'll never lay eyes on a better fellow to get Union men out of the rebel country.' That's what he said. He said you're one of the best stampeder pilots there is."

"I'm obliged for that sentiment," Greeley replied, thinking that soon folks would be saying that Greeley Brown *used* to be one of the best stampeder pilots.

"You don't need to worry about rebels much here in these parts, Mr. Brown," the outspoken young fellow continued. "This here is as solid a bit of Union country as you'll find in this end of the state. Ain't nobody here but wouldn't be proud to help Greeley Brown and his stampeders. Where you aiming for? Knoxville?"

"That's right."

"Well, you won't have to go that far to find the Union lines."

"What do you mean?"

"The Yankees are closer than that. There's a passel of them right now in Sevierville. You ain't got much farther to go."

This was agreeable news indeed, and the men acknowledged it with cheers. Once they encountered the first sizable body of Federal soldiers, they would be safe, truly safe for the first time in many a month.

"I thank you for that bit of intelligence. You're sure of it?"

"I seen them with my own eyes. You go to Sevierville and you'll see them, too."

"I believe we'll do that. What's your name, son?"

"Beasley F. Boyd. Little Bee, they call me, though I hate it. Sounds like a baby name. My pa's Beasley R. Boyd, he's Big Bee, and my grandpa is Beasley W. Boyd. He ain't called by no size of bee, just by Beasley W. Boyd. Likely you've heard of him. He's got a lot of land and once owned upward of fifteen slaves, including one who was big as a tree and would whup other fighters in show fights, but that one got drunk and fell out of a loft onto a pitchfork and died. Grandpa sold his other slaves out before the war come along. He's an important man. He's been to New York City twice, and has met three different congressmen. One time, he seen Abe Lincoln with his own eyes, but Abe wasn't president yet, then."

Greeley hadn't heard of any of the various Beasley Boyds, but he didn't let on to the boy. "You come from fine and important stock, it's plain to see. I appreciate your information and your aid, Little Bee . . . I'm sorry—Mr. Beasley F. Boyd. And when you see that Carter County uncle of yours, you thank him for saying such a kindly thing about me. Maybe I know him. What's his name?"

"Deeroy Boyd. You know him?"

"Think I might have heard of him." In fact the name meant nothing to him.

"Maybe you can meet him when you head back there after this run of yours."

Greeley's smile was small and quick. "Maybe so."

Little Bee Boyd performed his ferrying with skill and cheer-fulness, and Greeley parted company with the youngster much refreshed. He had a high opinion of boys, enjoyed their ways and their words, particularly those of bright and friendly types like Little Bee Boyd. Maybe someday fortune would bless him with a boy of his own like that, and a fine wife and whole houseful of other young ones besides. He hoped so. Greeley could conceive of no finer treasure a man could have than a good family.

Chapter 4

Greeley walked alone, bearing nothing but his haversack, his rifle now in the hands of Hennegar, who hid with the rest of the stampeders in the trees off the road. They had scattered off to both sides as soon as they heard the sound of someone approaching around a bend ahead, and Greeley was proud of how quickly and efficiently they'd hidden themselves, especially considering that some had feet so sore and swollen that he was beginning to doubt they would ever make the final few miles to Sevierville. He had slipped his rifle to Hennegar at the last moment, having decided not to hide from whoever was coming, but to stride along as if he were a lone traveler and perhaps pick up some verification about the location of the Yankees. Greeley slapped an expression on his face in imitation of the look of a dim-witted cousin he'd played with as a child, and sang a children's song off-key. Folks didn't bother idiots, beyond making fun of them, and Greeley had taken on that guise a time or two before in situations much like this one.

He sang a little louder as the slow, rumbling sound drew closer. A big, empty ox cart came around into view, pulled by a pair of oxen, upon one of which sat a young, muscular black man. He eyed Greeley suspiciously, maybe thinking him drunk, but when Greeley got closer, the ox-cart driver took on a different look.

"Howdy-do, boy," Greeley said, lisping.

"Howdy-do, yourself," the black fellow returned.

"Them's pretty cows," Greeley said.

"Them's oxen, not cows."

"I'm Johnny."

"I'm Hobert."

"Howdy-do, Hobert."

"You already said howdy-do. Now it's time to say bye-bye." Hobert rode on past, the oxen plodding heavily, the wheels of the ox cart turning so slowly a man could get sleepy watching them.

Greeley was privately amused at the disrespectful way Hobert had spoken to him. Most likely he'd never dare speak so insolently to a white man who didn't so obviously lack his full faculties. Greeley didn't resent the disrespect. If he had spent all his life having to nod and yes-sir every white man who came along, he'd take advantage of any safe opportunity for insolence as quickly as Hobert had.

"Hey, Hobert? You a rebel soldier?"

The dark face turned back to him, scornful. "I ain't no soldier of no kind, and I'd be no rebel if I was! I'm for the Union. All the slaves is for the Union! You got no sense about you at all?"

"I'm for the Union, too."

"Good for you. Maybe you ain't as stupid as you 'pear to be."

Greeley spoke normally this time. "Indeed I ain't and my name ain't Johnny."

Hobert pulled the cart to a stop, turned, and looked as scared as any young man Greeley had ever seen.

"And I ain't simpleminded, neither," Greeley said. He strode toward the cart. Hobert looked like he might pass out.

"Mister, I'm sorry, mighty sorry. I thought you was . . . I was speaking in such a way 'cause I thought that . . ."

Greeley reached the cart and stuck out his hand. "My name's Greeley Brown. I come from Carter County, and I need to know a thing or two from you."

Hobert took the offered hand with a look of disbelief and

mistrust, as if he expected Greeley would yank him right off
the ox's back. But Greeley merely shook the hand. Hobert dismounted on his own, ready now to show all the deference in
the world in the hope that he wouldn't receive trouble for
having been so insolent before.

"What do you need to know, sir?"

"First off, what's the leaning of the master of your house?
He a rebel?"

"No, sir. He owns me and another slave, but he's Union. He
tells us that once the war ends and we're free, we can work for
him and he'll give us board and food, and pay soon as he can
afford it."

"Sounds like a decent man. The kind of man I might be in
need of. If a band of stampeders come by, say with a bunch of
them so sore-footed they could hardly walk, you think he'd be
the kind of man to loan them the use of this cart, and you for a
driver?"

"Yes, sir, I believe he would. He's got two sons in the
Yankee army already. They stampeded theirselves to Kentucky
back in 'sixty-one, not even having no pilot."

"Well, I am a pilot, and in these woods around us there's
about thirty men hid and watching us, all of them stampeders
bound for Sevierville."

Hobert peered around like a man looking for ghosts in a
graveyard.

Greeley continued, "They've come for many a mile through
frozen mountains and rivers and everything, and some have
feet bad swole. If the worst of the crippled ones could ride to
Sevierville in this here cart, it'd be a blessing."

"You want me to drive, sir?"

"If you'd be allowed by your master, I surely would. You
could bring your cart back here, you see."

Hobert grinned and nodded. "I'll go and tell Mr. Neff right
now, sir, and I believe he'll be glad to help out, sir."

"You're telling me true when you say he's Union?"

"Yes, sir. Mr. Neff is a man you can trust, sir. You want to
come with me to meet him?"

"I believe I would. Hold up just a minute, though." Greeley
went into the woods, rousted up Corny Shelton, told him what
was going on, and instructed him to keep the men hidden until

he was back. Greeley retrieved his rifle from Hennegar, returned to Hobert, and hopped into the empty cart.

"Roll on, Hobert," he said.

Hobert slid into place on the ox's broad back, and they lurched into motion. It was slow, but it was pleasant to be riding instead of walking, so Greeley had no complaints.

Not only did Mr. Neff prove out to be as good a Union man as Hobert said and agree quickly to Greeley's proposal, he went further and provided Greeley a substantial amount of flour, meal, and coffee from a secret hoard. With the foodstuffs loaded into the cart, Greeley and Hobert rode back to the place where they had left the stampeders, Neff coming along on a sad, old, absurdly swaybacked horse that he said was the best animal he had other than his oxen. "I swear I'd shoot this old mare, but she ain't worth the cost of the lead," he said, then roared with laughter while everyone else merely smiled.

Neff scrawled out a letter for Hobert to carry, explaining that he was out on approved business for Jeremiah Neff of Cosby Creek, so on and so on. Then, abruptly, Neff declared, "By gum, the devil with pass notes and such! I believe I'll just go along with you."

And so he did, after sending Hobert back to the house on the run to give the news to Neff's no doubt exasperated wife. Neff did not remain mounted, however. Like so many in the region, he had heard of and admired Greeley Brown the stampeder pilot, and insisted that Greeley be given the honor of the saddle. Greeley argued, but Neff would not yield, and soon they really were moving along, Greeley plodding on a horse so swaybacked he felt like a comic figure, the men with swollen feet riding in the ox cart, the others walking around and behind them, and Hobert sitting astride his ox, driving the cart while Neff walked beside him with the air of a general leading his army.

Greeley hoped they were past rebel territory, because they made up quite a conspicuous circus at the moment.

After four miles rolled away under Hobert's cartwheels, Greeley was over feeling embarrassed by his swaybacked mount and not even worrying about rebels anymore. Instinct declared this particular stampeder run all but finished. No dangerous encounters, no serious injuries among the men, no sickness or death by misadventure, as had happened once when a panicked stampeder impaled himself on a sharp tree branch while running in the night. They had made it through. Greeley was beginning to feel very relieved.

"*Rebels!*"

The shout rose from somewhere among the stampeders, generating an instant and spectacular effect. The "cripples" in the ox cart came out and over the sides with astonishing fleetness, two of them badly spooking Greeley's horse and making it buck. Quite a buck it was, too, for a swayback, and Greeley was caught so unaware that he pitched right off the saddle onto the ground. One of the stampeders trod Greeley's right hand as he raced for the nearest brush, then something far heavier than a human foot crushed down on his left ankle, twice. Pain shot up his leg, through his torso, out his mouth as an agonizing scream. He looked and saw that the bucking mare had come down two times right on his ankle with one of her front hooves.

Another stampeder's foot kicked Greeley in the belly as he rolled to one side. Someone fell atop him. It was Hobert, scared out of his wits and running because everyone else was. He came up off Greeley and ran on.

Neff was over on the far side of the emptied ox cart, saying "Hold on, now!" and "What's all this?" and "Rebels? Them ain't rebels!"

Greeley tried to get up, but the mare shifted around and bumped him down. A hoof almost trod his ankle again, but he managed to roll away and come to a sitting posture in the road. Greeley winced, his ankle throbbing with some of the worst pain he had ever felt. He knew better than to try to stand.

"Them ain't rebels!" Neff repeated. Greeley looked up to see that not only were "them" not rebels, they were not even men. A sizable parade of women, white and black, some bearing children on their hips and others carrying brooms, mops, pails, and so on, had walked into view, setting off the great panic. Greeley grimaced, shaking his head. His men, going off with the intention of fighting armed Confederate soldiers, had run from a gang of broom-wielding females.

"Good day, Mrs. Newburn," Neff said to one of the women,

a large woman with dirt-colored hair. "And what are you fine women up to today?"

"Hello, Mr. Neff. You're looking well. We've just come from cleaning up Maude Orr's house. You know, where the fire was a couple of nights back. We've been scrubbing ash off the walls, mopping the floors, and such."

"That's fine charity."

"What's this?" Mrs. Newburn asked, waving at Greeley, who still sat on the road gripping his ankle, and at the stampeders who were slowly reemerging from the various hiding places to which they had fled. Most looked quite abashed to realize that what they'd taken for rifles on the shoulders of rebel soldiers were merely mops and brooms on the shoulders of women.

"Well, these men are Union men, heading for the good army in blue," Neff said cheerfully. He turned to Greeley. "Don't you worry about me telling them that, Mr. Brown—all these women can be relied upon."

"All but Mrs. Sparks," Mrs. Newburn amended. "Her husband is a Confederate, and she's not at all trustworthy." With this she turned and shook her head sadly toward one of the women, who glowered back. "But I'm sure you won't cause these men any trouble, will you, Mrs. Sparks?"

Mrs. Sparks, a very large and unpleasant-looking woman, scowled and grunted what sounded like a no.

Greeley rubbed his ankle and felt something like hot lightning rip through it. He bit back a yell, then wondered if in all the wide fields of the war, any scenario more absurd than this one was now being played out.

"That man on the ground is Greeley Brown, the famous stampeder pilot," Neff said. Greeley's eyes bugged. Did Neff know no caution at all? He thanked the Lord that the Union line was near. With Neff along, they'd be cheerfully betrayed in no time.

"I'm afraid I haven't heard of him," Mrs. Newburn replied, looking at Greeley but addressing Neff as if Greeley couldn't hear. "Why is he sitting on the ground that way?"

"I don't know. Mr. Brown, are you hurt?"

"The horse trod my ankle. I don't think it's broken, but it's hurt a right smart."

"Oh, that's no good. We'd better put you in the cart for the rest of the way, then."

Corny Shelton, looking very ashamed of himself for having bolted, came up to Greeley. "Sorry," he muttered. "I reckon we panicked."

"I reckon."

"Can I help you up?"

"Yes, and you'll have to help me get to that cart, too, because I can't put a bit of weight on this left foot."

There were many mumbled apologies from the embarrassed stampeders. Greeley knew their shame was three times greater simply because they had displayed such cowardly behavior to feminine eyes. Good, let them feel ashamed, he thought. They ought to feel ashamed, having run like that, having knocked their very pilot off his horse and gotten him injured.

Greeley was disgusted, considering what this injury meant. At the very least, he would have to lay up for a while until his ankle was strong enough to bear his weight. Maybe some kindly Sevierville resident would give or rent him a room or loft, or perhaps the Union soldiers stationed there would make some arrangement for him in return for all these fine recruits he was bringing them. Fine recruits? he thought ironically. Fine enough, maybe, as long as the rebels didn't send up against them any armies of women brandishing mops.

Chapter 5

Greeley rode the rest of the way to Sevierville in significant pain, his ankle swelling so badly against his boot that he was forced to take it off despite the cold. His mood was dark. The stampeders prudently kept silent around him, knowing they were to blame for his injury. Only Neff kept heedlessly chattering on, his cheerful voice as perpetual as smoke from a smoldering cheap cigar, and almost as annoying.

Greeley's acrimony mostly was directed at fate, however, rather than at anyone around him. He had planned to leave his men at Sevierville, set off in the direction of home, then quietly veer back toward Knoxville and from there to . . . he hadn't really decided. Kentucky, perhaps, or maybe Nashville. Maybe a point much farther away than that, someplace where the war was so remote as to be nonexistent. He might have gone as far as Canada, like many of the slaves who had escaped along the Underground Railroad over the years. He had money in his pocket from the fees from this stampeder band and a meager savings earned in earlier expeditions. Enough that he could live for a while until he found work. Greeley never worried much about taking care of himself financially. He had always been able to make do on very little, and to find work when he needed it.

Now this sprained ankle threw a kink into his plans. He wouldn't be traveling even as far as Knoxville for a while. His ankle throbbed with each jolt of the ox cart. He'd be forced to lay up in Sevierville, maybe for days, spending his money on a room unless he chose to camp out with the army itself, like he usually did . . . but he didn't want to do that this time. There would be questions, talk about his plans, about future runs that he knew would not ever happen. He'd receive the usual praise for his heroism and courage. He'd feel odd about hearing all that, knowing he was quitting.

They reached Sevierville and found the Union presence was strong. The stampeders one by one pumped Greeley's hand, thanking him for his guidance through the wilderness, some pressing coins into his palm, almost all apologizing profusely for having panicked earlier on. He managed to grin and tell them it was nothing.

A soldier whose medical qualifications were never made clear was brought in to examine Greeley's ankle. Greeley was told what he knew already: It wasn't broken, but badly hurt, and he should stay off it several days if he wanted to avoid walking with a limp the rest of his life.

Greeley was offered lodging within a house that had been commandeered for officers' quarters, but made an excuse to refuse it, saying he had a cousin in Sevierville who would put him up in his own home. The officers had Greeley fed until he felt he could not eat again for a week, then Neff helped him back onto the ox cart and asked for directions to the cousin's house.

Greeley had to be honest. There was no cousin, he told Neff. He simply hadn't wanted to remain with the soldiers this time. Though Greeley gave no explanation for this reluctance, Neff declared that he certainly understood the sentiment, yes sir indeed, and chipperly added that if Greeley didn't have a place to stay here, why, he would just ride him back to his own house and let him rest up there. Greeley could head on back to his home county when his foot was healed.

No, but thanks, Greeley replied. It was painful to ride; he needed to remain in Sevierville for now. Neff scratched his chin, thinking, then grinned and declared he knew just the place. An old friend of his ran a boardinghouse in the north part of town. He'd take Greeley there, and if the army hadn't taken over the place for quarters, he could find a good room and bed—just the domestic kind of setting where a man with a busted ankle could heal up fine. Furthermore, Neff figured he could talk his friend into putting Greeley up at a low price, maybe even for free. Good Union man, this fellow was. He'd probably be thrilled to help out the heroic Union pilot, Greeley Brown.

Greeley endured one more jolting ride on the ox cart, feeling self-conscious as he bumped through town with Hobert astride the guiding ox and Neff walking along beside the cart, grinning broadly, talking endlessly, waving at people along the way and pointing at Greeley. "This here's a hero!" he declared to one group of boys they passed. Many adults were within easy earshot at the time. "That man there is Greeley Brown, the great stampeder pilot. Look on a great man, boys!"

Greeley quickly begged Neff not to advertise his identity so openly. The Confederates had a price on his head, and the fact that the Union momentarily held the town didn't mean there weren't Confederate-supporting citizens around who wouldn't mind trying to collect the reward. Neff apologized deeply, then proceeded to embarrass Greeley all over again by declaring to those they encountered: "Don't mind us! Pay us no heed! Just heading for the boardinghouse, that's all!" By the time they actually reached the boardinghouse, Greeley felt like he had been the unwilling honoree of a ridiculous town parade.

The boardinghouse was a big, two-storied brick building of the Federal style, with big chimneys on either end and a two-level railed porch fronting both floors. Hobert parked the cart and dismounted, wandering off across the street to a clearing where several other black men were trying to keep warm beside a bonfire. Neff bounded onto the porch and into the front door without knocking. Greeley was left alone for a while. He shifted his foot about to make it as comfortable as possible, and sat there in silence, watching his breath steam before his face.

A couple of minutes later three of the gang of boys they had passed earlier approached the cart, having followed. "Are you really Greeley Brown?" one of them, apparently about fourteen years old and with a quivering, changing voice, asked.

"Nah," Greeley replied, grinning. "That was just Mr. Neff joking. He likes his jokes. I ain't no Greeley Brown. I don't even know who he is."

"Greeley Brown? Why, he's a Union pilot. He's guided six or seven thousand men out of the mountains to the Union lines. He's bushwhacked upward of a hundred rebels. He's famous!"

Greeley was privately amused at this absurd exaggeration of his career, and a little bothered, too, by this further reminder of just how well-known Greeley Brown was getting to be. It reconfirmed that he was right to be leaving his piloting work behind. With a price on his head, such mounting fame was dangerous. If the Union folks knew him this well, the Confederates surely did, too.

"So this Greeley Brown's a Union man, is he?"

"Yep. Just like my pa and my older brothers. True to the red, white, and blue."

"My pa favors the Stars and Bars," another of the boys said. "But Pa don't take no part in the war. He's stayed neutral. He's too crippled up with the rheumatiz to fight, anyhow."

Greeley was glad to hear about the neutrality. "I'm crippled myself just now," he said. "Not for good, I don't believe."

"How'd you hurt yourself?"

"Just a little riding accident."

The third boy in the little gang nudged the second and pointed. "Hey, Billy! Look! There she is!"

A girl of about fourteen or fifteen had just come around the side of the house, preceded by a running kitten whom she had been trying to catch. Clad in a dull-colored, ragged dress and a pair of worn-out boy's shoes, she nevertheless was a remarkably pretty young girl, eyes brown and large, features perfectly formed.

Her arrival took the boys' attention off Greeley. They immediately headed toward her; she froze and stared at them, looking scared.

"Hey, girl! You going to talk to us today?" the boy named Billy asked.

She remained unspeaking. The kitten ran under the porch.

"Hey, why won't you ever talk? What's your name?"

Still no answer. Her eyes flitted toward Greeley, then back to the boys.

The youths trudged toward her; her big eyes grew bigger. She turned and ran back around the house.

"Hey, come back! We just want to talk to you, that's all!"

She didn't return. The boys came back to the ox cart, looking puzzled and disappointed.

"I believe you scared her," Greeley said.

"She always acts scared," Billy replied. "Won't say a word, never. Just stares and runs."

"You boys are bolder than me. When I was your age, I couldn't even look a girl in the eye, much less talk to her. And that girl's even a mite older than you, it appears to me. I'd sure have never had the boldness to talk to an older girl."

Boy number one snorted. "Ain't no point in talking to her, anyhow. I swear I believe she's a mute. I ain't heard her make so much as a peep."

"Awful pretty, though," Billy added. "Prettiest girl in this town. Dang, I'll talk to her even if she is older than I am! I ain't shy!"

"She lives in town?"

Billy pointed at the boardinghouse. "Just a guest, I reckon. I ain't never seen her before a week ago."

Neff emerged, grin broader than ever. "Howdy, young men! You talking to my heroic friend, are you? Whoops! Sorry about that, Mr. *Smith*." He gave a big, obvious wink as he said the false name. "Pay me no heed, boys!" he said. "Just teasing with my friend here. He's no Union hero, not this one!" Another wink at Greeley.

Good Lord, Greeley thought. Save me from this chattering menace. He glanced at Billy, the son of a rebel sympathizer, and thought the boy had a knowing look on his face. He'd seen right through Neff, no question about it.

The boys headed off, looking around the side of the building and talking to each other as they withdrew, no doubt about the girl.

"It's all worked out," Neff said. "My landlord friend, Dero Campbell, has agreed to take you in and give you the best room he has, one he doesn't even normally let out. His son's room, you see, and he's off in the army and so now it's empty. No charge at all, and he'll charge you only his cost for any meals you take."

"That's kind of him," Greeley said. "Does he know who I am?"

"Yes, which is why he is so pleased to help you. He's agreed that while you're here, we'll call you Mr. Greeley Smith. That was my idea. Keeps your identity secret, you see. Not Greeley Brown, but Greeley Smith! No one would ever guess! Brown, Smith, two entirely different names, just the thing to—"

"Very clever of you," Greeley interrupted. "But let's make it George instead of Greeley."

"Oh! Yes, even better. *Much* better! George Smith it is. Can't beat you out for cleverness, eh . . . *George?*" Neff winked again.

With Neff's help, Greeley worked his way out of the ox cart and up onto the porch. Neff fetched his haversack and rifle, and together they entered the boardinghouse.

Dero Campbell, the landlord, was a corpulent man with three chins and a bad slump. He smiled with broad, tightly closed lips, and fiddled with his small-lensed spectacles as he studied Greeley up and down.

"Mr. Greeley *Smith*, I presume?" he asked in a tenor voice.

"Mr. George Smith," Greeley replied.

"Whatever, sir. I know who you really are, and I'm glad to be of service. George Smith it is."

"I appreciate the lodging. I'll try not to remain any longer than need be."

"Eager to get back to your piloting work, I suppose."

Greeley let that one pass.

"I'll show you to your room," Campbell went on. "It's on the lower floor here, so you can avoid the stairs. Would you like a basin of water to wash in?"

"That'd be prime," Greeley replied. "I'm mighty begrimed."

"You'll have it, and anything else you want, as long as you're with me. Let me take your arm, Mr. *Smith*, and we'll let you get your weight off that ankle."

With the washstand pulled close to the bed, Greeley was able to wash without having to stand. The water was warm and fresh, soothing. He washed slowly, first his face, then his hair, then he stripped off his clothes and gave himself the best bath he could, head to toe, drying off with a soft, clean towel. The ankle was red and puffy, but didn't throb quite so badly as before. He hoped it would heal quickly.

He had a change of clothing in his haversack. The feel of clean cloth against clean skin was deeply refreshing. He washed out his dirty shirt in what remained of his wash water, wrung it out, and hung it to dry inside the big oaken wardrobe in the corner, leaving the wardrobe door open to let fresh air inside. He sponged off the worst of the soil from his old trousers and hung them beside the shirt. Then he stretched out on the bed, flat on his back, propping up his injured ankle on one of the bed's two feather pillows.

The curtains were closed, but thin, and afternoon light streamed into the room. Greeley stared at the ceiling, hands behind his head, the soft pillow billowed up around his ears. He tried to recall if he had ever resided in so fine a room, and couldn't remember any time that he had.

Though Greeley seldom slept during the day except when hiding out during stampeder runs, the soft mattress made him relax and his eyelids grow heavy. The light from the window bothered him, however, so he reached to the bedside stand and picked up a newspaper lying there. Spreading it over his face to block more of the light, he closed his eyes and fell asleep.

He was awakened about an hour later by the muffled but distinct sound of a fussing baby. He moved the newspaper off his face and listened. The crying was coming from the room above. Spitting, infantile crying, with a croupy edge to it. It sounded like a sick child, which was disturbing, but his weariness overcame him again and he fell asleep once more, this time without the newspaper over his eyes.

The next thing that woke him was a knock on his door. "Mr. Smith? Are you there?" It was the landlord's voice.

He opened his eyes, rubbed his face, and propped up on his elbows. Mr. Smith? Oh, yes. He had forgotten his own alias. "Yes, I'm here."

"We'll be eating supper in about ten minutes, if you'd like to join us."

"Yes, yes. Thank you. I'll be there."

"Will you need someone to help you walk to the table?"

"No, no. I'll make it."

"Good. By the way, I'm leaving a crutch outside the door here, if you want it. I had to use it four years ago when I broke a leg. It might be a little short for you, but you're welcome to it."

"Thank you. That's very kind."

"See you at supper, then."

Greeley struggled to reorient himself. He had napped for almost three hours and felt quite groggy. He looked in the mirror and groaned at the mop-haired, ragged man who looked back at him. He dug a comb from his sack, dipped it in the cold basin water, and combed his hair into shape. His beard was long and untrimmed, something he usually never noticed or thought about, but in this homey setting he thought it made him look like a wild man from the hills . . . which, come to think of it, was pretty much what he was. Greeley Brown had never been a townsman, and it showed.

He smoothed the wrinkles of his clothing, rubbed his eyes and combed his beard, then rose and hopped on one foot to the door. He opened it slightly, reached around, and found the crutch. It was undersized, but serviceable. He cleared his throat, threw the door open wide, and hobbled out.

Greeley made his way to the back door, visited the outhouse in the backyard, and returned to the house, following his nose to the table in the big front dining room. Campbell was there, with a tall, thin woman who was setting a bowl of boiled potatoes onto the center of a long, narrow table.

"Hello, Mr. *Smith*," Campbell said. "Have you been resting that foot?"

"Yes. Comfortable bed you've got in there."

"Good, good. Mable, I want you to meet that special guest I was telling you about. This is Mr. *Smith*. Mr. Smith, let me introduce my wife."

"Good to know you, ma'am. Your hospitality is mighty fine."

"I'm so glad you're pleased, Mr. *Smith*," she said, and Greeley knew that Mable Campbell had been told his true identity. Greeley wondered if everyone he was to meet in these parts was going to have the lack of subtlety that these folks, and Neff before them, were demonstrating.

They helped Greeley settle himself into a chair at one end of the table, Campbell taking his seat at the head of the table across from him. Others, all men, began to drift in as Greeley was being seated; he nodded and spoke to them as Campbell bade them meet "Mr. *Smith*, our new guest for a few days until his injured ankle is healed."

Through the dining room door came two more guests, slipping in silently as ghosts but drawing Greeley's immediate attention.

The first was a woman, a little over thirty years old, with a face remarkably beautiful and remarkably sad. She looked weary. Auburn-haired, slender, brown-eyed, with a nose and perfect chin a sculptor might have chiseled on his presentation of ideal feminine beauty, she had about her something that seemed inexplicably familiar to Greeley, though he could not believe he had seen her before, for surely he would have vividly remembered a face like hers.

The mystery's solution followed the woman through the door in the form of the same young, silent girl Greeley had seen outside. The similarity between her and the older woman was striking and told Greeley he was looking at a mother and daughter.

"Ah, Mrs. Fry!" Campbell said, smiling. "Glad you could join us. How is the little one?"

"Sleeping now," she answered. "He cried a long time."

"Yes, I heard him—not that he was any disturbance, mind you. We've no problem at all concerning you being here. Though we don't normally like to take in such young children as your son, we're certainly glad to do so in your case, considering your circumstances."

"Thank you. Your kindness means a lot. May I ask you one further favor?"

"Certainly." Campbell was the image of ready cordiality. Greeley glanced at Campbell's wife, however, and saw a quite different kind of look. He coughed to hide a smile. Obviously the man of the house was taken by his beautiful young boarder, and the missus didn't much care for it.

"Might Cecilia take her plate back to the room and eat there, so that we don't leave him alone? He's coughing so much today. This morning he almost choked, even changed color, it was so bad, and I don't want to have him untended."

"We don't allow food in the rooms," Mrs. Campbell said firmly.

"Mable!" her husband remonstrated. "Surely you can see the need to make an exception here!" He turned back to Mrs. Fry. "Of course Cecilia may take her plate to your room. I'm sure she'll be very careful not to spill anything."

"Thank you. Mr. Campbell, you are so kind to me." She gave him a smile, which, though weary-looking and forced, would seem a treasure to any man fortunate enough to receive it. Greeley was actually jealous of Campbell for a moment. Glancing at the other men around the table, he saw them all staring transfixed at beautiful Mrs. Fry, and knew they were jealous, too.

Mable Campbell turned and stalked out the far door of the dining room, and out and down to the cellar kitchen below. Greeley suspected they would see no more of her for the duration of this meal.

Campbell didn't seem to notice his wife's angry departure; he had already grabbed a plate and was beginning to load it with far more food than petite young Cecilia Fry could hope to consume.

"There we go!" he said, handing the silent girl the plate. She accepted it without looking at him.

"Thank you," her mother said, and Greeley wondered why so polite a woman as Mrs. Fry hadn't taught her own daughter that she ought to say thank you for herself.

A glass of water was contributed, and Cecilia left the dining room, her light footsteps receding.

"You'll be remaining with us, I hope?" Campbell asked Mrs. Fry.

"Yes, thank you."

The chairs adjacent to Campbell's at the head of the table had been taken by two male diners. Campbell evicted one by saying that since his particular chair was the most comfortable of the lot, it should go to the lady. The man took a place nearer Greeley, muttering to himself, while Campbell ushered Mrs. Fry into her chair with all the attention of a waiter in a fine restaurant. His cordiality with the young woman was so great it seemed fulsome, but Greeley suspected it possessed the utmost sincerity. He made a mental pledge that when he reached Campbell's age, he wouldn't let himself act foolish over some pretty woman far too young for him, especially one who was married besides.

The meal, set into motion by a long prayer delivered by Campbell, went on with little true conversation, the talk being dominated by the landlord. Campbell talked ceaselessly, entirely to Mrs. Fry, who had only to occasionally nod and voice words of agreement to keep up her end of the exchange.

Greeley was glad for his position at the other end of the table, which allowed him to keep an eye on her without being obvious about it. At first he simply admired her beauty, but after a time he began to examine her manner as well, and realized something interesting: She was very subtly but deliberately playing up to Campbell, acting far more interested in what he had to say than was merited by his shallow babble, and sitting with her chair much closer to his than to the man on the other side of her. This was a woman who was knowingly playing Campbell as if he were a puppet.

Greeley watched her almost the entire meal, a simple repast of beans and potatoes, and dropped his eyes only when hers shifted toward him. Whenever that happened he would wish he'd combed his whiskers a little more carefully before coming to the table.

Mrs. Fry finished before the others, begged to be excused, and departed. Campbell smiled and nodded as she left, watching her, then seemed to deflate once she was gone. He sighed openly and looked wistful.

Mrs. Campbell came back into the room with biscuits in a basket, eyes burning like stove fires. She plopped the basket onto the table roughly, then swept back out.

Dero Campbell sighed again. He was moody now, lost in thought, picking at his beans with a bent fork. Someone else tried to start up a conversation about the weather, but it sank like a leaky boat. Greeley finished his meal, listening to the big grandfather clock on the far wall ticking away the minutes, to Campbell sighing beneath his breath, and to Mrs. Campbell banging away loudly in the kitchen below. As he stood and excused himself, he again heard the muffled cry of the Fry baby.

"Give my compliments to your wife for her fine cooking," he said to Campbell.

"I will, Mr. Brown . . . Mr. Smith, I mean. Glad you liked it." Campbell sounded sullen and distracted.

Greeley propped the crutch under his arm and hobbled out of the dining room and up to the front door. He let himself out onto the porch, settled down in one of the rockers there, and sat rocking for a few minutes until the cold drove him back inside.

He went to bed early that night, lacking anything else to do and figuring his ankle needed the rest. He stared at the ceiling, thinking about the beautiful woman in the room above, hearing footsteps moving about, and hearing the baby cry, off and on, long into the night.

Chapter 6

Greeley awoke long before dawn. The house was quiet except for those structural creakings always heard by night, and for the faint sound of someone snoring off in another room. Greeley lay with eyes open, thinking about the beautiful woman in the room overhead, the silent daughter, the sickly baby. He wondered where Mrs. Fry's husband was. Off to war, probably. Maybe dead. Widows were common now. The country was filled with women who had never figured to be alone until they were old, and with the graves of men who had never dreamed, when they marched off to war, that they would never march back again.

In the moments before sunrise Greeley's thoughts drifted around to the tragedy of the Wilmoth family. He was haunted by it. That same hopeless feeling that had kept him locked in his hut for days began to whisper again, scaring him. He sat up, then stood up, hobbling with the crutch over to a chair by the window, where he eased down and settled himself. He peered out through the thin curtain, waiting for the coming of day, telling the demons of the Wilmoth tragedy to go away and leave him alone. He tried to think bright thoughts, tried not to remember what it had been like to hear the blast of Florence

Wilmoth's shotgun, or to see the bloody insignia of Fletcher's cross on the gray and frozen faces of two hanged corpses. He blurred it out and let his thoughts go back further into the past, but they betrayed him, settling on another sad day, when he sat beside the bed of poor Sam Colter and watched him die young of a wound inflicted by one even younger, a boy who had learned to hate amid the atrocities of the mountain war. Greeley gave up trying to control his dark thoughts and let them flow freely, until they at last expended themselves and left him alone.

When light began to grow outside, Greeley saw on the floor the newspaper he'd used to cover his face during his nap. He bent over and retrieved it. He hadn't read a newspaper in a long time.

This one was a copy of the firebrand journal called *The Knoxville Whig and Rebel Ventilator*, published in Knoxville by famous old Union champion William "Parson" Brownlow, a man whose sense of restraint was as insubstantial as his chin. Greeley grinned, knowing he would be entertained by the Parson's rebel-baiting words. No man alive hated the Confederacy more than did Parson Brownlow; few were hated so badly in turn. Greeley had never laid eyes on Brownlow, but felt he knew him well. Brownlow was one of those figures almost everyone in the eastern end of Tennessee felt he knew, and held some strong opinion toward. The fighting Parson left no room for middle ground on himself or the issues he aired. His diatribes against Confederates were scathing, bitter, and personal.

Brownlow had been silenced for a time by the Confederacy, ousted and driven north, but after Knoxville fell to Burnside, he returned and resumed publication of his newspaper. The copy now in Greeley's hand was of the *Whig*'s newest incarnation.

By the rising light of morning Greeley read the newspaper, both its news and commentary, the latter of which roused a few chuckles and shakes of the head at the Parson's forthrightness. "Ah, me!" Greeley muttered after picking his way through a long editorial—he had always been a slow reader—and moved on to the next one, much briefer.

He had grinned over the first editorial, but his smile faded.

Pulling the newspaper closer, he studied the second editorial with a frown, his mouth forming the words silently, one at a time. When he was done, he laid the paper on his lap and stared at the backlighted curtain, mouth slightly open, forehead creased.

"Caesar Augustus!" he muttered. "Who'd have thunk it!"

He scanned over the brief commentary one more time, then gently tore it from the newspaper, folded it, and laid it aside for keeping.

After dozing a few moments in the chair until the sounds of increasing activity throughout the boardinghouse roused him, he groomed and dressed himself, and left the room to head for breakfast. Beyond that stretched what promised to be a long and dull day of sitting in a stranger's boardinghouse, bad ankle propped up before him and time ticking on, one slow moment at a time, just like the cursed war itself.

The weather warmed a little, so Greeley Brown became a porch dweller. Bundled up in coat, vest, and hat, he claimed one of the porch rockers as his own and resigned himself to a long stretch of idle rocking. He hated living like an old invalid, but at least on the porch he had the passing traffic to watch.

Three times during the morning the lovely Mrs. Fry brightened the scene, coming into the yard or onto the porch to walk about with seeming purposelessness. Greeley greeted her each time and found her polite but nonconversational. She seemed preoccupied, probably over her sick baby.

Mrs. Fry remained outside only a few minutes at a time. Once, young Cecilia appeared. Greeley's quiet greeting to her drew no response at all, other than a cautious glance his way.

Cecilia soon spotted the kitten she had been pursuing the day before and began to chase it about again. Never once did she call for it or speak to it. The kitten was a skittish and shy little creature, but no more so than Cecilia herself seemed to be. Greeley wondered how a child so appealing had managed to become so withdrawn, and if her lack of speech resulted from inability or her own choice.

• • •

Over the next two days meals at the long table became a great source of private amusement for Greeley. The sadly smitten Campbell spent each meal trying to appear suave and worldly in the eyes of Mrs. Fry, while Mable Campbell spent them storming about, glaring at him while she slammed laden bowls and dishes onto the table and tempestuously jerked empty ones away. The dishware was pretty good stuff, so Greeley was surprised at how roughly she treated it. Only a very perturbed woman would be so hard on her own dishes, especially in these days when domestic goods were so valued and hard to replace.

A middle-aged boarder became Greeley's mealtime companion. He was John P. Williams of Nashville, a shrimp of a businessman who was in Sevierville doing commercial scouting for the Nashville-based plow and farm implement company that employed him, and which had plans for expansion into East Tennessee at the war's end. Williams seemed to find the little Campbell romantic drama as amusing as did Greeley, and the two of them began exchanging pointed glances during meals and struggling not to grin. Though their interaction was limited to these silent communications—no authentic conversation had passed between them yet—Greeley thought that Williams might be a man he could like, except for one thing: the hungry way he eyed Mrs. Fry when she wasn't looking. His leers were so openly lustful it was disgusting to see them.

Later in the week, while Cecilia was in the corner of the yard, lovingly scratching the kitten's head and seeming so wrapped up in it that Greeley was listening to see if she would speak, Williams emerged from the boardinghouse and sat down beside him.

"Good morning, Mr. Smith," he said. "How's that ankle coming along?"

"Right well, thank you," Greeley replied. "I believe I'll be on my feet again in a day or two."

"Good! Very good." Williams gave one of those meaningless chuckles humans had used since the dawn of time to fill gaps in conversation. He pulled a couple of cigars from his pocket and offered one to Greeley, who gladly accepted. They lit up from the same match and settled back, the rockers creaking rhythmically beneath them. Greeley's impressions of Williams jumped up a few notches.

Williams waved his cigar at Cecilia. "Pretty little gal there. Wouldn't you like to see what she's going to look like in a few years, eh? Heh heh heh."

Greeley let the comment pass as his view of Williams promptly dropped back down again.

"That mother of hers is quite a vision, ain't she? The good Lord outdid himself when he molded her! Mmm mmm, yes indeedy!"

Greeley, who had had respect for women irrevocably hammered into him by a stern father, began hoping for something to divert Williams.

This was almost instantly provided when a band of blue-clad soldiers rode by, tipping their hats at Cecilia and nodding greetings to Greeley and Williams on the porch. Greeley looked closely to see if any of them were from his latest stampeder group. None were.

"What do you think of the progress of the war, Mr. Smith?" Williams asked after the soldiers were gone.

Greeley eyed him sidewise. "That's a question a man is hesitant to answer unless he knows the leanings of the one doing the asking. I ain't one to get into arguments with folks about politics and such."

"Well, I'll tell you first where I stand, then, to make it fair. I come from Nashville, rebel country. And I'm a good southern-born fellow and like the concept of states' holding out for a full share of rights. And I do believe the United States government has not always had the best interest of the South at heart."

"Well, I can understand how a man could feel that way," Greeley replied noncommitally. "You're a Confederate sympathizer, then."

"At the beginning, yes . . . but not now, and not wholeheartedly even from the start. You see, I'm a man of commerce, and I've always known that we here in the South are more dependent on our northern neighbors than we would like to admit. Let me give you an example. I was briefly in New Orleans back in 'sixty-one, and toured a shoe factory with a business friend of mine down there. He was hot for Secession, full up with the conviction that the South could stand alone, take care of all its own needs. He led me around that factory, pointing out all the big machinery, steam-run, showing the pieces and parts and so on that went into the actual shoes, the packing facilities where the finished product was put in wooden boxes for shipping. All of this, he said, showed how far the South has come, how we are becoming industrialized and independent. I nodded and went along, but I couldn't help but notice something: Virtually every machine in that factory had been manufactured in Boston. The wood from which the shoe pegs were cut came from Massachusetts. The leather came from somewhere up the river, I don't recall where, and even the wood for the packing boxes was shipped in from Illinois. I tell you, sir, I came away from that little tour with some strong second thoughts about the realism of our grand Confederate enterprise. It's the old battle between the ideal and the actual. I may like the idea of an independent South, but I have my doubts that it's going to happen, or even that we would be truly better off if it did. And hang it all, how would the Confederacy ever hope to keep unified itself, if it's based on the notion that a state can just secede anytime it likes?"

Greeley nodded, puffing the cigar. Cecilia Fry lost her kitten and began chasing it again. "Well, sir, I'd say you're right about that," he said.

"Are you a Union man, Mr. Smith?"

"Most folks on this end of the state are."

"Yes, I'm well aware of that. And I can understand it. Your economic interests in this section have been much less dependent on southern ties than ours over in Nashville and Memphis."

"I reckon so. But that ain't what makes me Union. For me, it's just a matter of being true to what my people before me done. My forebears fought mighty hard to bring about these United States, and I just ain't seen good reason to go against what they done. That's simple reasoning, maybe, but it seems right to me."

"Carrying on the old tradition! We all seek to do that in our various ways, don't we? Heh heh heh! I will say that many of my Confederate friends would reply to you, however, that what your ancestors truly fought for was independence and freedom, and that the government they created, though devoted to those principles initially, has become oppressive, and indifferent to our interests in the South."

"I suppose your Confederate friends would say that, yes."

"Yes. Well." Williams coughed and cleared his throat. Obviously there would be no substantive political debate erupting on this porch, this day.

Williams leaned back, rocking in silence a half a minute, pulling on the cigar and blowing smoke toward the bottom of the upper porch. "I'll be honest with you, Mr. Smith," he said. "I came out here and joined you for a reason. I've heard a rumor or two about you here lately, and I'm curious."

"What kind of rumor?"

"That . . . uh, forgive me if I'm intruding here, and I swear to you that you can trust me to keep my mouth shut . . . that your name isn't really George Smith, and that in fact you are one Mr. Greeley Brown, who I know is noted in the mountain regions here as a guide for Union men fleeing to join the Federals."

Greeley eyed him sidewise. "That's what they say about me, is it?"

"That's what I've been hearing."

"Who told you that?"

"Well, I wouldn't want to betray any confidences. . . ."

"Mr. Williams, I'll talk as straight to you as you have to me. If I was this Mr. Greeley Brown, and if I had chose to use a different name during the time I'm laid up here, wouldn't you figure that there was probably a good reason for it?"

"Yes, I suppose so. But . . . are you Greeley Brown?"

"Dang, you're persistent, ain't you!"

"I was a journalist once, sir, and I developed the habit of asking a lot of questions."

"Questions can sometimes get folks in trouble."

Williams paused, then sighed. "Yes, you're right. I do apologize, Mr. Smith."

"Brown."

"What? So you are Greeley Brown?"

"What's the point of denying it? I came into town in an ox cart with a loudmouth trumpeting who I was to everybody who could hear. And since I got here, every time our good landlord and his wife call me Smith, they say it like they're trying to make some old deaf person understand them. I believe who I am is pretty much an open secret."

"Well, I'll be! So you really *are* him!" Williams grinned like he had won a prize. "You can trust me, of course, not to say anything to anyone."

Cecilia caught the kitten again. Greeley waved his cigar toward her and decided to shift the conversation in a new direction. "Now, there's something to do with that little gal there that I could ask a question or two about my own self. You notice she doesn't speak?"

"I have noticed."

"I've wondered if something's wrong with her. She seems . . . different."

"She does. All I know about her is that she and her mother were traveling east and had to stop here when the baby became ill."

"Where's the father of the family?"

"According to our landlord, she presented herself here as a widow."

"War widow?"

"I suppose. That's one of war's chief by-products, widows."

"Going east, you say. I wonder where?"

"What was that county? Carter. Yes. Carter County."

Greeley pulled the cigar from his mouth, stopped rocking, and looked at Williams. "Carter County?"

"What? Is that significant?"

"It's just that I wouldn't recommend anybody going into Carter County these days. You get back in some parts of them mountains and you can find yourself plenty of trouble. Bush-whackers, Home Guards, and such. A lot of folks are wanting to get out instead of in—believe me, I know."

"Well, I don't know why she's going there. All I know is what Campbell told me."

"Campbell must talk a lot."

"He does."

Greeley asked, "What's wrong with the Fry baby?"

"I don't know. Campbell said that Mrs. Fry told him it had been sickly from birth and has gotten worse during their trav-eling. I saw it once—a little baby boy, as pale and weak as

you'd ever see. He sounds bad when he cries. You can tell
something isn't right."

"I know what you mean, sir. I saw Mrs. Fry rocking that
baby in the front room yesterday. I caught myself thinking that
it looked like it was bound to die. It's a sad thing when a child
dies." As he said that, Greeley's mind flashed painfully back to
a past day when he had watched a child of his own die as a
newborn, its birth taking the life of its mother as well. He had
laid them away in a common grave, the still babe in its
mother's pale arms.

"Sad, yes. Very sad." Williams flicked his cigar.

The men rocked in silence a minute or so, watching Cecilia
and the kitten. It ran away again. Cecilia didn't give chase this
time. She came back onto the porch and went back inside
without looking their way.

"I hope they don't go into Carter County," Greeley said.
"Especially with a sickly child. Over in those mountains,
people are suffering for lack of food, lack of shelter. It's no
place for a sickly baby."

"You sound very familiar with that county."

"It's where I come from."

"Oh, yes. I should have remembered. Thatcher said something about you being from Carter County."

Greeley's rocker stopped cold and he twisted to look fully at
Williams. "What did you just say?"

Williams grinned. "I'm sorry. I couldn't resist letting the
name slip like that, just to see how you would react. There's
been a reason for my curiosity about you, Mr. Brown. You see,
I know your brother. Worked with him for a while in New
York."

"You know Thatcher?"

"Indeed I do. Back during my journalist days, we worked
together on the staff of the *Illustrated Weekly Alliance*. Are
you familiar with the *Weekly Alliance*?"

"Yes, I know of it. I know it's a powerful pro-Union
journal, and the rebs hate it."

"Yes. Well, Thatcher and I were friends, not the closest of
friends, not having that much time together, but we got on well
enough. Took a few drinks together in the saloons after work
was through. Not that Thatcher Brown was around New York

all that much. He's a travel journalist, mostly, running all over the country and sending back stories."

Greeley shook his head wistfully. "I ain't seen Thatcher in years and years."

"He told me you two hadn't seen one another. But I can tell you that he keeps you in mind. He's proud of his big brother Greeley, guiding the Union men out of the mountains."

"So you've talked to Thatcher since the war commenced?"

"Yes. In Nashville, in fact."

"Thatcher was in Nashville?"

"He was, back just before Sumter. Traveling on the sneak, using an assumed name like you are here."

"Why?"

"He was beginning the grandest expedition of his career. He knew I had left the newspaper trade and gone into business in Nashville. So while he was in town, he looked me up. He told me about what he was doing. The *Alliance* had sent him down from New York, you see, to explore the South and get a firsthand account, but secret, of the developments of Secession and the war. He told me all this openly because he knew I could be trusted to keep his secret—and I assure you, Mr. Brown, that you can have the same confidence in me. In any case, he was just then beginning his tour of the South, using this or that pretext to explain his traveling and question-asking, the real reason, of course, being the series of articles he was writing. 'A Journey into the Heart of Secessia,' he was calling it—had plans to make a book out of it, too, at the war's end. We had quite a nice visit, and he told me all about you. All he knew, at least. Back in our New York days, he never spoke much about his early days in the mountains. I had heard him mention a brother once, but nothing more about his family or background."

Greeley was not surprised. There had been much sorrow and distress for Thatcher Brown as a boy. Family problems, a mother who blamed him for the accidental death of her husband—an accident involving a rifle Thatcher had dropped. It discharged, sending a ball hurtling fatally into his own father's body. . . . Greeley still felt pain at the memory.

Greeley asked, "Where is Thatcher now?"

"I have no idea. Continuing his tour, I'm sure. Lord only knows where he's gone or what he's done. Whatever he's done, I'm sure he's done it well. He's a capable journalist. The best I know."

"How did he send his stories to New York without giving himself away?"

"He explained it to me, but it was complicated and I didn't quite understand it all. It has something to do with a code he's worked out with the publisher. Words that meant something other than their common meanings, phrases and markings and such. Subtly slanting his words in varying directions, so that a slight leftward slanting paragraph was to be read to mean the opposite of whatever opinion it expressed. Referring to Secession leaders by innocent-sounding code names: Jefferson Davis being 'Uncle Godfrey,' for example. Like I said, I didn't quite follow it all, but seemingly it worked. Very sophisticated! He would produce his communiqués, have some associates rewrite them and forward them on to various people along a line that ultimately led to the *Alliance*. Not much different than spying, all this subterfuge he was up to. But oh, he was enjoying it! He saw it all as quite an adventure."

"Quite a dangerous adventure, I'd say."

"Indeed."

"What's he look like these days?"

"Very much like you, sir. I noticed it the first time I laid eyes on you. A remarkable resemblance. You're so much like him, in fact, that's what caused me to ask our landlord about you."

Greeley felt a warm burst of pride, a renewal of family linkage to a brother long gone from him. *Thatcher looked like him!* He had lost touch with his brother over the years, their lives being so vastly different, so separated by miles. The early family tragedies had led to Thatcher's being sent away, raised by relatives in the North. He had never come back to the mountains, not even as a traveling journalist. Greeley had understood. The memories for him there were too painful.

Greeley asked, "Have you seen anything he's written during his tour?"

"After the Federals took Nashville, the northern publications began reaching the city again. I did see a couple of articles, early on, but they've ceased. Right about the time of Vicksburg, they stopped."

Greeley frowned. "Vicksburg . . . he was there?"

"I think so. All I know is that until Vicksburg I saw some of his reports—under a pen name, but he had told me himself the pen name he would use—and after Vicksburg, there were no more."

Greeley stared across the yard. If Thatcher's dispatches north had abruptly ceased, he must have been stopped from producing them. Detected, caught, imprisoned . . . worse?

"I hope I haven't worried you, Mr. Brown," Williams said. "But I knew you would want to know that he seems to be missing."

"I'm glad you told me. I hope Thatcher is well."

"I do, too. For what it's worth, he's a surviving kind of fellow. Very clever. Much like you must be yourself, to do the work you do."

They fell silent, finishing their cigars. Greeley stared at the gray sky and thought about his brother.

After Williams went back inside, Cecilia came back onto the porch and descended the steps to the yard, not looking at Greeley, who watched her, preoccupied, as she began to look for the kitten again. A few moments later someone came onto the porch above. Mrs. Fry, certainly. He heard fitful, weak crying; she was holding the baby.

"Cecilia, come back in. Jimmy needs . . . I need you," she said.

The girl looked up, turned, and went back into the boarding-house. Greeley heard Mrs. Fry also reenter, above, the baby's weak crying muffling away as the upper door closed.

Mrs. Fry was absent from the supper table that night, and Campbell was sullen, slumped at the head of the table with Mrs. Fry's chair empty on his left. He looked dejected. Not only that, his face was bruised under the left eye. Someone inquired; he replied in a low voice that he had run himself into a door.

When Mrs. Campbell appeared with the usual load of beans and potatoes, Greeley noticed that two fingers of her right hand were splinted. She and her husband would not look at one another.

It must have been quite a row. Greeley figured Campbell would be doing much less flirting with the widow Fry from now on.

Chapter 7

The disturbance came just past midnight, awakening Greeley from a deep slumber.

He sat up in his bed, frowning into the darkness. Heavy footfalls sounded on the floor above; he heard the muffled sound of Mrs. Fry's voice, distressed. The baby was crying, louder than usual, but the cry was odd, disturbing. He heard another wail, from a different source, a keening, high sob filled with terror . . . Cecilia?

He got out of bed too quickly and winced as weight descended onto his injured ankle. Shifting to the other foot, he hopped to the wardrobe and dug out his trousers. Doors were opening throughout the boardinghouse, other voices sounding. He heard someone pass his door and pound up the stairs. Campbell's voice came through the wall from his room, and as Greeley slipped the crutch under his arm, he heard Campbell quickly going up the stairs.

Greeley hobbled as fast as he could to the door and opened it. Mrs. Campbell, clad in a pale nightgown, was standing in the door of her room, a lamp in her left hand, the other, with its splinted fingers, pressed to her bosom. She looked worried and confused.

"What's happening?" Greeley asked her, fumbling to close and button his shirt. The air in the hallway was cold on his face, the crutch's curved support cool under his arm.

"Something is wrong upstairs," she said.

"The Fry baby!" Greeley said, and headed for the stairs. Mrs. Campbell followed, then passed him halfway up, because he was slow on his crutch. The bowl of the lamp brushed his arm as she passed, warm but too freshly lighted to be hot.

Greeley reached the top of the stairs and saw commotion at the door of the Fry room. Mrs. Fry was in the hall, weeping. The keening, unearthly cry of Cecilia echoed out from the open door.

"What's wrong?" Greeley asked Mrs. Fry.

"The baby . . . oh, poor little James!"

Williams, barefoot, dressed in unhitched trousers and an open shirt, came out of the room and almost knocked Greeley down. Campbell, wearing a woolen nightshirt and a stocking cap, followed him, spouting the names of streets and talking about right turns and a big tan-colored house on the left, across from the church and near the stables. Williams nodded and headed fast down the stairs.

"He's going to fetch a physician?" Greeley asked Campbell.

"Yes, yes. But I fear it's too late."

Mrs. Fry put her face in her hands and sobbed.

Campbell turned to some of those just now arriving in the hall and began waving them back toward their rooms. "Please, please, everything is being taken care of. There's a sickly child here and the doctor is on his way. Please, just go back to your rooms."

Greeley went to Mrs. Fry. "Ma'am, is there anything I can do?"

"No," she said without lifting her face. "No. I don't think there's anything anyone can do. He's not breathing, not at all. I've been sure a long time he would die, but I didn't know it would be like this. It's like he just can't pull in his breath."

Cecilia's crying declined from the high wail it had been to an almost steady moan, softer but equally terrible to hear.

Greeley frowned, thinking. "Can't pull in his breath . . ."

He recalled a time when Thatcher, as a baby, had been sick and abruptly ceased to breathe. His father had cleared sputum out of Thatcher's throat, then blown his own breath into Thatcher's lungs, and it had caused him to start breathing again on his own. The passing of life, his father had later explained it. A mystical process: You breathe into the mouth of one who can't, and sometimes the life force goes in with the air and living begins anew. . . .

Greeley slipped toward the door and into the room. A single lamp, hurriedly lighted and poorly adjusted, burned, sending a line of oily smoke toward the ceiling. Greeley saw Cecilia, in her nightgown, squatting in the corner, hands pressed to her face, her big eyes staring straight forward and full of tears, that strange low wail exuding from behind her half-open lips. He looked for the baby, saw it in a wooden box on the floor, a makeshift crib probably provided by the Campbells. The tiny, drawn face was oddly colored. Greeley cast his crutch to the side and knelt, ignoring the pain in his ankle. The baby was not breathing.

He reached into the box and picked it up. Its small arms and oversized head fell back limply. His mind raced: What would make a child stop breathing? Choking on something, maybe?

He rolled the baby over, facedown, and gently pressed between the small shoulder blades. Something sodden and wet fell from the mouth—a wad of thread! The child's sheet, Greeley realized at a glance, was simply a cut-out portion of a full-sized sheet, unhemmed around the edges, plenty of threads sticking out. Obviously the baby had gotten one into his mouth and slowly pulled out more and more in the night, wadding it with its tongue and at last inhaling it.

He rolled little James back over, hoping for a sudden gasp of air. None came. Greeley felt sharp panic, but controlled it. He'd do what he had seen his father do, and hope it worked. Bracing the head with his hand, he pressed his face toward the little open mouth.

Cecilia, watching, let out a louder moan, stood, came toward him. He did not look at her, but gently breathed into the baby's mouth like he had seen his father do many years before.

Suddenly Cecilia was grabbing at him, her fingers filling themselves with his hair and pulling back. He had not been expecting it, and let out a screech of surprise and pain, almost falling over as a young, feminine face with an expression of absolute ferocity glared down at him.

"No!" Greeley said. "No! I'm trying to put the life back into him!"

"Leave him alone, Cecilia!" It was Mrs. Fry, who had come into the room behind him. "Maybe he can help. . . ."

Cecilia let him go, stepped back, and leaned her back against the front of the wardrobe, her face wild and eyes bigger than ever. She was silent now, no moaning. Her mother went to her and put an arm around her.

Greeley pressed his mouth to the tiny face again and blew in another gentle breath. He waited; no response. He tried once more, praying hard, trying to will the life back into the body.

The child moved in his hands, its body giving a tiny, spasmodic jerk.

He gave the baby one more breath. James Fry sucked in air of his own, then spat and coughed . . . and gasped in more air, and let it out. Then again.

The baby was breathing.

Greeley pressed the small body to his chest and closed his eyes, exhaling deeply. He stood, so full of relief he didn't even notice his painful ankle this time, and limped over to Mrs. Fry. He held out the baby.

"Your son, ma'am."

Mrs. Fry held out her arms, but suddenly Cecilia was there, sweeping up the baby before Mrs. Fry could. She withdrew to her prior spot and held him to her bosom, weeping and stroking his fine hair, kissing his brow. The baby cried weakly, fitfully.

Greeley watched, thinking it odd that the sister rather than the mother held the baby at this moment, marveling at the intensity of love she was heaping on the child.

He looked at James. He was sure that he had saved the child's life, but not at all sure it would be for good. The face had been hot against his lips when he breathed in his air. James Fry was a very sick baby.

But for now he lived, and that was good. Greeley stepped back, still watching Cecilia hold and caress little James Fry . . . and then his eyes narrowed and he noticed something that left him frowning in puzzlement. He glanced at the face of the widow Fry, and back at the baby, and from Mrs. Fry's expression realized that she knew what he'd just noticed, and what it had to mean.

She stepped forward quickly, taking and squeezing Greeley's hand. "Thank you," she said softly. "You've saved him."

"I saw my own father do the same with my baby brother once, long ago," he said. "It's the force of life, you see. It comes through the breath. That's how he explained it to me, leastways."

"Thank you, thank you so much. God bless you, Mr. Smith." She was still clasping his hands.

"T'wasn't much." Her touch was like a lightning tingle. It had been the longest time since a woman had squeezed his hands with such affection.

When Williams showed up some minutes later with a breathless doctor in tow, all had returned to their beds but Greeley, the Fry family, and the Campbells, and the latter pair looked none too comfortable lingering around the Fry room. Greeley figured it had to do with black eyes, broken fingers, and an old landlord's inability to control a childish infatuation. He could guess why they were loitering about. This was their boardinghouse. They were waiting around to see if a baby was going to die on their property.

Greeley went on to his bed a few minutes later; Williams, worn-out from running across town and telling how being stopped and grilled by two Union sentinels had delayed his effort, returned to his bed as well. The doctor did not leave. Greeley lay awake the rest of the night, unable to rest after all the excitement. Above him he heard footsteps, quiet conversation, and, at the beginning, the cry of the baby, still sounding distressed and sick. The cry became weaker, more fitful, as the night went on. Greeley prayed for James Fry but suspected the matter was beyond praying over. From the look and general feel of that poor baby, divinity had already made its decision, and James Fry's life would be a very short one.

Shortly before dawn he heard Mrs. Fry suddenly weeping above, and with her sobs the low, odd moans of her daughter, softer this time than before, but heavy with grief.

Another baby leaves the world, Greeley thought. The Lord

must like babies quite a lot, for He surely takes plenty of them to be with Him these days.

He rose long before breakfast time, readied and dressed himself, and headed out to receive news he already knew.

Greeley was touched by the way that the little community of the boardinghouse, and the broader community around it, came together to give comfort to the bereaved widow Fry and her unspeaking daughter. The Campbells showed the best side of themselves in providing a space for the tiny grave in their own family plot. Mr. Campbell no longer put on airs before Mrs. Fry, and even Mrs. Campbell seemed to have put away any hard feelings she might have had over her husband's boyish flirtations of before.

Greeley attended the burying, carried out free of charge by a local preacher who said just the right things in just the right way. Greeley pondered how preachers in general were getting mighty good at funerals these days. Plenty of opportunity to keep in practice, with a war on.

Greeley's ankle was much better, and he had replaced the crutch with a borrowed cane. Before long he intended to throw that aside, too, and set off for Knoxville on foot. Though he could find better means of traveling than hiking, he was accustomed to walking, enjoyed it, and felt very flabby and weak now that he hadn't been able to engage in it for days. He was ready to heal up the rest of the way, walk some strength back into his ankle and muscles, put this little unplanned Sevierville interlude behind him.

Only one thing gave him any reluctance to leave Sevierville, and that was the widow Fry and her daughter. He sensed their grief quite keenly and it roused in him something protective and fatherly . . . fatherly, at least, toward Cecilia. His attitude toward the widow was equally as protective, but not at all fatherly. He couldn't recall having ever met a more appealing woman, beautiful even in her sorrow.

And intriguing. There was a mystery about her and her daughter, things that were hidden or presented with a false face. He had ferreted out one hidden truth by sheer accident

there in the room with the dying baby, but even it raised new
questions. He knew the affairs of the Fry women were not his
business, but he was intrigued by them, especially now that he
knew the place they were bound was the very place from which
he was fleeing.

He didn't like the notion of them going there. How would
they travel? Did they know the way? Would they go alone, just
a woman and a mute young girl?

Most of all, did they have any clear idea of what they were
getting into, or any kind of protection at all?

He wanted to go to Knoxville. Needed to go. That unexpected little editorial in the *Whig* had been like a beacon call,
reminding him of a promised duty that had already gone unful-
filled for longer than it should. The best opportunity to fulfill it
that he was likely to find was open to him in Knoxville.

So he would go there, soon. But not until he had sat down
for a good, honest talk with the widow Fry, and let her know
how terrible was the mountain world into which she was
heading. She had a right to know. An obligation to know,
in fact, considering that she was going to be taking Cecilia
with her.

Chapter 8

The opportunity for such a talk came far sooner than Greeley had anticipated.

More than twenty-four hours had passed since James Fry had been laid in his tiny grave. It was night, the boardinghouse dark, and Greeley Brown couldn't sleep. Williams had given him a cigar that afternoon—an early parting gift, because he was planning to head to Knoxville, of all places, his anticipated departure a day or so away. Greeley, sleepless, decided a cigar could fill a restless hour more pleasantly than could tossing on his bed. But he'd not smoke it indoors. Cigar smoke had a way of penetrating right through walls and ceilings, and he didn't want the smell to bother anyone's rest, particularly that of Mrs. Fry in the room above.

He rose, picked up his cane, then laid it aside. He'd give it a try without any kind of support; this depending on wooden props was getting wearisome. He dressed and slipped on his boots, leaving the left one loose because of that ankle's lingering soreness.

Throwing on his coat and hat, he made sure he had cigar and matches and left his room, walking carefully for the sake of silence and his hurt limb. He reached the front door, then decided on the back porch rather than the front. On the back porch he would be hidden from the view of anyone on the street. More comfortable for a man accustomed to hiding.

So he reversed course and walked back through the boarding-house, testing his ankle and feeling pleased with the relative lack of pain. Perhaps he'd be back to his old self sooner than he had anticipated.

Above, a figure as quiet as a ghost appeared at the railing, looking down on him, but as he passed beneath, concentrating on his walking, he didn't notice.

The night was too cold, really, for sitting outside just for smoking, but Greeley didn't heed it any more than he usually did. He was used to cold. Sort of liked it most of the time.

He seated himself on an old nail keg, stretched his left leg out before him to take the pressure off the ankle, and lit the cigar. He puffed slowly, letting the smoke curl up around his head and spread when it hit the brim of his hat.

The door opened and she emerged, unexpected. Despite the darkness, he knew at once that it was she, if only by the form of the silhouette, the way she moved, the way she smelled.

He stood, touched his hat. "Mrs. Fry," he said, just to make sure she knew he was there. It came to mind that most likely she had just come down with the intention of heading to the privy out in the yard, and this embarrassed him because he feared it would embarrass her.

She didn't prove embarrassed, nor surprised to see him, when she spoke back. "Good evening, Mr. Smith," she said. "I hope you don't mind that I've come down here after you."

After him? What did that mean? "No, of course not."

"I wasn't able to sleep and went out into the hall. . . . I saw you moving around down below, and that you came out."

"I couldn't sleep either. Since I hurt this leg of mine, I'm resting so much more than I'm used to, I get so caught up on sleeping that I can't sleep anymore." He paused. "Of course, I know that you've got a lot more reason than me to be sleepless. I'm surely sorry about that little baby boy. I ain't just saying that neither. I lost a child of my own once, so I have an idea what you're suffering."

"Thank you. It's because of James, partly, that I've come out here. First, I want to thank you for what you did, saving him from choking. We would have lost him sooner than we did if you hadn't helped him."

"You've already thanked me. No need to do it again. Besides, I wasn't able to do anything lasting for him."

"He was a very sick and weak baby. He was from the day he was born. And his birth . . . that's the other reason I came out here. We need to talk. You know what I'm talking about, don't you?"

"I believe maybe I do." He looked down as he brought the cigar to his lips.

"Tell me if I'm wrong, Mr. Smith. You saw Cecilia's gown, and the moisture and stains on its bosom. The stains of mother's milk. And you realized when you saw it that James wasn't my son at all. He was Cecilia's."

"Ma'am, none of it is my business."

"I suppose not. But Cecilia is my business, and it's for her sake I wanted to talk to you about what you saw. I don't want you to have any false impressions."

"Ma'am, really, you needn't talk about it to me. It's not my affair and you needn't—"

"Please, Mr. Smith. Hear me out. I know I'm a stranger to you, and Cecilia is, too, but it would bother me greatly to have you go away from here with misconceptions about Cecilia. I know how bad it looks, a girl so young, a child herself, having a child of her own. I mean, it's the very reason we presented James as my child, publicly. For people to know that a girl of fourteen had given birth to a bastard child . . . it wasn't tolerable. So we altered the truth a bit, made me the mother rather than Cecilia, made James her brother rather than her son. But of course only Cecilia could give him nourishment."

"Yes, no . . . of course." He pulled harder on the cigar, making it glow red and bright.

"But I want you to know something, Mr. Smith. Not everything is what it appears to be. Cecilia is *not* at any kind of moral fault in this matter. It wasn't her choice, you see. There was a man, a very wicked man, who took advantage of her, who forced her—"

"Please. I understand."

"Cecilia has had a difficult life, sir. She's suffered more losses than she should. But she's a good girl, a decent girl, and that's why I came down here tonight, to make sure you understood the truth about her, and don't judge her wrongly based on what you saw."

"Well, I'm glad you told me. But what a terrible thing to happen to so young a girl, just a child. Poor thing. This man who did this to her, was he caught? Punished for what he did?"

She drew in a long breath. "Yes. He was punished."

"So he's gone now? Locked up, jailed, dead or something?"

"He's gone. He'll not be back. Ever."

"That's good. I believe any man who would do such a terrible thing, especially to no more than a young girl like that, has no right even to live."

She wrapped her arms tightly around her midsection and shivered, saying nothing.

"You're cold, ma'am. Let's step back inside. I just came out to smoke this cigar, that's all."

"No, please, I would like to stay out here a moment. The air is cold, but it's fresh."

"It is at that. Nothing like cold air to clear the mind. That's what I always say." He puffed on the cigar.

Miriam Fry smiled. "Some people might think it not proper, me being out here in the night with a man."

"Well, maybe. But I don't know that there's anybody even knows we're out here. And I've never been one to care much what busybodies have to say, anyway."

"What a refreshing attitude!"

"Just comes natural. Where's your daughter, by the way? Asleep?"

"Yes. Very soundly. She always sleeps soundly when she's sad."

"So she loved the child? Even despite how it . . . oh, listen to me. What right do I have to ask that kind of question? I'm sorry."

"No, don't apologize. It's a natural question. I asked it to myself for months on end, waiting for James to be born. I wondered if Cecilia, or even I, could ever love a child that resulted from so wicked and vile a thing as what was done to my poor daughter. But it's odd, Mr. Smith, hard to explain. As soon as I saw little James, I realized that he and the awful thing that led to his conception were . . . I don't know, two different things. It wasn't his fault who had fathered him, or how. And believe it or not, it was the same for Cecilia. She despised what happened to her. Blocked most of it from her mind, I think. But she never allowed her hatred of the man who misused her to transfer to James. He was a dear, sweet child. We both loved him very much. But Cecilia loved him, I think, more like a sister than a mother. She was just too young to see him any other way."

"Was James always sickly?"

"Always. When a baby's mother is no more than a child herself, things can be wrong. They were."

"I'm sorry."

"So am I." She shivered again, and her voice tightened. "I'll miss that dear little fellow. So will Cecilia."

"Ma'am, I'm going to ask you something, and I hope you won't think I'm prying. But I heard somebody say that you and your girl were bound for Carter County. Is that right?"

"Yes," she said, looking at him, her face a dark silhouette, features invisible. "Who told you?"

"Mr. Williams did, the same man who went for the doctor. He seems to know at least a little of everyone's business."

"Well, I've made no secret of my business. We were on our way to Carter County when James became sick. We stopped here because Mr. Campbell was so kind and willing to take us in. No charge, he said, me being widowed and having no money. No charge. It was so kind of him."

"Yes. To tell you the truth, he gave me a free room, too."

"Really? I wonder how he makes a living, giving away rooms. May I ask why he would give you a . . . no, forgive me. Like you were saying, it's not my affair."

"Aw, that's all right. He give me a free room because he likes some of the things I've done." A cryptic answer, but he wasn't sure he should say more, not really knowing her or where she stood on the war. If she favored the Confederacy and found he didn't, she might end a conversation that he didn't want to stop just yet.

"Things you've done?"

"Yes, ma'am. Just some things having to do with the war. Was that how you lost your husband, ma'am? The war?"

"No. A bad heart. It killed him young, like it had killed his father years before. But you were asking me about Carter County. Why?"

"Well, Carter County happens to be where I live. And the place I've left behind."

"You're from Carter County? So you know how to get there, know your way around?"

"Well, surely I do. I been living there for years."

"Oh, thank God! I've been hoping for someone like you to come along! When will you be going back?"

"I wasn't planning to go back at all. Not until the war was through. It ain't the kind of place anybody should want to go just now, ma'am. It's bad there in them mountains."

"The war?"

"Yes. Can I ask you why you're going there? You got people?"

"I do. My sister, and her husband. She's dying, Mr. Smith, and I'm going to join her and care for her until the end comes."

"I'm sorry. Maybe I know your sister, or her husband."

"I doubt you do."

"What's their names?"

She seemed reluctant to answer, but after a couple of silent moments during which she seemed to be struggling for an alternative, did. "Fitz. His name is Vaughn Fitz. Her name is Jane."

"I don't know them."

"You don't?" Why did she sound relieved?

"No. Are they new to the county?"

"Somewhat. I think they moved there a little before the war began."

"That doesn't surprise. Ain't many coming in *since* the war. I believe you're the first human being I've met who's actually wanting to go *into* the mountains instead of leave them."

"You understand that I have no choice. She's my sister."

"Are the Fitzes Union or Secesh?"

"Does that matter?"

"It might. It's the Union folk who suffer the most in those mountains. So it seems to me, at least."

"Which are you, sir?"

"I'm Union. Always have been."

"Well, Vaughn Fitz isn't."

"Is he an active rebel?"

"He's not a soldier. To my knowledge he doesn't take any active part in the war. But he favors the Confederates."

"Maybe that's for the best. You'd be safe from the rebs, at least. They don't often bother their own."

"I don't know why either side would bother me. I don't favor either side—I don't favor there being a war at all. All I want is peace for myself and Cecilia."

"You won't find peace in the mountains these days. I hate to tell you that, but it's true. Ma'am, there's folks being shot and hung, men and boys being dragged off from their homes and never coming back again. There's bushwhackers and down-right sorry thieves and robbers with no stake in either side of the war. If it's peace you're after, you don't want to go to the mountains."

"I'd love to have peace, surely but that's not why I'm going there. It's for my sister, like I said. And I never said I wanted to go there. I'm going because I must. Jane's dying. She needs me."

He thought about it and nodded. "You're right. When it's your kin in need, you go to them."

"Do you have kin, Mr. Smith?"

"A brother, but he's off somewhere a long way from here. That's all. No one else."

"No wife? No children?"

"I had a wife once. She died in childbirthing, and the baby, too. I told you I'd lost a child—that was the time. Later on I asked another woman, but she turned me down. It maybe was for the best she did, for that was when the war got to rolling, and I commenced to doing what I do for the Union."

"What is it you do, if I may ask?"

"I'm a pilot. I guide Union men out of the mountains to the Federal lines. Mostly men who intend to join the army."

"Have you ever guided women?"

"No. Why do you ask?"

"No reason. Just curiosity."

Greeley took a couple of puffs on the cigar, then made a

decision. "Mrs. Fry, having told you as much as I have, I may as well tell you the rest. I'd appreciate it if you'd not spread it around, though."

"Certainly."

"My name ain't really George Smith. It's Brown. Greeley Brown. I'm not only a guide, but also a recruiting agent. The reb government hates me so bad they've got a reward posted for anyone who'll kill me or bring me in. The place I live in Carter County is no more than a hovel, because the rebs burned out my real house long ago. That's who I am. I'm using the false name of Smith while I'm laid up here, because of the price on my head."

"I hardly know what to say, Mister . . . Brown."

"Don't say nothing. I just wanted you to know the truth about me. And call me Greeley. When there's nobody else around, anyway."

"Very well, if you'll call me Miriam."

"Miriam. Miriam Fry. That's a pretty name, Miriam."

"Thank you, Greeley."

She reached out her hand; he shook it, and was reluctant to let it go.

"You know, Miriam, you don't belong in those mountains. Not just because of the war dangers, either. You ain't right for them. The way you talk, the way you look, and behave, the manner you got . . . you just don't belong in them mountains."

"I have to go."

"I know. But you can't go there alone. Not just a woman and a girl."

"I have no choice. I must go to my sister."

He puffed on the cigar. She remained silent, arms wrapped around herself.

"Miriam, can I ask you something about Cecilia?"

"Yes, I suppose."

"Don't answer if you don't want to. I was just wondering if Cecilia ever speaks. I've never heard a word from her."

"She does speak. Sometimes. But usually only to me. And she would speak to James, whisper in his ear. I don't know what she said to him. And she'll whisper to animals sometimes, dogs and cats and so on. She loves pets."

"But she won't talk to other people?"

"Very seldom. Only if she knows them very well or trusts them very deeply. Even then she doesn't have much to say. She says little enough even to me. It's been that way ever since . . . *it* happened."

"I see. So she don't speak because she don't want to speak."

"That's right."

Conversation waned. Greeley sensed it was time to part from her. He cast down the cigar and crushed it out beneath his foot. "Well, I believe I'll be heading back in. Don't stay out here and catch cold, Miriam."

Again he sensed her unseen smile. "I won't. And Greeley . . . thank you for understanding, about Cecilia."

"Thank you for telling me. I enjoyed our talk." He stood. "Well, good night, Miriam."

"Good night, Greeley."

Chapter 9

Greeley Brown walked with rifle in hand, snow around his feet, a cabin at his rear, a ridge rising before him. Oddly, his ankle felt no pain and he did not limp, but a tremendous sense of dread overwhelmed him.

There were other oddities as well. The mountains were different. Taller, pointed like hounds' teeth and leaning toward him at the tops, closer together than they should be and seeming to grow closer by the moment. What had been the beginning of a ridge rising beneath his feet was suddenly a hollow, the ridge suddenly ahead again, as if it had nudged forward when his foot touched it. He went on to it and began climbing again, this time ascending, but his legs grew heavy, and though he trudged hard, he did not seem to be going anywhere. Up the ridge he struggled, higher, higher, and yet whenever he looked, he was still where he had been before.

The mountains were taller and closer still. He was trapped in them, and there seemed no way out. . . .

He was back in the hollow once more. Beginning to panic and feel breathless, he mounted the base of the ridge again and began the straining climb anew when the sound of a shotgun blast, muffled by walls of the cabin behind him, jolted him and made him weak with horror.

Greeley jerked awake in his bed in the Campbell boarding-house and stared at the dark ceiling above him. His entire body was rigid, his fists clenched. He wondered if he had shouted.

He listened to the night sounds around him. No one was stirring or moving. If he had yelled, he hadn't awakened anyone.

His nightmare left him uninterested in sleep. Morning would be here soon. He propped himself up on his pillow, hands behind his head, and studied the dimly visible lines of the paneled ceiling, letting his thoughts drift up through it to the beautiful woman in the room above, and her daughter. He thought about them with a surprising sense of affection, and then about the grim mountains to which they were bound.

He rolled onto his side, hugging his pillow, and knew that he had just made a significant and unexpected decision.

That Knoxville errand he'd been planning would have to wait. Or perhaps be done through a surrogate. Of course! Williams. He was going to Knoxville anyway. He'd surely be glad to deliver a letter, if asked. Williams was no true friend of his, but they did have Thatcher in common. Williams would surely do him the favor for Thatcher's sake if no other.

He'd ask him, tomorrow.

Breakfast was a somber affair. Both Miriam and Cecilia Fry were at the table, and the presence of the newly bereaved made the other diners just uneasy enough that conversation was stifled. Campbell had nothing at all to say to Miriam Fry; he declined even to look at her. This, Greeley noticed, seemed quite pleasing to his wife, the only person there showing any sign of cheer, except for a man who had arrived late the night before and knew nothing of the Fry baby or its death. His big grins, loud banter, and attempts to spark conversation presently died in the unhospitable atmosphere like a candle flame extinguishing inside a closed jar. He sat with a glum look, wondering what sort of dismal little society he had wandered into.

Miriam glanced at Greeley several times through the meal, their eyes meeting and seeming to communicate, though

Greeley was not quite sure what was being said. All he knew was that every glance simultaneously thrilled him and left him confused, and wondering how she would react when he asked her—no, *told* her, because he wouldn't accept a refusal.

After breakfast, Greeley bought stationery from Mrs. Campbell—the authentic stuff being rare, what she sold him was actually some cut-out pieces of old wallpaper—and an envelope. He borrowed a pen and a little bottle of polkberry ink and retired to his room to begin what was for him a rarely performed act. Though Greeley was literate, writing had always intimidated him, so he never took up a pen unless it was unavoidable. This was one of those times.

He struggled for three hours before he felt he had done an adequate job. Carefully blowing the ink dry, he read through his work twice, trying to perceive with the viewpoint and feelings of the one who would be receiving it. He wasn't fully satisfied, and wondered if he might have been better served to impose on the more fluent Williams to have done this job for him. No, that wouldn't have been right. This was a message he was honor-bound to write for himself.

Greeley folded the letter, which was fully covered with his rough, purplish-blue scratchings, and put it into an envelope. He sealed it with a few drips of wax from a candle and carefully wrote the name of its intended recipient on the front.

"Well, that's done," he said aloud to the ghost of his lost friend. "Maybe not exactly as you wanted it done, Sam, but as close as I can come just now."

He left the room, still limping but getting on quite well now without either crutch or cane, and went looking for John P. Williams, envelope in hand.

After meeting with Williams and receiving from him an agreement to personally carry Greeley's letter to its addressee, Greeley began another search, looking for Miriam Fry.

She was not inside the boardinghouse nor in the yard. Cecilia Fry was not to be found, either, and Greeley's concern grew. Had they set off from Carter County since breakfast, while he was sitting in his room struggling with pen and ink?

He encountered Mable Campbell at the door of the cellar kitchen. "Pardon me, ma'am, but do you know where Mrs. Fry and her daughter might be?"

Mention of the Fry name brought a twitch to the woman's left eyebrow and opened a Pandora's box of diatribe. "No, I cannot, but I can tell you where they will *not* be soon enough! They'll not be spending many more nights in this house, not now that that poor baby has gone on to glory. Don't think me a hard woman, sir, but my husband and I operate no charitable house of refuge for poor folks who pay not a cent." Her face changed as she recalled that Greeley, too, was not paying for his room. "I'm not speaking about you, of course, oh no. You are a hero, sir, and we're glad to help you, and the room you're in, why, it doesn't lose us a cent for you to be there, for we don't let out that one in any case. But that Fry woman, she's of a different stripe. There's scandal in that family, I believe. I'm too good a Christian woman to speak my suspicions, but suffice it to say I believe the widow Fry is a woman of doubtful repute, and she'll not be lingering long under my roof!"

His choice of words made her pause, her frown growing darker. "You'll be tossing out the widow and her fatherless child, will you?"

"All I'm saying, sir, is that the reason my husband was so kind as to allow them to stay at all was that he felt for the poor sick baby. Now there's no reason they shouldn't be on their way to wherever they're going, and so they shall be."

Greeley wished he had picked someone else to ask about the whereabouts of Miriam Fry, someone not so full of bile.

"So you don't know where Mrs. Fry is just now, you say?"

"No sir, I don't. But if you find her, send her to talk to me. There's someone waiting to take that room they're in, someone able and willing to pay."

Greeley told Mrs. Campbell good day and limped back on around the front of the boardinghouse, testing his ankle and finding it in pretty decent shape. That was good. He would need it back to full strength for what he had in mind.

He heard rough, boyish laughter from across the street. Squinting against the winter mid-morning sun, he saw one of the boys who had been among that original gang he met coming into town. This fellow, the big one who declared his father was a Confederate, had his hand held high above his head, and in it was the kitten that had been Cecilia Fry's object of affection for the past several days.

Before him stood Cecilia herself, her face invisible to Greeley from where he was, but her tense posture showing that she was upset and scared.

The boy twisted the kitten about above his head, then swept his arm in a great arc that threatened to bump the furry head against the ground. All the while he made extreme, mocking faces at Cecilia, and occasionally said words that Greeley couldn't make out.

"Dang!" Greeley muttered. He began trudging as fast as he could across the yard and toward the street. He told himself to go easy on the fellow, he was just a boy . . . but knowing what he knew now of Cecilia's past and what she had suffered, he felt a burning fury at this ugly, grinning tormentor.

When he was almost across the street, Greeley bellowed, "You there!" and instantly wished he hadn't, because Cecilia reacted far more extremely than did the young man, who merely blinked in surprise and grunted a "Huh?" Cecilia, with her back to Greeley, screeched and sank to her haunches, hands clapping over her ears as if Greeley had fired off a pistol just behind her head.

"I'm sorry, Cecilia, didn't mean to startle you," Greeley said, stepping around her and going straight for the boy, whose face was going through some odd contortions. "Boy, give me that kitten, right now."

The boy hesitated and tossed the kitten to Greeley, who instinctively but vainly tried to catch it and got himself badly scratched. The kitten hit the ground on its feet and bounded off. Cecilia, wiping tears, ran after it, back toward the boarding-house.

"Boy, don't you be bothering that girl no more. Her little baby has . . . her little baby brother has just died."

"I wasn't hurting her, or that kitten."

"She was crying. That's all I needed to see. What was your name? Billy, wasn't it?"

"Maybe it is, maybe it ain't. Just like you."

"What's that supposed to mean?"

"Whatever I want it to."

"You're a smart-tongued little devil, ain't you!"

"So?"

"So you'd best tuck your little forked devil tail between your legs before I yank a knot in it. Get on with you, and leave her alone from now on, boy."

"You ain't my pa. I don't have to do what you say. I'll talk to her if I want to! She's pretty."

"That's right, too pretty for you! Don't let me catch you around her no more. Hear?"

Greeley turned and headed back across the street, hardly noticing that anger had given him vigor and almost eliminated his limp.

The boy yelled after him, "I know you, mister! You really *are* Greeley Brown—my pa seen you setting on the porch and said you was! And he knows, 'cause he's seen you before! My pa says that someday somebody's going to put a ball through your brain off in some mountain holler and be rid of one damned old Union dog!"

Greeley ground his teeth but would not respond. He kept walking.

"You hear me, Greeley Brown? You're a Union dog! Union dog! Union dog!"

Greeley pondered how great would be the pleasure of testing out his ankle by kicking a certain young Confederate rump.

He headed around behind the boardinghouse and found Cecilia sitting on a stump on the far end of the yard, stroking the kitten and occasionally wiping at her cheek. Her back was toward him; her shoulders slumped and small.

He stopped and watched her, wondering how it could be that any man could abuse this young girl as she had been abused. He recalled the torments of his own late wife as she suffered in her ill-fated childbirthing, and wondered how hard it must have been for one so young and small as Cecilia to give birth. He imagined the terror and confusion she must have felt in addition to the pain.

He wanted to go to her now and make sure she was all right, but did not. He wondered if a girl who had endured what she had would be terrified by any kind of confrontation with a man. He was repelled by the notion of being an object of fright to her.

So Greeley merely headed back around toward the front again, to settle in on the front porch, if the sharp-tongued rebel boy was gone from across the street and the breeze didn't get too cold.

The boy was gone. Greeley eased onto the porch and settled into his rocker. The breeze was cold, but light enough to be endured. He rocked slowly, wondering where Miriam was and wishing Williams would show up and give him another of those excellent cigars.

Miriam had been at the grave of her grandson, grieving alone so that Cecilia wouldn't have to see it. "Sometimes she looks to see how I'm feeling, and lets her feelings follow mine," Miriam explained to Greeley. "So I try to be strong when I'm with her, so she'll try to be strong, too."

"Cecilia had a little spell of trouble while you were gone," Greeley said.

"What? What kind of trouble? Is she all right? Where is she?"

"Whoa, Miriam, be calm. She's fine, and it wasn't nothing serious. There's some boys in town here who've noticed how pretty she is, and one was teasing her some, keeping that kitten away from her to see if he could make her talk to him. I stepped across the street and had a word with him, and Cecilia came on back. She was out back petting the kitten a few minutes ago, and as far as I know still is. She's fine, just a little upset."

Miriam, who had been standing against one of the porch rails, now settled into the empty rocker beside Greeley's. "Poor Cecilia," she said. "She's so easily frightened now. She's so delicate. . . . She trailed off.

Greeley rocked in silence, the breeze feeling colder all at once.

"We're leaving here tomorrow, Cecilia and I," Miriam said.

"Tomorrow? Have the Campbells told you you must?"

"No. But I want to leave before they have the chance.

Before *she* has the chance, rather." Miriam smiled and cut her eyes toward Greeley. "To tell you the truth, Greeley, I believe I could stay here almost forever, if it were up to Mr. Campbell alone. I do believe he finds me . . . appealing."

"You noticed that, did you?"

"Yes. And I must admit I've taken advantage of it. A woman can sometimes benefit from the silly infatuations some men get. It's not the first time I've allowed some ridiculous man to do me a favor in return for a smile and a limpid gaze." She sighed. "Why am I so open with you, Greeley? Here I am confessing my soul, and I hardly know you."

"Ain't much to know. I'm a simple man."

"No, no . . . I don't think simple is the word. Uncomplicated, maybe. Honest. Authentic. That's it. You strike me as an authentic man."

"You speak well, Miriam. I don't know many folks at all who speak so fine as you do. It's one of the reasons I say you don't belong in them mountains. A lot of mountain people ain't been out of the hills in their whole lives, ain't seen nothing but a few square miles of mountain land. But you're different. Well-spoken, educated. There's an air of the broad world about you."

"I'm not all you think, Greeley. I'm not worldly or educated. Any education I have is through my own efforts. And if I speak well, it's only because I've made a point of imitating people of a higher station. Sometimes, Greeley, I've found that I've had to make my own way in whatever way I can. Sometimes the only way open to me has been to be something of . . . an actress, I suppose you could say."

"So you're saying that sometimes you act like somebody you ain't."

"It sounds bad when you put it that way. I'm not sure I can explain just what I mean."

"Well, I hope you've been honest with me, because I'm going to make you an offer. And I'm going to insist that you accept it. I don't want you and Cecilia going into the mountains alone. I mean, it's an absurd notion any way you look at it. You'd get lost, eaten by some critter, killed by bushwhackers, or you'd freeze to death. You just can't do it, no matter how bad your sister needs you."

"Greeley, don't think me rude here, but that's a matter that isn't up to you. This is my situation, and I'll decide what notions are absurd and which aren't."

"Fine, as long as you decide that the notion of me coming with you as a guide is one you can agree with."

"You mean you'd come with Cecilia and me?"

"That's right. And don't pretend the thought of that didn't cross your mind when you found out I'm a pilot."

She slowly smiled. "Greeley! What a fine offer! Yes, of course it crossed my mind, but I didn't dare ask, especially since you told me you didn't plan to go back at all."

"Well, I didn't plan to. But considering your situation, I'd be a pretty sorry excuse for a man if I let you head into them hills alone, and me go running off somewhere else just for my own benefit."

"I can't believe it! You'd really pilot Cecilia and me?"

"I made the offer, didn't I?"

"Oh, Greeley! Thank you! Thank you so much! Oh, you truly must be sent of God to help us!"

"Oh, I ain't nothing nearly that special. I just happened to stumble onto the scene, that's all. Limped onto the scene, maybe I should say."

"Oh, that's right—your ankle! How soon will you be able to travel on it?"

"Tomorrow, maybe. But I'd prefer to wait until the day after tomorrow, just to play safe. Don't worry, by the way, if the Campbells try to oust you between now and then now that the baby's no longer to be considered. I'll pay for your room for any extra nights you stay."

She squeezed his hand tightly, beaming, eyes brimming with happy tears. "Thank you."

"You're welcome."

"Did you say Cecilia is around back? I want to go tell her."

"Last I saw her, she was sitting on that stump back there."

Miriam rose lightly, glanced around, then bent over and kissed Greeley's bearded cheek. "I hope you don't find me forward for that. You just don't know how grateful I am."

He hadn't expected the kiss. It stirred feelings in him he hadn't known since his late wife had still been at his side. He muttered, "Why, I'm just trying to be helpful, that's all."

She left him, hurrying around the big building. Greeley sank back in his rocker.

Well, he'd gone and done it. Despite all he had pledged to himself, he was going back to Carter County after all. Despite all the deprivation and suffering, the men shot in mountain hollows, the tense awakenings at midnight to listen to the forests on the other side of the wall and wonder all in a sweat what was that odd sound just heard. Despite poor old Flory Wilmoth, who chose to die because going on living in the hell of the mountain war was more than she could bear. Despite those dark days of struggling alone in his hut with a devilish depression that had made him wonder if he would end up following Flory's example himself before it was done. Despite all that, he was going back.

He was still rocking and marveling over it all when Miriam came back around the boardinghouse, Cecilia with her. They walked onto the porch together, Miriam moving to the side, Cecilia standing before him, looking at him. She had the kitten in her hands, a white little puff with two slanting eyes that gleamed out at Greeley.

"That's an appealing little partner you're holding there," Greeley said to her.

Cecilia held the kitten out to him. He took it from her and patted it gently, scratching it around the ears. It wriggled, mewed, licked him. Grinning at Cecilia, he made a show of really enjoying the opportunity to play with the kitten, then handed it back to her with a feigned look of reluctance.

Cecilia Fry took the kitten, smiled at him, and for the first time spoke to him. Just a tiny whisper, barely audible: "Thank you."

He was so stunned to hear it that he didn't reply with anything more than a smile.

She smiled in turn, and ran off the porch and around to the back again. Just a child, she seemed. More childish than her years. Fourteen, almost old enough for marrying off by the standards of certain parts of the mountains, yet still playing with a kitten with the enthusiasm of a child of nine or ten. But Cecilia was older than her years, too, considering her experience of being forced into an early motherhood by the unthinkable wickedness of some man. Greeley felt deeply for Cecilia, and regretted the scars that marred what should have been a carefree young mind, and would for the rest of her days.

Miriam had said that Cecilia's abuser had been punished. Greeley was glad. He only wished he could have inflicted it himself. He could think of some choice and fitting torments to administer to any man who could take pleasure in hurting a child like Cecilia Fry.

Part II

FLETCHER'S CROSS

Chapter 10

Greeley had never undertaken a mountain journey quite like this one.

In all his stampeder runs he had never guided females, and now he had two of them. It lent a strange and not always comfortable ambience to the whole business. He was self-conscious every moment, and had to struggle to forget himself and maintain his concentration. He pondered with private amusement that there would be many who would click their tongues over the notion of a single fellow like him traipsing through the wilderness, unsupervised, with a beautiful woman and her almost equally beautiful daughter. But Greeley was a guardian, not a threat. In his company mother and daughter were not only protected, but respected.

Awkward as it was to be traveling with women, Greeley had to admit he enjoyed it more than not. Being in Miriam's company would be a pleasure in almost any circumstance. She looked beautiful despite the fact she was clad, like her daughter, in male garments that Greeley had scrounged up in Sevierville, including a flop hat that hid her bundled-up brunette hair. He had argued back and forth with himself before deciding to have the females dress this way. Considering the Home Guards and other rebels who might be scouting the forests for stampeders, it didn't necessarily heighten Miriam's and Cecilia's safety to appear to be men when viewed from a distance or through a veil of trees, but all in all the disadvantages of trying to travel through the wilderness in feminine garb outweighed all else, and Greeley had opted for the change of clothing style, Miriam concurring.

Several times Miriam repeated her conviction that Greeley was a godsend, telling him that she had not had even the vaguest notion of how she would have completed her journey had he not come along.

She told Greeley some about her and her daughter's pilgrimage eastward. The journey had commenced, under somewhat pressing circumstances that she declined to explain, in a little Middle Tennessee hamlet called Livingston, where she and Cecilia had continued to live after the death of Mr. Fry well over a year back. Their journey toward Carter County had been carried out by a hodgepodge of means. At times she and her daughter had traveled on foot, carrying the baby; other times they had ridden by stage and train—though soon their money almost entirely ran out—and once they had been given rides on horseback by a helpful, respectful, but rough-cut and anonymous group that Miriam suspected were some of the Cumberland's famous bushwhackers. Mile by mile, means by means, the pair of them, with the weakening baby, had made their way as far as Sevierville, using one invented story after the next to explain who they were and why they were traveling, playing on the sympathies and infatuations of many a man along the way, and always presenting little James as Miriam's child rather than Cecilia's.

Greeley didn't like hearing Miriam talk so casually about all the deceptions she had foisted throughout her journey. He wondered despite himself if he really knew the truth about her, if she really thought as highly of him as she avowed, or if he was simply one more helpful dupe along the way, fed stories that might be true, might not.

He didn't let those doubts linger, too overwhelmed by Miriam to stand for them. In mental lectures to himself, he affirmed that Miriam was simply a splendid woman in hard circumstances. She was who she claimed and what she claimed. She meant it when she declared him a godsend. That was that.

Besides, he had more pressing matters than doubts about Miriam Fry to occupy him, not the least of which was making sure he kept these women safe while also respecting the privacy they required. Greeley made sure their mountain camps were set up in the most discreet manner, taking such pains to give the women a reasonable seclusion without straying too far from them, that he suspected Miriam was laughing at him about it from time to time. Well, let her snicker. A girl who had suffered what Cecilia had surely was wary around men. He wanted to do nothing to make her feel invaded or afraid of him.

The silent and rather mysterious Cecilia gave Greeley much to ponder. She was an unusual girl, mixing childhood and maturity in strange ways. Here was a girl who could keen over her dying baby and weep over his grave like any mother, then be childishly absorbed in play with a kitten the next, seemingly having all but forgotten the lost child. Cecilia had seemed as upset over having to leave that kitten at the boardinghouse in Sevierville as over leaving her baby in a cold grave. Yet this gave Greeley no sense that the girl's relative values were out of balance. Cecilia had simply been handed too much to deal with, at too young an age, to have any hope of maintaining perspective. She had been knocked off her proper course by the wickedness of some violent man, and it was no casual cliché to say that God only knew if she would ever find her way back on again. Poor, silent child. There was something about her that broke Greeley's heart again and again.

The second night into the journey, they found shelter at the home of a lone mountain woman. To avoid difficult and complex explanations, Greeley presented himself as the brother of Miriam, uncle of Cecilia, traveling with them toward their old home place in Carter County, where they would be seeing to the care of his aged mother.

The old woman was deeply lonely and sad. Only a week earlier her husband, a crippled and ancient man, had been shot to death by a group of young bushwhackers trying to steal a hog from its hidden pen. "Our last hog, just a thin old thing, but all the meat we had. Zeke had been keeping it hid and was ready to butcher it, and when he caught them trying to take it, he couldn't abide it. He went out after them, with his rifle. They shot him right outside the gate you come through earlier this evening. If it hadn't of been dusky-dark, you could have seen his blood still on the stones. They shot him dead, like he was of no count at all, like he was less than that hog they wanted.

"And then they took the hog, with Zeke lying there in his dying blood. They never even give him another glance. Killed my husband, took my hog. Three laying hens, too. Took and wrung their necks right there and slung them over their saddles. I'm left with so little, I swear I don't know how I'll live out the winter. But what I have I'll share. It's them who won't share with others that the good Lord allows to starve, and them who don't forget to share that he blesses in his own good time."

Greeley glanced at Miriam's somber face and hoped that she was beginning to see why he'd warned her against coming into the mountains. The farther east they went, the more rugged the land became, and the more brutal grew the wartime world around them. Dying sister or not, if Miriam made the first sound about turning back and abandoning this journey, Greeley would take her and Cecilia out of these hills so fast they'd be astonished. He had sworn never to return to the mountains until the war was finished, anyway. Nothing less motivating than Miriam Fry could have made him go back on that intention.

That night by the light of the cabin fireplace, Miriam asked Greeley to tell her more about the realities of war in the mountains. It's ugly and sad, he warned her. It doesn't matter, she replied. I need to hear.

He told her with an honesty almost as brutal as the war atrocities themselves, ticking off case after case.

"It's hard to know where to begin," he said. "There's been deaths and killings from the beginning, on both sides, the Union folk taking the worst of it, in my view. Many a man who has met his end slumped over a stump out in some holler, tol ball through his skull. I've known men to be put on horses, noosed around the neck, and the horses rode out from under them so they're left to choke. I've known men and even boys to be lined up and shot for no crime other than being at the wrong place at the wrong time, and women to be insulted and shamed because they wouldn't tell where their men were hiding out. I've known of young women kidnapped from their families, and held hostage for the ransom of the last of the food the family was counting on to hold them through the winter. I've known of old women lashed with switches and dottery old men strung up with their toes just touching the ground, so they have to stand on tiptoe or choke, unless they tell where their son, or their daughter's husband, or the neighbor's boy, is hiding. I know of one young boy shot through the head by rebels while he begged them to shoot him anyplace but there, for he knew his mother would want to stroke his hair before they buried him and he didn't want it bloodied.

"That's the war in the mountains, Miriam. That's the way it's fought. You wake up some bright morning in them mountains, the sun shining down, the birds singing, and you think that there can't really be no war going on, people can't really be doing them kinds of things to one another. You manage to forget it all, because it don't seem real in the bright day. Then you get out with your rifle to do some hunting, and about dusk you find a man hanging in the shadows from a limb on some hidden ridge side, his flesh mostly gone and his eyes eaten out by birds, and then you remember, and know the war is real."

"How many people have you known who've died in such bad ways, Greeley?"

"I've known many of them personally, or in some cases, folks who were their close friends or kin. Let's see . . . back in June of last year, maybe July, there was Henry Archer, over on Stony Creek in Carter County. He was hiding out to avoid the conscription. Some rebs found him hiding in a thicket, hauled him off to Elizabethton. Throwed him in the jail. Before long they declared he was guilty of this or that, and decided to shoot him. They took him out of the jail, bound his hands behind him, and began marching him to the Narrows, where a lot of men are took to be shot. His wife followed them, baby in her arms, begging and crying for them not to kill him. They just pushed him along, keeping her behind and away from him, and she was still begging and wailing for him when she heard the shot. Later on she and a couple of men went and found him. They'd stripped him bare and left him lying, blood all over. No reason he should have died. He wasn't fit for military service anyhow—that's one reason he never stampeded.

"Then there's Andy Ward, one of the first ones killed. He's been dead now since the big rebellion after the bridge burnings of 'sixty-one. The rebs was hot mad when those bridges went up, and began rounding up Union men every which way. Lank Ellis, a sorry Secesh even if he is kin of Dan Ellis, arrested poor Andy, who was a loyal man of my own county. He was innocent—no crime, nothing to justify him being arrested, but he was a Union man and that's all that mattered. They tried to make him take the Confederate oath, and he wouldn't do it. So a rebel soldier shot him dead, right there. Ten or eleven days before Christmas.

"And Fiddler John Smith. Oh, yes, there's one I'll never forget. Fiddler John lived in Turkey Town, about the Lyons community, and got accused of robbing a Secessionist's house, though I don't believe for a minute he done it. He was locked up, no death sentence or nothing, but after a time he and some others were took out of the jail and told they was being marched to Bristol. A few miles above town, all at once Fiddler John was pulled off away from the others and marched off toward the Narrows. God knows, if there's really such a thing as haunting, the Narrows will surely be haunted from now till doomsday, so many have been slaughtered there. Anyway, they shot Fiddler John dead, then cut off his finger to get at a ring he was wearing.

"Berry Pritchard died in much the same way, shot to death for being a Union man. And there was Hiram Main, back in the winter of 'sixty-two. He lived in the Third District, just a young man, liked by everybody. He was off visiting a neighbor when a couple of so-called conscription officers out of North Carolina found him. There was a fight, and when them conscription men left, Hiram was dead.

"Then there was John Tilly, a few months later. He lived in Johnson County, on the Little Doe. Had a fine wife name of They robbed him and argued over who would get to 1. His widow still mourns him."

Greeley paused a moment, pulling other cases from his mind. "Right about the same time John Tilly was murdered, or maybe some weeks earlier, there was a little group killed over on the Watauga, near Fish Spring. One was James Taylor, who had been in a reb prison for serving as a Federal conscription officer. He'd escaped and was trying to make the Union lines when they caught him. He was with three other men, Sam Tatem, and two name of Kite and Rugger.

"These four together were scouting over along the Watauga, waiting for the water to go down some so they could cross, when a band of Johnson County Home Guards and some of Colonel Folks's rebels come along and saw them. They fired some shots, killed James Taylor right there, and shot Tatem a few minutes after. Then they took their forage ropes and strung up the other two. They left thinking they'd done some fine work, killing four Union men, but Tatem had skunked them. He'd fell shot, but he wasn't dead, just playing 'possum, and he's survived and healed up good since then. They call him by the nickname of 'Dead Yankee' Tatem to this day. You don't hear many tales like that. Most who get caught don't survive.

"But worse than any of these is what happened over on Limestone Cove just this November past. Over yonder stands the Bell house, where lived a couple of brothers named Bell, James and David, and they had a good house that was open to any Union man who needed food or shelter. David Bell was a physician, too, and helpful to the Union men in need of care.

"One morning a gang of maybe fifty stampeders out of North Carolina showed up at the Bell house, looking for something to eat and trying to find theirselves a pilot to guide them on to the Union lines. They were setting in the yard, resting after an all-night trek, when up rides Colonel Witcher and a big group of his rebel soldiers, and surprises them. They took off running, but the rebs was mounted and run them down easy enough. They shot them like boys shooting rats in a barn. Just massacred them right there, and them not having any real chance at all to resist. Ten or so men were slaughtered that day. James Bell was one of them who died. They shot him, wounded him, then laid him out and pounded on his head until there wasn't a brain left in it that hadn't run out onto the ground around him. They burned the house, too. Witcher kil' some others that day, too, who weren't at the Bell house. William Bird was one, and Commodore Sloan. They shot Sloan at his own house, before the eyes of his family.

"But it ain't just Carter and Johnson counties that see such things. All through the eastern end of Tennessee folks suffer in just the same way. And when you get over into the Carolina wilderness, it's worse. Men shot, hung, stuck to trees with bayonets like moths pinned to a board. Widows and children robbed of food and even their clothes. Cabins burned, livestock stolen, old men and women shot or hung. Women who have husbands out on the scout tied up and made to watch their children being tormented until they agree to betray their own husbands. Children herded up and made to lead the search for their own pappies out in the mountains, yelling and calling for them with the rebels sneaking along behind. Young woman captured and—"

"Enough," Miriam said. "I understand. You needn't say no more." She shuddered. "The cruelty of it! Those that do such things, I hope they suffer it all in return, a hundredfold."

Greeley replied, "They will. There's always a season of reckoning. A leveling of the balance. I used to preach about how that kind of vengeance ain't right, how it just keeps the wickedness going on and on. I suppose that when I said that, I was right—but the more time that goes by, the more I see people I know and love suffering, getting slaughtered, the more I crave that revenge for myself. It don't seem so wrong anymore."

"So you believe in vengeance, Greeley?"

"I don't know I believe in it. I know I want it."

"Does the moral law change, though? If it was wrong before, it's wrong now."

"I don't think the moral law has changed. But I believe maybe I have. I ain't trying to justify it." He looked closely at Miriam. "Does that bother you, hearing me say that?"

"Maybe some. Maybe what bothers me worse is that I understand so well what you're talking about." Her eyes made a subtle shift toward Cecilia. "Vengeance doesn't always feel so wrong when it's yourself, or your own, who is being
1."

looked around at the group. Their old hostess sat th eyes closed, tears streaming down her face.

Cecilia stared at the fire with a cold look of horror deep in her eyes. Miriam, after her last comment, had pressed her lips together tightly. They were whitening around the edges.

Greeley tugged at his beard, regretful now for his own unmerciful honesty. "I reckon I've spoken too freely," he said. "But what I've said is truth, and you may as well know it. This war has cast a dark cloud over the mountain country. It's a grim and bloody place sometimes. And if you want to turn back, Miriam, I'll gladly lead you back the same way we've come."

He saw the temptation playing in her eyes, but in the end she shook her head. "We must go on," she said. "For my sister."

He nodded. He would not have chosen any differently under the same circumstances."Then go on we will," he said.

Chapter 11

They traveled along the side of a mountain, moving more slowly than Greeley would have liked, but making up for slowness by steady progress. Walking ahead of the females, Greeley caught himself wondering at some moments just why he was doing this, going back on his own promise to shun these charnel hills, but a glance back at the struggling women, their faces reddened from exertion and their feet sore from the rugged trail, made him remember. He could endure one more journey into the mountains for their sake. He'd take them in, see that they were safely ensconced at their destination, and *then* he could leave, and put the mountains behind until the war was through.

So he told himself. But a deeper and more persuasive voice told him that once Miriam Fry was in these mountains to stay, he would find it quite difficult to leave. Her presence would tie him to these mountains with a bond stronger even than his desire to get away. He couldn't just abandon such a woman, and such a forlorn, silent child, in the midst of war; could he?

The sky was clear as they moved along the mountainside. The rugged land was to all appearances peaceful. But Greeley kept his eyes trained on the valleys and fields below, and before long he saw what did not surprise him, and paused to point it out to Miriam and Cecilia.

"Yonder," he said, pointing. "See them?"

They strained their eyes, unsure what Greeley was trying to make them see, but glad for the pause in travel. Cecilia gasped abruptly, pointed, and for only the second time in Greeley's experience with her, spoke: "Look!"

Miriam had seen them, too. "Who are those men, Greeley?"

"A band of raiders. Too far to tell for sure from here, but I'd say they're Home Guards. See them going in and out of that house? Taking goods of some kind. Food, probably, maybe weapons or clothes. They probably came on the excuse of looking for some poor old conscription dodger, but most likely what they had in mind all along was taking whatever they could get."

They watched the distant drama below for a minute or so longer, then Greeley told them it was time to move on. Farther into the wilderness. Farther into the land of mountain war.

They were still on a remote mountaintop, well away from roads and settlement, when Greeley called the halt for camping that night. He built a small fire; they cooked some bacon Greeley had brought from Sevierville, and sliced off hunks of bread from two drying loaves he had fetched along as well. They put the bacon between the bread slabs, and Cecilia and Miriam devoured the sandwiches like the half-starved refugees they very nearly were.

Greeley ate more slowly, making his food last. "Miriam, tell me again the name of your brother-in-law."

"Fitz," she replied. "Vaughn Fitz."

"Fitz, that's right." He took another bite, the firelight playing across his face. "It seems odd to me that I don't know him. Dang, I know almost everybody in Carter County, especially around the Limestone Cove."

"Well, I've told you he's not been there all that long."

"Yeah, that's it, I reckon. I just never happened to meet

him." Another bite, another long chew. "Fitz. Unusual kind of name."

In answer to an imploring look from Cecilia, Miriam asked, "Is there enough bread that we can have a little more?"

"Some. Take some, but keep in mind we need to make our rations last."

Cecilia pounced on the bread like that kitten back in Sevierville would pounce on a rolling ball of twine. The childish eagerness with which she assailed her next slice made Greeley smile. She was an endearing, appealing girl, even if a bit odd, even if the memory of what she had endured still hung about her like an unseen cloud.

They traveled safely but with difficulty while on the mountains, with greater ease but less protection while crossing the valleys and streams. The farther they went, the more familiar to Greeley the land grew, the more progressively uncomfortable Miriam seemed to grow. Greeley wondered, hopefully, if she was having doubts about the wisdom of going on. He asked her about it, just one more time, and she said what she always had: She was doing this for her sister, and had no other choice.

Mathen Ricker opened his cabin door with great caution, then, as usual whenever Greeley Brown came to see him, his eyes softened for a moment with a light of welcome, which he quickly replaced with a hard glare.

"I'll be!" the old mountaineer said. "There he comes again, that cussed Lincolnite Greeley Brown! What are you going to do now, bushwhacker? Shoot me down for being a good rebel?"

"I ought to, you know it?" Greeley replied. "I ought to just lever my Henry here and rid these mountains of one more kisser of Jeff Davis's backside. When you going to give your loyalty back to the Stars and Stripes, old man?"

"When the Yanks drive the rebels from these mountains. When cats bark and cows fly and hell gets a foot of fresh snow. Come on in, Greeley. It's good to see you, it really is. I been worried about you lately."

Greeley stepped inside the familiar cabin. He loved this place, loved old Mathen, loved to banter with him and tease him about politics. What made it fun was that, in this one case at least, political differences didn't really matter. He and his former neighbor would never agree on governments, but they shared a bond of friendship neither would break for anything. Mathen, rebel sympathizer though he was, had given Greeley refuge many a time in this cabin, especially after Thomas's Highland Legion destroyed one of Greeley's residence huts on over the ridge and left Greeley momentarily homeless. Since then, Greeley had built his current hut elsewhere, the one which, when he had last left, he figured he was leaving for good.

Mathen went to the chest that he used to store his food supply. "Greeley, you ain't going to guess what I got in here," he said, eyes dancing with excitement. "Try and guess! Try!"

"Why, I don't know, old man . . . you've got a good cigar for me."

"Better than that. Guess again."

"Plum jelly."

"Nope!"

"A cooked rat, like them rebels in the big cities eat now that the Confederacy has ariz to give them a good life of joy and independence."

"No, no, no. I'll just tell you. I got coffee."

"What? The real thing? No roasted wheat nor dried pumpkin nor scorched okra?"

"Nope. Good coffee, true as the gospel!"

"How?"

"I got connections, Greeley. A nephew, to tell you the truth. Good rebel boy, a corporal. He come to visit me when he was on furlough. Took a mighty risk, coming along through these Lincolnite infested mountains, but he come right on, and glory be if he didn't have a sack of true coffee for me. He told me he couldn't tell how he come by it, and I didn't ask. Me and him shared a couple of cups, and I can tell you this ain't none of that coffee that the Yankee soldiers sell out of their rations, after they've done boiled all the taste out of it for theirselves. This is the fresh bean, and since my nephew left I've been saving the rest for some other special time. Like now."

"If you're brewing, I'm drinking," Greeley said. "I'm obliged, Mathen."

The old fellow, who moved slowly but was still very limber and spry, went to the fire and built it up, then checked the water level in his big coffeepot, which had received little enough use since the war brought its deprivations. Greeley watched him, then closed his eyes, settling into a state of restful content. Mathen Ricker's was always a refuge to him, a pocket away from worries and war. But he remembered Miriam and Cecilia hidden outside, awaiting his return, and opened his eyes again. He thought about asking Mathen if he might bring them in and let them have coffee, too, but didn't, though it made him feel selfish. Mathen had only half a sack or so of beans, not enough to share with too many if he wanted it to last. He'd leave it to Mathen himself to make the offer.

"What brings you here, Greeley?" Mathen asked as he poked up the fire a little more.

"Well, I'm on an unusual errand," Greeley replied. "I'm leading a couple of folks back into the mountains instead of out of them."

"Why's that?"

"It's two women. Well, one woman, one half-grown girl."

Mathen looked at Greeley in surprise. "Women? Well, where are they? You leaving them out in the cold while you're in here getting ready to drink coffee?"

"They're out there just now, yes."

"Well, you ungentlemanly scoundrel, you go out there and call them in, while I—"

"Wait, wait. Let me talk to you first. There's a thing or two I need to know."

Mathen went back to his coffee preparations. "What's that?"

"Do you know a man at the Limestone Cove named Fitz? Vaughn Fitz?"

"I've heard of him, can't say I really know him. All I know is that he moved into the Cove about the beginning of the war, and he's a supporter of the Confederacy."

"That's all you know?"

"That's all."

"You don't know what shape his wife is in, do you?"

"Why, shaped sort of like this, I suppose." Mathen turned to Greeley, very straight-faced, and with his hands traced out the outline of a shapely woman in the air. He abruptly cackled with laughter. "That's how I remember them looking, anyhow. It's been a mighty long time since I had a good enough look at one to be sure."

Greeley grinned. "You'll see a pretty enough woman when I bring in Miriam. Miriam Fry's her name, and her daughter is Cecilia. Miriam's the sister of Vaughn Fitz's wife, and she's come to take care of her. It seems that Mrs. Fitz is mighty sick and expected to die. That's why I asked you about her."

"Oh, I see. But no, I got no answer. I don't know the woman nor a thing about her health. She may have died for all I would know."

"I hope not. Miriam's already had a death in her family. Just the other day. A poor little sickly baby boy, name of James. It was pitiful. I hope her sister is not only still living, but getting better. Miriam says she'll never get better, though. Something chronic and fatal, I guess."

"You know where Fitz lives?"

"Not exactly. I was hoping you would."

"I do, matter of fact."

Greeley had expected no different. Mathen Ricker knew pretty much where every mountain family dwelled, the one exception lately being Greeley himself. Greeley, though recently a neighbor of Mathen's, had moved elsewhere not only because the rebels had ferreted out his former dwelling, but because he'd become concerned that some Secesh desperate to earn the reward posted for his head might give old Mathen some trouble, trying to get his friend to tell where he was. So now Greeley made sure Mathen didn't possess that information. He worried occasionally about having holed up here so many times in the past. Word had a way of getting around, and if the rebels of the mountains began to perceive Mathen as a harborer of the enemy, it might bring him harm. Greeley hoped that would never happen.

"Tell me how to get to Fitz's."

Mathen gave a description of the route to Fitz's place relative to dwellings whose locale Greeley already knew. He described the house, a very isolated new cabin, and the lay of the land around it and how it stood in relation to the nearest watercourses. When Mathen was finished, Greeley could have walked straight to Fitz's door as if he had done it a dozen times before.

Mathen added, "Don't you be going to Fitz's place yourself, him being Confederate."

"I won't. I'll take the womenfolk as close as I can, but I'll make sure Fitz doesn't lay eyes on me. I've come to learn lately that I'm a far better known man than I wish I was. Strangers recognizing me and all. It's frightening."

"There's a lot that's frightening these days," Mathen said seriously. "There's new dangers in these mountains for Lincolnites."

"You thinking of a man name of Fletcher, maybe?"

"The same. You ain't run across him, have you?"

"Just his handiwork. He hung Tom Wilmoth and his youngest son. Carved an X mark on their jaws. I'm told that's his sign, like a cattle brand."

"Aye. Fletcher's Cross." Mathen coughed and spat into the fire. "He's a rebel, Greeley, and you know I favor the rebel cause, but I hear this Fletcher is dangerous even to his own kind, if he so much as suspects a betrayal. He's naught but a murderer. You stay clear of him."

"I'll stay clear," Greeley said. "How's that coffee coming?"

"It's coming. And I'll make plenty. Run out and fetch them gals, Greeley. Why, I don't know how long it's been since there's been a gal of any kind to set foot in this place, much less a pretty one. Go fetch them in!"

"I will. Oh, let me tell you—the daughter, Cecilia, doesn't speak. Except to her mother, and to animals, and a couple of times to me. It's a long story as to why she don't talk, and I don't know as I'm free to share it. Suffice it to say we'll probably hear nothing from her today, and if she seems afraid of you, it ain't nothing personal. She's been through some things."

"What about the mother? She speaks?"

"She speaks. Talks really fine, like a schooled woman, though she says she ain't."

"She your woman, Greeley? I'm asking so as not to offend you if I decide to ask for her hand, you see." His eyes laughed, but Greeley knew the old man was truly interested in whether his younger, lonely friend had a prospect. Mathen had been urging him to find himself a wife for a long time now.

"She ain't my woman. I wouldn't mind it if she was, though. She's a fine lady."

"I'll make sure I don't let my charm overwhelm her, then, so as I don't ruin your opportunity. You been behaving yourself with her out on the trail, ain't you?"

"Now, what gives you the right to ask me that, old man? But yeah, I have."

"That's good. Be a gentleman. Always respect the ladies, and behave yourself with some class and dignity. That's Mathen Ricker's motto." He punctuated the comment with a grimace and a loud, resounding belch.

"That's what you consider dignity? You been living alone too long, Mathen." Greeley rose, went to the door, and headed out to get Miriam and Cecilia.

Over at the fireplace, the water was starting to steam and before long would be boiling.

The coffee was as good as Greeley could have hoped. He and his two fellow travelers brought out the last of their provisions, and, combining these with some of Mathen's own food, made a very fine meal, the coffee serving both as beverage and dessert.

They didn't leave Mathen's place that day, though Greeley hadn't intended they would stay. Mathen himself made leaving impossible because of his hospitality and obvious eagerness for company. Despite his promise not to overwhelm with his "charm," Mathen in fact swept away both mother and daughter. With Greeley alone he was pleasant and mildly clever; in the presence of congenial femininity he was a riotous country wit and rough-cut raconteur. Greeley could only sit back, sip his coffee, and grudgingly admire the old fellow's way with the ladies. Cecilia in particular was delighted with Mathen, her eyes bright, her laughter ringing. But no words. Greeley wondered in the midst of all the fun how deep her sorrows and suffering must have run to make her withdraw so willingly from the world she knew.

Greeley slept on the floor and near the door that night,

Mathen snoring away on his own feather tick bed, Cecilia and
Miriam sleeping on blankets near the fire. Greeley didn't sleep
much, still operating in the cautious, guarding mode that came
naturally when he was piloting. He listened to the world
beyond the door, but heard nothing threatening.

Maybe he could endure the mountains some more after all.
Maybe he could bear to stay around, at least for a while, just to
make sure Miriam and Cecilia were safe and well at their new
home.

The weather grew colder in the night. When they awakened
in the morning, two inches of snow lay in the forest and clung
to the trees. They had a small, quick breakfast with Mathen—
including more coffee, at his insistence—then set off on the
final stretch of their journey, aiming for Limestone Cove and
the house of Vaughn Fitz.

Chapter 12

Greeley was unhappy about the snow, which left their tracks clearly behind them. By mid-morning, however, new snowfall began, and thickened, and the tracks filled. But travel was harder in the stinging flakes, so they moved more slowly and expended more energy than they would have on a snowless day.

As they approached Limestone Cove, Greeley began to feel glum and tense. The glumness came from the impending separation from Miriam, the tension from some vague sense of threat that hung in the air behind the white veil of snow. Greeley grew increasingly cautious.

He kept ahead, as usual, but as they neared the cove, Miriam called to him. "Greeley, please wait. Cecilia needs to stop a moment."

He halted and turned, noting that even after miles of mountain travel, nights spent in the woods and on cabin floors, and no good opportunity to wash away the grime of travel, Miriam still looked remarkable beautiful. "Need privacy?" This had become their polite code for referencing calls of nature along the way.

"Yes."

Greeley nodded. This privacy business was one aspect of piloting females that he had been forced to accustom himself to. The men he usually led didn't worry about it, simply slipping off the trail a moment to deal with matters with great dispatch, usually right in open view.

"Tell her not to wander far. In this thick a snowfall you can get lost before you know it."

Miriam went back to Cecilia and spoke to her; the girl turned and wandered into the trees and out of view. Miriam returned to Greeley's side, standing close to him. Because of the cold? Probably. He wouldn't have minded thinking there was more to it than that.

Miriam said,"Greeley, I owe you so much. You've gone so far for me and Cecilia, and me unable to pay."

"I wouldn't have wanted your money. Why, it was no more to me than just coming home." He let pass the fact, which she knew, that it was a home he would not have returned to at all if not for her.

"I'm glad we met you. If we hadn't, I don't know we could have done this."

"You'd have found a way, somehow. Tell me something, Miriam. Your sister does know you're on your way, don't she?"

"Yes, of course she does."

"And her husband?"

"Yes. Him, too."

"Since they asked you to come, how'd they intend for you to get here?"

"Well, any way I could, I suppose."

"They invited you but made no arrangements to help you come to them? It ain't an easy journey."

"There were no arrangements, but under the circumstances there really wasn't anything else to be done. Vaughn couldn't leave Jane alone, in her condition, to come get me. I let him know I would make my own arrangements and arrive when I could."

"When did they invite you?"

"November, last year. Vaughn wrote it himself. Jane is a much better pensman than he is and generally was the one to write the letters, but she has rheumatism in her fingers and so she had him write it."

"That's been quite some time. Think they're still expecting you?"

"They knew it would take me time to make my arrangements, especially considering how hard it is to travel in wartime. They're expecting me, but not on any particular day."

"Think it will be safe for you to just walk in and surprise them?"

"Oh, certainly. Jane will be thrilled to see me. Vaughn will, too, I'm sure."

"Do they know about little James?"

"How could they? He only died days ago."

"No, I mean, do they know Cecilia had a child, and how it happened, and all that?"

"They know."

"Kind of them, being ready to take all of you in. They must be good folks, even if they are Secesh."

"Thank you for saying that." There was the faintest trace of sarcasm in her tone, and Greeley was reminded that Miriam, even if not a Secessionist, was also not a Unionist.

"Well, I hope your sister gets better, even though you say she can't. What was her name—Jane?"

"Yes. Jane McCoy Fitz. McCoy was Jane's, and my, maiden name. And Jane will not get better, Greeley. She's known for some time that she'll not survive her illness. She's not yet thirty years old, and slowly dying. It isn't fair."

"I'm mighty sorry. What will you do once she's gone?"

Miriam smiled again, as if at a secret but not particularly funny joke. "I believe that Mr. Fitz might have some ideas in mind for me."

Greeley wondered what that meant, but could tell that she desired no further inquiries. A few moments passed in silence. The snow fell more thickly, piling around their feet. She scooted closer to him, and he had no complaints.

After a couple of minutes went by Greeley said, "I wonder how far off Cecilia wandered?"

"I was thinking the same thing," Miriam replied.

"We'll give her a minute more."

The minute passed, and no Cecilia appeared.

"I'd best go look," Miriam said.

"You'd best. But if you ain't back in a couple of minutes yourself, I'm coming after you. Don't get lost."

She vanished into the swirling white. Greeley huddled in his coat and pulled his hat lower. The cold, wet and piercing, ate through him.

A minute passed. Greeley was about to set out on his own when he heard Miriam's voice calling his name. She sounded disturbed, and also far away, but Greeley figured the wind accounted for the latter phenomenon. What accounted for the former he couldn't guess, and dreaded learning. He followed the sound and went into the trees.

He found them not forty feet from where he'd been waiting. Miriam was at Cecilia's back, her arms draped protectively around her daughter. Both of them were staring at something that swung in the wind, back and forth.

It was a man, or what had been a man long before. Now nothing remained but bone, a few scraps of hide and hair, and the tattered remnants of a shirt. The lower half of the skeleton had broken free and fallen to the ground and was buried somewhere beneath the snow. A fraying rope was around the bony neck, and a placard of some sort, the words now weathered off and indecipherable. Whether this man, whomever he was, had died at the hands of Unionists or rebels could not now be determined.

"Cecilia found it," Miriam said, and Greeley thought that "it" seemed the appropriate way to refer to the gruesome thing before them. There was nothing that seemed particularly human about this entity. But Greeley knew it had been a man nonetheless, some poor fellow who left home one day and never returned. He wondered if even now his wife still glanced out her shuttered window and hoped against hope that her missing man would return after a long and unexplained absence.

"Who is he?" Miriam asked.

"No way to know," Greeley replied.

"Why would anyone do this?"

"Plenty of reasons. Maybe he was a bridge burner back in

sixty-one, like me. Maybe he was caught trying to stampede. Maybe it was bushwhackers, punishing somebody for taking a different side than they take. It don't matter now. A dead man has no politics."

"It's terrible."

"Yes." He turned and looked squarely at them. "Ladies, welcome to the mountains. If you stay, you're likely to see more of this, or worse. I stand ready to head straight back with you right now, if you want to leave. Just say the word and we'll commence from this very point. This will be the last chance I have to make you that offer, before we reach your sister's house."

For an instant it seemed that Miriam might agree. One look at Cecilia's face revealed that she would walk out with Greeley in a moment, but it was left to her mother to make the decision. Greeley was disappointed but not surprised when Miriam made the same decision as before: She had to go to her sister, because she must.

He put out his arm and led them away, leaving the hanging skeleton where it had been from season unto season, and where it might well remain until there was nothing left for the rope to hold.

They stood at the head of a long, beautiful, white hollow, watching the snow fall and chimney smoke rise from a cabin below. The smoke dispelled in the breeze until it was one with the whiteness of the sky.

"There it is, if Mathen directed me right, and Mathen ain't ever directed me wrong before," Greeley said. "That's your new home, ladies. Looks like they got a good fire going." He turned a forced smile on them, working hard to hide the sorrow he was feeling at the impending separation. "Well, I can't go down there with you. Mr. Fitz is Secesh, and I'm a bit too wanted by the rebs to go shaking his hand. So I'll leave you to make the final stretch by yourselves. When you get in hollering distance of that house, Miriam, let out with some good yells and tell them who you are. People are edgy these days, and you don't want to surprise them. And don't tell them it was me who guided you there. Don't mention my name at all. Just make up a name for your guide, and say he's gone. Safer for me that way."

"I understand," she said.

"Well, it appears this is good-bye, though I hope to see you both again, lots of times, when this war is through." He looked at Cecilia, whose eyes were wet and seemed bigger than ever before. "And you, Cecilia, I hope you and me can sit down someday and have a good, long talk. If ever you want to, and only if you want to. I'll bet you have the prettiest voice that's ever been, from what little I've heard of it."

Tears overran Cecilia's eyes and spilled down her face, which she turned and buried against her mother's shoulder. Greeley thought perhaps he had said the wrong thing, but Miriam's face bore no remonstrance.

"It's been good to travel with you ladies, and I hope I've been the gentleman I said I would be. I do want you to know I think I've never met no finer a pair, and I'm glad I could be of service." He touched his hat, struggling hard to feign a bright demeanor. "Miriam. Cecilia. Good day to you both."

Miriam came to him and kissed him. Some of her tears clung to his face when she pulled away.

"Thank you, Miriam. God bless you both. And . . . take your hats off as you go down to the house. Let your hair fall out so they can see it from a distance. And don't forget to give a holler before you get close."

Miriam nodded and removed her hat right there. She pulled a hairpin from her bundled locks, and they fell, loose and shining, onto her shoulders. Greeley could have stared at the vision of it for a long time.

"Good-bye," he said.

"Good-bye, Greeley." Miriam's voice was quaking.

He nodded, turned, and strode away the way they had come, not looking back for a long time because he didn't want Miriam to see that all at once hers were not the only tears on his face. Finally he did turn, and looked down into the hollow. He could scarcely make them out a long way off, two forms in the white distance. He heard Miriam's voice calling out to Vaughn Fitz. Good for her. She was doing it just like he had told her.

"They're yours now, Mr. Fitz," he said. "I wouldn't have minded them being mine. You take good care of them, rebel. You better, or I'll come after you and make you wish you had."

He turned and trudged off, not really sure where he was going. Right then it felt good merely to be walking.

He reached a burying ground he hadn't seen before. A family plot, probably, or maybe a little community cemetery. Nicely hidden and remote, in any case, and as good a place as any to stop for a while.

The best thing about snowy skies was that they tended to mask smoke, so he gathered some sticks, peeled the bark off to expose the dry wood, pulled out his match case, and soon had a nice fire going. The smoke vortexed in the wind, swirling and breaking and vanishing into the snowfall. He leaned back against a gravestone and warmed his hands, mentally apologizing to whomever occupied this grave and telling them he meant no disrespect, perching above them like he was. It was just that the tombstone did a nice job of keeping the wind off his back.

There was no sensible reason to linger anymore in these mountains, he knew. Meeting Miriam and Cecilia had been a chance deviation from his intended course, or maybe fate, but either way they were at their destination now and needed him no more. Miriam's kiss, the memory of which still tingled on his lips, had been sincere and touching, but it had marked only an ending, not a beginning. Miriam's life was now entirely her own, and his was his, and that seemed to be how it would stay.

But the more he thought about that, the more dissatisfied he became. He began to feel that if he walked away from these mountains right now, he might leave behind something terrible—the mountain war—but he'd also be leaving the finest woman he had met since his own wife passed on.

He felt a quick, rousing impulse to make a fighting effort for her. Why let such a woman simply drift out of his life? Miriam had said something about Fitz having some "ideas" for her future once her sister had passed on. What did that mean? That he would marry Miriam in her sister's place?

"No, sir!" Greeley said to the wind. "No, sir, Mr. Fitz, I don't know that you'll be doing that at all!"

Maybe, instead of letting Mr. Fitz develop "ideas" for her future, Miriam ought to make a few plans of her own. Maybe those plans should include Greeley Brown! And maybe she needed to hear that from Greeley Brown himself.

Greeley stood, swelling with determination. He would *not* simply leave these mountains right now. To the devil with the war! And to the devil with Fitz! Secesh or not, Fitz was about to receive a visit from a Lincolnite named Greeley Brown, and if there was risk involved, it wouldn't be the first risk Greeley had faced.

He had to tell Miriam how he felt. He had to let her know that he was willing to stay in these mountains until the war ended and until her sister had passed away. He was willing to wait for her to finish her duty, and then he'd like the opportunity to court her with an eye toward marriage. He wanted her to be his wife, Cecilia to be his daughter. He wanted to be there when Cecilia decided her world was good enough to communicate with again. He wanted to be the man who would help make her world good enough.

He couldn't leave these mountains now. They weren't the same mountains he had fled earlier. They were transformed. *She* was now a part of them.

Greeley kicked snow onto the fire and fought back his impulsiveness just long enough to consider his options. Was there a way to let Miriam know he was still about that didn't involve marching right to Fitz's door? He mulled it for two minutes and couldn't think of anything. Probably best to be open and bold anyway. Maybe Fitz would prove to be a Mathen Ricker kind of rebel, opinionated but not hostile.

Weary and cold as he was, Greeley felt more full of life than he had since the war had commenced. For once he had something bigger and more important than the cursed war itself to fill his mind. Finding Miriam had given him purpose and hope, made him aware of life that would go on when the fighting ceased. It felt good. More than good. If not for fear he'd accidentally sprain that ankle again, he might have leaped up right there in that cemetery and clicked his heels, like he'd done to impress the girls when he was just a boy.

As a safer alternative, he began to whistle. An old Irish jig, one whose name he had never known but whose tune was a favorite. He was only six bars into it when his eyes swept over the tombstone he had leaned against, and the music droned into a low, sliding downtone, then silence.

He knelt, brushing snow off the stone and reading it three, then four times, just to make sure he was reading it rightly:

To the memory of
JANE ELLEN MCCOY FITZ
Beloved Wife of Vaughn P. Fitz
b. Jan. 2, 1836 d. June 4, 1863
ASLEEP IN JESUS

There was no mistake. The sister for whose care Miriam had come this far was already dead. Greeley stood, clenching and unclenching that nearly nerveless left hand, scratching his beard with his right and trying to reconfigurate his thinking along new lines. What did this mean? Well, surely it meant that the reason Vaughn Fitz had invited Miriam to join his household last November no longer applied. . . .

November? Greeley looked at the gravestone again. Was he remembering wrongly? No, he was sure he was right: Miriam had told him that Vaughn *and* Jane Fitz had invited her to come to their household late last November . . . but Jane Fitz was already dead last November. Dead for five months at that point.

A fragment of the conversation he and Miriam had shared earlier came to mind: *What will you do once Jane's gone? I believe that Mr. Fitz might have some ideas in mind. . . .*

Suddenly it was all clear in Greeley's mind. Vaughn Fitz, apart from being a sorry Secesh, was surely also a liar and a lecher. Lonely here in these mountains, he had cast his thoughts toward his widowed, beautiful sister-in-law, sent her a letter telling her that her sister was still alive and needed her. It wasn't rheumatism of the fingers that had kept Jane Fitz from writing that letter! Jane Fitz was long dead and gone before that letter was written.

As far as Greeley was concerned, Fitz had just kidnapped Miriam and Cecilia, or come just short of kidnapping them, anyway. As isolated as Fitz's home was, and lodged in the midst of war-torn mountains, Miriam and Cecilia were little more than prisoners once inside his door. It was no doubt part

of his vile plan. With Miriam in his house, Fitz would play on
her forlorn situation, and his, to pressure Miriam into taking
her sister's place. Miriam surely had held a dim notion that her
brother-in-law might be one to think along these lines when
she had talked in that cryptic way of Fitz's likely "ideas" for
her future once her sister was dead. What she hadn't known
when she said it was that the future was already at hand, her
sister already dead.

Greeley wouldn't stand for it. He'd not let himself be so
duped. He'd played a big part in getting Miriam here, and he
wasn't about to let a lousy backwoods Secesh use him that
way! He would march down to Fitz's house, tell Fitz that his
wife's own tombstone had just revealed the truth of his little
plan, and tell Miriam that she needn't stay with Fitz, that
there was another man in Carter County who could give her
more security than Fitz ever could, and ten times the love and
devotion.

He had marched a hundred paces from the burying ground
before unwelcome new thoughts came. There might be another
way to interpret the situation. Maybe Miriam herself knew all
along that her sister was dead. Greeley felt himself deflate,
hating the doubt that suddenly filled him. Maybe Miriam
hadn't been duped at all, but was the one doing the duping.
He remembered how slow she had been to answer when he
first asked what was her brother-in-law's name. Might she
have been afraid he'd know Fitz, and that Fitz's wife was
already dead?

No, he told himself. No. Miriam wouldn't have lied to me.
Miriam's no liar.

The other voice, as hated as it was reasonable, countered
that with the obvious. Of course Miriam was a liar! She had
told him story upon story of other men she had duped along the
way, tales she'd told at the expense of helpful or romantically
smitten men to benefit herself and Cecilia. She had claimed
that James was her own baby—a well-intended lie, but a lie
nonetheless. And he'd watched her play on the landlord's
infatuation back in Sevierville, pretending fascination with him
and the foolish things he said. . . .

Like maybe she's pretended to think highly of me, Greeley
thought. Maybe her kind words, and her tears of parting, are all

part of that business of playing the "actress" like she told me she does sometimes.

And so the battle went on inside him, trust of and devotion to Miriam Fry going up against mistrust of the same woman, and troubling questions that made more sense than he wanted to admit.

He went on, moving more slowly, deciding to keep an eye on the Fitz place for a while and see if he might gain a bit better perspective that way.

Might as well, he thought. He surely had nothing better to do.

The perspective came more quickly than he would have liked, and after he gained it, he wished he hadn't.

He had been perched hidden on a hillside for no more than an hour before he saw Fitz emerge from his house, rifle in hand, looking about. Greeley wondered if the man had seen or heard something suspicious, or if he was merely on edge the way most mountain folks were these days. Greeley wished he had a spyglass; he'd like to see what this Fitz character looked like up close.

While he watched, the door opened again and Miriam emerged. Again Greeley wished for a spyglass. Was she upset at this moment? Were there tears on her face, shed because she had learned that her sister was dead long before she knew it, and the wicked Fitz had brought her to his home under false pretenses?

What happened next made his heart ache. Fitz turned, went to Miriam, put his arms around her, and kissed her on the lips. Greeley saw no sign that she was surprised by this, and no sign of resistance. It was a long, seemingly passionate kiss they shared, full and heartfelt. Greeley's own kissed lips suddenly tasted bitter.

He vanished into the woods, knowing now who was the liar and who had been the fool. He wanted to cry as bitterly and full-heartedly as he had when he lost his father as a boy, but he wouldn't let himself do it. No sir. Not over a lying woman. Not over the likes of *her*.

He told himself that it really didn't matter, though he knew it did. He told himself he would quickly get over the hurt, though he knew he wouldn't. If there was anything he told himself about this turn of events that could really be believed, it was that his future was suddenly more clear. It was time to get out of these mountains and stay out, just as he'd already tried to do once. And it would take more than a pretty face and a sad story to get him to come back here next time!

He wondered how much else about Miriam Fry was false. Maybe Miriam Fry wasn't even her true name. Maybe even sweet, young, abused Cecilia wasn't what she pretended to be. Maybe when folks weren't around, she chattered to her mother like a trained bird, and they laughed together at the poor male dupes they fooled and misguided all along their sorry way. Dupes like Greeley Brown.

At a less distracted moment he wouldn't have let himself be taken so easily. He would have sensed the presence of the riders, heard them, felt them, even smelt them on the cold wind. But his guard had been low. He had been thinking of Miriam, concentrating on his feelings, for once, instead of watching the dangerous land around him.

The snow had begun falling hard again, and they reminded him of statues there in the woods. They were mounted, armed, semicircled before him in the swirl. One of them stepped his mount forward.

"My name is Fletcher," the man said. "Drop that rifle, sir."

Greeley let the Henry fall into the snow at his feet.

"Does anyone know him?" Fletcher asked his group, without taking his eyes off Greeley. Greeley stared at him in turn, taking in this vision from hell even while cursing himself for having allowed himself to march into the midst of it. Fletcher was a bearded, fleshy man, brown of hair, whiskers and temples specked with gray. His eyebrows were extraordinarily thick and hung down into the cavities of his eyes. He wore an enlisted man's heavy greatcoat, tall boots, and, despite his Confederate status, a Union field officer's Kossuth hat, very battered, its dark wool now snow-dusted almost white.

"I know him," a man said. "That's Greeley Brown. He's a Union pilot, Cap."

"Anybody else can confirm that?"

Several voices rose. Greeley pictured himself riding in an ox cart through Sevierville, a cheerful loudmouth at his side, bellowing his name, boys approaching, knowing him and talking him up. He should have let that be a warning. He had simply become too well known, and now it was going to be the death of him.

"Mr. Brown, is that indeed who you are?" Fletcher asked. He had a voice that was deep and penetrating even when hardly raised, and he barely moved his lips when he spoke. "I do believe you are. I've heard of you, Mr. Brown. You're a right troublesome man, from all I hear. What a stroke of luck I should find you here."

Greeley knew there was no hope. They would either stand him against a tree and shoot him, or hang him. He could buy himself some time by claiming he had a stampeder band awaiting him at some distant spot, and offer to lead Fletcher to them, but in the end the lie would be known and the situation would be the same. So he simply turned and ran, straight into the thickest of the trees, hoping that he could gain some distance where horses couldn't go, and that any shots they fired would happen to miss.

Rifles cracked behind him; balls slapped trees and sang through the air. He grinned and ran harder. Not hit so far! Then he felt something like a club smacking his left shoulder and knocking him down front first. He buried his face in snow and felt a slow, spreading throb ripple off his shoulder. He was shot, sure as the world.

Someone grabbed his ankles and dragged him back. He grunted and scraped over rocks and roots, and then they rolled him onto his back, whacked him on the side of the head with a rifle butt, and he felt himself being half carried, half dragged. His shoulder hurt very badly.

Someone hit him again and he enjoyed the mercy of being stunned. Worry faded, and what he saw through half-closed eyes seemed as unreal and miragelike as the curses and cold laughs he heard, as if through cotton, as they discussed their plans for him. He watched as a man scrambled up a tall, thin sapling, followed by another. Higher and higher, laughing and making chattering sounds like squirrels, then laughing some more. What were they doing? Then the sapling began to bend over, others gathered to get hold of it and hold it down, and he knew. He watched with odd dispassion as they tied a forage rope around the bent young tree, and a crude sliding noose in the other end. Then he was being dragged again, by someone who grunted and sniffed, and whose nose dripped on him, and his head went through the noose. He began to black out and was glad for it, because unconscious, he couldn't feel it when it happened.

But some consciousness still lingered as Fletcher came into his field of blurred vision and knelt, grinning, with a knife in hand. Greeley's face was pushed to the side, and he grimaced and moaned as Fletcher carved a cross into his cheek, starting above the beard line and extending down into it. It hurt, the blade like fire. The blood ran hot on his neck and soaked his whiskers.

"There we go," Fletcher said. "Now let him fly, boys."

Greeley saw no more after that. There was a jerking, a tug, a constriction of the neck that cut off his wind as effectively as a slice through the windpipe. He felt himself pulled up, his feet kicking in the air. They began to beat him as he swung, pounding him with the butts of their rifles, cracking arm bones and ribs. As consciousness began to give way, the last he heard was the diminishing sound of their laughter, and the last he felt was the dull pain of being beaten while dangling in air, and the sharp, lingering sting upon his face of Fletcher's cross.

Part III

BEN AND NANNY

Chapter 13

Early evening, Knoxville, Tennessee

John P. Williams, journalist turned man of commerce, pulled his coat tighter around his frame and tried to button it. The button, loose for days and given no remedial attention, popped off, and Williams let out a moan of disgust. He looked about for it, saw it lying beside the railroad track. "There you are, you sorry bugger! Pop off on me, will you? I ought to put you on the track and let the next train squash you flat."

His voice was slurred, for good reason: He was thoroughly drunk. There was good reason for that, too, at least in his own estimation. He had come to Knoxville with great expectations, only to have them destroyed like eggs beneath a fallen brick.

He grunted, squatted, and tried to keep from flopping to the side. Reaching for the button, he found it just out of reach, and scuffed toward it, still squatted. A titter of childish laughter made him turn his head to see three ragged black children over near the train station, watching him.

"Get off with you, you nigras!" he slurred. "What you doing, standing there laughing at a white man? You nigras have no respect anymore?"

The children trotted off, still laughing. Williams reached for the button again and fell over, flopping like a noodle onto the railroad track. "Aw, hell!" he muttered. Pushing up, he managed to stand, and staggered back off the track, waving dismissively at a button that would go forever unretrieved because the effort just wasn't worth it.

He stumbled over to a nearby shed and sat down, leaning against the wall. Pulling a flask from his coat, he took a big swallow, corked it shut again, and burst into tears.

"Oh, Maribell, how could you have done that to me?" he slobbered aloud. "Don't you know I love you? How could you do it to me, sweetheart?"

A mental vision of the face of the object of his frustrated affection hovered before him. A plain woman, really, but to him beautiful, all he had ever wanted in a female. He had hoped to make Maribell Bewley his wife, as soon as he dealt with the troublesome fact that he already had a wife back in Nashville.

His illicit love affair with Maribell Bewley had been going on for about a year. A widow since the Fish Springs battle, Maribell had been intensely lonely, and he, unhappily married and not overly burdened with scruples, had been happy to give Maribell the attention she wanted. Since meeting her, he had found reason after reason to make "business journeys" to East Tennessee, each of those journeys involving a few days of visiting his Knoxville lover.

They had talked big about marriage plans. Maribell had been breathlessly eager, and he knew his slowness to deal with the ugly necessity of divorce had grown frustrating to her. He had not, however, expected to find her frustrations had become so great that she'd married somebody else since his last visit.

But she had, and he'd discovered it early that afternoon in the clumsiest, most painful way possible. Showing up at her door, flowers in hand, he was met by a burly, sour fellow who asked what in the devil he thought he was doing at this house and why did he have those flowers? Maribell had appeared in the doorway behind her new husband, her face full of horror. She ordered Williams away, and none too politely. Told him she was married now, that she couldn't see him anymore, and would he please just leave and never come back.

Williams took another swallow from his flask and cried some more. He heard a noise and saw those same black children watching him again. He roared at them, clawed at them with his hand. They ran off.

"Useless contrabands!" he muttered. "Flooding every city in this state! You can't walk the streets anymore without nigras all over the place, taking up the boardwalks, squatting in the alleys, disrespecting white folks. . . ."

He slipped the flask back into his coat and detected an unremembered something in the pocket. Pulling it out, he stared at an envelope, and read aloud the name written across it in an unfamiliar hand. Miss Amy Deacon Hanover, Knoxville, Tennessee. What was this?

His beclouded memory slowly returned. Oh, yes . . . this was that letter given him by Greeley Brown back in Sevierville, the one he was supposed to deliver on Brown's behalf to Amy Deacon Hanover. Brown had said she shouldn't be hard to find, because she was entering the newspaper business, was from a well-known lineage, and would be known all through the city. Very important that she receive this message, Brown had said. Make sure you see it go into her hand, will you, Mr. Williams? Carry it to her personally?

It had seemed an easy favor, and Williams told Brown he would certainly deliver the letter. Now he swore, roughly shoved the letter back into his pocket, and wished he'd declined. He had rather liked Brown, who was the brother, after all, of an old professional compatriot, but here on the other side of his rude parting with his beloved Maribell, the whole thing seemed a tremendous bother. Williams decided to forget the letter for the moment and deal with it later. He had problems enough of his own for now.

He again produced the flask and took one more swallow. All he intended to do this evening was drink and drink some more, until the pain of the day was fully numbed. He stood, staggered a little farther down the track, looking for a more private spot to finish off the flash. The train yard was beginning to fill with refugees and contrabands, and Williams wasn't in the mood for company.

The next morning

The boy ran full-speed through back lots and backyards, climbing fences, leaping flower beds full of last year's dead beauties, tramping through garden beds of twisted brown vines that would soon be burned off and plowed under to make way for the early spring garden crops. Dogs barked at him, cats scurried beneath porches. A few folks yelled at him to watch what he was treading on, but most didn't bother. They all knew Sammy Culver, and that he wasn't the kind to mind adults anyway. He didn't mind his own parents, much less his neighbors.

Sammy clambered over one final fence and leaped with feline agility into the backyard that was his destination. A slightly smaller boy with a similar head of reddish, tousled hair looked up from the pipe he was lighting behind the Culver family outhouse, which hadn't been cleaned out in far too long and made the neighborhood reek.

"Hey, what you doing, Sammy? Want a smoke?"

"Bert, you got to come!"

Bert Culver, younger in years than his brother but every bit his equal in proud misbehavior, drew a rich mouthful of pipe smoke, blew it out, and clamped the pipe stem between prematurely yellowing teeth. "Come where?"

"The train station! There's a man been run over by a train down there! The darkies are all talking about it!"

The pipe left his mouth. "Run over? Dead?"

"They say he looks like a pile of fresh meat. Sort of a little man, they said, and he went right under the cowcatcher. They said about half a long train passed over him before it spit what was left of him out on the side of the tracks. Come on! Let's go see him before they haul him off!"

The pipe was dropped on the spot and lay smoking in the snow. Sammy Culver turned and went back over the fence, followed by his younger brother. More barking, more fleeing cats, more yells of warning from the neighbors. The brothers ran on, heedless. A man, run over by a train! This was a sight any sane boy would want to see, a terrible vision to experience and treasure and paint with gruesome words in countless conversations with boys not so fortunate as to have seen the thing for themselves.

They ran fleetly and tirelessly, covering ground they knew so well they could have run it blindfolded, two young Mercuries sailing through the back lots of Knoxville on winged feet.

The disappointment of the Culver brothers was deep. The corpse had already been carted off when they arrived, and there was nothing left to ogle except a huge smear of blood all down the track and pooled where the body had at last emerged from beneath the big grooved wheels. They meandered around the bloody place, trying to console themselves. It wasn't often one received the chance to actually see a man who had been hit by a train, so this was a true opportunity missed.

There were plenty of idle contrabands hanging around, three of them witnesses. The brothers quizzed them thoroughly. Was it a local man? No one knew. Did he try to get away from the train? No, he was passed out on the track, nobody noticing him until he was already struck. Drunk? Yes, young sirs, most likely he was.

Dogs, attracted by the little crowd and the smell of blood, began to arrive and went to work cleaning up the mess. This made for a nicely gruesome show in itself, and the boys watched silently for a while.

Sammy followed the bloody smear up the tracks, pacing it off to see how far the fellow had been dragged. Halfway along he stopped and ceased counting, and bent to pick something up.

"Hey, Bert, come look at this."

The brother trotted over. Sammy held out something ragged, torn, bloodied. "What's that? Part of his clothes?"

"No, it's a letter, I believe. See? There's an envelope, or part of one, and some of the letter still inside."

"Who's it to?"

Sammy, who badly needed spectacles but didn't know it, squinted at the smudged handwriting on the outside of the envelope. He was a poor reader, all the poorer since war closed down the schools and left him with no reason to read at all, and he had to piece the words together letter by letter. "It's to a woman named Amy Deacon Han. Or Han-something. Part of the name looks like it's tore off."

"Hanover, I'll betcha."

"You know her or something?"

"I know who she is. She's that woman that Pa thinks is so pretty, who's going to start a newspaper in town. I heard him talking about it. Her father was that Deacon fellow who lived in the big house on the hill that burned down. Remember him? He put out a newspaper, too, all in favor of the rebels before the war came."

"Oh, yeah," the other replied, though he didn't really remember.

"Doc Deacon was right famous, and his daughter kind of is, too. She did something that made her father mad at her and he run her off from Knoxville back before the war started. Pa's talked all about that. Don't you ever listen to him?"

"Sure I do." In fact he never did, unless motivated by a whipping rod. He'd never been able to understand why his brother actually found reason to pay attention to things the old fool had to say from time to time.

"Well, Amy Deacon got married and run a newspaper with her husband in Nashville, but somebody shot him dead— blam!—right in the street. Lots of blood, I'll betcha. She come back to Knoxville after that, maybe a month or two ago. You know what? She's an ab'litionist."

"No fooling?"

"That's right. She wanted to free the darkies a long time before Lincoln signed his paper. Pa says that he can't figure it out, a woman smart enough to run a newspaper being in favor of free darkies having the run of the country."

"Pa don't like her, huh?"

"Likes to *look* at her, when Mam don't see. Me and him was walking up near the Custom House last week, and he seen her and says, Mmmm mmmm mmmm, that there's one fine-looking woman, but I shouldn't tell Mam he'd said it."

"I want to read the letter."

"Let me. I read better than you."

Sammy handed the envelope over; Bert took it carefully, avoiding touching the blood on it. He pulled out fragments of two pages, unfolded them, and read aloud, but so much was gone that what he read didn't make much sense. He quit reading and shrugged.

"Well, none of that means poot to me. There's a Sam it talks about, though, did you hear that, Sammy? Somebody named Sam, like you. And it's wrote by somebody named Greeley. Greeley with a capital B and the rest cut off. Greeley Breckinridge, I'll bet you. Greeley Brady, or Brody. Or Belcher. Or just Belch."

"Or maybe it's an Injun, and his name's Greeley Blowing Wind."

"Hah! Or Greeley *Breaking* Wind."

They both had a good laugh over that one, and came up with other crude juvenile variations: Greeley Butt, Greeley Breast, Greeley Ballocks.

When that rich well of amusement ran dry, Sammy gave a sudden frown, evidencing the rising of a new inspiration.

"Hey, let's deliver this letter to Amy Hanover."

"Why?"

"Because she's got money. That husband of hers who got shot was rich, or almost. She'll pay us for bringing this to her, I'll betcha!"

"Yeah! Let's do! You know where to find her?"

"Yep. Over on Gay Street. Here, put these pages back in the envelope and let's go."

They left the railyard so quickly that dogs barked at them. The contrabands watched them go, fleet and fast-disappearing as two sparrows, then settled down idly in the cold. It had been a good day so far, the drunk beneath the train making things exciting, but the rest of the day would surely be long and dull. For folks who had no work and no real place to be, all days were long, even the short, gray days of winter.

Chapter 14

His name was Ben Scarlett, and he strode along snowy Gay Street with a strong, fast stride. He was swinging two arms but only one hand, the left one having been lost to an amputating knife long ago. A hook served in that hand's place, working pretty well now that he was used to it. Though to his regret the hook did scare little children, it also scared off a few other folks Ben didn't mind doing without at all. Some who might be prone to harass him—and for Ben Scarlett there had always seemed to be no dearth of harassers—thought better of it when they noticed the hook.

Ben was walking much faster than he had in days of old along this same avenue in this, his home city. The best he could usually manage back then was a drunken saunter, along with the occasional brief run when merchant Daniel Baumgardner chased him for stealing, or for sleeping off his latest drunken spell in the shed out back of his store. Nowadays he walked fast most of the time. Moseying was part of an alcohol-hazed past he was glad was gone.

He passed the building that had housed the old Baumgardner Mercantile Store, and paused to look through dusty windows into the now empty interior. He gave a small gulp of sadness. Dear old Mr. Baumgardner . . . against all odds, the merchant had become a great friend to him before the end. After years of yelling at Ben, running him out of his storage shed, threatening him with imprisonment, torture, and death by flaying, Baumgardner, softened and made lonely by the loss of his sons in this cursed, endless war, had become Ben's finest Knoxville companion. It was still hard to believe the veteran merchant was dead and buried, and his store closed and empty.

Though the emptiness of the building made Ben sad, it also gave him some hope that the war was winding down some. A few months ago any such vacant building would have been quickly taken over for use as a military storage facility or hospital. Now such commandeering wasn't happening quite as much; even some of the churches whose buildings had been taken over for hospitals were reportedly about to have their facilities turned back to them for their intended use. Ben was no judge of politics and war, but dared to hope such developments hinted the war would end before long, and that for Knoxville, maybe had substantially ended already.

He brushed away an icy glaze on the window glass and peered more deeply into the store, looking on through his reflection, which was slowly beginning to smile. He'd developed a thought or two about this location over the last week, and was about ready to share them with his employer, Mrs. Amy Deacon Hanover, the young widow of a Nashville newspaperman, and herself about to become publisher of Knoxville's soon-to-be-born newspaper, *The Knoxville Sage*. Miss Amy, as Ben always called her, had chosen that name for her upcoming journal as a tribute to her late husband, whose Nashville newspaper had been named *The Nashville Sage*. Ben had been pressman and general office assistant at Nashville's *Sage*, and would be again for the new Knoxville incarnation, if ever he and Miss Amy could work out the endless details that came with trying to start a newspaper in wartime, when paper and ink and so on were so hard to get. There was also the difficulty of occupying a building that wasn't really well-suited for a newspaper facility. This was why Ben's thoughts lately had centered on Baumgardner's big, empty store building.

Ben turned away from the storefront and continued down the street. As he approached the current would-be headquarters of *The Knoxville Sage*, he saw the front door open. Nanny, an escaped North Carolina slave woman who had come to Knoxville at the end of '63 and now was a servant for Miss Amy—a *paid* servant, for Amy Deacon Hanover was as hearty an abolitionist as had ever walked, and would not have dreamed of Nanny working for nothing—stepped out and held the door open as two young boys spilled out after her, each with a grin and a bright coin pinched between thumb and forefinger. They raced past Ben without a word, their heels kicking up dirty snow behind them.

Nanny, having seen Ben coming, held the door for him.

"Thank you, Nanny," he said. "Who was them boys? More of Miss Amy's mountain refugees?"

The reference was to an interest that had overwhelmed Amy Hanover since her arrival in Knoxville. In fact, it was Nanny's arrival that seemingly had prompted her obsession. Ben had stumbled across Nanny hiding in an old warehouse, hungry and ragged, weary after a long and dangerous flight from servitude on the far side of the mountains in lower North Carolina. He'd brought her to Amy, knowing that his kindhearted young employer, who had been his benefactor when he was no more than a common drunk, would be equally helpful to this poor refugee. And so she had been, giving Nanny food, shelter, work—and listening with fascination to Nanny's descriptions of her difficult flight and her tales of how so many people in the mountains were suffering, particularly those who held faithful to the Union.

Meanwhile, Knoxville had begun to fill with Unionist refugees, many of them from the mountains, seeking the relative safety of a Federally held city. Entire camps of them were forming in and around the city, segregated by race, posing problems for the occupying Federals and creating occasional ill feelings among the city's regular inhabitants. Amy had begun seeking these refugees out, talking to them, collecting their stories of atrocities, poverty, and rebel abuse in their home districts. She was infuriated at the Federal government just now for its failure to supply sufficient sustenance for these refugees, and its equally galling failure to apply sufficient military manpower to battling the bushwhackers and guerrilla bands operating from Knoxville eastward. Amy was becoming obsessed with the refugees and the mountain war that they shunned. Ben had a certain ambivalence about the issue. Certainly, interviewing refugees and being concerned about their problems was worthwhile and good . . . but wasn't the main goal right now to bring a newspaper into being?

"Them two warn't refugees," Nanny said of the two running boys. Her voice bore its usual lifeless inflection; she had a generally cold quality about her that made Ben struggle to feel much liking for her. The truth was, Ben thought Nanny acted downright ungrateful sometimes, failing to respect either Amy or himself, despite all they had done for her, and despite the fact that they were white and she was black. The latter consideration might not hold any bearing in the liberal mind of abolitionist Amy Hanover, but it surely did in the not-nearly-so-liberal private thoughts of former town drunk Ben Scarlett.

"Who were they, then?"

"Local boys."

Ben could see he'd have to pry for each fragment of information. "Where'd they get them coins?"

"Miss Amy, I reckon."

"Why'd she give them coins?"

"Don't know."

"Well, why did they come here?"

"They brung her a letter." Nanny paused, then for once actually volunteered something. "It was all tore and bloodied."

"Bloodied? Some kind of battlefield letter, maybe?"

"I don't know."

Ben caught himself thinking of something that came to mind almost every time he got irritated with Nanny, something a local street boy had told him about three weeks ago. Apparently Nanny had made a slighting reference to Ben behind his back, calling him "Mr. Hookfinger." It made Ben seethe. *Mr. Hookfinger.* A good name for some ridiculous puppet character in one of those traveling wagon shows, maybe, but no way for Nanny to be talking about the very man who had brought her to this place of refuge. So far, however, Ben had refrained from saying anything about it to Nanny.

"Where is Miss Amy?" he asked.

"In her office."

Ben headed for that office, a room that had been sectioned off from the rest of the building, about halfway back.

The door was closed, to his surprise. He rapped it gently. "Miss Amy?"

He heard paper shuffle. "What is it, Ben?"

"I wanted to come talk to you a minute, if you'd let me. Got us a good idea having to do with the newspaper and the old Baumgardner store building."

"Oh . . . I see. Uh, might you come back in a few minutes?"

"Why, surely."

"Thank you."

He walked away, thinking that *there* was a first. Amy seldom closed her office. He'd never had to talk to her through the door before.

He went over to the big wooden crate that held the press, and almost lovingly laid his hand on it, wishing the press was already set up and slapping out crisp new newspapers. It had arrived only two days before, shipped in from Nashville. Ben had come to love working with that press during his Nashville sojourn, and was eager to get at it again.

He sat down by the stove for a while, enjoying the heat, but Nanny was meandering around the room, making a token show of cleaning, and he soon found it annoying. So he rose and headed onto the street again, figuring just to walk around awhile and come back when Amy wasn't busy.

He was scarcely out the door before a grinning Skunk Linden greeted him.

"Hey, Ben! Hey! How are you there, friend?"

"I'm doing fine, Skunk. Just like you'd be doing if you'd be as smart as I was and put that whiskey behind you." Ben had tipped many a bottle in many an alley with Skunk Linden in years past, and, if he were honest with himself, would have to admit he now rather enjoyed letting the light of his newfound sobriety shine down to expose the ongoing drunken sinfulness of unrepentant old "Skunk the Drunk," as the street children called him.

"Well, Ben, you know, I'd say you're right about that. Sure need to give up the liquor. Then I could get me a job like you got, and have money like you got . . ."

"Don't waste your breath heading down *that* road! I ain't giving you money for whiskey, Skunk. How many times have you asked me, and how many times have I said no?"

"I didn't ask for no money, Ben, no sir, all I said was that if I had a job like you got, why, I'd have money already, and I could afford to buy myself food and keep a roof over my head. It's cold out these nights, Ben, and I've been sleeping in the alleys and so on. You remember doing that, don't you? I'll bet you don't remember it much at all when you're lying in that bed up in your room at night, all warm and cozy. . . ."

"I can't let you stay in my room, neither, Skunk. Miss Amy don't allow it. Now, if you'll let me by, I'll be about my business." Ben pushed on past him and started walking down the snow-dusted boardwalk.

Skunk fell in beside him. "Oh, yes, I know her, that Miss Amy. She's your boss woman. Got to do what she says! Got her rules, got to follow them!"

"That's right," Ben said. "And one of them rules is that I don't let nobody else share my room, especially folks I used to drink with. If I broke that rule, you know what would happen, Skunk? She'd fire me faster than a horse drops its poot. She's told me that very thing, all but the horse part, and I know she means it."

"Hard woman, that one is. Why, I bet she don't let you drink no more, neither."

"She don't, no, but me not drinking no more ain't really nobody's choice but mine. I'm a different man than the one you used to drink with, Skunk. I've put the past behind, asked the Lord above to forgive me my sins, and now I ain't going to drink no more."

"What if you did drink?"

"I won't."

"But what if you did? What if you showed up drunk before your boss lady one of these days? Huh? What'd happen then, huh?"

"I told you: I'd lose my job. That's her second rule. As long as I work for her, I don't get drunk. I don't even *drink*, not a drop."

"Pretty gal's got Ben all wrapped up like pork sausage! You do everything she says, Ben? What is it? You going to marry her?"

The question actually stung, but not because Ben held any secret ambition to marry Amy Hanover. There had been a time that such a fantasy would have appealed to him, but the kind of feelings he held for Amy had changed. The prior year he had almost found again a woman, Angel Beamish, who once had been his fiancée. Almost found her . . . but only almost. Now she was dead and gone. Ben did love Amy Hanover, no question, but the love was not of the marrying sort, and the snide way Skunk asked roused Ben's ire.

"Skunk, I ain't going to marry nobody. And all I can say is, it's too bad that your own wife ever married you. I feel sorry for her, having to put up with you."

"She don't put up with me no more. She's been gone for upward of a year."

"She left you?"

Skunk frowned and would not reply. Ben Scarlett was taking over control of this conversation in a way Skunk didn't like.

"So she *did* leave you! Well, I don't blame her. And you know what? Right now you're getting left again. By me. Have you a good day, Skunk. I'm gone."

Skunk reached beneath his coat and dodged around in front of Ben, forcing him to stop. From beneath the coat he pulled out a little bottle of whiskey. Pulling the cork, he stuck it under Ben's nose.

Ben Scarlett's face turned red. His breath came fast and quick, and for a second all that mattered in the world was encased within the glass walls of the bottle before him. The rising whiskey scent filled his nostrils, his brain, and his hands rose of their own accord, reaching. . . .

From somewhere the will came, and Ben grabbed not the bottle, but Skunk's arm, and pushed it away. Ben turned his back, feeling breathless. Skunk laughed and tilted up the bottle, letting it gurgle, making sure Ben heard him enjoying what Ben could not.

Skunk smacked his lips, corked the bottle, and put it away. "You can turn around now, Ben. The old devil in the bottle is gone! No more whiskey under your nose to tempt your righteous soul to drink!"

Ben faced Skunk, anger rising to the steaming point. "I ain't righteous, Skunk. I don't know I'll ever be good enough to be called righteous. But I ain't a drunk no more, and I am a man what tries now to live like a Christian should, and being that I try to live like a Christian should, I ain't free to tell you just how sorry and mean a son of a bitch I think you are, and how I'd like to tell you to jam that bottle of yours up somewheres where you'd have a mite bit of trouble getting it out again."

"I believe I've got your goat, Ben Scarlett! But we can be friends! Come back here and take a swaller or two with me!"

Ben put his hands over his ears and walked on down the street.

"Come on, Ben! Come have a drink, like in old times! We can have some good times together, me and you, now that you've got some money about you! Come on, Ben!"

"Get thee behind me, Satan!" Ben hollered back, drawing an odd stare from a man walking up the other side of the street.

"Satan?" Skunk chortled. "Satan? No, that ain't me, Ben. You got me mixed up with my pappy." He laughed, high and wheezing.

Ben, still walking, began to sing aloud about standing on Jordan's stormy banks and casting a wishful eye to Canaan's fair and happy land.

"Come on, Ben! Come back!"

Ben clasped his hands tighter over his ears and sang more loudly.

"You'll be back!" Skunk yelled. "One of these days, Ben, you and I will tip the bottle again, just like before! You'll be back!"

A woman emerged from a bakery beside where Skunk stood yelling, two loaves in her hand. Skunk looked at her. "He'll be back," he said, pointing after Ben.

The woman pulled the loaves close to herself, protectively, and hurried on in the opposite direction as fast as aging limbs could scuttle on a cold and snowy day.

Skunk Linden watched Ben go out of sight farther down the street, shook his head, and said, "Ah, me!" He took another drink from his bottle, rolled it around in his mouth before swallowing it, then enjoyed a deep sniff of the scent spilling out of the bakery. He was hungry, and hot bread would be delicious, but food was expensive in wartime Knoxville, and Skunk didn't have enough money in his pocket to buy bread even if it were cheap.

Chapter 15

Skunk Linden had been much more unsettling than Ben would have wished possible, and he walked in the snow beside the river for nearly an hour to let his mind and spirits grow calm again. He sang a few old songs aloud, softly, drawing a compliment from a woman passing by. "You have such a beautiful voice, sir, like an angel singing." Ben thanked her without his usual self-deprecating comments. He knew that he truly did have a good voice. He'd sung quite a lot when he was young, people oohing and aahing over how fine he sounded, and girls looking wistful and moonstruck while they listened. He'd lost his singing voice during his years in the bottle, when he lived much of the time out of doors in the elements, but now the innate richness of his voice was returning to him, mellowed and actually enhanced by the years. He welcomed it back like an old friend.

He allowed plenty of time for Skunk to wander off somewhere before he headed back up the street toward the soon-to-be *Sage* office. Along the way he prayed. Lord, I'm sorry I come so close to taking that bottle from Skunk. Lord, I'm sorry I called Skunk a bad name. Lord, I'm sorry that it seems like when I think I'm walking on the dry, I look down and find

SEASON OF RECKONING 141

myself sinking in the mud. Mostly I'm sorry that I've always got so blamed much to be sorry about.

He made it back to the office with no further Skunk encounters. Taking off his coat and hat, shaking off the cold as best he could in a ramshackle building that leaked in icy air at every seam, he looked around for Nanny, didn't see her, and headed back toward Amy's office. The door was open this time.

She was at her desk, writing on a pad. Working on her notes about the mountain refugees again, most likely. He wished she'd devote as much interest in the newspaper, else they'd not get to press for the first time until sometime in the summer.

Amy looked up, her face pretty as always, but slightly puffy, tired-looking, already starting to show the signs of wear, age, and stress. Ben thought what a wretched thing it was that a woman so young should already be a widow. Terrible, what losing a husband did to a woman. He didn't consider the fact that Amy had another reason to look bedraggled. She was pregnant, carrying the child who was all that remained in the living world of the late Adam Hanover. When Amy was seated at her desk, the steadily increasing swell of her belly mostly hidden from view, it was easy for Ben to forget that she had been with child for months now.

"Can I bother you a minute, Miss Amy?"

She smiled, but he thought she seemed preoccupied. "You're no bother. You work here, don't you? Come on in."

He slid into the creaky wooden chair that sat across from Amy's battered desk, which had been in the building when she rented it, hadn't been removed by the owner, despite notification, and therefore had been commandeered. "Miss Amy, I was doing some thinking today, about the newspaper. Seems to me that this building here is a little on the shabby side if you want to look businesslike, perfessional, like you'll want to."

Amy Hanover stifled a smile. It was inherently funny to her a man with a hook hand, rumpled clothing, muddy boots, and the war maps of endless years of drinking and neglect etched in wrinkles across a weathered face, talking about the need to look "perfessional."

"It is shabby, no doubt, but it was the best available when we came to Knoxville."

"Well, that's true, but there's another place open for rent

now, right on up the street. A lot better place, tight against the wind, good roof on it, three stoves inside. The old Baumgardner store building."

"Yes, I know."

"You do? Well, maybe you've thunk my thinking ahead of me. Were you thinking we might look into renting that place for the newspaper?"

"I was. But not now. I looked at the price. Far too expensive."

Ben saw a dream that had become a pet fantasy crushed at once beneath the finality of her tone. Oddly, he was suddenly annoyed, though Amy seldom roused that emotion in him.

He spoke with more forthrightness than he would have shown had he given it a moment's further thought. "Too expensive . . . but you don't think it's too expensive to be paying rent on a drafty building that leaks and ain't set up right for a newspaper, paying me pressman's wages and free board for wasting my time on this and that piddling errand, paying Nanny to burn breakfast and sweep the dust from one side of the room to the other and back again . . . and paying attention to all them poor mountain refugees and their sad tales, instead of paying attention to getting the *Sage* going. To tell you the truth, Miss Amy, I believe you care more about all them woeful mountain tales than about this newspaper." He paused. "There, I said it. Reckon I shouldn't have."

Amy's brows arched. Ben had never spoken so petulantly before. Surprise became quick anger. "No, I don't believe you should have, Mr. Scarlett. And perhaps you should consider that there are certain advantages to yourself in us keeping this building instead of moving, one of the key advantages being that this building is also where I allow you to live in a room at no charge, in a city in which lodging is growing so expensive it can bankrupt a person."

For a moment there was tense silence between them. Then Ben remembered who had the most to lose here, and thought: Uh-oh.

He prudently conjured up a don't-pay-no-heed-to-dumb-old-Ben chuckle. "Oh, listen to me, Miss Amy. I didn't have reason to speak to you that way. I'm sorry."

The rigidity of her jawline slowly relaxed. "Apology

accepted." She cleared her throat and sat up a little straighter. "In fact, Ben, your perception may have more truth in it than I want to say. I've been meaning to have a talk with you for a few days now. I have a confession: You're right that I've been paying more attention to the refugees I've been interviewing than to the newspaper. The things I've been hearing from the Union people who've been driven out of the hills, out of their homes and communities, who've had husbands and sons shot or hanged, houses burned down, women mistreated, children left orphaned . . . those things compel me. They move me. They dominate my mind. I'm sorry if I've let that push the newspaper aside lately." She paused. "But I'm not sure I'm *particularly* sorry. I'm thinking that maybe all this has been orienting my mind in directions that might actually be more important than the *Sage*."

Ben looked confused, then scared. "More important?"

"Ben, don't read too much into anything I say just now. I'm thinking, that's all. I came back to Knoxville, back home, in such a stunned condition, with Adam being gone so quickly and unexpectedly. I made decisions fast, because I felt compelled to. Maybe I made them too fast." She drew in a deep breath. "For one thing, I hadn't anticipated how much opposition we would receive from Parson Brownlow. He's determined to be *the* Unionist voice in Knoxville, and he resents me for daring to compete with him. He says some dreadful things about me in print—one of them being, by the way, that my 'staff' is comprised of a one-handed town drunk—and he says worse about me, and you, in conversation. A lot of it gets back to me, you know. I'm sure he intends that it should."

Ben laughed, openly relieved. "So it's Brownlow who has you down? Pshaw! I don't care what Brownlow says about nothing! He can throw his insults around all day if he wants to! You know what somebody told me? Back when he was publishing his newspaper over in Jonesborough, he once wrote something about how anybody could look at his paper and see that it beat any other paper in the country for attacking folks, getting hateful and personal with them. Did you know he spent two years putting out a weekly paper devoted to criticizing some preacher he didn't like up in Sullivan County? Two

years! That's plain old meanness, that is, and folks know that
Brownlow is just that way. Even them who agree with him
about a lot of things take him with a grain of salt."

"I'm aware of Parson Brownlow's nature," Amy replied.
"I'm also aware that he is well-established, while we're not,
that he has good facilities, which we don't, that he has more
years of experience than I do, and established advertisers. I'm a
woman of some means, Ben, but even so, I'll need to break
even at the very least, and make a profit if I can." She looked
away from him and her eyes became moist. "I'm losing my
confidence. In myself, in my plans . . ."

Ben frowned. "You ain't going to do it!"

"What's that?"

"Start up the *Sage* again. I can tell, listening to you, that you
ain't going to do it. And it's the very reason we moved here!"

"Ben, the reason we moved here is that I had to leave
Nashville. I couldn't bear to stay, with Adam gone. The awful
way he died haunted me every moment I was there. I came
here to escape that, and the only reason I brought you with me
was that—" She stopped abruptly, looking trapped.

Ben could easily guess what she didn't want to say, so he
said it for her, quietly. "You brought me with you because I'm
one of your charity cases. The old one-handed drunk that Amy
Deacon Hanover pulled out of the alley and into the pressroom.
And you knew that if I didn't stay tied to your apron strings,
I'd fall right back into drinking again."

"Ben, that's not how it is. The way you make it sound . . .
that's not it at all."

"So how is it?"

"How it is, is . . . well, yes, it's partly because I did think
you needed the support I was willing to give you, to keep you
away from the bottle. That much is true. But Ben, I swear, it
was as much for me as for you. I'd just lost my husband, Ben.
And as you may recall, our newspaper was failing in Nashville
even before Adam died. I felt weak, defeated . . . I hated feeling that way. I knew I had to leave Nashville, but I couldn't
have borne leaving without something, somebody, who I could
rely on. Somebody who cared about what happened to me, and
worried for me. That was you, Ben. I brought you with me not
only because you needed me, but because I needed you, too."

The floor between his feet suddenly held his rapt attention. "Well . . . thank you for saying that," he mumbled. A pause, then he chuckled. "Dang it, all I come in here for was to say maybe we ought to rent the Baumgardner place, and here we are talking gush!"

Amy paused, then burst into laughter. Ben always had a way of putting life into perspective, of stripping away pretense and self-importance. She laughed well, but her eyes remained moist, and she still looked very tired, as if the laughter could turn to weeping very easily.

Ben looked up at her. "You seem awful tired, Miss Amy. I believe it ain't good for you, hearing all them woe-tales from the hills."

"I have to hear them. I know it's what I'm supposed to do right now. And that's why, partly, I've been thinking about changing our plans some."

Ben instantly worried, but was glad to note she had used the word "our."

She went on. "I'm a writer, Ben. Not really a person of business, but a writer. I communicate ideas. I force people to face realities and think them through instead of ignoring them. For years it was the wickedness of slavery that I tried to communicate, and I think I did it well. But slavery is dying away. The situation is different, and will be. The challenge for the freedmen, and for all of us, really, is to see how former slaves are going to find their own place in society. There will be poverty, and hate, and jealousy. It's already happening—you know how people here hate seeing the streets full of contrabands, roaming around, looking for work, places to stay. Even when the Negro men join the army, there's still their families to be dealt with. . . . But enough of that, for now. There'll be time to deal with all those matters later."

Amy was speaking faster, more intently, leaning across her desk like the Amy of old, the one Ben enjoyed most. "What is even more pressing and urgent right now is what's happening in the mountains and the foothills. We're fairly safely ensconced here in Knoxville, Ben. We have the protection of the Federal army, and I doubt the Confederates will ever hold this city again, even if they try. But head east, out toward Morristown and Bean Station, up to Greeneville, Johnson's Depot,

Taylorsville, Elizabethton . . . go into the North Carolina mountains around Warm Springs and Marshall, into the hills around Asheville and over in all those isolated little coves and hollows, and there you find people in the midst of the worst kind of war. Not just soldiers, either—but common, everyday mountain people, suffering and fighting and being abused in so many ways. Not just the Union people, I know—there are sins done on both sides in this cursed war—but it's the Union people who have caught my heart, because they've done nothing to bring this terrible situation onto themselves other than being *loyal*. There's the key of it all! By doing nothing but remaining loyal to what they've believed in for years, they've had suffering brought down upon them. The rebels and their sympathizers are the instigators of this conflict, as I see it. What suffering they do, they've at least in some measure helped to bring upon themselves."

Ben sat there nodding, thinking how it all made perfect sense to him, yet knowing that an articulate Confederate could lay out the same facts from the opposite viewpoint, making the Unionists the villains, and that would sound just as sensible. He had often bemoaned to himself the miseries of being a simple-thinking man. It was like being a puff from a cattail plant, blowing about in whatever direction the wind was blowing most strongly at any given moment.

"So what I'm considering, Ben, is maybe not going into the newspaper just now . . . eventually, yes, but maybe not just now. Maybe when the war is over, and maybe somewhere besides Knoxville." She pursed her lips at him a moment. "In fact, I've been thinking about a town you've already mentioned today. A place where I wouldn't have Brownlow throwing up obstacles."

"A town I already mentioned . . . Jonesborough?"

"Yes. Or maybe Elizabethton. Somewhere in that region, close to those mountains. I think about going there, and it draws me, somehow. That's where the *Sage* needs to be. Not Knoxville."

"But not until after the war is through . . . you did say that, didn't you?"

"Yes. But I admit it absolutely tugs at me, every time one of these Unionist refugees tells me a story, to go there right now.

Don't worry, I'm not actually going to do it. But to get right into the midst of it, to help expose to the world the things that are happening there—I wish I could go. I'd go tomorrow, I swear I would!"

"I'm glad you ain't. It would be foolish to throw yourself into the midst of all that, considering the baby."

"Yes, yes. I know." She grew wistful. "But if only . . ."

Ben thought how strange a female Amy Deacon Hanover could be, sometimes wanting to get into the thick of the very situations other folks tried to avoid. For example, he'd never known a living soul, until he met her, who actually relished arguing over the miserable subject of slavery. Most people preferred not to think about the sorrowful aspects of that institution, but Amy not only stuck her face right into it with eyes wide open, but tried to smear it in everybody else's as well. Who but she would *want* to plunge into the midst of a cruel mountain war?

"I hope you won't do nothing to get yourself in danger, Miss Amy."

"Well, like you said, there's not much I can do right now, considering the baby." She brightened instantly. "But I *am* going to write, or at least start, a book about what I'm learning from these poor refugees who come to the city. I could do that right here in Knoxville, print it right on our press, find some bindery equipment. . . . We could become a book publisher, Ben. Small-scale, local, but it would be a feasible alternative to the newspaper, and I think we could at the very least recover our costs and keep afloat until situations change and we're able to move over to Jonesborough or Elizabethton and get the paper cranked up. My own father got his start in publishing by writing and publishing a home medical book right here in Knoxville, years ago. Did you know that?"

"I surely did." Ben was relaxing some; it seemed that whatever her plans were, he was not being eased out of them, and that ultimately her plans were getting bigger, not smaller.

"And if creating an actual bound book proves to be too expensive, I think we could publish, to begin with, in something like newspaper form, stitching the pages together by hand, if need be. Once again, I've sort of borrowed the idea from my father. We'll be as innovative as necessary—we're in the land of wartime makeshifts, after all, and we can makeshift as well as the next people, can't we, Ben?"

He smiled, very relaxed now, and nodded. For a while there the world had looked mighty uncertain. Though Ben had far more confidence in himself now than he had during the drinking years, he knew he was still not so far past that stage that he felt he could float entirely on his own. Amy had been right when she said that the need situation between herself and himself went two ways.

His eye caught a glimpse of something odd on Amy's desk. It was a tattered envelope, really little more than half an envelope, and splattered with something initially liquid but now dried to a brownish stain. *Blood!* He recalled the two boys who had run out the door earlier, and what Nanny had told him. Curiosity to know more arose, and he decided to play the innocent and see what she would tell.

"Miss Amy, pardon me for switching the subject, but I swear it looks like somebody's bled onto some of that paper on your desk. That there envelope—is that blood on it?"

She lifted her brows again in that way he had seen so many times. "Yes it is, and oddly enough, Ben, you haven't really changed the subject at all." She picked up the envelope, not seeming to mind touching the blackened blood, and Ben thought it funny how women were generally less squeamish about blood than men. "This letter was brought to me today by two boys who found it on the railroad tracks. Did you hear about the man run over by the train this morning?"

"No!"

"There was one . . . I paid another little boy to run over and talk to the authorities for me, and from identification they found in his pockets, it was apparently a businessman from Nashville, named Williams. I'd never heard of him. But this letter apparently had fallen out of his pocket and been mostly torn up by the train. And you can see it's bloodied pretty badly. But my name is visible on the front of the envelope. See?"

She held it up. Ben gave a quick glance and a quicker nod.

"The letter, sorry to say, is so torn up, so much of it missing, that it's impossible to make any real sense of it. It's from someone with the first name of Greeley and a last name that begins with B—and the odd thing about that, Ben, is I've heard just such a name many times while I've been talking to these mountain refugees. That's what I meant when I said you hadn't really changed the subject. There's a stampeder pilot out of Carter County by the name of Greeley Brown. Have you heard of him, by any chance?" She paused, staring. "Ben, is something wrong? You look pale."

Ben held up his left arm; the hook glinted in the light. "I've not only heard of him, but I've met him. It was Greeley Brown and a band of his stampeders who found me on a mountain one night, sick and out of my head with a putrefied hand wound. It was Greeley Brown who cut off this very hand and saved my life, Miss Amy."

Her eyes glittered with astonishment. "Truly?"

"Truly. I swear."

"Ben, that's remarkable. Remarkable. Almost . . . scary. I've heard his name mentioned by so many people I've been interviewing, and now I have a letter fragment that he might have written . . . and now this, about your hand! Ben, if there's a destiny, and I'm not at all sure there is, but *if* there is, mine must certainly have some link to Greeley Brown."

"What's the letter say? Oh, I'm sorry. That ain't my business. You needn't tell me."

She paused, then placed the letter in a drawer of her desk and closed it. "It's impossible to tell what it says," she replied. "Too much of it is cut off for it to make sense."

"Oh."

She smiled broadly. "Ben, we've had quite a talk today! I'm sorry to have thrown so many changes at you so quickly. And keep in mind that nothing is set in stone. I'm just . . . reconsidering. Rethinking. Making sure of what I need to do before I set out to do it. And whatever happens, I want you to know that you are still my employee, still my professional aide and companion. Still my friend. I want you to work for me even when I'm not quite sure what the work is! Do you mind that?"

"Miss Amy, I'll dig ditches with this hook for you, if that's what you want."

"What I want is for you to stay with me, to work with me, to be open to whatever I finally settle upon . . . and to stay away from liquor. That's important, Ben. And it's one of the few things that could make me change my mind about you. I'll be a faithful friend and employer for you as long as you keep working as hard as you have, and as long as you stay away from whiskey. I liked you the first time I met you, Ben, that evening when you helped me hang broadsides all up and down this very street. But I like you much better now. You're a far, far better man without whiskey. Stay away from whiskey, Ben."

She had given that warning many times before, and he knew she was not one to repeat anything without reason. This was a prohibition that she truly meant. He thought of how close he had come that very day to violating it, and inwardly shuddered. "I'll stay away from it, Miss Amy. I will. I won't go back to what I was before, not ever."

"I'm glad," she said. She stood as he did, and gave a quick grimace, her hand groping to her abdomen.

"Miss Amy, are you all right?"

She straightened, smiled, put her hand to her side again. "I'm fine, Ben. Just a little pain, that's all. Stomach trouble. My mother had it all her life, and I believe I've inherited it."

"Nothing to do with the baby?"

"No, no. Not at all."

"Good. Got to take care of that baby, you know."

"Of course."

He turned away and left the office. She sat down quickly, touching her abdomen again, brows knitting. In a few moments the pain was gone. Just a stomach cramp, nothing more. Nothing to be concerned about.

A few moments later she rose and quietly closed the door. Removing the bloodied letter from her desk, she pulled the damaged contents from it and spread them on the desktop. Resting her hands atop her pregnant bulge, she studied the scrawled words closely. Whoever had written this letter, whether Greeley Brown or some other Greeley, wrote in large, blocky letters. He was not educated, clearly, nor accustomed to writing. Producing this letter had probably required much effort and concentration. Now very little remained from the results of that labor, and what did remain provided more mysteries than answers.

Even so, what she had told Ben Scarlett wasn't fully true. She thought she *could* detect a trace of the letter's meaning . . .

maybe. And that maybe was enough to fill her with excitement and dread all mixed together.

"Sam," she whispered. "Sam . . ." The name was there, but the surname, like that of the writer himself, was not. It was deeply frustrating. Might this be the same Sam she had thought of a thousand times or more, especially since Adam had been killed?

She read: "Mrs. Hanover, Sam wanted me to be sure that you was told about . . ." She cut off reading at the point the words themselves were cut off. Told about what? *What?* And how could she hope to find out?

There was only one Sam she could think of who could have any meaningful message for her, and she had seen or heard nothing of him since the time she was still in Hannibal Deacon's household and Sam Colter had mounted his horse and rode out of town in the wake of some trouble involving his brother in North Carolina. But she had known that was not the sole reason he had left. Sam had been in love with her, had asked her to marry him, and she had turned him down. It wasn't because she couldn't have loved him in turn, but because war had come and she was wrapped up in it, determined to play some role on behalf of the Union she so deeply supported. At that time she had been unable to conceive of getting married. Her only husband at that point could be the great Cause itself.

Since that time, much had changed. She had become involved in the smuggling of counterfeit Confederate currency on behalf of the Union's underground warfare efforts, gotten herself shot in the process, and wound up in Nashville. There, she had met Adam Hanover, and all her big talk about not marrying before the war ended had blown away like dust. She *had* married, and lost her husband to an assassin's bullet mere months later.

And now, this tattered letter, this indecipherable communication, this tantalizing mention of someone named Sam who had a message for her . . .

She picked up her pad and began to write. Whatever this message meant, and even if it did have to do with Sam Colter, she couldn't let it concern her now. Too many important things to do. She couldn't let herself become preoccupied with meaningless messages and memories of a young man whom she had already declined as a husband.

But as she wrote, the image of Sam Colter stayed in the back of her mind, and nothing she could do would erase it.

Chapter 16

Supper was cooked by Nanny, as was becoming the custom, and eaten at the long table in the *Sage* office. Amy was quieter than usual, picking at her food, and Nanny had nothing to say at all, so it was up to Ben to try to keep up some chatter so the meal wouldn't be utterly silent. He talked about everything that came to mind—the weather, a recent fire that had burned down one of the city's oldest houses, the astonishing speed with which refugee camps were springing up around the city—but no one would pick up on his talk and he finally gave up. When the meal was through, he excused himself and headed out of the building for a long walk, this one fortunately avoiding Skunk, then up to his room.

He settled himself by his window and watched the street below. Ben often passed the early evening away in this manner. It was relaxing, and in a city full of soldiers and refugees in addition to its resident citizens, a man could often witness some interesting human dramas playing out on the street below. Tonight the stage was disappointingly empty. He was about to turn away from it when he saw the side door of the *Sage* office open—his room was above the rear portion of the L-shaped building, and gave him a clear view of the side door—and Amy emerged, bundled up in her big coat and furred cap. She walked to the street and down it to her own small house, a little three-room affair that sat back off the street and was full of clutter. Amy was no housekeeper, that was certain. The street curved slightly in front of the *Sage* office, so Ben was able to watch her travel the full distance to her humble home. He watched her until she was safely indoors, and wondered how in the world a woman such as Amy, who seemed more suited to living in a man's professional world than a woman's domestic one, was going to be able to adjust to being a mother. That was going to be an interesting spectacle, sure as the world.

A refugee wagon, laden with furniture, came rumbling up the street. He watched it pass, studying the people on it. A man, wife, and couple of little children. He wondered from where they had come, which side of the war they supported, if any, and if they, too, would wind up as pages of notes in Amy's pad. He mulled over the book notion she had shared with him, and decided he favored it. Writing a book wouldn't be so stressing for Amy as putting out a newspaper, and Brownlow might let up on her, too, if he didn't see her as a competitor. The more Ben thought it over, the better he liked it. Amy could write her book, print it up and sell it, give birth to her child, and maybe make things easier on herself for a while until the war was finished. A book such as hers would sell a lot not only in the immediate area, but also in the northern cities, where awareness of the Unionist refugee problem in Tennessee was beginning to gain much attention and relief societies were forming right and left. The book idea made a lot of sense on several levels, and Ben admired Amy for coming up with it—and appreciated her for being willing to keep him employed even if there wasn't going to be a newspaper for a while.

Ben wished he was as clever as Amy. It would be fine to be able to write books and so on. He had the occasional fantasy of becoming a writer of sorts himself, and in fact was making headway toward it, though in a far different manner than Amy.

Opening the little drawer in the table beside him, he pulled out a notepad of his own and studied the rough but rhyming lines he had written there. Six lines so far . . . not much to show for several evenings of chewing on his pencil and scribbling.

He wasn't even sure what this would be when finished. A poem, perhaps, but more likely a song, if he could find some old folk melody that would fit with the words. His own song, his own private statement, the words of a man who had spent a life fighting a private war with liquor, observing the tragedies of a public war being fought by two factions within one nation. Nothing anybody else would probably ever see or hear, but it was a satisfying effort anyway.

He scratched in another line, read it, shook his head, and crossed it out. It was cussed hard, trying to make words sound right and fit with what came before. Deciding he wasn't up to the effort this evening, he put the pad away, then glanced out the window again.

Nanny had emerged from the *Sage* office and was looking around furtively. Ben frowned. Why was Nanny outside? He knew that Amy had firmly ordered her to remain in her own little quarters—a cot and table in a little storage room at the back of the office—after dark.

Ben really wasn't surprised to see Nanny violating the order, for it seemed in her character to resist doing what anybody told her. But it made him mad anyway. Nanny could make him mad just by looking at him. He'd never met a colder, more ungrateful person than her. He had listened to Amy's lectures about how white people should try to understand and be kind to freed slaves, considering all that so many of them had suffered, and he'd tried. But something about Nanny just always made it impossible. He'd tried to like her, tried to be her friend, but it just hadn't worked out that way. Nanny didn't seem to want his friendship, which was a little insulting, considering how he had brought her to Miss Amy and given her a home, paid work, and status that was probably the very best of any black refugee in the entire city.

He leaned over and blew out the light burning on the table, not wanting Nanny to look up and see him illuminated in the window. What was she up to? He settled down to watch.

Nanny, meanwhile, was leaning up against the front of the office building, but back in the most shadowed area, as if trying to be inconspicuous. Suspicions crowded Ben's mind, shaped and fed by his conception, typical of the time and culture, of almost all blacks as inherently dishonest, sneaky, and immoral.

Was Nanny stealing food or other items and selling it? Worse still, was she prostituting herself?

The latter suspicion loomed larger when Ben noted the approach of a male figure down the street. Huddled in a ragged coat, the man was moving in a way to suggest secrecy. He paused on the far side of the street from Nanny, looked in both directions, and strode across quickly. Nanny stood up straighter as he approached. Ben looked closely in what meager light was available, and saw that the fellow was black. One of the many contrabands now in the city, maybe. But as Ben peered harder, he believed the man looked much like a freedman who had been around Knoxville for years, a poorly reputed fellow who went by the name of Cat Kingsley, and who always seemed to have money in his pocket although no one could say just where he got it. Ben had figured Cat for a thief, and maybe a blackmailer, for years now.

Ben watched Cat and Nanny converse and wished he could hear what they were saying. From their motions he suspected that Cat was trying to get Nanny to let him into the *Sage* office, but Nanny was refusing. Ben tensed like a panther waiting to spring. By heaven, if she let Cat in there, they'd have Ben Scarlett to contend with on the spot! He'd as soon see the office doors opened to the devil himself as to Cat Kingsley! But they didn't go in. Instead they slipped onto the street together, hurried down it, and vanished into the shadows. Ben had lost track of them before he could figure out just where they'd gone.

He moved away from the window and closed the curtain. Should he tell Amy what he had seen? Part of him wanted to, but Ben had been raised by a father who despised "tattling" above all other sins, and the lessons had stuck and been bolstered by his own life in the streets, where a man minded his own business and let other folks mind theirs.

He wouldn't tell Amy, not yet. But he'd sure be keeping an eye on Nanny from now on, and might just confront her with what he knew, if this kind of suspicious behavior kept up. Anybody who was fooling with Cat Kingsley was probably up to no good. Cat had never done a decent thing in his life, as far as Ben knew, and if Nanny was having anything to do with him, it did nothing to make Ben think higher of her.

• • •

An hour later Cat Kingsley sat back against the wall of the shed behind the old Baumgardner store, the look of satisfaction on his face illuminated by the light of the single flickering candle stuck onto one of the empty shelves. Nanny was standing, adjusting her clothing hurriedly, slipping on her coat. He watched, grinning, pulled the stub of a chewed cigar from his pocket, and popped it into his mouth. Cat never smoked cigars, just chewed them.

"What's the matter, Nanny? You cold?"

"You know I'm cold. There ain't no heat in here."

"We had the right kind of heat a minute ago, didn't we!"

Nanny didn't reply. She pulled her coat up around her neck and sank down onto the floor, shivering.

"You know, we could be a lot warmer these evenings if you'd just let me into your room. Ain't no reason we should have to be sneaking around in old sheds and such when you've got that nice warm room we could use."

"I done told you, I can't let you in there. I'm afraid you'd steal something. And if Ben Scarlett or Miss Amy caught us, that'd be it for me. I'd be on the street right off."

"They wouldn't catch us."

"They might. That Ben Scarlett, he stays up late sometimes. He might hear."

Cat looked around the shed. "Ben Scarlett used to sleep in here, you know?"

"He did?"

"He sure did, back when he was a drunk. Know what I think? I believe he'll be a drunk again, too. Once a drunk, always a drunk."

"He's a religious man now. Goes to church. He won't drink nothing now."

"He'll give in. Just you wait. Ain't nothing no church can give him sweeter than whiskey."

"Don't you believe in God, Cat?"

"Ain't never met the man. Don't believe there's such a feller anywhere to be found. What? You don't believe in no God, do you?"

"I don't know."

"The white folks made up God. Helps keep niggers in their place, telling them they can have all the good things in heaven when they die, while the white folks have all the good things while they live."

Nanny said, "I don't know nothing about that. But I don't believe Ben Scarlett will drink no more."

"You like Ben, do you?"

"I don't know. No, I don't reckon I like him. But it was him who brought me to Miss Amy, and she's been good to me."

"How much she pay you?"

"Nothing. Just gives me my food and room. That's why I have to do this."

It was a great and resounding lie, and Nanny hoped she made it sound convincing. She knew the kind of man Cat was, and that the worst thing that could happen would be for him to find out she received wages. He'd be after her money right away if he knew. Her purpose in these secret rendezvous with Cat Kingsley had nothing to do with the meager money he gave her in exchange for her physical favors. She accepted that money only to keep him from realizing the true reason she shared herself with him.

"Well, I reckon you've earned your pay tonight," he said, reaching into a pocket and producing a couple of bills in Confederate currency. "Here you go."

"That ain't no good to me here. Give me greenbacks."

He grinned, put away the Confederate bills, and produced United States currency in their place. She took it, counted it, stuffed it in her coat pocket.

"I'll bet Miss Amy's got a lot of them greenbacks, don't she!" he said. "I hear that her husband was a rich man."

"I don't know."

"I'll bet she's got all kinds of money. And she don't share it with you, does she!"

"I don't know how much money she got."

"Hey, I got something else to give you," he said. From the other side of his coat he produced a dark, squatty, stoppered bottle, and handed it to her.

She took it. "What's this?"

"French pills. Pills for women. You take them if you get a 'complaint,' and they make it go away." He winked.

"What do you mean, complaint?"

"I mean, if your monthly don't come, you take some of them pills, and before you know it, you're healthy again."

She looked again at the pills as understanding came. "You mean, if there's a baby in you, you take these, and the baby dies?"

"That ain't the way to put it, Nanny! There's ways folks say that without saying it, you know. Say a woman's been sporting, and misses her monthly, she can go to the right kind of places, where there's special doctors, and say, 'Doc, I've got obstructed menses.' That's how you say it—'obstructed menses.' And the doc will give her a bottle of pills like that, she'll take them, and all of a sudden them menses ain't obstructed no more."

"Where'd you get these?"

"Old Cat gets whatever he wants."

"Why'd you give them to me?"

He laughed. "How stupid are you, woman? The way me and you do, one of these days you're going to have some obstructed menses, and when you do, you just take them pills."

She stared at the bottle, her impassive face not showing the feelings stirring inside her. Had she vented them, she might have thrown the bottle into Cat's face and let him know that the very reason she "sported" with him at all was so that she *would* become pregnant!

But he would never accept that. He couldn't possibly understand the pain that motivated her. He couldn't know how, since arriving in Knoxville and watching Amy Hanover's pregnancy advance, she had developed a longing ache for a child she had left behind in North Carolina when she made her break for freedom. At the time she had truly believed she didn't love that baby and wouldn't miss it, if only she could be free. Freedom from slavery had been her only goal. But life had its ironies: Now that she was no longer a slave, the child she'd given up had begun to haunt her. She saw it every time she closed her eyes at night, and felt its absence from her arms every waking moment.

The child she abandoned had left a void in her life, and she intended to fill it. The day she suffered from "obstructed menses" would be a day of joy for her. There would be no desire for the benefits of Cat's "French pills." And no more desire for Cat himself. There was nothing this man could give her that she would want other than another child in her womb, and then in her arms, filling the emptiness her abandoned child had left behind.

She could not let him know any of this, of course. She nodded and put the bottle of pills into her coat pocket. "Thank you, Cat."

"You don't lose them pills, hear? And you keep them hid. Don't you let no Ben Scarlett nor Miss Amy find them. We don't want them knowing about the good times we been having of a evening, do we!"

"No." It was the first truthful answer she had given him that night.

He gave her a warm grin. "Come here and sit beside me. I'll keep you warm."

"No. I need to get back to my place, case somebody finds I'm gone."

"I said for you to come sit beside me, woman." There was no grin this time.

Nanny went to him and sat down. He slipped his arm around her and nuzzled his nose against her cheek. The cigar in his teeth stunk. She sat unmoving, expressionless, and said nothing more to him that night.

Chapter 17

Nanny thought there was something odd about the way Ben Scarlett looked at her over the breakfast table the next morning, and throughout the day, as he came and went, she caught him staring at her from time to time. Coldly, it seemed to her. She found it very disturbing.

Miss Amy also didn't seem like her usual self. She seemed preoccupied, and a couple of times through the day, Nanny saw her wince as if with pain and put her hand to her belly. She asked Amy about it once, indirectly, and Amy said she was fine, nothing but a touch of stomach trouble.

Nanny had another rendezvous that night with Cat Kingsley, and he talked more about Miss Amy's money, how she surely had lots of it. He asked her something new as well: "She got a safe or a lockbox in that office?"

"Yes." It was a truthful answer, for once, given quickly before any thought, and Nanny wished she had followed her usual habit of lying.

"I figured. I figured. Full of money, I'll bet."

"I told you, I don't know nothing about her money."

"Nanny, think how it could be, me and you, if we was rich. We could go off somewhere and live a fine life. Think how

grand it would be if me and you had a lockbox full of money
our own selves."

The next day passed with more staring by Ben Scarlett,
more signs of sickness on Miss Amy's part. Nanny began to
feel that the world beneath her feet was unstable. Something
was amiss, and she was beginning to grow frightened.

That night Cat brought up Miss Amy's lockbox again, and
Nanny knew it wasn't random conversation. She wished she
had never begun meeting Cat Kingsley. The more she was
around him, the more she sensed that he was a bad man, and
that his interest in Miss Amy's lockbox was growing.

That night, sneaking back to the office with her mind full of
worry, Nanny happened to glance up at Ben Scarlett's window.
It was dark, but she thought she detected a movement of the
curtain. He was up there, watching. Cold dread filled her. She
wondered how many times he had watched her come and go.
Ben knew that Miss Amy had ordered her to remain in her
room at night. Now she understood why he'd been looking at
her the way he did lately, why he never had anything to say to
her anymore.

The next day he stared at her again, and this time she stared
back. The communication was silent, but understood by both
of them. While Miss Amy was closed in her office, interviewing another Unionist refugee, Nanny and Ben slipped to
the front of the building, near the stove, and faced one another.

"You going to tell her?" Nanny asked.

"Nanny, would it break your jaw to call me 'sir' every now
and then?"

Her teeth clenched tightly; she felt the impulse to spit at
him. But she forced it out: "You going to tell her . . . *sir*?"

"I hadn't planned on it. Not at first. But I been seeing you
sneak out like that for three nights running. What are you up to,
girl?"

"Nothing. Sir."

"Nothing, huh? What's Cat Kingsley got to do with that
'nothing'?"

He knew more than she had thought. She fished in her mind
for the best answer, but could come up with no more than,
"Cat's my man."

"Your man? How do you mean? Your beau?"

"I don't know what that is."

"Your beau. Your sweetheart."

"Yes. He's my sweetheart."

"He ain't much of a sweetheart, Nanny. Cat's a dangerous man. He's one wicked man. You in love with him?"

Nanny nodded, not knowing what else she could do.

"I'm going to ask you something straight out, and it'll probably make you mad. You acting the whore for him?"

It did make her mad, and it showed in the flash of her eye and a quick grinding of her teeth. But she restrained any greater reaction. "I ain't, no sir."

"Well, good."

She couldn't hold it back. "You think every nigra woman is that kind of woman, *sir*?"

"No. But I got my questions about them who sneak out night after night, 'gainst the rules, and slip off for an hour or more with the meanest darky in the city."

She clamped her mouth shut and stared at him hatefully.

"You'd best not be sneaking out at night no more, Nanny. I'll be watching from my window to make sure you don't."

"You going to tell Miss Amy?"

"I don't know. I might. I ain't generally one to tell on folks, but I don't like nothing that has to do with Cat Kingsley. If I see you sneak out again, I will tell."

"I won't sneak out no more . . . sir."

"That's good. Tell me something: Is it true that you called me 'Mr. Hookfinger' behind my back to the local children?"

Her chin thrust out. "Yes, I did. Sir."

"Don't call me that no more. I don't like it."

He turned and walked out into the street, leaving her fuming, angry, wanting to cry. But that she would not do. She had endured hells that no white-skinned person could know. It would take far more than the likes of Ben Scarlett to wrench tears from her eyes.

That night, Cat Kingsley made his usual approach to the *Sage* office, but found no Nanny waiting for him. Puzzled and beginning to grow angry, he cussed beneath his breath and looked around, wondering what was wrong. Minutes passed and she didn't appear. He thought about knocking at the office door, but feared someone else might be in there tonight. Maybe that was what kept her from coming. He left.

Above, Ben Scarlett's curtain fell in the darkened window and Ben stood, nodding with satisfaction. Nanny had been true to her promise, and there was one Cat that would have to prowl elsewhere that night if he wanted to find a willing kitten. Ben retired to his bed, feeling he'd taken care of one problem that Miss Amy hadn't even known she had. He was rather proud of himself.

The next day, Ben gave Nanny a little smile the first time he saw her. She gave him a stare in return. That night Ben watched again, and Cat showed up as before. Again no Nanny. It seemed she was going to mind even if she didn't like it.

When Cat showed up, this time he found a scrap of paper lying beneath a stone on the spot Nanny had formerly awaited him. He picked it up, sneaked into an alley, and examined it by the light of a match. It was a crude sketch of the side of the *Sage* building, with an arrow pointing at a particular window. He knew that window, having examined it once while thinking about breaking into the place, but it had been nailed shut, its glass panes replaced with wood.

Maybe not now, though. He set fire to the sketch and let it burn to ash. Then he headed for the *Sage* building again and slipped into the alleyway on the side of the building opposite to and therefore out of view of Ben Scarlett's window.

The wood-paned window slid open easily. Someone had removed all the nails. He grinned. Nanny was turning clever on him! He liked that. He looked down the alley, put a leg through the open window, and slipped inside.

He stood in the darkness. "Nanny?"

"I'm here, Cat."

"I found your map. Where you been these last nights, woman?"

She approached him in the darkness. "I was caught, Cat. I couldn't come out, or else Miss Amy would have knowed."

"Who caught you?"

"Ben Scarlett. He'd been watching us out his window, when you'd come meet me."

"Damn his damned old hook hand! What he do, say he'd tell on you?"

"Yes. He said I couldn't slip out no more. So I waited two nights to let him see I wasn't sneaking out, then I put that paper out there. Oh, I hope he didn't see you finding it!"

"You think he might have?"

"He might have . . . I hope not. I was taking the chance he wouldn't watch three nights running."

"You took the chance . . . woman, you're a fool! If he saw me, he might be fetching the law right now!"

"He didn't see you, Cat. Come here, come to me. I been missing you." A match struck; in its light he saw her the first time, lifting the bowl of a lamp and reaching the match toward the wick.

He lunged toward her. "Put that light out, woman! He'll see it!" Cat grabbed her wrist and shook the match out. "You should have found some other way to get that map to me, Nanny. He might be on his way down from that room of his right now!"

He was squeezing her wrist very tightly. It hurt.

"But hell, now that I'm in here, I may as well take a chance of my own. No sport tonight, woman! Where's Miss Amy's lockbox? Tell me quick!"

Nanny recoiled, and at that moment her own folly laid itself out before her. She had let Cat into this building for one reason only: because she was angry at Ben Scarlett, and wanted to outwit him. If he sought to thwart her from going to her nightly rendezvous, she'd thwart him by bringing the rendezvous to her. It would have been easy, of course, for her merely to have left through that same window herself and met Cat back at the Baumgardner shed, Ben Scarlett none the wiser, but it seemed better, more cunning, to do it this way. Now she and Cat could have their time back in her room, and should someone come in, she could hide Cat behind her cot and play the innocent. And if challenged by Ben about whether she was keeping her promise not to leave the building by night, this way she could say that she was and not even lie about it. Nanny thought it a fine scheme, a great way to be one up on old Hookfinger. She was determined to become pregnant, to fill that hunger in her heart that only a child of her own could satiate, and Ben Scarlett would *not* stand in her way!

But anger at Ben Scarlett had muddled her thinking and made her overlook something that would have made her think twice about her scheme: all Cat's covetous talk about that supposedly wealth-laden lockbox of Miss Amy's. Now, with Cat looming before her, virtually drooling for that lockbox, she couldn't fathom how she could not have realized this would happen. He intended to take that box, obviously—and she had let him in, *invited* him in, to do it!

Her failure to answer angered him. "I asked you where that lockbox is, woman! Tell me, or I'll bust you a good one right across that pretty face!"

"I don't know where it is . . . Miss Amy took it, I think. Maybe she locked it in the bank."

"You're lying!"

"I ain't!"

"Where's her office room?"

"I don't know . . ."

"You *are* lying!" He drew back his hand and struck her so hard she fell. "You know where that box is, damn you, and you can just go fetch it, right now! Get up from there and get me that box!"

She rose, hand on her jaw, and stumbled crying toward Amy Hanover's office. The door, though closed, was not locked, and she went in. He followed, looking around as if expecting someone to come in at any moment.

Nanny would not try to deceive him further. His blow had hurt, and she had realized he was the kind who would kill her if he thought it would serve him to do it. Tears streaming down, she went to the most cluttered corner of a very cluttered office and scooted back a stack of books; they tilted and fell, tipping over a shelf, which crashed down as well. Startled, Nanny stepped back, tripped, and knocked an unlighted lamp off the desk. It shattered on the floor.

"Woman, you trying to make all that noise?" Cat said urgently. "Damn you, you trying to get somebody in here on me?"

"No, Cat, I ain't. I just fell, that's all."

She got up again and poked about for the lockbox. It was

dark in the room, so she worked by feel more than sight, and discovered the lockbox by the cool touch of its smooth metal surface. She hefted it up, found it heavy.

"That it? You got it, woman?"

"Yes."

"Bring it here, quick!"

Moving in the dark, she tripped over some of the spilled books. The lockbox hit the floor with a loud thud that shook the building.

"I'm going to kill you, woman! You trying to get me caught, ain't you!"

"No, Cat, I swear I ain't!"

"Let me have that box." He strode forward, around the desk, and reached down for the box. As he lifted it, the corner of it struck her face, scratching it deeply and making her yelp in pain.

"Hush that, woman!" He kicked her, hard enough to hurt, not hard enough to make her scream.

After that everything happened fast. Cat said something threatening to her, but was interrupted by the rattling, then the opening, of the front door of the office building. Ben Scarlett's voice echoed back through the building: "What's going on in here? What's all that noise? Nanny, where are you?"

Cat Kingsley swore loudly, and this time when he kicked Nanny, he kicked very hard. She took it in the ribs and let out a yell. Almost passed out, she heard Ben Scarlett running through the building, back toward the office, while Cat tried to make his way too hurriedly out of it. He tripped and fell, grunting and swearing as he came down atop the angular lockbox. She heard him getting up as Ben reached the office door.

"What's going on in here?"

The next sound was Cat cursing Ben, followed by a metallic, clicking sound. Nanny realized it was the sound of a cooking revolver and let out a scream that sounded in tandem with the firing of the shot. She heard Ben grunt and fall, and fainted away in shock as Cat Kingsley swore some more and ran out of the office, over Ben's body, and out through the building toward the same window through which he had entered. The window slid up, then down; Cat's footsteps, moving fast, receded and were gone, and for a time there was nothing in the *Sage* building but its usual nocturnal silence.

Chapter 18

Nanny did her best to hold Amy Hanover's gaze, but for once her iron will failed her. She hung her head and fought the urge to cry, and wished Amy would say something, anything—anything but continuing to burn her with her silent, hurt stare.

But the stare continued another half minute before Amy spoke. Her voice was quiet. "He's injured, Nanny, but it appears he'll survive. The bullet struck him in the lower right shoulder, thank God, so that nothing vital was damaged. A little lower and it would have struck his lung. But even now there's the danger of mortification. And Ben is a man who damaged his own body for years with the way he lived. His system isn't as strong as the average man's. We can hope he will pull through, but there's no full assurance yet."

Without looking up, Nanny asked, "Is he awake?"

"No. Not yet. Whether that is from the bullet wound or from him striking his head so hard on the press crate when he fell, I can't say. The doctor seemed almost as worried by him striking that crate as he was by the bullet itself. The bullet is out of Ben, though. Thank God we were able to find a doctor so quickly."

"It wasn't me who shot him, Miss Amy."

"For heaven's sake, Nanny, I know that. You've told us already. But it was you who let this man into the building. And so deliberately! Removed the nails from a sealed window to do it! Tell me the scoundrel's name again."

"Cat. Cat Kingsley. He's a freedman."

"Why did you let him in?"

Nanny had mastered the art of the lie years ago, and had come to rely on it as her path through life. But this time the skill failed her. She was shaken deeply, and spoke with honesty.

"I been . . . seeing him. He's my—" What was that word Ben Scarlett had used? "He's my beau."

"Your beau. What do you mean, beau?"

"I mean . . . sort of like my husband. You know."

Amy drew in a slow breath, trying to calm a rising fury within her. "Yes, I believe I do. So you've been using this place, the very room I've given you, as a place to give yourself, your body, to some man."

"No, Miss Amy, I ain't. Up until tonight, we been slipping off together into a shed on down the street."

"Oh? So you've also been violating my rule about not leaving this building after dark."

"No, I ain't . . . yes. Yes, I reckon I have."

"So why did you let this 'beau' of yours in here tonight, instead of going to that shed? Were you trying to help him rob me?"

"No! I done it because Mr. Hookfinger . . . Mr. Ben, I mean, he'd caught me slipping out, and he'd told me not to do it again, or he'd tell you."

Amy stood, pacing about to let her temper calm. They were in her cluttered office, and outside, the sun was beginning to rise. The pistol shot that felled Ben Scarlett had generated investigation by a Union street sentinel who had been passing within range of the sound, and from then on the night was a flurry of wild activity. Amy had been roused from her little house down the street, a doctor was summoned, police came and asked abundant questions, scribbling notes, drawing crude sketches of the scene. They were gone now, having reluctantly accepted Amy's request that Nanny not be hauled off and locked up. Amy had taken responsibility for Nanny, who after all had not been directly responsible for the shooting, and the police had gone along with it, after some argument.

"Nanny, I don't know what to say to you. I'm shocked. Disappointed." Amy turned and faced her. "No, it's more than that. I'm *furious*! How *dare* you abuse the kindness I've shown to you! How *dare* you play games with me, and with Ben, and with the rules I've laid down! If Ben dies, God forbid, or if he suffers any kind of permanent damage from that wound or that fall, as far as I'm concerned, you'll be almost as responsible as the scoundrel who shot him!"

"I'm sorry, Miss Amy. I didn't know none of that would happen."

"This 'beau' of yours took my lockbox, Nanny. Was that part of your plan, too? Did you and your 'beau' intend to divide the money between you?"

"No, no! The robbing was just his doing! I didn't know he'd do that! I swear!"

"You swear. You swear. What good is your word, Nanny? How can I be expected to trust you now?"

"I don't know, Miss Amy. I'm sorry. Are they going to hang me?"

"No, they won't hang you. Though I don't know that you don't deserve it. Tell me: Why did Ben come down when he did? How did he know something was going on?"

"Because of the noise. Things falling over and such."

"So you two were stumbling around in the dark, robbing me blind." Amy paced some more, face reddened with anger, eyes red and strained from lack of sufficient sleep. "Well, thank God there was no money in that lockbox. Papers, some letters that were important to me, a couple of pieces of cheap jewelry that I'll never see again, but that's all."

Nanny imagined Cat, finding that his long-desired theft of Amy Hanover's lockbox had brought him so little gain. It might have been funny at some other time, but now it was frightening. What if Cat got angry, came looking for her to expend the anger at her expense? She had only realized this evening what a fearsome man she'd been dealing with.

"Nanny, why have you been doing what you have with this man? Don't you know it's wrong? What would have happened if you should have gotten with child? Did you expect me to say nothing to you about it? Did you just presume I'd gladly take on the expense of a bastard child in this household?" Amy in fact would have taken in the child; an illegitimate black baby, offspring of an escaped slave, would have been just the kind of person to most deeply appeal to her progressivist sympathies. But just now it wasn't the progressivist incarnation of Amy Deacon Hanover doing the talking.

Nanny felt again a strong urge to lie, because Amy had reached an area in her life that held her most hurtful secret and touched her deepest personal wishes. But the image of Cat, furious and dangerous, was strong in her mind, and she sensed that her best hope lay in the unfamiliar world of honest truth.

"I just wanted to have me a baby, Miss Amy. I never thought much about what would happen after it come . . . I just wanted it so bad!" Nanny began to cry.

"Why would you want a baby? You have no husband, no good means to support a child on your own."

"I had a baby once before, ma'am. Back in Carolina. I was married, you see, married to a white man, and—"

"You were married? To a *white* man?"

"Yes, ma'am. He and me, we was married, not in no white folks' kind of marriage, but we had stood up before a preacher, a nigra preacher, and said our vowels."

"Your vows, Nanny. Vows. Well, where is this husband of yours now? And the baby?"

"My husband, he got killed. He was stampeding north, and got killed running from the rebels. And my baby, I had to leave him behind when I run for freedom."

This news struck Amy into a couple of moments of silence. "What do you mean, leave him behind? Where?"

"With the other slaves, Miss Amy. They was taking good care of him, and I never was much good at mothering, so I left him. I wanted to be free so bad."

Amy stared at her. Her voice became very quiet, yet in its quietness, as condemning as the voice of God Himself, standing in judgment. "You abandoned your own child? Left him in slavery—so you could be free?"

"Yes, ma'am. I thought it wouldn't be bad to do it, thought I could bear up . . . but I miss him so! I'll never have him back, I know, but I thought if there was another baby . . ."

Amy could scarcely believe it. In earlier days, before she had a child of her own developing within her, when virtually the sole afflatus of her spirit was her driving hatred of slavery, she might have viewed Nanny's case with some empathy, even held it up publicly in her writings as a tragic example of the evil upon evil that slavery fostered. But she was a mother now, already feeling a strong bond between herself and the life within her, and the thought of abandoning a child in the midst of such a tragic state as enslavement strained her substantial ability to understand and accept. It galled her beyond words.

Amy sputtered, exclaimed, but could find nothing to say. Her heart hammered in her chest, her face reddened further, and anger overwhelmed her. The progressivist, abolitionist, liberal Amy Deacon Hanover vanished, and the Amy Deacon Hanover who emerged in her place was a stranger not only to Nanny, who witnessed the transformation through widening eyes, but to Amy herself. Had she been able to step back from herself and witness her actions as if performed by another, she would have been appalled at what she saw, for what she saw would have been a feminine version of her own late, bigoted, hate-driven father.

She leaned toward Nanny and fired her words point-blank. "You are a wicked woman, Nanny. A selfish, wicked, dishonest, worthless woman, and I despise you."

Nanny put her hands over her face and cried into them, her shoulders heaving. Amy jerked the hands away. "You look at me, Nanny! Don't you try to hide your face! Show some backbone, girl!"

Amy went to a shelf and picked up a bottle she had placed there earlier. Bringing it to Nanny, she grabbed the crying woman by the hair and held her head upright, not at all gently. Nanny gasped in pain and bit her lip.

Amy shook the bottle in her face. "Tell me what this is, Nanny."

Nanny's eyes grew large as she recognized the bottle of "French pills" that Cat had given her.

"That's just . . . how did you get that bottle? That's mine!"

"That's right, Nanny. It is yours. The policeman found it hidden under your bed. And you know exactly what it is, what it does, don't you! Here . . . let me read some of what this label says to you. 'Dr. Montgomery's French Periodical Pills—warranted to have the *desired effect* in all circumstances . . . These pills regulate the system and produce the monthly feminine turn . . . they restore debilitated constitutions to their proper energy and healthfulness by removing from the system every *impurity* . . . the only precaution necessary is that married ladies should not take them if they have reason to believe they are enceinte, as they are *sure to produce a miscarriage . . .*' " Amy jerked Nanny's hair again. "These pills are designed to end a pregnancy, Nanny. An odd item for someone to possess if that someone is wanting to have a baby, don't you think?"

"They ain't mine, Miss Amy! They was given to me by—"

"Not yours? You already said they were yours! They were under your cot, Nanny, hidden!" Amy jerked Nanny's hair yet again, hard, then let go and turned away like something disgusting had just been presented to her. She threw the bottle of pills across the room. Nanny jerked and made a small yelp as it crashed loudly against the wall. "You never wanted a baby, Nanny! All you wanted was your own carnal fun . . . or maybe he was paying you for your service! Was that it? You were his Cyprian? Yes, that is it, isn't it! Those pills, those are the kind of pills you'd find in any whore's crib."

Nanny yielded. She would give no further defense. Clearly there would be no point. She rubbed the place where Amy had pulled her hair and cried louder.

Amy had to wait a few moments before her voice was steady enough to speak again. Fury that boiled out of her now was generated by more than Nanny's betrayal and Ben's shooting. This was the fury of a widow still in grief, a woman living in a hundred different tensions all at the same time. "Nanny, I no longer trust you. I think you are a liar, a thief, a *prostitute*! I've given you home, wages, an opportunity, and you've done nothing but abuse it. Because of you a good man has been hurt, maybe mortally. Because of you my place of business has been invaded and robbed—and even now you lie to me, trying to get my sympathy with talk of wanting a baby, when all the while you have pills on hand designed to kill any baby that might be conceived." Amy laid her hand on her bulging belly. Her voice became quieter, though her fury was not at all lessened. "You know who my father was, Nanny? He was Dr. George Deacon, one of the most ardent Secessionists this city ever knew. He viewed your race as little more than animals, useful only for what labor they could give. I despised his view, but you've done something no one has ever been able to do before: You've made me wonder if maybe I've been wrong, and he was at least a little right. You know what you are, Nanny? You're no more than a foul, miserable *nigger*!" That word had never before escaped Amy's lips, but now it burst out, propelled by the force of every previously unvented tension inside her. "You're a nigger, Nanny, not worthy of the refuge I've given you! You're a disgrace to your race, and I hate you! I *hate* you!"

Something changed inside Nanny. She was full of fright, but now anger came along with it. She stood, pointing at her abuser. "I hate *you*, Miss Amy! Because I been telling you the truth, and you won't believe me! I *did* want a baby! I wouldn't have took them pills! I wouldn't have killed no child inside me, and all the things you been saying, they ain't true!" She lunged forward, shoving Amy to the floor. Amy looked up in terror. "I curse you, Miss Amy! I curse you and the baby inside you! I curse it to die! Then you'll know what it feels like to have a child and then not have it no more! Then you'll know why I wanted so bad to have a new baby in place of my poor little lost Joel! I'll laugh the day your baby dies, Miss Amy! I'll *laugh*, and I'll thank God above that it's dead! And I hope you suffer worse than I ever have, if there is such a suffering as that!"

Nanny burst into sobs again, and fell to her knees.

Amy, terrified, crabbed back from her and stood, shaking. "Get out," she whispered. Then it became a shout. "Get out! Go away from here and never let me see you again! Go off to the contraband camp . . . go off to hell! You have no place here anymore."

Nanny stood and staggered to the office door. She ran sobbing through the building and out the front, coatless, leaving the door open behind her. A cold wind sailed through the building, blowing papers from tables and shelves.

Amy went to her desk and slumped into the chair. Sitting heavily, she stared blankly at the open office door, mouth open, tears streaming down. She laid her head over on the desk, resting it on her arms, and thought that she had never felt so sick and exhausted. In three minutes her eyes were closed and she was breathing with irregular heaves, her body tense despite the fact she was asleep.

Ben Scarlett lay pallid and still in a long, corridorlike hospital room, his chest moving slowly up and down but his eyes still tightly shut, not having opened since the bullet pierced him, and his head, now bandaged, had smacked against the hard side of the wooden press crate. Amy sat in a chair at the bedside, gazing at the opposite wall, listening to the combination of moans, snores, and low conversation common to hospitals. The prior year she had grown quite used to such facilities, working as a volunteer nurse in Federal army hospitals in Nashville. During that time she had become inured to the worst horrors a medical facility could present. She had carted off amputated limbs, taken splatters of blood across her clothing, even her face, without a flinch, listened to men scream hopelessly for relief, heard their voices fade slowly until death came. She had been able to endure it all, but today, despite the relative peace and lack of intense suffering in this particular ward, she was numb with horror and almost sickened by the smells that hung in the foul air.

She told herself that her pregnancy accounted for this in large part, but knew there was more to it. This hospital sickened her because of who lay in the bed beside her. Dear old Ben, a man who had stumbled into her life while still a drunk on the streets, who had chanced his way to her again during her brief and ill-fated career as a counterfeit currency smuggling agent for the Federal government, then found her yet again in her Nashville days, when he came to that city on a doomed quest to regain a woman named Angel Beamish, whom he had once planned to marry. Ben hadn't been away from Amy since, and their bond was all the stronger since her husband was killed.

Not that Ben Scarlett could ever be a man she would consider marrying. She knew he loved her deeply, and she loved him as well, but their love was not of the romantic variety. Once or twice during the time Ben had helped her with her currency smuggling, she suspected that he might have seen her in a romantic light, but time and experience had changed that. She and Ben knew where they stood with one another. Their relationship was close, but not one of those varieties for which a single handy tag had been created by whoever it was who built languages. Ben was to Amy just . . . Ben. There would never be another, no one who would ever play the exact role that he played in her life, and the idea that she might lose him was intolerable. This time it was no stranger occupying the hospital bed beside her, someone to receive a generalized kind of sympathy and care, like those poor soldiers hospitalized in Nashville. This man was part of her. This was *Ben.*

Amy tried to concentrate on praying for Ben, but her mind would not remain still enough for that. She thought of their past times together, of her life when she first met him and her oppressive father was still living, of the companionship they shared on so many occasions, of the way Ben had listened and responded to her in ways no one else could. To lose him would be almost as difficult as it had been to lose her husband . . . dared she to think it, she might have said it would in some ways even be worse.

Her mind ultimately drifted to Nanny and the terrible encounter they'd had. Amy was repelled at the awful thing that Nanny had said to her, the cursing to death of her own baby . . . and though Amy was far from superstitious and did not believe curses held any power, it was appalling to know that another human being could actually hold such a hatred toward her that such a vile thing could have been said. *I'll laugh the day your baby dies, Miss Amy! I'll laugh, and I'll thank God above that it's dead!* Amy would never be able to forget what it was like to hear those words. Awful words, dreadful words. Could Nanny have possibly meant them?

She had to ask the same question about the almost equally horrific things she had said to Nanny. Amy was mortified to realize she had insulted Nanny on a racial basis. Amy Deacon Hanover: abolitionist, progressive, social free-thinker—and that very Amy Deacon Hanover had insulted Nanny on the basis of the color of her skin. She deeply wished now that she hadn't. Nanny had deserved much of what she'd said . . . but not the racial slur. It distressed Amy to realize that, despite all her idealism, she might have more of her racist father buried inside her than she had realized.

But her anger at Nanny was still far stronger than any regrets. Nanny had pushed her down! Pushed her, and her being pregnant, and at the same time invoking a death curse on the unborn child! Amy could conceive of nothing more spitefully wicked. Though she disbelieved in curses, it made tears rise each time she thought of it. Nanny's actions and words would be hard to forgive.

Amy closed her eyes. This was no time to be worrying about Nanny. Nanny was gone, Lord only knew where, and maybe that was best. Let her go, and be forgotten. What mattered now was Ben Scarlett.

She looked at him, his face gray and pale, his breathing slow and seemingly painful. His eyes were still tightly shut, and he seemed more sick and weak than the injuries he had suffered justified. What if he was more deeply hurt than even the doctors knew? *Please, Lord, please.*

She laid her hand over and touched Ben's arm beneath the sheet, realizing only then he was still wearing his hook. That wouldn't do. When he came around again, he might injure himself with the hook. She pulled the sheet down, loosened the leather ties that held the hook in place on his stump. She lifted it off and laid it in her lap. Looking down at it, her chin trembled and she began to cry, clutching it close and praying very hard for Ben Scarlett to open his eyes.

Part IV

THE CONTRABANDS

Chapter 19

Try as he would, it was hard for the thin man in the ragged civilian clothing to keep from smiling.

He had very little to smile about, really, but for a man accustomed to the conditions under which he had been living for the last several months, very little was enough. What had him prone to grin was the sheer simple pleasure of actually traveling, going *somewhere* after months of being unable to go anywhere at all. He settled his slender frame back against the seat and enjoyed the rocking of the railroad car, stifling his grin because he knew it would look ludicrous. But when he glanced at the man beside him, who wasn't nearly as thin as he but certainly was not the corpulent fellow he had been in their days of freedom, the smile came bursting out, and the other man smiled, too. Moments later they were both chuckling.

Two bored-looking, gray-clad guards sat across from them in the compartment. One, who had been seated with head back and eyes shut, almost sleeping, opened his eyes at the sound of their chuckling and peered oddly at them. He elbowed the more alert guard beside him.

"Take a look at that, wouldja? Setting there giggling like girls, and them in the fix they is."

The other guard replied, "They won't be giggling once they hit Salisbury. No sir. They know how to keep 'em in line at Salisbury."

The thinner man scratched at his beard and eyed the guards with poorly disguised contempt. "So you believe we'll have it worse there, do you?"

"Did you hear somebody say something, Henry?" the second guard asked, staring straight into the thin man's face.

"I believe I did, but I don't know how they was invited to speak," the first guard replied.

"Sounded like Yankee talk," the first one said. "Ain't no sound uglier than Yankee talk."

The thin man who was the butt of this hostility smiled anew and resettled himself. "Rockwell, did you hear somebody say something?" he asked the man at his side, imitating the guard's South Carolinian drawl. "I swear I did, and it sounded like reb talk."

"Why, that was reb talk? I thought it was just somebody passing bad wind."

"You two shut up, damn you," the first guard said. "You'd best quit your blab and enjoy the ride, for you'll have little enough to enjoy once it's over."

"Why, who can say?" replied the thin man. "We might just escape between here and there."

"Yeah? Then what? You'd run into the mountains for the Union lines? There's plenty who tries that, few who makes it. You put you Yankees out in the mountains and you'uns is fish out of water."

"I'll have you know I was born in the mountains, my good man," the thin civilian replied.

"Northern mountains is dunghills compared to ours down here." The guards laughed.

"Odd to hear somebody from flat old South Carolina talking that way, when there's big mountains aplenty in the North," the civilian replied. "And I'll have you know that I wasn't born in the North anyway, you goober-chewing rebel. I come from the mountains of this very state of North Carolina."

"Is that right? Well, you should have stayed. Should have been a good Confederate and not gone Yankee on us. That way you wouldn't be in this mess."

"I've been in worse."

"Huh! You been in Libby Prison, Yank. It don't get worse than that."

"Except at Salisbury," the other guard threw in.

"Yeah, except at Salisbury."

"Really? As I hear it, Salisbury is something of an improvement. At least there's a yard to walk in."

"You'll know soon enough. What's your name, Yank?"

The thin man smiled and dipped his head slightly, and for a moment seemed almost elegant despite his rags and emaciated, unshaven condition. "My name is Brown, sir, Thatcher Brown. Civilian correspondent for the *New York Weekly Alliance*."

"The hell! That Lincolnite rag? No wonder they locked you up! What were you doing roaming around in the Confederacy?"

"My job, sir, that's all. Corresponding on the progress of this great Secession cause of yours for my newspaper. But my friend and I managed to get ourselves caught trying to float past the Vicksburg batteries on some cotton barges, and since then the wise Confederate government has decided that we should be held as prisoners of war."

"Spies, that's what you'uns are."

"Correspondents, sir. We do not work for the United States government."

The second guard waved a smelly cigar stub at the other man. "So you're a scribbler, too?"

"Yes indeed. My name's Rockwell Griffin, traveling correspondent from the Boston *Union Argosy*. My friends, like Thatcher here, call me Rockwell, or sometime R.W. You two, however, can just call me 'sir.' "

"Huh! Call you turd, that's what I call you! So you'uns figured you could get past Vicksburg, did you? Reckon you larnt different."

"Reckon we did," Thatcher said, again imitating the drawl, to his companion's amusement. "But think of all the hospitality we'd have missed in Libby Prison if we had made it through! We've 'larnt' quite a lot about your famous southern hospitality, living in that swine sty."

"Better'n you deserve. Why they moving you to Salisbury, Yanks?"

"Ask the Confederacy's grand and wise old Secretary of

War. It's his decision, as illegal and unsensible as any other the Confederacy has made in regard to Rockwell and me."

Rockwell contributed, "By all rights, we were supposed to be paroled by now. There were several journalists captured together with us, and all of us were given paroles to return home. The others have all done just that. The paroles for Thatcher and me have been ignored."

"Ignored, and now officially revoked by Secretary Seddon after we petitioned him for a review of our situation," Thatcher said. "We're being held as hostages until the end of the war, held with reference to southerners jailed in the North."

"Tit for tat, lean for fat," one of the guards said, and the other laughed as if that cliché was a new one on him.

Rockwell Griffin continued, "Why we've been transferred to Salisbury, we couldn't tell you. Just more of Secretary Seddon's all-wise plan, God bless him."

The second guard said to Thatcher, "Hey, if you was born in Carolina, why'd you leave?"

Thatcher's lip curled, not quite a smile. "Family reasons," he said.

"Well, if you'd stayed you'd be better off. You'd be a rebel."

"Don't know about that. The area I come from, most people are Union. I have a brother there who's as Union as any man can be, and in fact has made something of a name for himself by guiding Unionists north to join the Federal army."

"What's your brother's name?"

"Greeley Brown. Last I've heard of him, he's living in the mountains of Carter County, in Tennessee, and guiding hundreds of men off to become soldiers and shoot at you gray boys."

"I ain't never heard of no Greeley Brown."

"You go a few miles west of here, into the mountains, and say his name a few times. You'd find folks there know who he is quite well."

"Well, maybe he'll traipse over to Salisbury and march you out of that prison, if he's so wondrous."

"Maybe we'll just march out and go meet him on our own," Thatcher replied.

"You'll not get out. Nobody does."

"Some do."

"They're caught and brought back."

"When I get out, I won't come back," Thatcher said.

The first guard laughed. "Yeah, you won't, because the odds are that when you get out, you'll do it in a wood box."

The conversation waned. The train chugged on through the night, heading for Raleigh, where the prisoners would be placed in a boxcar and taken, still under guard, to the grim place that was to be their home until it all was over, whatever and whenever "over" would be.

Knoxville, the next evening

Ben Scarlett opened his eyes at dusk and peered around, blinking, wondering why the ceiling of his room had suddenly vaulted up by ten feet or so and changed color. He felt something tickle his cheek, and turned his head slightly to see the top of a woman's head lying over on his mattress, just above his shoulder. Her hair against his face accounted for the tickling.

"Pardon me, ma'am," he said in a voice dry and scratchy. "But if you'd tell me what in the devil is going on here, I'd appreciate it. And can you scoot your head some so I don't get such a tickle on my face?" He lifted his left arm to scratch his face, then remembered that he didn't have a hand on that arm, and noticed that somebody had removed his hook, too.

The feminine head beside him lifted slowly, and a familiar, sleepy, pretty face, momentarily branded with the wrinkle lines of the sheet against which it had been lying, looked rather stupidly at him. Then Amy Hanover's eyes widened and a smile broke across her splotched face.

"Ben! Oh, thank God! Ben, you're awake!"

"Howdy, Miss Amy. Lordy! Listen at my voice, scratching like claws on slate! Is there some water around here . . . wherever here might be?"

"Yes, there is . . . I'll get you some. . . ."

She was up in a moment, running to a nearby table upon

which sat a pitcher of water and several glasses. She poured a glass full and all but ran back to the bed with it. Kneeling, she cradled Ben's head gently, lifting it just enough to let him drink.

When he was done, he lay back, licking moist lips. "That's better, yes sirree. Where am I, Miss Amy?"

"You're in the hospital, Ben."

"Hospital? How'd I get here from there?"

"From the office, you mean?"

"No, from *there*! That place. That place I've been."

"You've been right here, Ben, ever since it happened."

"Since what happened?"

"Since you was shot."

"Shot?" He laughed, but pain hit and he quit. "I ain't shot, Miss Amy. I never seen a single gun nor nothing at that place. Nothing but . . . light, and people, and things that I can't hardly say what they were . . . good things, though. It was a good place. Finest I've ever been."

"Ben, I think you're addled. You did strike your head when you fell. If you reach up you'll find it's bandaged—but don't reach up, because it will probably be sore. I'll get the doctor."

"I ain't addled. I remember it well. A dark kind of tunnel, light at the end of it, me looking at it and thinking, 'That there's a mighty pretty light,' and heading for it up that tunnel. Then I come out at that place, and there was folks and things, and it was all real fine. I stayed a good while, and then I hear somebody saying, 'Time to get back, Ben!' and now here I am!" He sounded remarkably cheerful, not at all like a man who had been lying wounded with his medical fate uncertain.

"Ben, wherever your mind has been, your body has been here the entire time. You were shot by a thief at the *Sage* office, and brought here straight from there. You haven't been any-where else, Ben, and you've been unconscious."

"Well, if I was unconscious, conk me in the head again and send me back. I liked that place. And you know, I been there once before, though I didn't remember that I'd been there until I got there this time. But it was all familiar. I seen it when I was just a boy and had me a bad fever for a week. They told me when I got well that I had liked to have died, but I didn't believe them, 'cause I'd just been having a fine time scampering about in that same pretty place. And before that, I'd been floating around the room, looking down on myself, watching myself lying in the bed. I floated out and looked around in the yard and such, and even seen my pap out in the field, working. He was digging a finger in his nose up to the first knuckle, not knowing nobody was there to see, I guess. I remember laughing at him, and when I come back into myself and got well again, I said to him, 'Pap, did you ever get that booger picked out when you was there in the field?' and he looked as surprised as get-out, I'll tell you! It all got forgot, though, like I said, until this time." He frowned suddenly. "Shot? You said I was shot?"

"Yes. It was Nanny's fault, in a way. She had let a thief named Cat Kingsley into the office through a window—"

Ben jerked and groaned. His face went gray and his body collapsed back heavily, as memory crashed in all at once and something fundamental in his look and demeanor changed. His eyes had been bright and clear, but suddenly they clouded with pain and he seemed to decline a little even as she watched him. "Now I remember," he said, his voice lower and more strained. "It was Cat Kingsley. Nanny'd been sporting with him in the Baumgardner shed, and I'd made her quit it, but she'd let him in through a window, and I heard the sounds of things getting knocked about. I remember it now . . . running down from my room, going in the front way, and then there was Cat, and . . . oh, I do remember. I remember how it hurt, and burned. And my head, my head . . ."

"You're alive, Ben. You're back with us, and you'll be better now."

"My shoulder hurts, my chest, my head . . ."

"I'll get the doctor." She touched herself just under the right shoulder. "That's where the bullet struck you, Ben. It didn't injure any vital organs, but the doctors said the shock of it was dangerous to you, and the blow to your head might have killed you."

"Might have killed me . . ."

"But it didn't. That's what matters." She bent over and kissed him lightly on the forehead, making him grin for a moment. Pain took away the smile almost at once, however. "I'll go fetch a doctor to look you over now that you're awake.

Close your eyes, Ben. Rest. Maybe you can go back to that place you had dreamed about."

"Place? What place do you mean?"

"What you were just talking to me about . . . the dream place, the one with the light and the tunnel and the people. . . ."

"I don't think I remember . . . I don't. I don't remember it now."

She was not surprised. In her work in the Nashville military hospitals, Amy had encountered more than one person who had come near death and returned talking about a tunnel and light. A vivid dream, she supposed. A trick of the mind to make dying easier to endure, and generally forgotten fairly quickly once consciousness returned. But some she had known did remember, and seemed awed and changed by that memory. But it was a trick of the mind. Amy was sure of it—even though she couldn't quite account for the phenomenon of a disembodied Ben Scarlett as a boy watching his father from above in a field.

She patted Ben gently, and headed into the depths of the hospital in search of his physician.

Her little son Joel was in her arms again, and Nanny was at peace. She felt his warmth against her, looked into the eyes that bore the imprint of his father's before him, a father she hadn't loved but who seemed dear now because it was he who had given her Joel. Touching his hair, she caressed him gently, then bent to kiss his coffee-colored face.

A loudly shouted curse jolted her awake, and she sat up quickly, the dream image of her abandoned son vanishing like a bursting bubble of soap. More cursing assaulted her ears—two men spoiling for a fight in one of the muddy rows of dirty snow between the lines of tents and hovels that made up this refugee city. The contraband camp, polite people called this place. Less polite ones referred to it as the nigger camp. As far as Nanny was concerned, it might as well be dubbed "Hell," except that it was far too cold for the name to really fit. Nanny, having left her coat at Miss Amy's, was having to make do for a wrap by bundling herself in an old blanket she had found when she entered this tent, and it wasn't doing much of a job keeping her warm.

She had hidden in this tent since she came to the camp. She did not know if she had permission to be here. All she knew was that its only other occupant was a very old, very sick black woman, seemingly with no family, and she had been in no position to protest Nanny's intrusion. Nanny was not even certain the old woman knew she was here. A time or two the woman had turned yellowing eyes in her direction, but whether those eyes could see was an open question.

Nanny hoped they could not see her. She wished no eyes could see her, that she could move invisibly through the world, heralded by no one, touched by no one, bothered by no one. She had spent most of her lifetime longing for freedom from slavery. She had that now, but now she ached as deeply for freedom from humanity itself. A world of her own, where no one would curse and fight, no one would insult and degrade her and call her "nigger," no one would accuse and condemn her like Amy Hanover had. A world that contained her alone . . . and Joel. Joel would be there, of course. And he would love her, and not care at all that she had abandoned him to find her freedom. She looked around the filthy tent. To find *this*.

Nanny's stomach grumbled, and she added a new ingredient to the private mental paradise she was conjuring: food. Lots of food, abundant and easy to find, and delicious. At the moment even bland food would be welcome. She had enjoyed plenty to eat at Miss Amy's, but here at the contraband camp she didn't expect to fare so well. The food here came from emergency rations issued by the army, from relief societies, from charitable citizens. There was little of it. Nanny closed her eyes and imagined that long table in the office of the *Sage*, and the smell of the food she had cooked herself. How had things fallen apart so quickly and utterly? She cursed herself, wondering why she had been so blind to the good situation she had at Miss Amy's. She should have never done anything to threaten it.

It was Cat's fault, really. If he hadn't been such a scoundrel, Ben Scarlett wouldn't have been shot and she wouldn't be in his piteous condition. She pictured Cat's face, and mentally cast upon him the same curse of death she had called down upon Miss Amy's unborn baby.

Nanny opened her eyes. She felt badly about having cursed that baby. What if the curse worked and the child really did die? Well, if that happened, at least she wouldn't be around to know about it. And if the baby died, who could say it was her curse that caused it? Probably there was nothing to curses, anyway. But just to be safe, she closed her eyes again, pictured Miss Amy's pregnant, bulging belly, and consciously withdrew the curse she had uttered. There. That should take care of it and if it didn't . . . well, let Miss Amy know what it was to feel the emptiness of arms and heart that a missing child created.

A general stirring outside the tent made Nanny crawl to the door and look out. She saw a wagon rolling to a stop, refugees crowding around. A fat white man and a couple of white women in black dresses like uniforms climbed onto the wagon bed and began handing out loaves of bread. Hands groped up for the prizes like the heads of hungry young birds in a nest. Nanny slipped out of the tent and joined the race toward the wagon. People were crowding, shoving, the man on the wagon calling for "you darkies to get yourselves into some kind of line," and no one was heeding.

Nanny found herself squeezed out, away from the wagon. Her stomach rumbled again. Someone bumped her; she bumped back, and got a curse from a fat woman who had only one good eye and a patch over the other one. The fat woman waded in against the crowd at the wagon, shoving people aside like a locomotive pushing through a snowbank. Her thick arms seemed extraordinarily long, and soon her hands were extending over the edge of the wagon itself, her deep voice bellowing for food.

Nanny was right behind her, having trailed in through the gap she made. The fat woman got her hands onto a loaf and yanked it from the donor's fingers. Then another loaf came within reach and she grabbed for it as well.

She got it, but in the meantime had lost her first one, because it had been snatched it from her hand. Turning, Nanny plunged back through the crowd, running over one frail old man who mischanced to be behind her. The big woman cursed at her and thrashed about in the crowd, trying to break out and pursue, but Nanny was small and fleet and soon lost herself amid the tents and shelters. It took a few moments for her to regain her bearings about where she was in the refugee camp, and she feared suddenly that she might not be able to relocate her tent, and that big locomotive of a woman would find her out in the open and thrash her to death. But Nanny spotted the tent a moment later and went into it.

The old woman was lying on her back, wheezing, her eyes staring up at the underside of the roof peak. Nanny studied her a few moments while she chewed on the loaf.

"Old woman," she said when the loaf was almost gone. "Old woman, you want some bread?"

The old woman groaned, maybe an answer, maybe just a groan. Nanny took one more bite, sighed, and went to the old woman's side with the remainder of the loaf.

"You got you any teeth? Can you chew?"

The old woman, eyes still staring straight up and more yellowed than ever, made a noise in her throat. Nanny tilted up her head and offered her a fragment of the bread. The old jaws chewed weakly, and after three efforts she managed to swallow the bite. Nanny gave her another, then another. The next bite, however, simply lay in her mouth; she was too weak to chew. Nanny laid the woman down again and rolled her onto her side. "That way you won't choke on it. Just let it sit in your mouth, and you can swallow it when you want to."

The old woman's wheezing was less now that she was on her side. She remained in that position the rest of the day. Nanny rolled her onto her opposite side when darkness came, and discovered the woman had soiled herself. She wrinkled her nose. "Well, I reckon you can't help it."

She cleaned the old woman as best she could, and disposed of the ruined garments. The woman was virtually unclothed now, so Nanny covered her with one of the three ragged blankets in the tent. She slept that night with only one blanket herself, wrapping up in it like a cocoon. A time or two she thought about moving close to the old woman for the sake of sharing heat, but the idea of doing that repelled worse than the cold stung. She stayed where she was, tossing and turning and cursing the season of winter.

Just before dawn, chilled to the pit of her being, she decided maybe it wouldn't be so intolerable to move a little closer to the old woman after all. She scooted herself over without ever leaving her blanket, and rolled up close, her back against the old woman. Closing her eyes, she tried to go back to sleep again, then opened her eyes again suddenly, realizing that she felt no movement against her back and heard no breathing but her own. She came out of her blanket quickly and rolled the old woman onto her back.

She was dead, all right. Nanny could tell it by feeling her face, and after she did that she wiped her hand hard on her blanket, trying to brush the death-touch off it. Nanny grabbed her wrap, and one of the old woman's, and went back to where she'd been before. She sat there, blanket over her shoulders, staring at the corpse, which was visible only as a dim outline inside the dark tent. Nanny wished heartily for day, but it was as if the bitter cold had frozen even time itself. Almost an hour dragged by before she decided she could not endure the company of the dead any longer. She crawled over to the old woman, took the third blanket off her, grabbed her ankles and pulled her from the tent. Dragging the body through the sleeping camp, she left it near the place where the bread wagon had sat earlier, and headed back to the tent to wait for daybreak.

Chapter 20

She was at his side as long as he was confined to the hospital ward, and when he was sent home, she took him to her own house and had his bed moved into a corner of the lone spare room, which was filled with a remarkable amount of clutter for someone who had lived in the place for such a brief time. Ben spent the first days staring at heaps of books and paper, mounds of old newspapers and out-of-season clothing. He wondered why Amy had never had Nanny come down here and clean all this up. She had been a paid servant, after all. But Amy had confined Nanny's duties almost strictly to the *Sage* office. Ben figured it was because she had hired Nanny more out of sympathy and her ideological desire to help out black people in desperate situations than out of any real desire for a servant. Maybe the notion of having a black woman cleaning up her dwelling would have smacked too much of slavery for Amy's abolitionist tastes.

Ben was glad Nanny was gone. It was easier than ever to despise her. He talked about it with Amy one evening. "Miss Amy, I know where you stand on darkies and slavery and all, but I got to confess to you: I never did like Nanny. I tried to think of her like you said I should, but I couldn't. She's always seemed spiteful, and I don't believe she ever appreciated what you done for her."

Amy replied, "Ben, I'll make a confession of my own. I've felt the same way. For a long time. I tried to pretend I didn't, tried to convince even myself that I could overlook Nanny's ungratefulness and attitude. But I couldn't. I always resented her in secret. And Ben . . . when I spoke to her last—really, it was more shouting than speaking—I uttered words I never thought I'd hear myself say. I told her she was a shame to her race, and I called her a . . . nigger. And I wasn't just mispronouncing the word, like some do. I was using it like a knife. I meant it to wound her. Can you believe that I, of all people, would do a thing like that? I'm ashamed of myself."

"Well, Nanny had done a mighty bad thing. She knew she wasn't supposed to let nobody in the building."

"Yes, but what did her race have to do with that?"

"Well, nothing, I suppose."

"That's right. So why did I call her 'nigger'? I'll tell you why: It's because no matter how much I claim to have freed myself of all the wrong racial attitudes of our little world here, I haven't. Not fully. There's some of my father hidden inside me."

"Don't say that," Ben said. "Your father and you, there was no two people in this world more different."

Amy was ready for a new conversation. "Do you think they'll ever catch Cat Kingsley?"

"Who can say? He's probably hiding somewhere. A man like Cat knows all kinds of places to hide. He's always been slick on the getaway, always one to land on his feet. That's why they call him Cat. What I wonder about is Nanny. I wonder where she is?"

"Maybe she's with Cat. She had claimed he hit her, even had a bruise on her face, but I don't know whether to believe that or not. I have no trust for Nanny anymore. I'm wondering if maybe she's in the contraband camp. I'd thought about going to look later on."

"No, don't you do that. You stay away from that camp. Nanny'd probably figure you'd come to do something bad to her. That's the way she thinks. She might try to hurt you."

Amy gnawed her lip, trying to decide whether she should

tell Ben more of what had transpired between Nanny and herself. She hesitated, then spoke. "She might hurt me at that. She tried once already, right there in my office, while we were arguing."

"What?"

"She pushed me down. And said something terrible to me. She said she hoped my baby would die. She put a curse or something on me. Just nonsense, of course. But it was awful to hear it."

Ben bolted up to a seated position as fast as a wounded man could do it. "She *hexed* you?"

"It was just words spoken into the air, Ben. There's no such thing as hexes."

"I don't know about that. I've heard tales about darky hexes. There's odd things that happen sometimes. I know a man who was hexed by a darky witch who didn't like the way he flapped his jaws bad about her all the time, and he cut his leg on a saw and ended up dying with the lockjaw."

"Ben, don't talk that way! It's nonsense and superstition . . . and it makes me nervous. You think I want to spend my time worrying that my baby might die because of something some ignorant servant girl said? Rationally, I know it's rubbish, but if you start planting notions in my head . . ."

"I'm sorry. Your baby will be fine, sure it will. It's like you say—rubbish." But Ben had taken on a somber manner that he couldn't quite fully hide. Amy wanted to roll her eyes. It was just like Ben to believe in hexes and so on. And just like him to be able to make her halfway believe in them herself. Ben had always possessed more influence over her than she could account for.

She rose. "Are you hungry, Ben?"

"Some, yeah."

"I'm going down to the office and fix us something." There were no cooking facilities in Amy's little house; all her meals were prepared and taken down at the *Sage* building. Nanny had handled most of the cooking before, but now, of course, it all fell to Amy.

"Don't go to no trouble. Just something easy. Bread and bacon would do just fine."

"I believe that's your favorite dish, Ben Scarlett. You eat any more bacon and you'll grow a snout. Need anything before I leave?"

"Just hand me that book there and I'll be fine."

She left him reading, and headed down the street toward what she and Ben still thought of as the newspaper office, though it seemed very doubtful now that any newspaper would ever actually be published in it.

Just before dusk in the Knoxville camp for contrabands

Nanny had found that the only reasonably effective escape from hunger was sleep. There was food at the contraband camp, but never quite enough, and little more than an hour or two a day passed during which her stomach felt adequately full. So she slept a lot, escaping the worst of the hunger, and also the isolation. The people around her were not companions, but living camouflage. Miss Amy had said no one was after her, no one would hurt her or lock her up—but Nanny knew that was before she'd gotten angry and pushed her down. Before she had cursed Miss Amy's unborn child to die. Hiding away here, Nanny found nothing unreasonable or even unlikely in picturing the entire Federal army and Knoxville police force scouring the country for her.

She huddled beneath her blankets, her back toward the flap of the tent. She always lay angled that way during daylight hours, never knowing when the flap might be pulled back and some uniformed white man might peer inside, recognize her, and lead her off to whatever fate the world of white law had in mind for her.

She was lost in the mental shadowland between thought and dreams when the light inside the tent changed subtly and she knew she was no longer alone. Opening her eyes suddenly and widely, she stared for a moment at the back of the tent, then sat up and turned simultaneously, and saw not the anticipated authoritarian white intruders, but the grinning visage of Cat Kingsley.

She leaped up to a squat and scuttered back to the rear of the tent. "Cat, you get away from me! Get away!"

He came the rest of the way into the tent. "Well, well, look here what old Cat's found! If it ain't Nanny herself, hid out amongst the contrabands!" Still grinning, he crept closer. "I figured you above all this kind of thing, woman. Hiding out amongst the hungry refugees, 'stead of working for the whites and living in a good warm room, lots of food . . . what happened, Nanny? Did dear Miss Amy toss you out?"

"Yes, and it was because of you, Cat! You *shot* him!"

"Is he dead?"

"I don't know. He wasn't when I left."

"I wish he would die, in a way. I never did like Ben Scarlett. But it's better if he lives. That way they won't call me no murderer."

"I don't want you in here, Cat. This is my tent."

"Your tent? How'd you get it?"

"I just . . . came in. There was an old woman, but she died."

"Well, I'm just coming in, too. It's our tent now, Nanny. Me and you."

"The law'll be looking for you, Cat. You'd best run."

"I will, I will. In good time. But I got business to do before I go, and in the meantime, they ain't going to find me here. Too many folks here. I'm just one more dark face among hunnerts. Like you."

"What business you still got here? Why don't you just leave and let me be?"

"My business is money that's owed me, that's what. A good bit of money, and I'll not leave until I get it."

"You got Miss Amy's lockbox. I heard her say there was jewelry in there. Take that and go. I scared of you, Cat. And if they catch me with you, they'll blame me right along with you for all you done. I don't want to be around you no more."

"Always thinking of yourself, ain't you, Nanny? Let's get this straight in line right now: I'm here, I ain't leaving, and when I do leave, you coming with me."

"I ain't!"

"You is. I like you, Nanny. I aim to keep you around."

"I won't go with you. You can't make me!"

"Yes I can, woman. Because if you don't go, I'll kill you. You know I'll do it, too."

"I'll go tell. I'll tell that you're here, and they'll come get you and lock you up!"

"Then when I'm out, I'll kill you. Or maybe I'll get some-body else to do it for me, even sooner. I can do that, Nanny. I know the ways to get it done."

Nanny dared not doubt him. She had no more to say, and knew she was trapped. His grin spread slowly. He knew she was trapped, too.

"I been missing you, woman. Missing them nights we've shared. Why don't you come here, right now, and let's make up for the time we missed. What you say? Come on . . ."

She tried to stifle her trembling, tried not to let the dread and revulsion she felt show. A smile whose generation required much effort warmed her face. "I missed you, too, Cat," she said. "I missed you, too."

He reached her, big hands touching her, grinning face moving in close to her own.

The well-bundled woman opened the door and hurried inside, fleeing the cold. At the desk on the far side of the head-belching stove that filled the center of the little office room, a desk-bound soldier looked up and, before he could restrain himself, lifted his brows in undisguised admiration of his new visitor. Then, as she turned from closing the door to face him, he noted the telling bulge of her belly, cleared his throat, and became the image of military decorum.

"Good day, ma'am."

"Good day, sir." She glanced at his shoulder. "Corporal, is it?"

"Yes, ma'am. Corporal Isaiah Petter. May I help you?" The corporal's diction was precise and clean, possessing neither a southern guttural slur or harsh northern nasality.

"I hope so. My name is Mrs. Amy Hanover. I've come trying to find someone. He may not be here now, in fact probably isn't, but I expect he's familiar here. His name is Greeley Brown. I don't know whether he is enlisted, or a civilian. I expect the latter."

"You're right, ma'am," Petter replied. "I don't know Mr. Brown personally, but he is a civilian. He works in recruiting for the army, though, mostly the Thirteenth Regiment of the Tennessee Volunteer Cavalry."

"Does he come to Knoxville?"

"Well, he hasn't that I know of, but I would expect he'd show up here now that Knoxville is occupied. It's a closer and safer way to reach the Federal army than going to Kentucky, like he has before."

"But he hasn't come yet?"

"No, ma'am. But I do believe I heard he showed up with some recruits in Sevierville some weeks ago. But I can't vouch for that personally."

Amy nodded. "I see. Well, I may be wasting my time. I received a letter from Mr. Brown, you see, but it was . . . damaged. I wasn't able to read much of it, and don't really know what he was trying to tell me."

"So you know Mr. Brown?"

"Well, no. And I don't know certainly that it was he who wrote the letter. Part of the name was torn off, you see, but the 'Greeley' was there, and some of what I could make out in the letter seemed consistent with it being Greeley Brown. . . ."

Corporal Petter stared at her in puzzlement.

"I'm sorry. I'm not making much sense. Here . . ." She dug into her bag and pulled out a letter. "I'd like to leave this here for Mr. Brown, if ever he should appear in Knoxville. It tells him that the letter he wrote to me was torn up and that I didn't really receive the message. It tells him where to reach me. Will you see that he gets it, if he comes?"

"I'll do my best . . . I can't promise you, there being so many things that could happen. I don't know I'd even know he was here if he came. But I'll put out the word."

"Thank you." She handed the letter to the corporal and turned to go.

"Wait, ma'am," Petter said. "I just had a thought. Though Greeley Brown isn't here just now, another pilot from his region is. Mr. Daniel Ellis. He's just come in by train from Nashville, which is where the Thirteenth Regiment is stationed just now. He took them some recruits, and I believe, ma'am, that he intends to remain around Knoxville for a few days, collecting letters and so on to carry back to soldiers' families in his home region. I should be able to locate him, if you would like a meeting."

Amy saw little to gain from meeting Ellis in terms of finding out what Greeley Brown had been trying to communicate to her in his letter. However, she had heard Ellis's name mentioned as frequently as Greeley Brown's by the many mountain refugees she'd interviewed since the beginning of the year. It couldn't hurt to meet him.

"I'd be pleased to meet him, sir, if you don't mind going to the trouble."

"Not at all, ma'am. If you'd like to have a seat, I'll find someone to fill in for me here, and see if I can locate Mr. Ellis for you."

Amy smiled and went to the nearest chair. Corporal Petter left, and Amy was alone for a couple of minutes until another corporal entered and gave her a nod in greeting. He seated himself behind the desk and lit a pipe. The clock on the wall ticked, and chimed three o'clock.

Amy let the heat from the stove bathe over her, until it became too hot and she moved to a farther corner. The clock chimed the half hour and she began to consider rising and leaving. Ben didn't know where she was and might be needing something, though he was healing up with remarkable speed and doing pretty well on his own now.

Amy was about to leave when the door opened and Corporal Petter came back in, followed by a lean, bearded stranger with keen and unblinking eyes, and skin made swarthy from weathering. He looked at her squarely, nodded, and came forward to introduce himself before Petter had a chance to do it.

"Daniel Ellis, ma'am."

She put out her hand. "Mr. Ellis, I'm Amy Deacon Hanover. I'm pleased to meet you."

"Amy *Deacon* Hanover . . . the same Amy Deacon who was daughter to Doc Deacon?"

"That's right. You knew my father."

"Knew his paper, knew his reputation. Didn't agree with much he had to say."

"Neither did I, Mr. Ellis."

"I understand you're asking about Greeley Brown."

"Yes. Do you know him?"

"I do. And I'm concerned about him."

"Concerned?"

"Yes, ma'am. Because from the time of his last stampeder run, nobody's laid eyes on him that I know of."

They pulled chairs together and talked for several minutes. Ellis laid out what meager facts he knew: Greeley Brown had taken a stampeder band toward Knoxville back in January, had diverted to Sevierville instead after learning that a Union force was in that town at the time, and according to rumor had somehow gotten injured and laid up for several days in Sevierville. Then he had left, and now no one knew where he was, though several men eager to form a new stampeder band for him to pilot had been trying to find him.

"So that's all that's known?" Amy asked.

"All that's known . . . though there is a rumor floating around. A false one, I hope."

"What's that?"

"There's a scoundrel in the mountains now, name of Fletcher—"

"I've heard of him." Seeing Ellis's surprised expression, she added, "I'm a writer, you see. I've been interviewing refugees from the mountains since the beginning of the year."

"Oh, I see. Well, if you know about Fletcher, you know he's a murderer and villain. He claims some sort of commissioned status, but there's nothing to it as best anybody knows. Just a story to excuse him for burning down Union folks' homes, stealing from widows and wives with husbands off fighting in blue, and murdering Unionist scouters. Being a Union man is good enough to give you a death sentence with Fletcher."

"What's the rumor about Greeley Brown?"

"That Fletcher caught him and hung him from a sapling. Supposedly Fletcher himself is bragging about it. Greeley would have been quite a prize for him. He's become a pretty well-known man in the mountains."

Amy felt a pang of sadness. Though she hadn't met Greeley Brown in person, she had met his spirit time and again in the words of refugees who knew and admired him. She hoped he wasn't dead.

"Do you believe this rumor, Mr. Ellis?"

"I've tried not to. But the more time goes by, the more I'm forced to think about it."

Silence held a couple of moments. Petter coughed over behind the desk. He had been busy during their conversation trying not to look like he was listening.

"Mr. Ellis, do you have any idea why Greeley Brown, who has never met me, would write me a letter?"

"No, ma'am, not as I can think of. Did he?"

"Yes, or I think he did. The man who was carrying the letter was struck by a train and killed. The letter was very damaged, quite a lot of it completely gone. The name 'Greeley' was visible on it. . . . Here, I'll show you the letter, if you'd like. I'm afraid there's some dried blood on it."

Ellis read the letter fragments with some interest but no sign that it meant anything to him. He handed it back to her. "It appears to have something to do with a fellow named Sam. Is this letter why you're trying to find Greeley?"

"Yes. From what I can tell, the letter was written to convey some message from this 'Sam' to me. There's only one Sam I've known well in my life, a young man who was a store clerk in Greeneville. His name is Sam Colter. Did you know him?"

"I'm afraid not, ma'am."

"So you don't know if Greeley knew Sam Colter."

"No, I don't. But Greeley and I ain't had much contact since the Carter County Rebellion back at the end of 'sixty-one, right after the bridge burnings. We've both laid low most of the time since then, and though we've been in the same line of work, our paths ain't crossed."

Amy nodded and stood. Ellis stood as well. "Thank you, Mr. Ellis. If you should happen to run into Greeley Brown . . ."

"I'll be sure to tell him about meeting you, and about the letter getting ruined. It may be, ma'am, that it was a different Greeley who sent that letter, though."

"Perhaps so. It's not that common a name, though, and the last name does start with B. That narrows it down quite a lot."

"Yes, I reckon it does. Well, can I do anything else for you, ma'am?"

"You can let me interview you. I'm writing a book about the plight of the Union people in the mountains."

"Well, now there's a book that needs writing. I could tell you aplenty of stories, for sure."

"Would you?"

"Don't see why not."

Before they parted, Amy and Ellis agreed to meet the next day at the *Sage* office. Amy parted company with the famed pilot with a combination of excitement over the pending interview and disappointment at being unable to confirm anything positive about the apparent Greeley Brown letter.

She hoped strongly that the rumor about Greeley's death was false. Selfishly, she wanted him to be alive so she could find him and decipher the message that had failed to come through. More importantly, she wanted him to be alive because she admired him. He, like Ellis, had done much for the Union cause. She'd like to have the chance to meet him someday.

It would be a shame if some murdering scoundrel killed a man such as Greeley Brown, she thought. Fletcher. Another man she had not met. But the more she learned about this ruffian, the more she was learning to hate him.

Leaving the little military office after thanking Corporal Petter for his help, Amy threaded her way along streets and boardwalks, heading back to her house and Ben Scarlett.

Chapter 21

Cat snored, loudly. This was a fact Nanny hadn't known until he intruded upon her here, because before, he had never slept in her presence. She'd told him about the snoring after the first night, and he had gotten angry, denied it, told her that the only people who snored were old and fat, and he'd never snored in his life and never would. She hadn't mentioned it again, and night after night had endured the railroad train rumble of it, hating the noise as much because *he* generated it as because it made it hard to sleep.

The time was shortly before dawn, and she'd been awake for at least two hours, listening to him. Through her mind several familiar, slightly varying fantasies had played: sneaking out, finding a policeman in town, bringing him here and letting him arrest Cat; sneaking out and *not* finding a policeman, just running, going as far away as she could as quickly as she could; sneaking to the other corner of the tent, finding Cat's pistol, or better yet, his knife, sneaking back over . . . ridding this tent of snoring once and for all, and herself of a big and dangerous problem.

The latter fantasy was the most satisfying, but Nanny knew she would not carry it out. Cat was the murderer, not she. She wouldn't carry out the other fantasies, either. Cat had said he would kill her if she didn't cooperate with him. She could not gamble that he didn't mean it.

He awakened when the light came, filtering yellowish-tan through the dirty tent fabric. He was grouchy, as usual, and glared at her as if she offended him by being there.

"I'm hungry. They brung in food yet?"

"Not yet. It'll be a long time until food."

He swore at her, vilely, as if it were her fault, and said, "Get out there, woman, and see what you can find me."

"How am I supposed to find you food?"

"Hell, how do I know? What do I care? Steal it! Just bring me something to eat!"

She nodded, though she knew she would fail. He'd sent her out on such a hopeless errand four times in the last several days. She had come back the first two times to report that she could find no food, but the treatment he'd given her those times taught her a new procedure: Leave the tent and don't return, no matter what, until food is brought to the camp.

She slipped out through the tent flap, blinking in the light, and stood, straightening her stiff back. Across the camp others were beginning to emerge, and smoke was rising in plumes from various fires. The sky was cloudy, and across the low sky-line of Knoxville a layer of black spread across the sky, beneath the clouds, spat up by a thousand belching chimneys. It was going to be an ugly day, in an ugly place, in an ugly time.

Nanny shivered in the cold and began trudging through the ice-crusted mud, beginning her feigned search for food. She walked to the end of the first row of tents, stopped, and stared with a frown at a sight she hadn't seen on such prior rounds on other mornings.

Two men who appeared to be policemen were walking from tent to shelter to tent, lifting flaps and looking in, poking their heads into shelter doors. Following them were three soldiers, bearing rifles and dangerous, warning looks.

She knew at once they were looking for Cat.

She stood unmoving, watching them, not sure what to do. Should she go back, warn Cat, let him hide, or escape? Yes, that was it . . . he would be grateful to her, treat her better . . .

No, no. Best to keep walking, to go elsewhere in the camp,

or out of the camp, and let them find Cat on their own. He couldn't blame her. It was Cat himself who had sent her out on this fool's errand. They'd catch him, haul him off, and she'd be through with him.

The latter option made the greatest sense, yet it frightened her deeply. Somehow, Cat would weasel his way out. They'd miss his tent, he'd detect them and slip out in some way . . . then he'd be angry and take it out on her.

She would warn him. Better to be in Cat's favor than not. Maybe this incident would scare him, make him give up on whatever debt he was waiting to collect and head for Nashville. He'd take her with him, of course, and Nashville was a place she didn't want to go. But surely, once they got under way, she would find opportunity to escape him. She couldn't lose Cat in this camp, nor in Knoxville, but out in the world at large, she could do it.

Nanny turned and headed back to the tent. Kneeling, she thrust in her head. Cat, who had almost gone back to sleep, grunted and frowned at her.

"Cat, they've come a-looking for you!"

"What?"

"They've come for you, Cat! They're coming from tent to tent, sticking their heads in!"

He swore, crawled to the tent door, and looked out cautiously. "I don't see nothing."

"You got to stand to see them from here. They're a-coming closer, though. You got to hide, Cat!"

He pulled his head back inside the tent, cursing.

By the time the policemen and soldiers reached Nanny's tent, they had each begun examining the tents and shelters, seeking to speed up the task. One of the two policemen knelt and stuck his head in. Nanny, lying down on the blankets, jerked upright as if just jolted from sleep. She stared at him, mouth open.

"You the only one in this tent?"

"Yes, sir. Only me."

"No man?"

"No, sir."

"You know anything of a nigra man name of Cat Kingsley?"

"No, sir."

He glanced at the muddied, large pair of boots sitting in a corner of the tent. "Them ain't yours, I take it? You ain't got feet that big, do you?"

"They ain't mine, sir."

"They don't belong to Cat Kingsley, do they, girl?"

"No, sir."

"Why you got them boots?"

"I found them, sir. I was going to sell them."

"Found them, huh? Stole them's more like it. You nigras are the worst race of thieves I ever seen."

She put on a face of someone caught in crime. "You ain't going to arrest me for stealing them, sir? Please don't, sir! I'll give them to you, if you want them, sir!"

The policeman laughed, and shook his head as he withdrew it.

Nanny waited for the sound of the policeman moving on down the row, but he didn't do that. Instead he paused, then his footsteps moved around to the side of the tent and toward the rear. . . .

Nanny lunged to the back of the tent, lifted the canvas wall. Cat was just behind it, lying on his side.

"Roll in, Cat!" she whispered sharply, and scooted back to give him room.

Cat rolled in quickly, and Nanny let the wall drop.

She and Cat listened together as the policeman reached the rear of the tent. He remained only long enough to see that no one was hidden there, and moved back up to the front and down the row. Cat had gotten inside just in time.

Cat let out a long, slow breath. "I owe you good for that one, Nanny. I owe you good."

"Just treat me kind, Cat, that's all I ask."

"Ain't I always done that, Nanny?" He laughed, and kissed her.

Ben walked slowly and silently into the little front room of Amy's house, and watched with concern as she reclined on the battered old couch there. Her head rested on a pillow, her face, pale and puffy, was upturned, eyes closed. Her hand touched her pregnant belly, rubbing gently, while her expression bore the look of someone in discomfort.

"Miss Amy?"

She opened her eyes quickly, startled. "I didn't know you were there, Ben." She began to sit up.

"No, lay on back, that's all right. Are you hurting in some way?"

"I'm fine. Just a little uncomfortable."

"You had a look of pain on your face."

"Ben, I'm fine."

"I ain't trying to worry you about this, Miss Amy, but with the baby and all, I feel concerned when I see you—"

"For heaven's sake, Ben, would you please hush! And quit treading so lightly around what you're trying to say. You and I both know you're thinking about that silly curse. I'm telling you that the baby is fine, any discomfort I'm feeling is coming from my stomach, *not* from anything to do with the baby, and there is nothing to fear from any silly curse!"

"I just worry for you when I see you looking so pained."

"Ben, I've told you before: My mother had a stomach condition. An ulcerated stomach, Father called it. It caused her quite a lot of pain sometimes, and it was at its worst when she had matters to worry about. I believe I have the same condition, and you're not doing a thing to help it by worrying over me like some doting old grandmother."

"I ain't going to get mad at you just because you scold me for worrying about you."

"Why are you up and around? Shouldn't you be resting yourself?"

"I'm doing fine. It wasn't that bad a wound. It's you I'm worried about."

"Well, look at us," Amy said in a sarcastic tone. "Worrying about each other. We ought to have a competition, give a prize to the one who worries the most."

Ben shook his head. "I wish you wouldn't take things as funny that ought to be took serious."

"And I wish you weren't such a superstitious old grandmother."

Ben lifted his right hand to point at her, but that made the wound hurt and he put it down again. "I ain't superstitious," he said. "Worrying about hexes ain't superstition. It's good sense, that's all. Don't you forget that fellow with the lockjaw."

"Sometimes I wish you'd get lockjaw, just to shut you up," Amy muttered.

Ben raised his brows, turned, and headed back to his room.

"Superstitious old grandmother!" Amy whispered. She liked Ben, loved him, but they'd spent enough time under one roof. He was beginning to wear on her, and probably she on him.

The next morning, Amy brought up the possibility of Ben's going back to his own room above the rear section of the *Sage* building, expecting to receive a quick agreement.

Ben surprised her. "I ain't going back to my room."

"What? Why?"

"Because I'm going to keep an eye on you."

"The hex, right?"

"You may think it's nothing. I don't."

"Ben, I regret the day I told you about that. You intend to stay right here in this house until doomsday?"

"If it takes that to make sure that baby is safe, I sure will."

"And what do you intend to do if something should happen? Are you a physician?"

"No, but—"

"If this hex is so powerful, like you seem to believe, how do you believe you can do anything about it, just by staying under my nose all the time?"

"Well, I don't know, but—"

"Ben, you *will* go back to your room. If you don't, I will. You can have the house, I'll take the room. But one thing I won't take is us trying to share the same space any longer than need be."

Ben straightened, frowning. "It wouldn't take much more of that to hurt my feelings, Miss Amy."

"Ben, you know I love you dearly. You're the best friend I have in the world. But we aren't meant to stay in the same house, especially for a reason as silly as this superstition of yours—and it *is* a superstition, that's all."

Ben stood unspeaking.

"Ben, as soon as you feel up to it, I want you to move back to your old room. You can still watch over me. You'll still be close by. I promise, if there's anything at all that seems wrong, anything that would indicate danger to my baby, I'll let you know at once. Ben, do you believe I'd be careless about my own child's welfare? Do you think I'd take my child's life lightly?"

"No."

"Then please . . . be reasonable about this. Don't let some silly fear get the best of you."

He took it in, thought about it, nodded.

Amy rose, came to him, and kissed his bearded cheek. "I knew you'd come to your senses. And don't think I don't appreciate your concern for me. It's very sweet and dear of you, in its own silly way—" She cut off and put her hand to her belly again, unable to stifle a wince.

"Miss Amy, are you—"

"My stomach, Ben. I swear. Just my stomach."

"Are you sure?"

"I'm sure."

The first night back in his own room, Ben sat by his window, looking out on the street, thinking. Snow was pouring down, lying eight inches thick on streets and roofs, piling deeper by the minute. Ben had despised snow in his days as a street dweller, but now it served as a reminder that he had a warm, safe place to live, and gave him a cozy feeling. The feeling faded only when he remembered that there were many out there now living in conditions similar to or worse than those they had known. Homeless, impoverished men, spending the night in sheds or outbuildings. And what of the refugees? Entire camps of them, black and white, living in wagons, tents, thrown-together hovels. He was a fortunate man in a time when misfortune reigned.

Tonight he could not feel the proper gratitude, however. He was preoccupied with the "silly" concern that Amy had so often derided. Perhaps she was right, perhaps his fear of a curse was foolish superstition. Amy was educated; he wasn't. He had no irrefutable evidence that curses held any power.

But, hang it, were there not some things a man just *knew*? Just as a soldier knew not to settle every one of his affairs before battle because it invited death, just as a bride knew not to let her husband-to-be see her on the day of the wedding, so Ben Scarlett knew it was not wise to ignore a curse, particularly one voiced in anger. Nanny's race added another worrisome matter. In Ben's perception, black folks knew things hidden to whites, had contact with a supernatural netherworld that educated, supposedly rational folk like Amy Deacon Hanover might deny, but not eliminate.

So Ben was faced with a problem. Amy clearly wasn't going to let him stay with her, and he couldn't forget her comment that there would be nothing he could do to overcome a hex anyway. That very comment was what had him sitting up tonight, watching the snow, pondering.

The more he considered it, the more he realized that Amy was right. Some things a man couldn't fight. If a curse was to be fulfilled, fulfilled it would be.

There was only one conclusion to draw: What a man can't fight, he can only remove. But how could he remove a curse? He puzzled over this, very fretfully.

He had been staring through the glass, at the falling snow, but now he looked instead at his reflection in the window, and abruptly laughed at the crease-browed, worrying fellow looking back at him. Suddenly the entire business seemed just as Amy saw it: silly, superstitious, a waste of worry. Amy was right. What Nanny had done was voice words in the air. Words held no power in themselves. Surely there was no cause to be concerned.

Ben instantly felt a great relief. He rose to go to bed, but glanced out the window a last time.

In the street below a man was staggering along, looking cold and weak. Drunk, most likely. He leaned against the wall of a building across the street, slumped over. His form was illuminated by the light of a lamp burning in a window beside which he stood. Ben stared closely. The man looked familiar. When he saw the fellow lift a bottle to his lips, he recognized him at once.

It was Skunk. Drunk as he could be, roaming and drinking

on a night when he ought to be sheltered somewhere. Ben frowned. He had always been careful even in his most extreme drinking days to watch out for the weather. Many a hard-drinking man had died of exposure long before the liquor got a chance to kill him.

Outside, Skunk strode on past the window, lifting his feet high above the drifting snow. He moved outside the range of the window light. Ben tried to see him, but lost him.

Ben stepped back into the center of his dark room, nudging at his chin with his prosthetic hook. A moral dilemma rose to drive worries about curses and unborn babies from his mind. He knew Amy's hard rule that he not allow anyone to share his room, particularly former drinking companions. But Skunk was far too drunk to be roaming like he was on a night like this.

Ben made up his mind. Slipping on his coat and hat, he headed out and down the stairs, stepping carefully because of the snow piled on the steps. Halfway down he called out, "Skunk! Skunk Linden!"

He reached the bottom of the stairs and entered the street. He peered about but could not see Skunk anywhere. He called again, and thought he heard a low moan in answer.

Ben headed into the center of the street and saw him. Skunk had fallen, facedown, and was lying in the snow, struggling to get up but unable to do so, either because he was too drunk or maybe too cold. Ben went to him.

"Skunk, it's me, Ben. Can you stand up?"

"Ben . . . howdy, Ben . . . pull me up from here."

"I can't. I got shot through the right shoulder and can't pull very hard. You'll have to get up yourself."

"Well, I'll try . . ."

Skunk struggled but couldn't make it. Ben turned and extended his left arm. "Grab hold, Skunk. No, not the hook, the arm. Pull yourself up on that, if you can."

This time Skunk made it. He stood, swaying like a tree in the wind.

"Lost my bottle," he said, looking around in the snow. "Where's my bottle?"

"Forget that bottle. You're best off without it. Come on, Skunk. I'm taking you up to my room. I'll not have you freeze out here. Miss Amy would understand."

"I want my bottle."

"Forget about it. Let's go."

Together, Ben and Skunk headed for the stairs, then up them, slowly and with difficulty, and into the room. Ben closed the door, shutting out the night and the storm.

Chapter 22

Morning came and revealed a city covered by nearly a foot of snow. Ben threw open the curtain and let the brilliant light of a clear day stream in, bringing a smile to him, eliciting a groan from the badly hungover Skunk Linden.

"Close that back, Ben, please!"

"Nope. Can't do that. You got to get out of here, Skunk. It's against Miss Amy's rule for you to be here at all, and I want you to go. You got someplace you can take shelter?"

Skunk sat up, looking unhappily around, forehead creased, eyes squinting. "No place so nice as this."

"I'd keep you here if Miss Amy would allow. But she won't, and she's probably right not to. You and your liquor are a source of temptation to me, and I truly don't need to be around you."

"I can't tempt you with nothing right now. My bottle's out there, in the street."

"Buried in a foot of snow."

"A foot! No fooling?"

"Come look for yourself."

"I can't. Can't bear the light."

"You'll have to. Get on up and out of here, Skunk, before anybody sees you."

"You got any food?"

Ben dug into his little box pantry and found a heel of bread and half a jar of apple jelly some local woman had given Amy, who didn't care for apple jelly and therefore passed it on to him. Ben dug out his folding knife, used it to spread some of the jelly on the bread, and gave it to Skunk.

"There's your breakfast, best I can provide. Now get on with you."

"You ain't much of a companion since you quit drinking, Ben. I hope you start again so you'll be more fun."

"I won't start again. I'll never touch another drop."

Skunk moved slowly about the place, collecting his boots, putting them on as slowly as possible, gnawing on the bread, dripping jelly on his clothing and the floor. That on his clothing he fingered off and ate. That on the floor he stepped in and ground into the wood. Ben found it frustrating to watch.

At last Skunk stood dressed, booted, and becoated, fingering the smashed-down top hat that always made him recognizable from far away to Ben. His pale face was pinched with misery. "You sure I can't stay awhile?"

"I'm sure. You go find yourself a warm shelter and wait out this bad weather. And don't drink. You'd have died last night because of your drinking, if I hadn't seen you. You'd have passed out on the street and nobody would have found you until the snow melted off."

Skunk frowned as if in deep thought, and Ben wondered if he'd gotten through to him at last. Since he'd quit drinking, Ben was evangelistic among other town drunks about the merits of going sober. Skunk had never given any heed to Ben's lectures before.

Nor now, his next words revealed. "How'm I going to find my whiskey in all that snow?"

"You won't find it. You'll leave it out there and forget about it and let some wagon run over it and bust it. You ain't going to drink another drop of it, because you're giving up the whiskey."

"I ain't giving it up. I live for it. Without it they ain't no reason to go on."

"You'll find more reasons than you could ever know, if you'd just go for a month without the stuff. Forget that whiskey. Get on with you."

Skunk left, suffering in the bright sunlight glinting off the snow, moving gingerly down the stairs, clinging to the handrail and testing his footing on each step. At the bottom of the stairs he paused and looked up at Ben. "Thank you for saving my hide last night, Ben."

"Think nothing of it, Skunk."

"I do appreciate it. I'll repay the favor for you one of these days."

"Fine, fine. You have a good day, now. Get out of the cold."

"I will."

Ben went back inside and began shoving wood into his small fireplace. When he had the blaze off to a good start he went back to the window, and frowned when he saw Skunk down there, kicking about in the snow, looking for his lost bottle.

A few moments later Skunk was struck hard in the side of the face by a well-packed snowball. He spun around, cussing, thinking he was being harassed by some of the hordes of boys who roamed this city without schools. But he saw no one but a family of black refugees, picking their way through the snow, probably on their way to the contraband camp, a couple of nicely dressed businessmen making their way to store or office, and a skinny black boy shoveling snow off the boardwalk. Skunk shrugged and went back to looking for his lost treasure.

Another snowball walloped him. He cursed and looked around wildly, with big, spastic motions.

"Skunk, you move on!" It was Ben's voice, coming from above. Skunk looked up and saw Ben back at the top of the landing of the stairs going up to his room. He was packing a third snowball, doing quite well at it considering he had to do it with only one hand. "You forget that bottle and get out of here, or I'll snowball you to your grave!"

"Damn you, Ben Scarlett!" Skunk yelled. "You're the sorriest, persnickitiest, most self-righteous old grandmother of a man I ever knowed! You mind your own damn business!"

The snowball knocked off Skunk's top hat. He knelt to

retrieve it, and when he stood again, Ben heaved yet another and hit him right in the face.

Skunk made a snowball of his own and tried to throw it, but it missed Ben by at least twenty feet. Ben laughed scornfully and threw another one that Skunk barely dodged.

Skunk knew he was defeated. He waved a dismissive hand at Ben, cursing him again, and began trudging down the street. He glanced up one last time and yelled, "You're just wanting it for yourself, that's all!"

"Nope," Ben replied. "I don't touch it no more."

Skunk went on, hungover and unhappy. Ben stayed on the landing until he was out of sight, and then went back in to finish readying himself for the day. He was eager to get down to Miss Amy's place and make sure she was well and didn't try to get out in a snow that was thick and heavy and could easily make a pregnant woman fall. Especially one as stubborn as Amy, who seemed to think herself invulnerable.

Ben was not happy with what he found. Amy met him at the door in her dressing gown, looking terribly pale, and he knew something was wrong. Miss Amy didn't sleep late. She admitted she'd been in bed. Stomach pain again, nothing serious. She'd been scribbling some outline notes for her refugee book, in fact.

Ben, who once again had flip-flopped on the hex issue and now was back on the side of belief, didn't think the problem was really her stomach, or nothing to worry about. Amy's trouble had to do with that baby, and he couldn't fathom why she refused to admit it. Was she so prideful in rejecting "super-stition" that she would actually let her child suffer harm, maybe even die?

He brought it up gently. She responded mildly. He put his concern out again, a little more forcefully. She replied in kind. He grew more forceful still, she did the same, and before long they were again in the midst of a fierce argument. When Ben left, it was because Amy ordered him to. He left with an insult ringing in his ears: She had called him a "worrisome old grandmother."

He strode back toward his room in an anger so hot it should

have melted the snow around him. Skunk had called him a grandmother, too. This was not an image of himself that Ben liked, nor felt he deserved. Was it bad that he concerned himself with the welfare of people he cared about? Shouldn't Skunk be glad there was somebody willing to care about him at all? Was it "worrisome" that Ben Scarlett cared about Miss Amy and her unborn baby and didn't want harm to come to them? What was wrong with folks? Couldn't they tell when somebody was just trying to do right by them, see to their welfare?

Sometimes life was frustrating. Sometimes it didn't make a lot of sense. Sometimes a man just wanted to get away.

So Ben did. He took a long walk around the city, not easy to do in a foot of snow. He let his mind run in whatever direction it wanted, allowed full vent to any thought that came, and in that way calmed down some. He decided he'd simply have to view Miss Amy as a hopeless case, a woman too blinded by her own supposedly progressive way of thinking that she just honestly didn't realize the full truth. The world as Ben Scarlett saw it was a far more complicated one than Miss Amy knew. It contained many more potential levels of being, potential realities, than she would ever admit to. In Ben's world, one didn't scoff at curses or the ability of one person's ill-willed mind to invoke harm on the mind or body of another.

He paused on his walk when he came in view of the contraband camp. Staring at the rows of tents and shelters, watching the plumes of smoke rise to the sky, he wondered if Nanny was in there somewhere. He doubted seriously that Cat was; an officer had visited Miss Amy recently and reported that a thorough search of the camp had failed to turn him up. Of course, the police had waited too many days before getting around to making the search, in Ben's opinion, and deep down he wondered if they had been so nonchalant about it because the victim of Cat's bullet was only old Ben Scarlett, former town drunk who they probably figured would someday be town drunk again. Nobody to get all that worked up about, especially since the bullet had done only superficial damage. Ben wriggled his shoulder and touched the place it had pierced him. A little sore just now from him throwing those snowballs at

Skunk, but surprisingly well-healed on the whole. He'd been lucky.

Ben stared at the contraband camp. Cat had probably come out lucky, too. They'd not search too hard for him now. Maybe not at all. It was just as well, Ben supposed. Ben had made it through without serious injury, and Cat hadn't managed to steal anything that important to Miss Amy. Those were the considerations that mattered. Let Cat go. If Ben never saw him again, that'd be a good enough resolution to the crime to suit him.

But what of Nanny? Might she still be at Knoxville? If so, Ben was sure the contraband camp was her likely hiding place. And as he thought that over, an idea came. A very good idea, he thought, one maybe he should carry out right now. But no, he was tired and cold, ready to get back and have a bite to eat and warm his feet by the fire, and his wounded shoulder was starting to hurt worse all at once. When the weather got a bit better, though, when he wasn't tired and hungry and sore, he'd come back and put his idea into motion. Maybe he could solve Miss Amy's problem on his own, and not even have to argue with her about it.

He began walking again, back toward his room. The snow crunched beneath his feet and sent bright sunlight shafting into his eyes, reflecting off the diamond crystals.

Ben was tired by the time he reached his destination, and trudged slowly across the street toward his stairs. The snow, pure and beautiful by morning, was now broken up and marred with mud by the day's traffic. Pretty things never lasted long in a city, Ben mulled. The thought struck him as deeply meaningful, and he considered trying to work it into the secret song he was writing. No, it wouldn't fit. The song was not about cities, but about war.

Maybe he'd work on that song a bit just to pass the time. Today was the kind of day he could most strongly wish that Miss Amy's original plan to revive the *Sage* here in Knoxville had worked out. He'd enjoy being hard at work today, setting type, spreading ink, watching the press create page after page. Even though Miss Amy was continuing to pay him out of her personal account, just as if he were working, it was not quite as satisfying to receive money in return for nothing. Miss Amy had her interviews and book plans to keep her busy, but he had to find his own ways to fill time.

As he neared the boardwalk, something moved beneath a corner of his heel. He paused and looked down, and realized just then what he'd run across.

He'd just found Skunk's lost bottle of whiskey.

Ben froze on the spot. Behind him a wagon creaked by. A man passed before him on the boardwalk, giving him a curious glance, probably wondering why this hook-handed man was standing like a statue at the edge of the street. A gang of white boys raced past, chasing a frightened-looking black girl, pelting her with snowballs and calling her contraband trash.

Ben lowered his eyes and saw a portion of the bottle gleaming at him through a hole in the snow. *Ben Scarlett, get hold of yourself. You don't need that bottle. You don't want that bottle.*

Only half the thought was true. He didn't need the bottle, but he did want it. Abruptly, unexpectedly, he wanted it badly. A snowy day, nothing to do—and a bottle. It was a combination that called with the sweetness of a Siren's song to something deep within him, a hunger and longing that was so ingrained in him that it was almost part of his very spirit and identity.

No. No! Ben Scarlett doesn't touch whiskey anymore. Ben Scarlett is a new man. Ben Scarlett wouldn't touch that bottle because Ben Scarlett wouldn't want to.

But Ben Scarlett did want to.

His mind scrambled for an escape from temptation. But it didn't scramble too hard. The bottle in the snow held him fast.

He began mouthing his favorite verse from the scriptures, one he liked because it contained a subtle and very appropriate play on his very name: *Though your sins be as scarlet, they shall be as white as snow . . .*

He glanced around. The muddy snow didn't look very white just now. And scarlet was an awful pretty color . . .

He gave his head a quick, hard shake, and forced a laugh at the mental games he was playing with himself. Of course he couldn't drink that whiskey! He'd given it up, hadn't he? Besides, Skunk probably had the stopper out of it when he dropped it, so there would be no whiskey in it anyway. All this inner struggle was probably going on over an empty bottle!

Ben bent down and picked the bottle up. The stopper was in it. The bottle was more than half full.

He stared at it like a man who had found a key that might open heaven, might open hell, and he wasn't sure which. Two choices faced him: a day of boredom, of lonely struggle against temptation . . . or a day with a pleasure he hadn't enjoyed in a long time. No one would have to know. He'd draw the curtain, close and lock the door, and if anyone came knocking, he wouldn't answer. He could drink, enjoy himself, then give it all up again when he was through.

He closed his eyes. *No.* With tremendous will, he bent again and put the bottle back into the snow. *Now break it, Ben. Stomp on it and break it.*

He didn't break it. He left it where it was, stepped onto the boardwalk and headed up the stairs so fast that he almost fell on the slick, accumulated snow.

Ben was at his window within five minutes, staring down at the bottle in the snow. The sun glinted on it and it was very visible to anyone who passed. Maybe someone would come along and take it away. He'd welcome that. Hate it, too. But it would be best.

He wished he'd left Skunk alone so he could have found the bottle this morning. That way this whole internal war wouldn't have been sparked.

People passed on the boardwalk and the street. No one noticed the bottle, or if they did, they didn't bother it. One woman came by, paused, stooped and picked it up. She looked at the label, shook her head, and tossed the bottle back into the snow. She went on, leaving the bottle even more exposed.

Ben stared at it from his window. His empty stomach rumbled, asking for food. He didn't notice.

The clock ticked away an hour, then two. He didn't notice that, either. Ben Scarlett sat in his chair by the window, staring at the bottle in the dirty snow.

• • •

There was no bottle in the snow when Amy Hanover came to Ben's place about dusk. She mounted the stairs carefully, conscious of the danger of falling in her condition. When she reached the top, she rapped on the door.

No answer came. She rapped again. "Ben? Are you home?" Surely he was. She had seen a light shining behind the closed curtain of his window.

Still no response. She knocked harder. "Ben! It's me, Amy. Please answer! I have some news for you I think you'll want to hear."

She heard movement inside. Then Ben's voice came filtering through the door, weaker than usual. "I'm here."

"Can I come in?"

"I'm, uh. I ain't decent. I'm sick."

"Sick? Let me in, then, and I'll help you."

"No. No. I don't want you to catch it."

She paused, filling with dread. "Ben, have you been . . ." *Drinking.* She couldn't ask it. She didn't really want to know the answer.

"I just been sick, that's all."

He didn't sound sick. He sounded drunk. But Amy accepted his word. She did not want to deal with the consequences of not accepting it.

"Are you sure I can't help you?"

"Yes." He paused. "Why'd you come up them stairs, Miss Amy? You shouldn't have done it. You might fall."

"I won't. Ben, I came to tell you that I visited a physician today. Because of how I was feeling. I wanted you to know that I was right. It is my stomach. It isn't the baby. He gave me medicine."

He was just on the other side of the door. She fancied she could smell his whiskeyed breath right through the wood. "That's good. I'm glad."

"Ben, are you sure you're all right alone?"

"I'm sure."

"You can quit worrying about the baby now, Ben. I wanted you to know that. The baby is fine. That's what I came to tell you."

There was a long pause. "Miss Amy, I need to tell you . . ."

"Yes?"

Another pause. "Nothing. Nothing. Never mind."

He sounded like maybe he was crying. Amy wanted to go in, tend him and make sure he was safely in his bed. But if she went in, she knew what she'd find. Ben was drunk again. After all this time, he had yielded.

But if she didn't see it, she could pretend she didn't know. He could tell his lie and she could claim to believe it, and maybe this wouldn't happen again.

"I'm going home now, Ben. I'll check on you tomorrow."

"All right, Miss Amy."

"Good night, Ben."

He didn't reply.

Chapter 23

He was putting on a valiant pretense, and she was tempted to make an equally valiant effort to believe him. But the truth was too easy to see. Despite Ben's forced cheerfulness and nonchalance, she read the reality in his eyes, in his manner, in the slight tremoring of his fingers, and smelled it in the subtle scent his pores exuded. He had been drunk the night before, on whiskey, and he couldn't hide it.

When she knocked on his door, he answered it instantly, so she knew he'd been waiting for her to come. Preparing himself, probably rehearsing his story and practicing his don't-you-worry grin since before dawn. Everything about him at this moment was false, from his smile to his happy report that, by gum, he was feeling much better this morning than he'd have thought, considering how sick he was last night. Amy smiled and went along, but it generated a deep ache inside as she did it.

"So . . . what was it you said yesterday evening?" Ben asked her after he had spewed his string of lies. "I was feeling so puny just then that I ain't sure I heard you right, you see, heh heh heh!" The fulsome smile he presented was so ghastly and transparent she wanted to slap it off his face.

"I said I went to a doctor, and that he told me the only problem I have is with my stomach. Exactly as I had thought. He said it probably came along about the time that Adam was killed, and hurts me most when I'm feeling distressed about something."

"So those pains you've had—"

"Have nothing to do with anything being wrong with the baby. Nothing to do with Nanny's silly curse. That's what I came to tell you last night. But, like you said, you were 'sick.' "

"Yes. That's right. Well, I'm sorry about your stomach, but glad the baby's fine."

"So I'll hear no more about all that hex silliness from you?"

"No. You won't." He meant this. He had already decided he would not argue uselessly with her any longer. Nothing she'd just said had changed his view about Nanny's hex, however. Just because the baby was healthy at the moment didn't mean it might not get sick later, or die by some accidental means either before or after birth. But there was nothing gained by pointing this out to her.

Amy was pleased with his seeming agreement. "Good. Well, I'm glad that's settled. Now, are you really feeling better?"

That absurd grin returned, masking nothing. "Much better, yes."

"When did you start feeling sick?"

"Oh, I don't know, sometime late in the day. Hey, what do you think of all that snow out there? How long's it been since we had such a deep snow in March, huh?"

"Ben, there's something we need to talk about."

He laughed. "Why, what? We've already talked about that curse and such. You've told me there's nothing to be worrying about. That's all settled now."

"That's not what we need to talk about. I just want to tell you, Ben, to remind you, that you'll always be my friend, but that it's important you obey my rules if you're going to be my employee, too."

"I do obey your rules, Miss Amy."

"I'm glad to hear you say that. Because if you broke them, especially the significant ones, you know that as much as I would hate to do it, I would have to keep my end of the bargain and let you go."

He laughed again, loud and false-hearted. "Why, of course! That just kind of goes without saying, don't it?"

"Maybe, but it's important sometimes to say it anyway."

"Well, all righty. You've said it, though I can't figure why. But you don't need to worry. I ain't going to drink no more."

"I hope you really mean that, Ben."

Another false laugh. "Listen at you! What's wrong? Don't you believe old Ben anymore?"

"Is there any reason I shouldn't believe you?"

"Why, no, no! Just the same old me! Sober as a judge and determined to stay that way!"

"I don't want you going back to drinking again, Ben."

"I won't."

"I mean it."

That spurious smile faltered and went away. He looked her in the eye, dropped his gaze a moment, but raised his face and found it again. "I mean it, too."

They looked at one another, wordless, and more communication passed between them in the next few silent moments than had been conveyed in any of the evasive words they'd just tossed back and forth.

"I really do mean it, Miss Amy," Ben repeated.

"I'm glad, Ben. Because it's important that a man who has become addicted to liquor not touch it at all. One slip is sometimes all it takes to lead to another slip, and another, and suddenly he's trapped again."

"I know, I know. Believe me, I do. I've slipped before." He paused, and added, "Back in Nashville. You remember that time."

"Yes. You slipped once, but then you put it aside again. There's no reason that one slip has to lead to another . . . right?"

"Right."

She reached over and patted his hand, smiling. "Ben, I was thinking, maybe you should come back and stay at my house again for a while. For *my* sake, of course. Maybe you should even stay until the baby comes. I'm getting farther along now, and I think I might feel more secure with someone close by."

"Maybe that would be a good idea, Miss Amy."

"That way, you see, you could keep an eye on me."

"Yes. I sure could."

"You'll move back in today?"

"I will. I surely will." The smile this time was genuine.

"Good. Now help me back down the stairs, would you? I'd hate to fall."

That night, Amy heard him singing. Quietly, in his room, the door closed. She was sure he did not know she could hear, so she stood quietly beside the door, listening to his voice and marveling at how remarkably beautiful it was. She had not had any idea that Ben Scarlett could sing so hauntingly.

The song was an old camp meeting repentance hymn. *I will arise and go to Jesus/He will embrace me in his arms/In the arms of my dear Savior/Oh, there are ten thousand charms . . .*

After that came another hymn, and another. She knew what she was hearing. Ben Scarlett was looking his failure in the eye and seeing it for what it was, purging it out of his heart through his songs to God. It was good. She was glad he was doing it.

She felt she was invading, but the beauty of his voice kept her where she was, unable to pull away. The last verse of the last hymn faded away, and she waited for another to begin. When it didn't, she turned to slip away.

But then a song did begin, but no hymn this time. This was a new song to her, both words and tune. Like the hymns he had sung, it had a minor, mountain kind of melody, mysterious and eerie and Celtic, not merely pretty, but entrancing, hinting of things deep and mystic, of history and centuries slipping away and leaving only their ghosts behind.

The words, though, captivated her foremost. Ben's song told a story that was sad and plaintive. It was a lamentation. Its subject was war.

Amy listened, almost breathless, to words and melody that caught and held feelings and thoughts she had known many times, but been unable to capture in her own writings. Hearing it in Ben's soft but splendid baritone made it all the more moving, and when the song abruptly ceased, seemingly incomplete, she touched her face and found tears there. She waited for him to sing the rest of the song, but he didn't. Perhaps he

had sung all of the song that he knew. She wondered where
he'd heard it, and why such a wonderful, sad, mystic song
could have remained so obscure that she would have never
heard it before.

She went to bed that night trying to remember the melody
and words, but they had escaped her.

She hoped Ben would sing that song again for her someday.

The next day brought mail, including an unexpected letter.
Amy ripped it open and read it in mounting excitement, then
put on her coat and hat, and with letter in hand headed through
the mushy, melting snow down to the *Sage* office, where Ben
had gone to do some cleaning. Mostly dusting and picking
things up, because the motion of sweeping hurt his healing
bullet scar. With Nanny absent, there was no one else to do it.
That suited him, really, because at least it was work, some way
to fill the idle hours.

"Ben!" Amy called as she came through the door. "Ben, are
you here?"

He came out of her office, broom in hand. "Everything all
right, Miss Amy?"

"Yes, fine. Ben, I'm to be receiving a visitor soon. Horatio
Eaton. You remember him, don't you?"

"Yes indeed. The abolitionist fellow who used to put out
that newspaper."

"That's right, the paper that published my very first abolitionist pieces. Well, Horatio has been in Boston for several
months, but now, since Burnside's invasion, he's wanting to
return to Knoxville. And listen to this . . ." She unfolded the
letter and scanned her forefinger down its lines. "The first part
of his letter is mostly his greetings, his regret about my husband's death, his pleasure at learning that I've returned to
Knoxville, that kind of thing. But then he talks about his own
professional interests . . . let's see, yes! Here it is: 'My concerns have shifted somewhat, my dear Amy, since the days we
were writing about the need for slavery's abolishment. With
emancipation and the war, new needs have arisen, and will out-
last the ending of the war. There are now millions of Freedmen
who must find their way into society, and a new way of life to

be imposed upon states that have formerly made their way economically on the back of slavery. There will be lingering hatreds, resentments, and jealousies toward newly freed Negroes from the lower working class of impoverished whites. It is my desire now to turn my attentions to these problems, to create a new incarnation of my publication that would explore this new form of American society descending upon us, and advocate for fairness for all members of that society." And he goes on awhile, and says he would like to make East Tennessee his base of publication again, that he's coming to Knoxville within a matter of days from now to explore the possibilities here, and that he hopes we can again work together. Oh, Ben, isn't it exciting!"

"Wait a minute . . . I thought you was all wound up to write a book and not get back into newspapering for a time."

"Yes, but this might be the best of both worlds. Look at the situation: Through my inheritances, I've gained a fairly substantial wealth. I own a good printing press, type, cases, all the supplies needed for a newspaper. I gather from the letter that Horatio doesn't have his own equipment now. I'm thinking that perhaps Horatio and I might be able to come together. I could continue to work on my book, contribute to his newspaper sometimes, like I used to, except this time out in the open, and he could handle most of the actual editor and publisher duties. It's exciting! There's something very provident in all this. Did you notice how his concerns and mine are so close?"

"Close, but not the same. He's thinking mostly of the freed slaves, and you've been looking at the Unionist mountain refugees."

"There's no reason we couldn't each concentrate on slightly different areas. We'd actually cover more ground that way."

"There's also the matter of what you said about moving closer to the mountains. Up to Jonesborough or Elizabethton, after the baby comes. Mr. Eaton's letter there said he wanted to set up in Knoxville. He might not want to go to them other towns."

"He didn't say Knoxville, Ben. East Tennessee. That's all it says." She held out the letter, pointing. "See?"

"Yeah. Yeah, I see. You're right. Well, now! Ain't that interesting!"

"You'd be the pressman, of course," Amy threw in.

"Good. Good." He smiled. "You know, maybe all this is provident, like you said. This could really work out right! When did he say he was coming?"

"No exact day given. But soon."

"How will he find you?"

"Through the army, I suppose. Or the police. They'll be able to guide him to me."

"I remember when Horatio Eaton was in town before. He wasn't what you'd call a beloved man."

"That's because he opposed slavery. He spoke the truth, and the truth is seldom pleasant to look at."

"You think he'd face a lot of opposition from the locals?"

"Some, I'm sure. But times are changing. We could alter our style, our approach, to make the paper the least offensive to the most people while still giving a strong and accurate message. Meanwhile, I could publish my book, begin lecturing, touring. . . ."

"Don't forget. You'll have a little one to deal with, too."

Amy paused and reddened. "My goodness, Ben, I'm embarrassed to say it, but I *had* forgotten. Look at me, big as a house, and I'd forgotten all about the baby! Can you imagine?"

"Well, you got me to remind you."

"Yes. And you're right. The baby will come first, naturally. I'll do all I can for Horatio and the refugees and so on—but the baby will come first." She paused and stroked her engorged middle. "Funny thing, Ben. Even feeling my baby moving inside me, it's hard sometimes to imagine that it's real. It just doesn't seem possible that I'll have a living, breathing baby in my arms before long. A living bit of Adam. It just doesn't seem real to me. Like it isn't really ever going to happen."

"Don't say that, Miss Amy. I mean it. Don't say that."

She smiled. "What? You're afraid I'll 'hex' myself or something? I thought we'd agreed that all that was rubbish."

"All I'm saying is, don't say what you said. Ill-spoke words can make bad things happen. That's what my father used to tell me when I was a boy."

She sighed, thinking that Ben must sometimes feel quite

burdened with all the superstitious baggage he carried. "I'll be more careful," she told him.

"Well, I'd best get back to cleaning. With a guest going to show up, we'll want the place looking good. Your office is still wrecked from when Cat was in there."

Amy shuddered. "I hope that man is long gone."

"Me, too."

"I do wonder where Nanny is, though. Maybe the contraband camp."

"Maybe. Or maybe she's gone, too. To Nashville or someplace. A lot of the nigras are going to Nashville."

"I wonder if she'll ever try to find that baby she abandoned."

"I doubt it. Nanny's too hardened in the soul. I'd say she's glad to be shut of it. I can't imagine her having either the love or patience to raise a baby."

"I don't know, Ben. You know what she told me? She told me she had been . . . with Cat Kingsley so that she could have another baby and replace the one she abandoned. I don't really believe it, because she had a bottle of pills that are made to make women lose babies in the womb. I don't know why she would have kept those about if she really wanted a child. But she talked about it with a lot of feeling. She really misses that child she left behind."

"Shouldn't have left her, then. Sorry, Miss Amy, but I can't feel too sorry for Nanny. She's too much like me. Most of her problems she's brought on herself."

"Some of them, yes. Not all. She didn't bring it on herself to be born in a race that others look down on without reason. She didn't bring it on herself to grow up in slavery."

Ben grinned. "No wonder people get so riled up at you abolitionists! You say all these dang annoying things."

Amy laughed, and tucked away Horatio Eaton's letter. "Ben, do you mind some company for a little while? I believe I'll try to straighten up my office, since I'm already here."

"Be glad to have you! But you let me do the real work, hear? Got to make sure that baby don't get strained."

"Agreed."

They worked together for the remainder of the afternoon, making play of the labor, enjoying one another's company, growing cheerful and happy in their mutual presence. The tensions that had affected them both for weeks grew irrelevant. Eaton's letter and the potential direction for them that it conveyed had blown a fresh wind into their spirits. During those afternoon hours, Ben thought that if life were like this all the time, no man would ever have reason to be tempted by whiskey.

He hoped maybe life would go on this way. Maybe it would once Eaton arrived, the baby was born, and the press still crated up in the corner was operating again.

Who could say? Maybe the war would end before long, too. Life would really be fine then. It would roll along in a pleasant, quiet stream, and nothing at all would ever come along foul enough to muddy its waters.

Chapter 24

The boy was thin, painfully so, his brown eyes deep-sunk and brooding. He sat on the edge of a chair across from Amy's desk, spine erect and not touching the chair back, staring at the corner of the desk and talking in a low voice accented in the manner of the East Tennessee or western North Carolina mountaineer. He was one of dozens of new refugees who arrived in Knoxville each day. His name was Ollie Cress, and his family, what remained of them, had arrived in Knoxville from Johnson County, on the same day Horatio Eaton's letter had.

Amy had pen in hand and a pad before her, and struggled to take notes. The problem was not that the boy spoke fast, because he didn't, but that the story he told was so difficult to hear. He spoke it without any visible trace of sentiment, which only heightened its impact on Amy's already volatile emotions. Worst of all, Ollie Cress's story was not exceptional. She'd heard the same kind of thing again and again as she talked to refugees from the hills.

"My father, he was a little fellow, like I'm going to be. Small of frame, and with a limp. He'd broke his leg once while he was little, for he was prone to fits all his life, and when one would hit him, he'd fall wherever he was. When he broke his leg, he was riding in the back of a wagon, and the fit seized him. He fell beneath the wheel.

"His name was Isaac Henry Cress, and he always went by I.H. That's what Mama called him, too. I.H. He was a farmer, and traded in horses. The land we lived on had come down through the family for years and years, on back to the war with England. My great-grandfather once killed three Cherokees right where our house sat. My father told that story quite a bit. One of the Cherokees had killed a great-uncle of mine the day before, and they'd come for my great-grandfather, but he defeated them, and cut off their fingers to make a necklace from the finger bones. He wore it until the day he died, tucked down under his shirt.

"When the war broke out, my father went strong for the Union, but there was nothing he could do, being prone to fits. He couldn't be no soldier. But when the rebels' conscript commenced, a man sent word to Papa that they was going to conscript him, fits or no fits, and if he tried to get out of it, they'd kill him. This was going to be done by a man who had not liked my father for years before, because of trouble they'd had over the sale of some horses a long time ago. That's the way it is with so many of the war troubles. Folks use the war as a reason for settling up scores that don't really have nothing to do with it, you see.

"Papa knew he'd have to go to scouting so they wouldn't find him. He called me to him and says, 'Ollie, while I'm in the woods it'll be up to you to do the work and see to the protection of your mama and your sisters. I'll be watching, all I can, but there'll be times when I have to be out of sight of the house, and those times, you'll have to be the man of the house.' I says, 'Yes, sir.' So he headed out into the hills.

"Sure enough, the conscript man come along two days after that, with a few soldiers, and they talked mean and asked where my father was, and I told them he was gone off to Knoxville on business and wouldn't be back until the end of the year. They cussed and threatened me, and told me they'd make my mother and sisters walk down the road nekkid— pardon me for repeating that, ma'am—if I didn't tell where my father was. But wouldn't tell. So they come up and got me, and tied me to a tree and whupped on me, but I wouldn't talk to them. My mama come out—"

Amy interrupted. "Wait, Ollie. Go back. You say they whipped you?"

"Yes, ma'am. One of them had a forage rope that he'd stuck nails and pins through, and they used that. It hurt bad, and I bled, but I wouldn't squall for them. They told me to squall, but I would have let them whip me to death before I'd have give them the satisfaction. Well, after a time my mama come out on the porch with a shotgun that ain't worked in ten years, and waved it around and told them to leave me alone. They laughed at her, but ceased from whupping me and rode off, saying they'd be back and they'd have my father conscripted or see him in hell one . . . pardon me again, ma'am.

"Papa had been up in the woods and seen them riding up, but he hadn't been able to see when they was whupping me. He come back to the house that night, after dark, sneaking in the back, to see what had happened, and when he heard they'd whupped me, he cried. I never seen him cry before. He said that if he'd knowed they was doing that, he'd have come down and let them take him. I says, 'No, Papa, don't you never let them take you, for they'll take you into the woods and shoot you.' He said he'd rather be shot than have his own family whupped and threatened.

"He went back out into the hills, and everything was fairly good for a long time after. The conscript man never come back, but every now and then the Home Guard would ride through and threaten to burn us out, and ask where Papa was, but one of them had been sweet on my mama back when she was a girl, and because of that, I reckon, the Home Guard never did burn us down.

"Papa got thin as a garden snake out there in the hills, and just as brown as a darky from the weather, but he did pretty well as a scouter compared to some. He's always been good in the hills. We all sort of got used to it, Papa living like that, most of the time within pretty easy reach of the house. Every now and then he'd come in, when we thought it was safe, and eat a meal at the table, and even spend the night in his bed, with mama. But most of the time he was scouting. He told us he hadn't had a single fit since he'd took to the hills, and that if he went much longer without fits, he might try to join the United States Army. But he never got the chance.

"Cap Fletcher showed up in Johnson County, you see, out of Virginia. Him and his renegades called themselves Home Guards, but that was just foolish lies, for they weren't no such thing. Just bushwhacking thieves and killers, that's all. And my papa was one of the first men they killed in Johnson County.

"I suppose that's how they was able to fool us, you see. They come riding in, wearing bits and pieces of Union uniforms, and claiming to be good Union men on the run from Bozen's rebels and heading for the Union lines, and Cap Fletcher talked such good Union talk that Mama believed him. He had a fine McClellan saddle, with about a dozen cross marks branded into it, which I thought looked odd, and a new army pistol. He points to me and says, 'If that boy there was a mite older, I'd just take him with me through the lines and let him become a Union soldier.' That sounded fine to me, though I knew I couldn't leave, Mama and my sisters needing me with Papa out scouting. Mama says, 'I'd be proud for him to be a soldier, but he's too young and we need him anyhow, with his father gone.' Fletcher says, 'Not gone to the rebels, I hope?' And she says, 'No, just gone off scouting. He's a Union man.' I wished right then she hadn't have said that, for it give me a bad feeling. Like my grandpap always said it, I just felt the hell-breath down my neck when she said that. Fletcher grins and says, 'Where's he scouting? We got some good whiskey we'd like to give him, and some dried pork and parched corn we'd be glad to share.' Mama, fooled by him, turns to me and says, 'Ollie, take these men up to find your father.' I says, 'No, Mama, we don't know we can trust them,' and that made Fletcher mad. Mama got mad, too, and said she knew a good Union man when she seen one. So she made me lead them up to where Papa usually scouted.

"Well, I still didn't trust them, so I took them a different place where I knew he wouldn't be, and says, 'Well, I reckon he must be gone off somewhere.' Fletcher pulls out a knife and tells me that, 'By Gee,'—though of course he said the straight-out blasphemy—I'd 'best roust out old Daddy right fast' or I'd be 'skinned and eat.' I knowed then they really wasn't Union and Mama had been fooled. I told him I wouldn't do it, and a couple of them jumped down and grabbed me and tied me to a tree, belly-in. I knowed I was to be whupped again, and steeled myself for it.

"This bunch was meaner than the Home Guards, and used a leather strop. It broke my hide before long, and I couldn't hold back from yelling. Fletcher says, 'You going to tell us where dear Daddy is?' and I says no. They whupped me some more until I passed out for a while.

"When I come around again, Papa was there, and they had him. I reckon he'd seen them and what they was doing to me, and had come to give himself to them. But then I looked and seen there was one of them dead, shot through the head. It was the one who had whupped me. Papa had shot him from hiding, you see, before he turned himself in. I was proud of him for shooting that man, but I wished he hadn't, too, for now there was no chance they'd let him live.

"And they didn't. They killed him right there. Stood him up against a tree and run a bayonet through his neck, pinning him up like a doll, and then Fletcher come over and carved a cross mark onto his face. Fletcher's Cross, that's what they call it in the mountains. It's his way of marking the Union men he murders. Then they backed up and commenced to target practice on Papa, shooting at his chest. They just shot and shot until there was nothing left of his chest but a big old red hole. Fletcher told them to quit, they was wasting too much ammunition. Then they cut me down from the whupping tree, drug me down to the house, threw me in the yard before my mama and sisters, and Fletcher blasphemes again and tells Mama that her 'Gee-damned old Lincolnite husband' was dead and gone to hell. Then they took Mama, and all my sisters, and tore the clothes from them, and made them parade around that way before them, them laughing and saying dreadful things, and making them say indecent things back to them. After that they took anything worth taking from the house, and set it afire, and made us watch it burn. The only thing they didn't take from us was a 'possum we had fattening to eat out in a pen behind the smokehouse, and that was only because they didn't see it.

"We went to a neighbor's place, about a mile off, and they give clothes to my mama and sisters, and cleaned up my back and poulticed it. Then they went and fetched Papa's body in and buried him. But these neighbors had already been robbed of most of their food by the Home Guards, so they didn't have much to feed us. They sent my oldest sister back to the house, and she brought in the 'possum. They killed it and used the meat in stew, and that's how they fed their family that night, and mine, too. And after that we just stayed with them, me healing up some, all of us eating as best we could, which wasn't much, and making plans to get here to Knoxville. We found somebody who'd guide us for free, and now here we are. We're living in the white refugee camp, and what'll become of us, I don't know, but Mama says that God provides."

He was finished with his tale, and stopped talking. Amy had quit writing halfway through, too entranced and horrified by what she was hearing, but it didn't matter. Every detail was lodged in her memory.

"Ollie, you don't have to do this if you don't want . . . but would you let me see your back?"

His face showed the first sign that Amy had seen of emotion. He flinched slightly. Amy quickly told him to forget the request, she needn't see his back at all, but he shook his head. "I'll show you, if you really want me to."

Amy nodded.

Ollie Cress stood, turned, and pulled off his shirt. His back was a hideous mass of scabs and fresh scars. Amy stared, then turned her head away. Ollie put his shirt back on and turned to her.

"Reckon I should go back now, ma'am. I hope I told you enough."

"You did. Thank you, Ollie. And I'm sorry. About everything you've been through."

"We'll make it, ma'am."

She gave him money, more than she'd promised when she recruited him as an informant, but he did not reject the gratuity out of pride, as some did. Ollie Cress accepted it with quiet gratitude, said a whispered God bless you, and turned to go.

As he exited the office door, Amy called to him. "Ollie, one more thing . . . have you heard of a Union pilot, not from your county but from Carter County, named Greeley Brown?"

"Oh, yes, ma'am. A great and good man."

"Do you know where he is now?"

"Not for sure, ma'am, but the story is that Fletcher's raiders caught him and hung him from a tree, and beat on his body while he was choking to death. As I hear it, Fletcher himself has bragged about that one considerable. His 'finest Lincolnite killing,' he calls it."

Amy nodded. "Thank you, Ollie."

"You're welcome, ma'am. I hope you have you a good day." He headed out the door, through the office, and into the street, leaving Amy at her desk, slumped, staring, and full of sorrow.

Amy fell coming home that night, on her doorstep. Ben saw it and ran to her. She'd fallen facedown, her weight striking hard on her enlarged midsection. With his heart palpitating wildly, Ben went to her and helped her up.

His face was pale as paper. "Miss Amy, are you hurt?"

"I don't know . . . I don't think so . . ." She stood, slightly bent over, holding her belly. "The baby's kicking. That's good, I suppose."

"It's my fault, Miss Amy. I should have cleaned all that slush from the walkway."

"Let me sit down, Ben."

He led her to the sofa and helped her ease down. Pulling up a chair in front of her, he stared into her face, holding her left hand in his right one. She looked up into his intense gaze and frowned.

"For heaven's sake, Ben, get that look off your face. I'm fine. Just let me sit here for a while to be sure."

He looked down, but didn't let go of her hands. And as soon as she looked away from him, he was staring at her again. She gave him another frown and pulled her hand from his.

"Ben, I asked you to stop staring like that. And quit thinking what you're thinking, too. It had nothing to do with what you think it had to do with."

"What are you talking about, Miss Amy?"

"You know what I'm talking about. This curse of Nanny's."

"Why, I didn't say a thing about that."

"You were thinking it."

"Well . . . you must have been, too. You brung it up."

Amy suddenly put her hand on her belly.

"Miss Amy . . ."

"It's nothing, Ben. That one was my stomach. I've gotten good at distinguishing my pains lately—heaven knows I've got plenty of them. The baby kicking, my joints aching, stomach burning . . ."

"When's that baby supposed to get here?"

"Sometime in June. Maybe the first part of July."

"Not all that long either way."

They didn't talk further for a minute or so. Amy sat concentrating on what her body was telling her, feeling her belly with her hand, brows knitting.

"Everything seem all right?" Ben asked.

"Yes. Yes. I believe everything is fine."

"Not just saying that?"

"No. Really, I don't think any harm was done. But that was frightening."

"Yes indeed. I'm going to be keeping a close watch on you this evening, whether you like it or not. We got to take care of that baby."

Amy smiled and patted the back of his hand. "I see that I was wise to bring you back here. You do take good care of me, Ben."

"I do my best. After all you've did for me, why, I owe it to you to make sure you are all right. And I feel like I owe it to your husband, too. Adam was good to me. Since he can't be here to see to you, I figure he'd want me to do it. Not that I think I could ever, you know, replace him or nothing."

"You're sweet, Ben. I'm sure Adam knows what you're doing and appreciates it as much as I do."

"You know what I'm thinking? I'm thinking you've been working too hard. You ought to give up going to the office and such. End these interviews with refugees and suffering folks. You need to be thinking good thoughts. Happy things. A woman with child ought always to be thinking on happy things. It's good for the baby, and the baby's what you need to be concentrating on these days."

"And since when did you become so expert on maternity?"

"It's just good common sense."

"You know, I suppose it is. Maybe you're right. Maybe I ought to end the interviews for now." Her face grew sad. "I heard the most terrible story today, about this ruffian named Fletcher. God help us, what a terrible story."

"See there? That's just the kind of thing you don't need to be hearing right now. Let it go for a time. Them refugees will be around for a long while yet. Let your baby come, then you can go back to what you do as soon as you're able."

"I'll think about it. But with Horatio coming, I'll still be needing to talk to him."

"Well and good. But even he'll keep. The thing for you to do is get yourself rested up. Get ready for Adam's little feller to come into the world all healthy and strong."

Amy nodded. She had been jarred emotionally even before the fall by the terrible story she'd heard from young Ollie Cress. The fall had shaken her even worse. For once, Amy Deacon Hanover was willing to listen to someone else's advice, even that of Ben Scarlett, who knew little more about maternity than a bird dog knew about the rules of Congress.

"I will rest. You're right. From now on, the welfare of my child comes first."

"Good. So you'll start taking it easy tomorrow, right?"

"Right."

Ben grinned and nodded.

He went to bed that night feeling pleased with Amy's new attitude. He'd long known she had been pushing herself too hard, not making sufficient accommodation for her pregnancy. Maybe that fall she'd taken, potentially harmful as it was, had actually done some good. Starting tomorrow, she was going to take better care of herself. She had promised that, and he'd hold her to it.

Ben fell asleep knowing what he would be doing come tomorrow. If it was possible, he'd perform the task that had come to his mind during that snowy walk when he had stood watching the smoke plumes rising over the contraband camp. He knew now that he should have gone ahead and taken care of that matter as soon as he'd thought of it that day, instead of heading home and getting drunk like a fool old sinner. If he hadn't put it off, maybe Amy wouldn't have fallen today. He knew what was behind that fall, even if she didn't. There were forces trying to harm her that went beyond her limited rationalistic understanding.

He went to sleep thinking how ironic it was that intellectual folks like Amy tended to believe in far too little. It was a good thing folks like her had good old common people like him to take care of them, folks not so blinded by education and intellect that they couldn't recognize a hex at work even when it literally knocked them to the floor.

Chapter 25

Skunk Linden eyed Ben Scarlett's window and noted that it was dark. Good. Old Ben was off somewhere, or maybe asleep. Skunk patted his bulging coat pocket, then felt inside to make sure the note was in there. It was.

He headed across the street, pausing at the area where he'd lost his bottle the other day in the now-melted snow. He sighed, wondering what fortunate person had found it. That had been some cussed good whiskey. Well, such was life.

He went a few steps farther, glanced about, and mounted the staircase leading to Ben's room. He climbed slowly, taking care to make very little noise, and at the top removed the contents of his coat pocket. He snickered to himself. A bit of sacrifice involved in this little gift, but worth it. Ben wasn't a completely ruined fellow—he had allowed him to spend the night in his warm room, even though it was against the rules—but Ben had a self-righteousness that galled him to no end. It had been downright cruel of Ben to make him abandon his search for his missing bottle the other day, and to humiliate him besides by hitting him with snowballs. Had Ben forgotten what it was like to be humiliated? Did Ben not realize that the way he had treated him was the very way uppity people had treated Ben not that long ago? In Skunk's opinion, Ben had become the very kind of man he had once himself despised.

Ben Scarlett was due a good taking-down. He and his big talk about never drinking again! It was giving up drinking that ruined Ben. But a ruined man could be unruined, and made to eat his prideful words in the process.

Skunk left what he had brought beside Ben's door.

Let's see how you resist temptation when it's right on your doorstep, Ben! Let's see if you never drink again! Let's see if you have any grounds to preach at me next time our paths cross!

Skunk slipped on down the stairs again, very proud of himself. He was a clever man, no question about it.

Ben Scarlett was frustrated. He had planned to go to the contraband camp on the sneak the first chance that came, but the day proved no such chances.

Amy, meanwhile, was proving true to her word. She had an entirely different mien than she typically displayed; it was as if she'd taken a burden off her shoulders and laid it aside. No talk about interviewing refugees. No realizations that she must run by her office and fetch this or that. She moved slowly, carefully, and was cheerful to the point of being lighthearted. Apparently she had meant it when she said she would change her ways until the baby was born.

There, ironically, was part of his problem. Amy kept him close at hand all day, doing tasks for her that she normally did herself, running errands that only a day or two back she would have never considered passing on to anyone else. The day slipped by, and no chance to go to the contraband camp came.

Ben retired that night in bitter defeat, wondering if it would be the same the next day. Probably so. He considered giving up his fears about Nanny's curse and adopting Amy's viewpoint. She was far more intelligent than he, after all.

But what if she was wrong? What could it hurt to go find Nanny and have her undo whatever mystical thing she had done? If matters were as Miss Amy said, and words really couldn't afflict supernatural harm on others, well then, it wouldn't hurt anything for Nanny to mutter a few more words. But if words *could* invoke true harm, if there really *was* something to curses and the like, having Nanny revoke the one she placed on Miss Amy's child could literally make the difference between living and dying.

Just as Ben feared, the next day was as busy as the last one. Amy undertook a great cleaning of her house. How had she so swiftly accumulated so much pure junk? Ben wondered. But of course the real work fell to him. Again a day went by with no opportunity to visit the contraband camp. Ben retired that night with visions of Nanny leaving the contraband camp, traveling toward Nashville, Louisville, some other distant city, going out of his reach forever while her lips continually renewed the evil curse she had placed on an innocent child not yet even privileged to see the light of the sun.

Ben slept fitfully that night, and the next day worked hard again, ironically restrained by Miss Amy's obedience to his own suggestion of a new, calmer, and safer way of life for her. He felt he might explode. Evidently he was going to have to come up with some pretext and get away from her for a few hours.

But as he thought of that, he realized part of the reason Miss Amy was keeping him so busy. It wasn't all for her own sake. It was for his. He knew that she knew he had gotten drunk despite his vows, and she was keeping him so occupied that he had no opportunity to get drunk again.

So he couldn't make some excuse and get away long enough to find Nanny. If he did, she would believe he was doing it merely to go out and drink.

He lay down that night puzzling over what to do, and fell asleep flat on his back out of sheer weariness from all the work she'd been putting him through.

Amy's scream awakened him just after midnight. Ben rose with a bodily jerk so hard it felt for a moment like he'd been shot all over again. He hit the floor on a run, pounding his head against the frame of his bedroom door in his hurry to get out.

He found her sitting up in bed, breathless but already beginning to look ashamed as she realized that she had screamed, like some impressionable little girl, over nothing more than a nightmare.

Ben sat down on the stool beside her bed. "What did you dream?"

"Nothing. Nothing important. Dreams are just thoughts. They don't matter."

Yes they do, dear stubborn Miss Amy, just like curses do, whether you admit it or not! "Tell me anyhow. There's an old saying that if you tell a bad dream to somebody while it's still fresh, you'll never have it again." Not bad for an old saying I just made up, Ben thought.

"I dreamed . . . I dreamed I lost my baby."

Ben's jaw grew rigid. *Lord, no. Don't let that curse be working here. Lord, put that curse on me, if that'll take it off her baby. Bring me the trouble, if there has to be trouble, but don't let it strike Miss Amy or that child.*

Amy looked at Ben and forced a smile. "I know you're probably thinking one of your silly ideas again, Ben," she said. "But remember, a dream really doesn't matter. And besides, now that I've told you what it was, I'll never dream it again. Right?"

"That's right." Ben didn't add that it wasn't a recurrence of the dream that concerned him, but the possibility that the dream might become a reality. He tried to sound as casual as possible when he said, "Miss Amy, would you feel better if I pulled up some blankets on the other side of your door there and stayed close by the rest of the night?"

"No, Ben. That isn't necessary. It was only a dream. Go on back to your bed."

He went back to his room, but did not get in bed. Instead he sat down in a straight-backed chair with a blanket over his shoulders and his door open. He stared the rest of the night at Amy's door across the hall, ready to leap up and bolt through it at the first odd sound or outcry.

None came. By the time dawn lighted the sky, Ben was freshly asleep in the chair, the blanket having slipped from his shoulders to the floor. Amy found him that way.

Poor Ben. He was such a worrier. It could get irritating sometimes, yet she had to love him for it. He meant well.

She returned to her room and began bumping about, making enough noise to waken him, so he wouldn't realize she had already been up, and seen him sitting there in his chair, a one-handed sentry guarding a widowed mother against the curse of a bitter slave girl. What an odd gang we are! Amy thought. When Adam had died on that street in Nashville, he had left her in a strange world indeed.

Horatio Eaton showed up the next day, just before noon.

Ben found meeting the man to be an odd experience, because he'd had contact with him once before, indirectly and in odd circumstances. A threat had been voiced against Eaton's life by none other than Amy's own father, and Ben was set up to be the scapegoat. He had sent Eaton a warning letter, then fled Knoxville.* Now, as he shook the nervous little abolitionist's hand, all that came back to him, and evidently to Eaton as well, because before they had finished the luncheon that Amy set out for them all at the *Sage* office, the matter had come up and been talked out. It wasn't a pleasant conversation for any of them, because it revived many tense memories, but when they were through, each had a sense of resolution. It was good that they'd talked. Then came up the matter of Amy's contact with Horatio Eaton's cousin, Jonathan Eaton, who, as an agent of the Federal government, had recruited Amy for the currency smuggling work that got her captured and wounded. Horatio felt partly responsible for what had happened to her, he confessed, and once again airing the affair and all the feelings surrounding it had a purging effect.

Conversation in the afternoon turned toward less stressful subjects: Eaton's ideas for reviving his old publication, and Amy's parallel concepts. Excitement grew between the pair, and Ben found himself slipping into the background. It was the first time in days that he saw an opportunity to get away and try to take care of the matter at the contraband camp. During a brief absence by Amy, Ben told Eaton that he was stepping out for a while and would be back that night. Would he mention this to Amy when she returned? Eaton naturally had no objection, and Ben made his escape.

He trekked through the town, thinking about what he was about to do and growing nervous. Right now a good drink

* See *The Shadow Warriors*, Book I of The Mountain War Trilogy.

would go far to settle his nerves. . . . Out of the question, of course. He trudged on, until the camp came into view.

His nerve failed him. The last time he'd seen Nanny had been the night he was shot. Though he had recovered well from the wound, the idea of facing her again revived all the fears that went with such a bad wounding. He didn't want to see Nanny, nor speak to her. And what if Cat Kingsley was in that camp? There was a face he truly didn't want to see again.

But as he thought about Amy's dream and the scream it wrenched out of her, he knew he had to go on. Nobody else was going to deal with this curse business. It was up to him, and he wouldn't fail.

A drink surely would be nice right now. It'd be a lot easier to do this job if I had a bit of something to steady my nerves.

He was striding toward the camp again when he saw the two boys who had brought that tattered letter to Amy back at the first of the year. They were hiding behind a woodshed on down an embankment upon which Ben was standing, unseen, smoking pipes . . . and they had something else, too. He paused and looked closely.

A bottle. These boys had a bottle of whiskey, passing it back and forth, turning it up to their lips.

Ben began to tremble. That bottle looked mighty enticing. Surely it wouldn't hurt to . . .

Yes, it would hurt, and he knew it. Steeling his will, he forced himself to look at those boys and see in them an image of himself when he was their age, sneaking drinks, putting his first footsteps onto the road that had almost destroyed him.

The righteous side of Ben Scarlett, the one that so disgusted Skunk Linden, asserted itself. Throwing up his chin, Ben came down the embankment like one of heaven's angels descending from heights above. His appearance was so sudden that both boys dropped their pipes in surprise and came to their feet.

"You boys! What are you doing there?"

"Nothing. Who are you?"

"Never you mind that. I know what you're doing here. You're back here drinking whiskey."

"What of it? Ain't your business, is it?"

"You bet it's my business, boy! I know what that stuff can lead to. I know what it can do to a feller. You give me that bottle right now, hear?"

"You ain't getting our whiskey!"

"What would your daddy say if he knew you was drinking that stuff, huh?"

"He'd say, what the hell you boys doing with my whiskey?" one of the two replied, and the other laughed.

"What about your mama, then?"

"She'd say, give me a swig of that, you little poots!" More laughter.

"Well . . . if your folks ain't going to keep you on the straight and narrow, somebody's got to."

"You ain't getting this whiskey, you big turd!"

The second boy asked, "What do you care what we do? What's any of this to you, old man?"

Had the boy been able to see into Ben's mind, he would have found the question he'd just asked had already crept up inside Ben. Why was he doing this? He had come down off that bank in a fire of righteousness, but already ideas not so righteous were beginning to creep in. If he could get that bottle from them, shoo them off . . .

"You just want this whiskey for yourself!" the first boy declared.

Yes, I do, Ben thought. No, I don't. *I do, but I don't . . . I won't.*

He'd smash that bottle, right before their eyes. Prove to them, and to himself, that he could do what was right.

"Give me that bottle, right now."

"I won't do it!"

"Hey, look there, Bert—he's got a hook for a hand!"

"That's right," Ben said, brandishing the fearsome-looking prosthetic. "And I'll hook your eyeballs right out if you don't give me that bottle. I'm going to save you boys from a life of drunkenness." *No, that ain't true. I'm going to get it and drink it myself! No I ain't! I'm going to smash it!* So went the struggle in his mind, back and forth.

Ben lunged quickly while the boys were still fixated on the hook. He snatched the bottle away before they realized it.

"Well! Now I got it!"

"Give it back!"

"No . . . no, I'm going to take it off somewhere and smash it."

"I'll bet he's just an old drunk, Sammy. He's going to drink our whiskey."

"That's not true. I was a drunk, but by the grace of the Lord Jesus I've turned away from my sin, and I don't drink no more."

"I didn't think the Lord Jesus liked stealing, fool!"

"Show some respect for your elders, son."

"He's a big liar, Bert. He's going to drink that, sure as the world."

"I won't!"

"Then let's see you smash that bottle right here and now!"

"Well, I . . ."

"See there? He's a drunk, sure as sin! He's stole our whiskey!"

Ben lifted the bottle as if to smash it, but his arm froze in place. He stood there like an absurd statue.

"Come on, mister! Don't smash that bottle! Give it back . . . we'll share it with you."

Share it . . . *A drink surely would go down good right now.*

Ben never knew how he summoned the fortitude to do it, but from somewhere, it came. He flung the bottle to the ground, as hard as he could. It smashed. The whiskey flowed out, soaking into the dirt.

"I be damned!" one of the boys murmured. "He really done it!"

Ben felt like laughing and crying all at once. Part of him wanted to sing a hymn, another to drop on all fours and lap the whiskey-dampened ground.

Suddenly he was weak. He wanted to sit down. To lie down.

"You boys . . . get on out of here."

"I'll tell our pa!"

"No you won't. 'Cause he'd flay you for stealing his bottle. Go on . . . get away."

They ran off, cursing at him as soon as they were well out of hook range. Ben let the abuse roll over him and off him. Then they were gone.

He didn't sit down. He stood looking at the broken bottle, then chuckled. "Look there what you done, Ben! Maybe you're a stronger man than you know."

He shook off his torpor and resumed his trek toward the contraband camp.

Chapter 26

They stared at him with hollow, hungry eyes, these people who had longed for freedom and now had it, only to find that it was no more than a new kind of bondage with evils all its own. Ben Scarlett moved up and down the rows of huts and tents, looking for the well-known face of Nanny among the scores of unfamiliar ones. He did not see her.

"Mister."

Ben turned. A small, dark girl in rags looked up at him. "Yes, honey?"

"You got food, mister?"

"No, honey, I don't."

Her sad face grew more so, and she turned away.

"Honey, wait." Expectantly she turned, eyes brighter. "Tell me something: Do you know a woman in this camp name of Nanny?"

The sadness returned. She shook her head, turned away again.

"Uh . . . hold on. Just a minute." Ben dug into his pocket and pulled out a coin. He handed it to her. "There you go. For your family."

She took it with a look of awe, and stared at him, too dumb-struck to say a thank you, but he knew, even without her saying it, what she felt. He smiled at her, and she smiled back, and ran away.

Ben went on, looking at all who were outside and, when he could, peering through tent flaps and shelter doors to try to make out the faces of those inside. No Nanny. He was disheartened, partly, also a bit relieved.

He went on, turned down another row, and noticed he was being followed. Children. Two of them, then three, then four. They had seen him give the little girl the coin.

Ben faced them. "I'm sorry. I got no more."

He saw their disappointment, and it broke his heart. They turned away, slowly scattering.

Ben cursed slavery. These people might no longer be slaves in the technical sense, but it was slavery that had brought them into a society that made no adequate provision for them to live in any state but bondage. Seeing their sorrowful condition, particularly that of the children, made him understand anew, and appreciate, what drove Miss Amy, and Horatio Eaton, and others like them who saw farther and deeper than most of the people around them.

It took longer than Ben had anticipated to tour the entire camp, and when he finally reached the end, Nanny remained unfound. He asked a question or two of some who didn't appear too frightened or cautious of him, but answers were not forthcoming. All he asked denied any knowledge of any woman there named Nanny. Soon Ben realized that he would probably receive no help even if those he queried *did* know of her. These people had no reason to trust a white stranger who appeared among them, asking unexplained questions.

He made another round of the camp, a little more quickly this time, hoping he would have better luck. He did not. He looked at the sky, growing cloudy and dark. The wind was beginning to blow in with the dusk. He realized how long he'd been gone, and that Miss Amy was probably beginning to worry.

Ben was full of distress. Nanny wasn't here, and the odds were he would never find her. He could only hope that Miss

Amy was right about hexes and so on, because it didn't seem probable that he was going to be able to do anything about it. Well, at least he'd tried.

But what about the baby? What if something bad happens to the baby? I'll spend the rest of my days wondering why I took so long to look for Nanny. I might have found her if I'd come looking sooner.

Dejected and very tired, Ben began trudging back toward home. His route out of the camp took him to a wooded stretch where a dirty, trash-filled creek flowed. A narrow footbridge made of two logs pinned together spanned the somnolent little waterway, just inside the shadow line of the woods. Ben set foot onto it and started across, watching his feet to make sure he didn't slip off the slick, worn logs.

"Well, look here!"

The voice, very slurred but instantly recognizable, made him jerk his head upright, then suck in his breath. On the other side of the bridge, in the woods, stood a dark figure he knew at once.

"Cat . . . I figured you were gone from here."

"That right? Then what'd you come here looking for?"

"I came looking for Nanny."

Another figure moved near Cat as he said that name. Ben squinted into the thickening dark. Nanny was there, staring at him with wide and fearful eyes.

"Nanny, huh? Why you want Nanny?" Cat sounded quite drunk, which put Ben on edge. Cat was known throughout Knoxville as being mean all the time, but all the meaner when he had liquor in his belly.

"Because she did something she shouldn't have. She put a hex on Miss Amy's baby. Hexed it to die."

Cat roared with laughter. Ben felt blood rising in his face, anger joining with his fear. How could he laugh at such a wicked thing as cursing a baby?

Ben looked away from Cat and at Nanny. "It was an evil thing to do, Nanny. I come down here to find you and get you to take off that hex."

Nanny had some trouble finding her voice. "There wasn't no real hex . . . it was just something I said. I was mad at her. I ain't no witch. I got no power to hex nobody."

"Well, maybe not. Miss Amy don't believe in curses at all, no matter who casts them. But me, I ain't so sure. I want you to take off that curse, just in case."

"I done did it. I done took it off . . . just in case."

"You ain't lying to me, are you?"

"I ain't lying. I took it off almost right away."

"I hope you really did. Because Miss Amy has fell once already, right on her belly, and that ain't even counting when you pushed her down. And she's took to dreaming about losing her baby."

Nanny's voice grew higher. "She ain't lost it, has she? Say she ain't!"

"She ain't. Not yet. I want to make sure it stays that way."

"I done lifted the curse, like I told you. But I'll lift it again, if you want me to. I lift the curse on Miss Amy's baby! There. Now you heard it yourself."

Suddenly Ben felt foolish. Hearing those meager-sounding words made the whole thing seem absurd. Surely Miss Amy had been right all along, and he'd wasted his time coming down here. But there was also a trace of relief. Who could know certainly that a tragedy had not been averted here? It was like he had said . . . it made sense to deal with even ridiculous possibilities, just in case.

"Thank you, Nanny. You done the right thing there." He turned his attention to Cat again. "You shouldn't have shot me, Cat. You might have killed me."

"Huh! But I didn't, did I? You look mighty strong and healthy to me, Ben Scarlett!"

"I was down under for some days because of that wound. They said it was the shock of it, or something like that. They said that for a while I could have died."

"So there ain't no danger now, huh? No reason for you to be down here bothering old Cat."

"I told you I didn't come here for you, Cat. I'd hoped I'd never lay eyes on you again. I come for Nanny. Now my business is done, and I'm going on home."

"Your business . . . but what about mine?"

"You got no business with me, Cat. You're danged lucky I don't go find me a peace officer and have you arrested. I could, you know."

"That's right. You could. And that's what my business is, Ben. I want to make sure that don't happen."

Nanny said, "Cat, no! Just let him go!"

"Let him go? How do I know he won't go straight to the law, huh?"

"I won't do that, Cat," Ben said. "All I want is to be through with you."

"Same way I feel about you, Ben." Cat reached beneath his coat and came out with a knife. "I want to be through with you once and for all."

Nanny began to cry, pleading for Cat to put the knife away.

"I'll put it away when I'm through with it."

Nanny said, "He's drunk, Ben. He's been drunk most the day. He'll kill you! Run!"

It sounded like a very good suggestion to Ben. He turned on the footbridge—too quickly. His feet went out from under him and he came down hard on the edge of the bridge, then off and into the stream, head downward. Something jarred hard against his skull, and it was almost like striking that press crate after Cat shot him, but this time he struck the other side of his head. His ears rang and his vision wavered. He thought, I need to get up . . . but his body wouldn't obey. Water washed over his face. He was in the stream, head submerged.

Water sucked into his mouth, then his lungs. Still he couldn't move. Panic filled him. He heard someone laughing— Cat. He tried again to move, and this time, praise be, his head came up and his face broke the surface of the water. He crabbed back toward the bank, spitting and coughing dirty water, and blinked until his vision cleared. He looked up and saw Cat coming toward him. He had come down the opposite bank and was splashing into the water, staggering drunk, grinning and swearing, knife glinting in his right hand.

Ben struggled to rise, but fell. His head seemed to be spinning. "No, Cat . . ."

Then Nanny was at Cat's side, grabbing his arm, pleading and crying and yelling, trying to pull him away. Cat jerked free, swearing at her. She grabbed him again by the shoulder, and he slashed at her hand with his knife. Nanny pulled her hand off at the last half second, and Cat drunkenly ended up slashing his own arm. He roared and cursed all the louder. Ben, still trying to get up, saw Nanny begin slapping at him, kicking, telling him she hated him, telling him not to hurt Ben Scarlett.

You tell him, Nanny. You just keep telling him. Ben pushed to his feet and tried to get up the bank, but it was muddy and slick and he fell again. Something grabbed his shoulder. Cat's left hand. Despite a strong urge to squeeze his eyes shut, he looked. Cat was swinging back his right hand, still holding the knife.

Now Ben did close his eyes. But the knife didn't strike, and Cat's hand pulled off his shoulder. Ben opened his eyes again. Nanny was on Cat, literally on him, legs wrapped around his middle, her arms around his neck and under one armpit. He flailed and swore, and Ben saw the knife suddenly dislodge from the massive hand and fall into the water.

For a moment Ben gazed stupidly at the knife, which moved and changed shapes beneath the prisming, slow-moving water. Cat fell, Nanny still clinging to him. The water whipped and flailed as if filled with frantic snakes.

Ben came to his knees in the water, mere feet away from the thrashing man-woman fight. He fixed his eyes on the knife, crawled toward it, reached . . .

Cat threw Nanny off himself; she came down atop Ben's outstretched arm, driving it, and him, down. His face submerged again and he could not lift it. He felt the knife beneath his hand, but with Nanny's weight crushing him, couldn't close his fingers around it.

Nanny rolled over him, then off him. He grasped the knife, pulled it up, but then something struck him—Nanny, slipping and falling as she tried to stand. Ben twisted his head and saw Cat lunging his way, splashing through the water.

Ben glanced toward the bridge, the bank, hoping to see people there who would intervene and halt this madness. But there was no one there. No one to see, no one to intercede.

Cat lunged at Ben, but Ben rolled away, just in time, and Cat missed him and came down in the water. Ben pulled up to a sitting position, then to his feet. The knife was in his hand.

Cat rose, very swiftly. He had a rock in his hand. He came at Ben from a slightly unexpected angle, so when Ben slashed at him with the knife, he missed. The stone in Cat's hand did not.

It hit Ben in the jaw, knocking him down, stunning him. Then Cat was somehow atop him, lifting the rock. Ben swung up his left arm and the hook there caught Cat in the fleshy portion under his right upper arm. The rock came down but missed Ben's head. Ben hooked at Cat again, failing to connect. His right shoulder had struck stones along the bank, sending pain ripping through the tender place the bullet had pierced him. Hot torment filled his side, his arm, and gave way to a fast numbness so thorough that he could not feel the knife in his fingers.

Cat brought the rock up, down. Ben took a glancing blow on the right side of his forehead, taking off flesh and driving Ben into the blackest of pits, where there was no more sound or vision, and all battling ceased.

He did not know what hour it was when he reached the base of the stairs leading up to his room. He did not recall that he was no longer living there, but down at Amy's house. For that matter, he did not recall how he had even traveled from the contraband camp back to this place.

All he knew was that he was battered, bleeding, sore all over, and that when he had come out of that black pit, Cat Kingsley had been lying dead in the stream, the knife that Ben had held stuck deep into his side. Nanny was nowhere to be seen.

I've killed a man, Ben thought. All I was trying to do was get away, and I've killed a man. I don't even remember doing it . . . but he's dead.

The stairs stretched up before him, seeming endless. He put his foot on the first one, grasped the rail with his still partly numb right hand, which required him to reach across himself and made his posture ill-suited for climbing. But he couldn't grip the rail with his hook.

He climbed slowly, taking an eternity. When he reached the top he was exhausted. He saw something there—a cloth sack, a note pinned to it, something inside the sack. Kneeling, he looked at it. The note was scribbled, hard to read, but he made out the words:

A litull somthing for you Ben from yur freind Skunk Linden

Ben pulled open the cloth sack. A whiskey bottle. Full.

There was no inner debate this time. No struggle at all, like there had been with that bottle he had taken from those boys. *Thank you, Skunk. God bless you.*

He made it inside the dark room with the bottle. Pulling out the cork with his teeth, he took a long swallow. It was purging, healing, everything he needed. *Thank you, Skunk. You're the best friend a man ever had.*

He leaned back against the wall, catching his wind, trying to relax and quit hurting. He took another pull of the whiskey, and began to cry.

"I've killed a man, Skunk," he said out loud to the dark room. "I've gone and killed Cat Kingsley. Killed him with a knife." He sobbed, and everything he said after that was blubber and nonsense.

He was drunk and almost asleep when he realized he couldn't stay where he was. His mind filled with images of policemen and soldiers, scouring the town for Ben Scarlett, the murderer. He was sure they would see it that way—murder. There had been no witnesses, except Nanny, and she was gone. And she'd as likely take Cat's side of things as his. She might have fought Cat, but when it came down to it, she and Cat were of the same race. They were lovers, too. She'd surely tell them that Ben Scarlett had murdered Cat Kingsley in cold blood, out of vengeance for the shooting in the *Sage* office.

He had to leave. Had to get away . . .

Miss Amy. What about Miss Amy? How could he go, just leave her right now, with her pregnant and nobody else to care for her?

Then he recalled there was somebody else. There was Horatio Eaton. He had come to Knoxville wanting to stay. Well, now he could. He could take over care of Amy Hanover. Ben knew he had to give it up now. Had to run. He'd killed a man.

"Good-bye, Miss Amy," he said aloud. "I got to go. I'll . . . I'll leave you a letter. . . ."

He half walked, half crawled to his table by the window.

Opening it, he found the pad upon which he had scribbled line after line of his secret song, his lament over the wickedness of war. It seemed foolish now. To the devil with it. Ben Scarlett had no songs left in him. He had killed a man, and now he was a drunk again besides. He knew he crossed a line when he drank from the bottle Skunk left him. It took the power of will not to drink, and he had no will left to draw on.

Ben found his pen and inkwell. Dipping the pen into the ink, too far, he flipped open the pad and began scrawling a message. He'd leave it right here, on the desk. She'd come looking here when he didn't show up at her house. She'd find it.

He wished he could see her again, talk to her in person. But obviously that couldn't be, if for no other reason than that he was a drunk again. She'd have to fire him. Well, he'd just save her that trouble. He'd fire himself, take off from here. Leave Knoxville behind. He had to leave anyway. He'd killed a man.

He finished his message, only half aware of what he'd written. He went to his closet, pulled out what clothing he hadn't taken down to Miss Amy's. Lacking a valise or carpetbag or any other real luggage, he pulled the case off the extra pillow on the bed and stuffed the clothing into it. He took another swig from the bottle, stoppered the neck, and threw the bottle in, too. Then he left the room and went out onto the landing. He made it halfway down on foot, fell the remaining half. He rose, then felt around on the pillow case and was glad to find his bottle wasn't broken.

He headed down the street, scared out of his rationality, hurting, and drunk. He figured he'd walk well out of the city, but he made it no farther than Baumgardner's old store before he knew he had to stop. He turned down the alley and found the door of Baumgardner's shed unlocked. Staggering in, he closed the door behind him, sank onto the floor in the pitch-blackness, and went to sleep.

Ben awakened the next morning, head aching. For a few moments he was puzzled at being in Baumgardner's old shed, but then he remembered, and sorrow came.

He rose and walked out into the light. The events of the prior evening played through his mind, sickening him. He remembered his maudlin hours of drinking up in his room, the note he wrote to Miss Amy.

The note . . . what had he written? He had been drunk and despairing when he penned it. He couldn't remember a bit of what the note contained. Better go back and see, he decided. He might have said too much. There was no reason for Miss Amy to know all that had happened. This was his burden and trouble. No reason that it should become hers.

Ben slipped through the alley and onto the street, but only after looking carefully about to make sure no one was likely to notice him. He headed up the walk briskly, feeling exposed, feeling like the law was around the next corner, waiting to apprehend him. Ben Scarlett . . . killer of Cat Kingsley. Ben knew nothing about what the law would consider murder, or what it wouldn't. He would take no chances. He'd spent too many drunken years on the wrong side of the law to start trusting it now.

He reached the base of the stairs leading up to his room and climbed quickly, despite a great soreness of body. His old shoulder wound throbbed. He was out of breath when he reached the landing. He fumbled for his key, found it, and as he extended it to the lock, the door pulled open and away from him and he found himself face-to-face with a haggard-looking Horatio Eaton. Eaton, as surprised as Ben, jumped back from the door with a yelp.

"Mr. Scarlett!" he said. "Merciful day, sir, you scared me! But thank God I've found you!"

"What are you doing up here?"

"Looking for you! I've been looking for you for hours! So did Mrs. Hanover, though I finally persuaded her to go to bed a couple of hours ago. I told her I'd keep looking the rest of the night, if need be. When you didn't return to the house last night, she became very worried. She gave me the key to your room here, and I've been here four times now, hoping I'd find you'd shown up since the last time. And I'm surprised to see that you have now . . . I just found your note, you see. I'd missed it the other times." Eaton held out the torn and scribbled sheet.

"My note . . . yeah. That's what I came back to find."

"I read it, Mr. Scarlett, but I could name little sense of it. Something about trouble, and you being sorry, and saying you had to leave Knoxville. That's why it surprised me so to see you at the door. I was just leaving to take the note to Mrs. Hanover."

"I want to see it first."

Eaton, looking thoroughly puzzled, gave Ben the note. He scanned it quickly, ashamed at how sloppily, drunkenly written it was, and the garbled content. He was deeply relieved, however, to note that he had written nothing about the fight with Cat, and the stabbing. Ben wadded the note and thrust it into his pocket. "No need for that, I don't reckon. You can give Miss Amy my message yourself."

"Mr. Scarlett, please come with me, back to Mrs. Hanover. She's been so worried, and she'll be relieved to see you are alive and . . . well." He said the last word tentatively, having looked Ben over and seen that he didn't really look well at all. He was bruised, with a large scabbed area on his forehead where skin had been abraded away almost to the bone.

"I can't go back."

"Look, sir, I don't know what 'trouble' it is your note was talking about, but whatever it is, I'm sure it can be dealt with. Please do come back with me."

"No, no. I can't sir, as much as I wish I could. Ain't no reason to talk about the trouble . . . it's my problem, nobody else's. Just tell Miss Amy that . . . tell her I broke her liquor rule, and that I know from how I'm feeling that I'll be breaking it again and again. Tell her old Ben's lost control, lost his will, but that he'll be fine. He'll get back on the track again, on his own. She won't have to nurse me through it this time."

"Sir, I wish you'd reconsider about—"

"No! Just listen, so you can tell her. Tell her that there's things that have happened that make me have to go away for a while. Tell her I'll be going east, probably, maybe to find some folks I've knowed before who was good to me and helped me out in other times of trouble. Tell her I hate to leave without seeing that baby born, but there ain't no other way. And tell her I ain't worried about that baby anymore. I believe now it's going to be fine."

"Mr. Scarlett, why not simply tell her these things yourself?"

"I don't want her to see me like I am now. But I will see her, later on. Maybe when she comes east herself, for she's been talking about that, heading in closer to the mountains where she can write about the troubles there."

"Yes, she told me yesterday about that plan," Eaton said. "You'll be in that area . . . Jonesborough, Elizabethton?"

"I expect so. But don't let her look for me. I'll come find her, when I'm back on the track again."

"Mr. Scarlett, please, do come with me. You don't seem in any condition to be making major decisions."

"The decision's done been made for me, sir. Take good care of Miss Amy for me, Mr. Eaton. Tell her that old Ben will be thinking of her every day, and that sweet little one when it comes along."

"Is there anything else, sir?"

"Just tell her that I love her an awful lot. That I'm still Ben, and still her friend, if she's willing to keep me. And I reckon that's all. I'm going now. Don't follow me. Don't you let her send nobody else to follow me, either. I mean it."

Ben turned and went back down the stairs. He remembered he'd left his pillowcase luggage in the Baumgardner shed. He'd fetch it, quickly, and head out of Knoxville by the hidden ways known to dogs, boys, and veteran town drunks.

Amy Hanover was past tears by the time a policeman came calling the next morning. When she opened the door to the uniformed man, fear jolted her. She was certain he'd come to tell her they had found Ben dead. She let him in amid rising dread and invited him to sit, but he declined.

His choice of words initially seemed to confirm her fear, but not for long. "Mrs. Hanover, I've come to tell you that a corpse was found yesterday morning in some woods over near the contraband camp. A local man, nigra, name of Cat Kingsley. The same one who robbed your building and shot your employee name of . . ." He consulted a little note pad. ". . . Scarlett. Benjamin Scarlett."

"Cat Kingsley is dead?"

"That's right, ma'am, and I figured you'd want to know. He was stabbed to death, left side. As best we can determine, he'd been hiding out at the contraband camp since he robbed your place. Some say he was with a woman, who may or may not have been that nigra gal who was working for you. It seems that earlier in the day, Cat had collected some money from another nigra that owed him a debt, and had been bragging about it around the contraband camp, and drinking whiskey all day like he was celebrating. We found no money on him, though, so we figure either some contraband robbed him and killed him, or maybe the fellow he'd got the money from decided to take it back, or maybe that woman he had took up with killed him. She ain't to be found nowhere, and we searched the camp thorough."

The only thing Amy could think of to say was, "I see."

"If Mr. Scarlett's about, I can tell him. He might be glad to know the nigra what shot him is dead."

"Mr. Scarlett is . . . busy. Not here just at the moment. I'll be sure he receives the word."

"All righty then. Thank you, Mrs. Hanover." He touched his hat. "Have you a good day, ma'am. And best wishes on that young one, when he comes along."

"Thank you, sir."

Horatio Eaton emerged from one of the back rooms when the policeman was gone. He had heard it all.

"Amy, I hate to speculate like this, but that 'trouble' Ben talked about—"

"I know," she snapped. "I've thought the same thing. He was gone the same night Cat Kingsley was killed. You said he looked scarred up and bruised, like he'd been fighting. Maybe the trouble Ben is running from is more than just that he's drinking again." She shook her head. "But Ben isn't a killer. I'm not sure he'd even kill in self-defense, if that's what it was. He's a gentle man." She shook her head. "No. No. Ben didn't do it."

Eaton said nothing.

Amy excused herself and went to her room, closing the door. She lay down on her bed, on her side, knees curled up under her pregnant belly. She stared at the wall a few moments, and her lip began to quiver. "Oh, Ben!" she whispered. "Oh, Ben, what's going to become of you now?"

Part V

THE CHARNEL HILLS

Chapter 27

There was an old story the mountain people told, mostly to the children. Somewhere among the highest, most remote peaks, they would say, God Himself lay sleeping, a handsome, ancient figure enwrapped in a long, white beard. Look for Him up there on some foggy, haunted day, and you might find Him—but don't awaken Him, for when He awakens, that's when He'll bring time to an end.

A little boy in Carter County, the story went, had heard the tale from his grandmother and decided to investigate. He packed himself food, left his home early one morning, and climbed high into the mountains, looking for God. He returned home the next morning with his clothing disheveled, his face scratched as if from running through brambles and laurel tangles, and a look of wild astonishment on his face. God is there on the mountain, true enough, he reported to his parents, who had not known where he was and had been frantic with worry. But He's different than what the preacher always says: He's old, but has no beard, for He's a woman, a hag, and furthermore, His face is wrinkled and ugly as sin itself.

The boy's report, once spread about, generated great mirth,

for all the older folks of the county knew that the boy had surely seen not God, but old Sally Clung. She was ancient—seemed she had always been ancient—had never been married as far as anyone knew, and lived an isolated hermit's life in a little cabin she built for herself. If God really did sleep in the mountains, some folks declared, it was a good question who had been there longest, Him or Sally. It was also a good question as to which of the two had the most mysterious ways.

Few ever saw her, though many who wandered in the vicinity of her hidden place often reported an eerie feeling of being watched. Old Sally, others would tell them. Old Sally was hid out and watching you.

Though mothers angry at children who wouldn't behave sometimes evoked Sally's name as a threat—go to bed or Old Sally Clung will come drag you off by the nose!—the occasional hunters who actually encountered the hermitess reported she was as friendly as could be. If she didn't try to find human company, neither did she reject it when it happened to find her. She would open her cabin, share her wild foods, hear whatever news there was. Strangely, though, Sally already seemed to know most of what went on in the hills—who had died, who had been born, who had gotten married, whose crops and cattle were healthy and whose weren't. It was a mystery, considering her general lack of human contact, and the best guess anyone could make, short of attributing some kind of mystical abilities to the old woman, was that she was maybe not so cut off from human life as it seemed. Old Sally goes creeping when no one knows, they would say, usually unseen but always listening. You'd best watch what you say in the fields, on the hunt, at the barn, at the graveyard, in the berry patch, at the mill—for you never know whether Old Sally Clung might not be behind the next bush or tree, taking it all in, then creeping back up to her little hidden cabin, treasuring her bits of information like jewels. That Sally did spy on people was no mountain myth. Occasionally, only occasionally, she had been caught at it. But no one grew angry for it. Everyone knew that Sally meant no harm. She was just being Sally Clung, doing what Sally Clung did.

The Union people of the hills in particular had come to love Sally over the past year. Many a scouter, visiting home, told stories of finding food, bandaging, herbal medicines, and the like, that had appeared as if by magic at their camps while they slept. Sometimes the items would be directly beside them, meaning that whoever placed them had been right there with them, close enough to touch, yet had not been heard. Old Sally, they said. It had to be Old Sally. No one else but she could be so subtle and silent.

Rebels out in the hills, however, had no such tales to tell. No mysterious benefactions came their way, and sometimes, worthwhile items they did have somehow vanished in the night despite all precautions. The Union folk loved to hear these tales, and contrast them with what the Unionist scouters told. It all added up to one obvious fact: Sally Clung favored the Stars and Stripes and disdained the Stars and Bars, and distributed her blessings and banes accordingly.

In war or out of it, Sally Clung knew the life of the Carter County hills. She was a shadow that haunted its perimeters, plumbed its depths, pierced its veils. A few said there was something about Sally that was mystical and a little beyond the merely human, that she believed the mountains themselves were living things, and sometimes they whispered to her old secrets. She had been known to declare that not all the old myths told by the Cherokee who had once hunted in these ranges were myths at all, that sometimes she had seen with her own eyes the odd beasts and beings of the Indian legends, and the Little People who almost never let the eyes of white folks find them.

That was Sally Clung. No one knew from where she had come, or when, and whenever life passed and she was gone, it would be likely that months would go by before anyone realized she was missing. That, of course, was assuming that Sally Clung would ever die. Most sensible folks figured she would, someday. Others declared, with seemingly honest conviction, that as long as the mountains stood, or at least until God rose from His secret sleeping place, untangled his white beard, and brought time to an end, Sally Clung would always be there in the high ridges, creeping, watching, listening, learning, knowing, just like she always had.

· · ·

He had run as hard as he could, as far as he could, and now he knew there would be no escape. Every time he looked back, they were still there, on his trail. His weapons were empty and discarded, his energy depleted, his will gone. He had nothing left with which to defend himself except a small knife and a tiny reserve of flickering strength. They would defeat him, but he would go down slashing.

But the end came less dramatically, and with no opportunity for him to fight back. He stopped, turned, faced them as they came, pulling out his knife, trying to find his voice to hurl a defiant word. A rifle ball found him first, piercing his hammering heart and stopping it cold. He crumpled to the ground, the knife falling from his fingers.

"He's dead?" one of the two pursuers asked, panting. He and the second pursuer were the youngest and fleetest of the band that had set out initially in chase of this scouter, and had left the others behind.

"He looks it," said the one who had fired the shot. He was sucking air hard, strained from the pursuit. He swore angrily and spat. "I didn't mean to hit him through the heart. I'd wanted to preserve him for a time, so the Cap could take care of him his way."

"He'll not be happy about this, that's certain," the other said. "The Cap likes to catch them alive."

They went to the fallen one and kicked him over. Indeed he was dead. The one who had shot him swore again, and knelt glumly beside the corpse to await the others.

Cap Fletcher, strong and vital despite his forty-plus years of age, was at the lead of the remainder of the pursuing band when they appeared about a minute later. Ten men, including Fletcher, had begun the chase of this scouter, whom they had driven out of his hiding place, betrayed to them by the scouter's own sister. She had not had a choice. Married to a Union man off with the Thirteenth Tennessee, now stationed at Nashville, the sister had seen the lives of her two children held hostage to her betrayal of her brother. So she had betrayed him. Fletcher would be true to his word. He would not now harm the children. He would, however, burn down their house. This was as much a given as the cross he carved on the face of his victims. It was not negotiable.

Fletcher, seeing the dead victim, paused and sat down on a log nearby, catching his breath. The other seven of the pursuers who had lagged behind reached the scene, most of them following Fletcher's lead and pausing for rest. A couple went on up and inspected the body.

"I'd hoped we'd get to hang him," one of them said. "A hanging corpse sends the best message."

"I didn't aim to kill him," said the one who had done it. "I was trying to bring him down wounded, but I hit him in the heart. Clean shot."

"It happens sometimes like that."

Fletcher stood and walked up, digging a cigar from his coat pocket. He lit up slowly, staring at the dead man through the smoke.

"I wasn't trying to kill him, Cap," the responsible party said.

"Well, you did anyhow," Fletcher replied. "So much for hanging him. Ah, well." He knelt, plucked the scouter's dropped knife from the ground beside him, and deftly carved the gruesome insignia of Fletcher's Cross onto the left cheek. The scouter was young, with a sparse beard. It allowed the mutilation to show up quite well.

"We'll take him back and hang him up by the heels in the yard of his sister's house before we set it ablaze. I'd say that'll give a few of these damn Lincolnites something to dwell on. And Roger, next time try not to kill 'em before we can capture them. Hear?" Fletcher stood, examined the knife he had just used, and shook his head. It didn't suit him. He handed it to Roger. "Here. You killed him, you keep the knife."

Fletcher turned and walked out into the woods some distance, smoking his cigar and still resting up from the run.

Roger squatted and cleaned the blade of the knife on the dead scouter's trouser leg. He removed the scouter's knife sheath, thrust the knife into it, and hung it on himself. "Well, I needed me a good knife anyhow. Hey, I dodged *that* bullet, didn't I? If the Cap had been in a sorry mood, he'd have cussed me from here to Tuesday."

The other grunted agreement and looked down at the mutilated face of the dead man. "The Cap is one hellacious mean man, ain't he!"

"Huh! You'd be mean, too, if what happened to him had happened to you."

"I know all about that," the other replied. "I wasn't asking *why* he was mean. I was just noting that he was."

"Well, you're right. He is mean, mean as a striped snake. Ain't no disputing that fact."

Ten minutes later, when Fletcher had had enough of the place, they headed back toward the mountain farm of a woman who would soon see her brother's murdered and marked corpse swinging from an apple tree in her own front yard while her house blazed to ashes behind him. Nobody wanted to carry the body, so they tied a rope around the ankles and dragged him. His corpse, hauling and bumping along on its back, sometimes turning and dragging facedown, plowed a wide swath through the leaves of the forest floor.

Above, the sky was clear. It was a beautiful, almost spring-like day, cold but with the hint of a coming season that one more mountain Unionist wouldn't be around to see.

Sally Clung emerged from the laurel thicket that had concealed her and looked off in the direction that Fletcher and his ruffians had gone. She wondered where the rest of the band was; Fletcher generally had more men with him than had chased down that scouter. Probably only the fleetest ones had joined the chase, the others remaining wherever it was they had come from, with the horses. Fletcher's band was generally mounted, taking to foot only when pursuit was required through areas too rugged for riding.

Sally eyed the swath the victim's dragging body had made through the leaves and shook her head. If they'd left him, she'd have seen to a good burial for him, as best she could, laying him away in a cave or sinkhole. Giving him honor. She had known that scouter—Hank Heth, whom she had watched grow up in these hills, hunting, trapping, chasing down straying cattle—and she had brought him an item or two in his camp. She'd even let him see her, and spoken to him just two days before. He'd told her that the war was surely winding down, that Longstreet was reportedly slipping out of East Tennessee and back into Virginia to join Lee. It surely meant better times would soon come for the mountain people . . . if only the bush-whackers and ruffians could be dealt with, somehow.

Sally did not know the word "ironic," but the concept was strong in her mind just then. Poor Hank, talking one day about better times coming, now being dragged dead and maimed through the same woods that had hidden him.

Sally squatted, face still turned in the direction Hank had been dragged off, and waited. Before long she saw the first white plumes of smoke rising, dimly visible through the tree-tops, thickening and blackening as the cabin caught better fire. Jennifer Heth Carswell's house. Hank's sister. She'd married Fred Carswell, who'd stampeded off the year before and joined the Thirteenth Regiment at Greeneville. Good folks, all of them. Sally had enjoyed watching them for years. It seemed that Fletcher always tended to go after the good folks. Sally knew he did. She'd been watching Fletcher, too, every chance she got. She knew almost every person he had victimized, almost every cabin he'd burned. She knew the repeating Henry rifle he carried had once belonged to Greeley Brown, the stamp-eder pilot. She knew how Fletcher had obtained it, and why Greeley Brown was no longer seen in these mountains and guided no more stampeders to the Union lines. And for this, most of all, she hated Cap Fletcher.

She knew a lot about Fletcher and his activities. She knew many of his temporary camps, the routes he took in and out of the hills. She knew some of those who gave him aid and some-times betrayed the location of scouters to him. These she hated almost as much as she hated Fletcher himself.

One thing, however, not even Sally Clung knew: the loca-tion of Fletcher's main camp. Somewhere in the ranges was his headquarters, hidden well, and perhaps not by Fletcher's clev-erness alone. She suspected that someone sheltered him from time to time, perhaps while his forty or so men were dispersed in small groups in various camps, making it impossible for all of them to be detected or captured at once. Perhaps Fletcher had several safe houses to which he took when times were hot. Perhaps only one or two. Sally had been frustrated at every effort to ferret out the truth.

Sally watched the smoke of the burning cabin for a while, then rose and moved silently back through the trees, over the wooded hills, down through gullies and hollows, until she reached a big, gnarled oak whose roots grappled out like witch fingers over a recess in a rocky bank. More than a depression, not quite a cave, this south-facing alcove had been home to Hank Heth since he'd become a scouter. He would need it no longer. Nor would he need the item that Sally had come here to fetch. She didn't know why Hank had run without taking it with him. Panic, she supposed. But it was good, in one way. If Hank couldn't use his fine Henry repeater, a battered but workable near duplicate of the Greeley Brown armament taken by Fletcher, Sally knew someone who could. She was glad Fletcher and his men had not examined this niche. They probably would have never expected a poor mountain scouter to possess such a good weapon.

She found the rifle wrapped in an oiled cloth, laid carefully back into the alcove, out of touch of the weather. She looked about among the late Hank Heth's other possessions, taking his meager food stores and anything else that was worthwhile, including, best of all, a sack of ammunition for the gun. The sack was half the size of a man's head and well-stuffed. Sally grinned toothlessly and nodded with satisfaction as she tested its weight.

She rose and moved off through the woods, bearing her new possessions. It had been a bad day for Hank Heth, to be sure, but what he had left behind would give meaning to his unjustified passing.

Sally moved with silence and swiftness, a hunched human ant crawling through a wooded terrain, while a mile away smoke rose from another burning cabin, and another corpse, hung by the heels, displayed the sickening stigmata of Fletcher's Cross for all to see.

Sally's cabin was low and built into the side of a hill, its roof covered with dirt, overgrown with moss. It had no visible chimney; Sally had cleverly vented her fireplace into a narrow, deep cavern behind her house. The cavern, too small to accommodate a human form, had a natural draw that sucked the smoke into the depths of the hill, where it evanesced away into nothing long before it could emerge through whatever other openings the cavern had. Sally's hidden cabin, though detectable to an experienced woodsman, could easily be passed by an average person without relinquishing any hint of its presence. She stooped to enter its low door. Anyone passing who had seen it might have thought he was observing some mountain gnome absorbing its form into the mountain itself.

The interior of the earth-shrouded cabin was dark, pungent with the scent of logs, soil, and the crevice of the cavern hidden behind the rear wall. Dried herbs and vegetables hung along the walls or filled containers, most of these made by Sally herself from gourds, log sections, or natural clay. A covered crockery vessel held water. There was no stove, only the fireplace, with hooks and kettles and a flat stone hearth. An old flintlock rifle leaned in one corner, a horn hanging from its ramrod. She set Hank Heth's rifle up beside it. The flintlock was Sally's weapon, used mostly in winter, when food was harder to obtain. Most of what Sally ate the rest of the year was vegetable, and what meat she obtained came mostly from snaring rather than shooting.

She had given the rifle more than its usual winter usage over the past several weeks, however, since she'd taken a new resident into her home. At the beginning he had eaten nothing but thin gruels and soups, but lately he began eating more normally, as his strength slowly returned and his battered body healed, and Sally had been required to work harder than usual to keep up a food supply.

He was asleep when she came in, but woke as she stirred about at the fireplace, building up a blaze. He watched her silently, eyes half closed, then smiled at her when she turned.

"Hello," she said. "How are you feeling?"

"About the same as when you left this morning." The man's voice was whispery, yet with an underlying, abnormal grating quality. "Where'd you go?"

"Out and about. Sneaking and watching." She lifted her head high, looking at him down her thin nose, brows lifting, voice becoming slightly shrill. It was her way when what she had to say was, in her opinion, significant. "I seen him again. Him and his wicked men, they've killed another. It was Hank Heth. I watched him carve his cross and drag him away."

"Hank . . ."

"You knowed Hank."

"Yes."

"It was Hank's sister betrayed him. Under pain or threat, no question. They burned her cabin and was talking of hanging Hank by his heels before it."

The man on the bed said nothing.

Sally's homely face took on an odd, intense expression. She went to the bedside and dropped into a squat, giving her a squirrelly look.

"Look at me," she said.

He turned his face toward her.

She looked closely into his eyes, silently, then nodded. Her voice was even more shrill when she spoke, a hallelujah-shouting kind of shrill. "Yes, *yes!* I see it in you, stronger by the day—the fire of life, burning brighter! Just the faintest of sparks when I cut you from Fletcher's noose, but now it burns bright and hot! Its heat is healing a throat that's been choked, returning a voice that's been stole, fusing bones walloped by the clubs of the wicked!" She all but chanted her next words, a rugged liturgy she had delivered in this way, with minor variations in the wording, almost daily since this man had come into her dwelling. "You was spared for a reason, Greeley Brown! You was spared to be the agent of God's own vengeance against the wicked man who has come to plague us! Your life was snatched from Fletcher's hand, but his will not be snatched from yourn! You was spared, but you will not spare in turn! Mercy was gave to you, but you shall not give it back!" She laid her gnarly hand on Greeley's scarred cheek. "You was pierced by Fletcher's knife so that Fletcher's heart may be pierced by yourn! You was spared for a reason, Greeley Brown. You was spared to rid these sacred mountains of Cap Fletcher and all the wicked ones who aid him!"

He had heard this ardently intoned descant more times now than he could count. At the beginning, when he'd resided in a semiconscious netherworld between death and life, unaware of where he was or who was the strange, slumped crone who moved in the shadowed borders of his vision, he had not really understood these intense words so often spoken into his ear. But as the spark of life remaining in him flared and grew, as healing began, he realized he was in the company and home of Old Sally Clung, that she had found and cut down his battered body after Fletcher had abandoned him for dead. He had begun listening to her chant. She drove it into his mind, day by day, word by word: He had been spared for a purpose, and that purpose was to destroy Cap Fletcher.

He was in no condition yet, however, to do that or much of anything else. Cap Fletcher had come close to destroying Greeley Brown. His ruffians had battered him severely while he hung choking, cracking, though not completely breaking, ribs and arms, damaging a kneecap, reinjuring the ankle that had kept him laid up in Sevierville at the first of the year. His skeletal injuries alone would keep him bedridden for weeks.

Potentially more threatening to him than those injuries, however, were the direct effects of the hanging. Sally had cut him down at the last possible moment; a few seconds longer and he would certainly have been beyond hope. His throat had been constricted, severely bruised, skin abraded so badly that a permanent scar was inevitable. His voice was entirely gone at the beginning, and was only just now beginning to return. Worse, he had been unconscious for two weeks, Sally tending to him even through he didn't know it. She purged and patched the bullet furrow in his shoulder—a minor injury, to his good fortune, though it had cracked his collarbone. She splinted his arms, bound up his ankle. She kept him alive by putting luke-warm broth between his lips and forcing him to swallow. She kept him watered in similar fashion. She cleaned his body when it was required. And through it all she whispered into his ear the chant that had become her private scripture, telling him to return, return, return . . . he had been spared for a purpose.

So he had returned. One day he had opened his eyes, and he was back as if from a long, dream-filled sleep. No voice at first, hardly even the ability to make any part of his body obey his mind . . . yet he was alive, and day by day, fed and encouraged and chanted to by his odd hag of a savior, he had become more and more the man he was. He could speak now, whispering, and had even managed to sit up a few times. It would be a long time before he was what he'd been before, if ever he achieved that at all—but if he doubted it, Sally didn't. Her claim that he had been spared by some greater design than human was not merely her way of encouraging him. She seemed truly to believe it.

"I brought you something," she said to him. "It was Hank Heth's. Now it's yourn."

When she held the repeating rifle before him, his eyes teared. "Almost like the one Fletcher took from me," he whispered.

"There's ammunition, too. Bullets. Yours now. One of them will end Fletcher's life."

Greeley looked away from the rifle, back toward the ceiling.

She knelt beside him, mouth almost against his ear. "You glad to have the rifle, Greeley Brown?"

"Yes," he said.

"You'll use it for the purpose it was brought to you for?"

"Yes."

"Do you believe, Greeley Brown, that you was spared for a purpose, and that purpose is the killing of the murderer Cap Fletcher?"

Greeley paused a moment, then said, "Yes."

"Do you believe it truly? Does it burn in your heart like the fire of God?"

"I do believe it."

"You'll slay him, Greeley Brown. Your hand will slay him. Do you believe me when I say it?"

"Yes," he said, and meant it.

Chapter 28

Rockwell Griffin stopped abruptly, bent over, and hacked with his hands on his slightly crooked knees until it sounded as if his very innards would be coughed out. Thatcher Brown stood beside his friend and fellow prisoner, feeling the helplessness he always felt when Griffin was seized in this way, and also the secret guilt of knowing that deep inside he was grateful it was Griffin and not himself who was so sickly.

When the fit was done, Rockwell Griffin straightened slowly, face red, lips wet with sputum. He pulled a foul rag from his pocket and swiped it over his face, tucked it away again.

"I swear, Thatcher, if it wasn't for this prison yard, I believe I'd be dead by now."

Thatcher did not dispute it. He believed the same.

Griffin looked around the broad, open, four-acre yard and smiled sardonically. "You know, a man could be fooled, looking at this place from the outside. A man could take this for a park, or some New England college campus. Oak trees, a good well . . . better than Libby Prison, certainly." The smile died away. "But I hate this yard all the same. It gives me sunlight, fresh air, a certain illusion of freedom . . . it keeps me alive, so that building yonder can take more time killing me."

Again Thatcher could not dispute Griffin's view. As fine as it was in this open yard on pretty days, as healing and pure as the air might be, what they experienced in the actual prison building where they slept was the opposite. Their sleeping quarters were overfilled, unsanitary, stinking of every kind of human and verminous filth imaginable. Thatcher seldom entered that hated structure without feeling as if every killing miasma known and unknown was filling his lungs and crawling over his skin. Yet, so far he had retained his health, or as much of it as any prisoner could hope to keep. Griffin, less hearty than him even in free and healthy conditions, was not so fortunate.

Griffin looked around, eyes flitting like those of a cat held too long in a cage. "I've got to get out of here, Thatcher."

"I know. I know. And you will. We both will."

"But I must do it soon. I'll die if I don't. You know it's true. You'll go out of the barracks one morning, wondering where I am, and you'll pass the hospital bench where they lay the dead. You'll throw back the sheet to have a look, and it'll be me staring back at you."

"That won't happen. Listen, Rockwell. The winter's past. The weather is warming, and if it only makes the indoors stink all the more, at least it makes the open air all the better and healthier. We have the run of the yard all day, and as long as we take advantage of every minute in the sun and fresh air, you can make it through. You can throw off whatever that place"— he tilted his head toward the barracks building—"puts upon you."

"Are you resigned to staying here until the war ends, then?"

"No. I want out as much as you do. But we have to do it carefully."

"Maybe. Or maybe not."

"What do you mean?"

"That perhaps boldness can compensate for caution. Think about it, Thatcher. Take Captain Reed. A blanket over his shoulders, a defiant attitude, and he walks right past the guards simply on his own word that he was supposed to be at head-quarters." Griffin paused to cough some more, not so bad a fit this time. "And what about those who have simply scaled fences, defiant of every precaution, or roped themselves down walls? I heard of several prisoners using croton oil to give themselves the appearance of smallpox, then leaping off the hospital wagons on the way to the pox ward. You and I both know of prisoners who have escaped by forging their own discharge papers. It's defiance and brazenness that make for a successful escape."

"Defiance, brazenness, and *opportunity*. Make a run at the wrong time, in the wrong conditions, and you'll certainly be shot or recaptured."

"You're strong, Thatcher. Healthy. Your constitution allows you to bear up. Mine is poor. I'll not survive if I stay here."

"You think your conditions would be better on the other side of the wall? What would you eat? Where would you go? These things must be planned. If you're ill now, you'll be ill out there. Most of those who escape are recaptured—you know that. It's because they don't have an adequate plan."

"I don't have time for an 'adequate plan,' Thatcher. I have to get out of here alive, soon, or else I'll be taken out of here dead."

Thatcher opened his mouth, closed it again. There was no point in argument, and no good argument to be made, anyway.

"Are you with me, Thatcher?"

He looked down at his battered boots, thinking, wiggling his big toe and having a full view of it because there was a hole in both his boot and sock. He looked up at Griffin. "I'm with you."

Griffin smiled and was about to speak, but a new fit of coughing struck, and by the time it was through, there seemed nothing worth saying.

Beneath the house of Vaughn Fitz, Limestone
Cove, Carter County, Tennessee

At least there was a cat to play with, a skinny, black and white creature who lived off the mice that scampered in Fitz's barn and beneath his house. Though the cat was a female, and showing some obvious signs that it was about to again fulfill its biblical duty to go forth and multiply, Cecilia had given it a man's name, Greeley. But only she and the cat knew it. It was their secret alone, because now the cat was the only living being to whom she talked. She did not even converse with her mother anymore, in the rare times they were alone. She was not pleased with her mother at the moment, not after what she had done. And Cecilia would never, never, have anything to say to Vaughn Fitz.

She was speaking to the cat now, there in the cool under-space of Fitz's well-built house, hidden behind the stone wall of the foundation. There were many gaps in the foundation, allowing her to peer out from the shadows without being easily seen from the outside. It was a marvelous place to hide away with Greeley the cat. This was a tiny, protected world, with openings to the broader world outside, but isolated from it all the same. Here she could see what happened without becoming part of it, and listen through the floorboards to all that was said in the house without being detected herself.

Footsteps thumped above her, making the joist creak. She put her mouth close to the cat's left ear and whispered. "Listen, Greeley . . . it's him. Let's be very quiet so he won't know we are here. He can't know about our place because he's awful and hateful and wouldn't let us come here anymore."

Speaking was not difficult for Cecilia. She declined to speak in the public world of humans not because she couldn't, but because she merely didn't want to. Ever since *it* had happened, that awful, barely remembered event that she had mostly expelled from her mind, the unspeakable violation of herself that had resulted in the conception and birth of poor, lost little James, Cecilia had found it perfectly sensible to hold her silence. Silence was a protective wall that she could keep in place, that no one could force her to remove. It was, to her, power, one of the few things in life that she could control.

From above, Fitz's voice filtered down. Cecilia whispered to the cat again. "He dares to call himself my father! Think of that! *Him*, my father! It isn't true, Greeley, so if you hear him say it, don't believe it. My father is dead. He was a good man, not mean and ugly like *he* is. *He's* not my father, he's my uncle. He might be married to my mother now, but he's still my uncle to me, and he'll never be anything more. I wish he wasn't even *that*!"

The cat moved, nestling against her shoulder, beginning to languidly wash its right front paw.

She listened to Fitz's voice, fussing to her mother about something. It seemed to Cecilia that Vaughn Fitz was fussing about one thing or another all the time. Quite often it was Cecilia herself who was the cause of it. He resented her silence to him. He'd tried to cajole her to speak to him many times, and grown bitterly angry when he failed. Fitz didn't like to fail. But fail he would if he thought he could bring her under his control! Cecilia was determined about that.

"Mama shouldn't have married Uncle Vaughn," she whispered. Her breath made the cat twitch its ear. "She didn't have to marry him. She could have married Greeley Brown. That's who I named you after! Did you know that? He was a good man, and I know he liked Mama. I could tell. She liked him, too. But she's been so afraid ever since she . . . never mind. You don't have to know about that. I wish she hadn't been in such a hurry. I wish she hadn't said yes when Uncle Vaughn asked her. I know she really didn't want to marry him. She didn't even want to come to the mountains. She only came because she believed they'd never find her here."

She scratched the cat around the ears. Its purring was loud in the enclosed, cool space.

"I like talking to you," Cecilia told the cat. "I miss talking sometimes. But not talking to people. I don't care if I never talk to people again."

Vaughn Fitz's voice rang down from above, but he was at the far corner of the house from Cecilia, and she couldn't understand what he said. But he was yelling, angry like always. Yelling at her mother, his new bride.

"I hate him," Cecilia whispered. "I hate Uncle Vaughn. And I hate this place, everything about it . . . except you." She looked out through one of the foundation holes, her window on the world. "I wish Greeley Brown would come back. I wish he could take us away again, and him and Mama could be married instead of the way things are now. I wish he'd come on a big horse, riding onto the road right up there, and then down to—"

As if response, a horseman appeared at the indicated place. Cecilia's eyes gaped wide and she wondered if . . . and then saw that it wasn't. Other horsemen appeared behind him and, as a group, began riding down the long slope toward the house.

Cecilia reached over, put her arm across the cat, pulling it close. She knew this band, and the man who led them. They had been here once before, and judging from the conversation her uncle had carried on with the leader then, the history between himself and this band went back to well before that visit.

As the horsemen came closer, generating noise, Fitz's voice above stilled. Cecilia heard him tromp across the floor to the front window. Her mother's lighter footfalls traced the same route.

Miriam's worried-sounding voice was barely audible to Cecilia. "Vaughn, is it—"

"Yes," Fitz cut in. "Fletcher. Go back into our room, Miriam, and wait. I'll go see what he wants."

"I don't like that man," Miriam said. "I know who he is and what he does. He's a murderer, and I don't like it that you befriend him, Vaughn."

Cecilia, watching the riders draw up to the front of the house, cringed back, squeezing her cat so tightly it struggled in protest. She was glad to be hidden. The last time these men had come, she'd been in open view, and the way some of them looked at her had reminded her of that gravedigger who came into her room back in Livingston, the dirt from her father's grave still clinging to his clothes. What happened after that she had chosen to forget.

"I don't 'befriend' him, Miriam," Fitz was saying above. "I give him aid when he asks it. Would you rather have me on his bad side? Would you?"

Miriam withdrew. Cecilia tracked her footsteps across the floor above her.

The front door opened, closed. Fitz's feet and lower legs entered Cecilia's limited window of vision, almost directly in front of the space in the foundation through which she peered. She could have almost touched his ankles if she'd tried. She cowered back farther into the shadows, hardly breathing. Her hand touched something cool, hard, pointed. Twisting her head, she saw that it was an old knife with a wooden handle and six-inch blade, very rusted. She swept it into her hand, finding it comforting to have a weapon in the presence of these frightening men, even one so inadequate as a lost, rusted knife.

"Good day, Captain Fletcher!" Fitz said fulsomely. "Pleasure to see you and your men!"

"Hello, Fitz. How you faring?"

"Fine enough, sir."

"How's the beautiful new bride?"

"Well, sir, she's fine as well. What can I do to help you today?"

"Not a thing, Mr. Fitz. Today is simply a brief social call. I've come to bring a proper wedding gift for your bride."

"A, uh, gift? Oh, yes indeed! Why, how kind of you, sir! If you wish to leave it with me, I'll take it to her."

"I wish to give it to her myself, Mr. Fitz. Is she here?"

"Well, to tell the truth . . . uh, yes indeed. I believe she is. I'll fetch her."

Cecilia thought: Don't go out there, Mama! They'll look at you, they'll smile the way they do, they'll say things to one another. Please don't go out there! She moved the knife in her hand, fantasizing about jabbing it into Fletcher's heart, then moving down the line of riders like a human tornado, killing them one by one. Two years before, such violent images would have never entered her mind. Two years before, though, many things that had happened to Cecilia Fry still lay in the future.

Fitz was already back inside the house, calling to Miriam. Cecilia listened as Miriam emerged from the bedroom and slowly advanced through the house, her dread evident in the very tone of her footfalls.

Moments later Miriam was outside beside her husband. Fletcher doffed his hat; most of his men touched theirs, and nodded greetings to her, subtle, ugly, hungry smiles on their bearded faces. Cecilia saw the eyes of several of them darting quickly about. *Looking for me. They want to look at me like they're looking at Mama.* It made her feel sick and afraid. She jabbed the air with her knife, killing them all again. She wished she had had this knife the night the gravedigger came into her room.

"Mrs. Fitz, ma'am, it's a pleasure to see you again,"

Fletcher said. "During our last visit to you, I'm afraid I was not quite the gentleman in that I had no wedding gift for the lovely new bride. I didn't know at the time, you'll recall, that my friend Mr. Fitz had took himself a new wife. So I've returned today with something I hope you'll find useful in your home."

"Thank you," Miriam replied. She sounded weak and afraid, something Cecilia was not accustomed to hearing when her mother spoke.

Fletcher reached behind him and pulled a cloth sack from where it hung on the rear of his saddle. Something inside clinked metallically. He swung down from his horse, approached Miriam, and handed it to her.

"I'm afraid it ain't wrapped up no more than being in that poke there, and I'm afraid it ain't new. But I recall that when I was here before and you brewed us up that punkin coffee, there was a leak in your kettle. So I've brung you a good one to replace it, and some coffee, too. Not much of it, but it's the real stuff."

Miriam accepted the sack, spread its top, and looked into it. Cecilia, from her angle of view, noticed something subtle and odd in her mother's reaction. She moved just a little, as if she had staggered slightly on her feet, like someone feeling faint or very surprised.

"Thank you," Miriam said again to Fletcher, her voice even softer. "I'll take it in now." She reentered the house a little too quickly to appear casual, which didn't seem to please her husband.

"Well, sir, that's fine, mighty fine!" Fitz boomed out, as if to cover his wife's abrupt departure. "What a fine thing indeed for you to think so kindly toward my wife. You've made her a happy woman."

One of the riders said, "And I'll bet that come nightfall, she makes you a happy man, eh, Fitz?" Laughter rumbled through the assembly.

"Eh? Oh . . . heh heh heh . . . uh, yes indeed."

Fletcher turned to his riders. "Men, I'll have no disrespectful and ungentlemanly talk here at Mr. Fitz's home. You understand me?" He faced Fitz again. "Very sorry, sir."

"Think nothing of it. Captain, might I invite you in? I can

have Miriam boil up that coffee you brought, and spread among us all, we'd at least have enough for a taste for each."

"Kind of you, Fitz, but we'll decline. We need to be moving on. We've been active the last few days, and it's prudent for us to retire for a time."

"You'll be at the camp?" He nodded his head to the left, farther down the narrow little valley in which the house stood.

"We will. And you'll see that no one approaches it, as usual." It was obviously a statement, not a request.

"Of course."

"Good day to you, Fitz. Enjoy that coffee." Fletcher looked around. "Where's your little mute girl?"

"She's off hiding somewhere, most likely. Playing with that cussed cat she likes so well."

"Lovely child, that girl. Too bad about her muteness. Well, we'll be off."

Fletcher went back to his horse and deftly swung into the saddle. Fitz, showing his relief, more than he realized, at seeing Fletcher leave, put on a broad, friendly grin that only betrayed his underlying nervousness. In a final effort at making congenial conversation, Fitz said, "Captain, that's a fine-looking rifle you got booted on your saddle there, judging from what I can see. That wouldn't be a Henry, would it?"

Fletcher pulled the rifle from its scabbard and held it up in one hand, turning it to give Fitz a good view. He was at this moment far enough from the house that Cecilia got a good view of the rifle, too.

"It is a Henry, yes sir. Sixteen shooter. Fine weapon. It came my way through an encounter with a damned Lincolnite stampeder guide whom we left twisting from a sapling back in February. There's his mark, right there." He pointed at the cross-mark brands burned into his saddle. "It's a good weapon, this rifle. It's serving me quite well."

"Well, perhaps one day I'll have one of my own."

"Good day, Mr. Fitz."

"Good day, Captain Fletcher."

The band rode on, kicking up abundant dust. Cecilia noted that they didn't head back the way they had come, but on farther past the house, toward the place where the ridges on either side of the farm came together into a narrow, canyonlike pass, opening into a hidden meadow beyond where Fitz had once grazed cattle.

They're camping back there, Cecilia thought. Uncle Vaughn is letting them hide on his land.

That thought bothered her, but something else bothered her more, a vague thing she could not quite grasp. She frowned in her hidden place, trying to figure it out, but it always just evaded her, teasing her like that cruel boy who had taken the kitten from her back in Sevierville, but for some reason far more distressing.

Cecilia was asleep at last. Miriam withdrew from the loft quietly, descending the narrow steps with care to avoid making them squeak. Fitz was below, seated in his usual chair, watching her. She avoided his eyes and sat down in what was becoming her own usual chair, a cane-bottomed rocker. She began rocking, staring toward the fireplace at the coffee kettle that Fletcher had brought her that day. So far she had not used it, though Fitz had asked her to boil a pot of coffee for supper. She had given no reason for not obeying.

"Miriam," he said, "I have a question for you."

She kept staring at the coffeepot. "What?"

"Why did you marry me?"

"Because you wrote to me and asked me to."

"I did. That's true. But why did you say yes?"

"Well, I suppose because—"

"Look at me when you answer!" He snapped the demand at her, then in a softer tone, added, "Please."

She shifted her eyes his way. "I married you because we had both lost our mates. We were alone. You needed a wife, I needed a husband."

"So that's it. Purely a functional marriage. A convenience."

"I would hope that no marriage would be merely a convenience."

"What I'm asking, Miriam, is whether you feel any true regard for me. Any affection. I'm asking whether you love me . . . or think you might someday."

"Vaughn, I have had a certain affection for you. For many years. I thought you were a good and loving husband for Jane, and I appreciated you for it. When Joseph died and you sent me the letter of proposal, it seemed sensible to me to accept what you offered. And I have, and did."

"A 'certain affection,' then, is all I receive from you? No more?"

"You must give me time, Vaughn. I can't so soon come to fully love a man when my own husband has been dead for hardly more than a year. When I came here, married you, I knew that I wouldn't instantly feel the full measure of love for you. But I came fully believing that it could develop. Over time." Her eyes left him again. Back to the coffeepot, hanging on its hook at the fireplace.

"Do you still believe you can learn to love me?"

She fought a tiny, sorrowful feeling that stirred inside and threatened to develop into a much deeper, larger emotion. "I don't know," she replied honestly.

"Why not? What has changed your opinion?"

She did not instantly reply. "You have."

"This Fletcher business. Is that it?"

"Yes."

"You think I'm doing wrong by allowing him to hide on my land?"

"Yes."

"Why?"

"Because he is a murderer. And a particularly vile murderer at that. Cruel." She looked at her husband. "Do you know what he does to the faces of the people he kills?"

"I know about Fletcher's Cross, yes."

"Doesn't it revolt you?"

"Yes . . . but so does the experience of having a father, old and sick, handed out and hanged by Lincolnites who've come into another state to punish Secessionists. So does having an aging mother stripped naked and mocked, then shot dead when she tried to reach a rifle to keep her husband from being hanged. So does having a wife killed by a Lincolnite bullet that was fired at a dog in sheer meanness, but ricocheted and hit a person instead."

"Those things have never happened to you!"

"No. But they did happen to Cap Fletcher. And that's why he is what he is, and does what he does."

"But the carving of the faces . . . it's brutal."

"War is brutal. And I hope you'll never have to see how brutal it can be. And perhaps you won't, if I continue to cooperate with Cap Fletcher."

"It's *wrong*, cooperating with a man like that!"

"Miriam, what are you running from?"

"What?"

"Tell me what you're running from. You didn't come here just to reach me, or these mountains. You'll recall that I sent you three letters of proposal, not just one. The first a month after Jane died. You refused me. The second three months after that. Again a refusal, even more firm. And then, me being the lonely fool I was, I dared to send you a third proposal, knowing you'd surely refuse it—and suddenly the answer is yes. I was astonished. Pleased, of course, but astonished. So I began making arrangements to have you brought here, or for me to go to you, and you say no, no, you'll come in your own time, you own way. It was as if you didn't want me to know just where you would be at any given time. It struck me as odd. What are you hiding, Miriam? What are you running from?"

Miriam stared at the coffeepot, unanswering, tense.

"Was it the scandal with Cecilia's child? Because I want you to know I was ready to overlook the circumstances of that whole sorry business. Though God in his wisdom chose to take the baby on and mercifully spare him the ordeal of a bastard's life, if that had not happened, I stood ready to take little James in, despite the scandal, and raise him as if—"

"Scandal! What 'scandal' do you mean? The only scandal in that business, Vaughn, is the scandalous thing that was done to my daughter. She was violated. Raped! Or do you doubt that?"

"Miriam, how am I to know? Cecilia isn't the kind of young lady that's easy to know or understand. She won't speak. She's *odd*. Perhaps some man misunderstood her in some fashion—"

"Cecilia has been 'odd' only *since* she was violated, not before! She stopped speaking *after* that event. What are you saying, Vaughn? Do you believe Cecilia, a mere *child*, seduced a gravedigger, of all things? The very gravedigger who had just put her father into the ground?"

Fitz exhaled loudly through his nostrils, lips clamped together. "I can see I'm sort of digging a grave myself, the more I say. You seem bound to misunderstand me."

Though Miriam wanted to shout it, she kept her voice very quiet for the sake of the girl who was the subject of the exchange. "What am I misunderstanding? Were you not implying that Cecilia's rape might not have been a rape? That *she* is at fault as much as the scoundrel, the *devil*, who did such a foul thing to her?"

He lowered his head. "Perhaps I was implying that, without meaning to. I'm sorry. You must understand that I'm very confused. By many things. By Cecilia disliking me like she seems to. Her refusal to speak. Your own acceptance of my marriage proposal after two rejections, and the odd way you dealt with coming here, as if you wanted to come in the back door, so to speak. And I'm confused by your own coldness toward me."

"There's one reason only for any coldness you feel, and that has to do with the bushwhacker you are hiding in your back meadow."

"He hides himself. He merely uses my land to do it."

"With your permission! And don't try to tell me that if you saw a troop of Union soldiers riding down this way, you wouldn't send warning to Fletcher."

"I would warn him. For the love of God, woman, we're on the same side of this thing! I may not be a soldier, but I am a Confederate, and proud of it!"

"Don't raise your voice. You'll wake up Cecilia."

"Confound it, I'm just getting weary of not being able to understand you, or why it is that you came to marry me! That day you first came, and I kissed you on the porch, you kissed me in return. You seemed to have the feeling for me that a wife should for her husband. But since . . ."

"But since, I've learned about Cap Fletcher. I've learned that you cooperate with murderers."

"Killing in wartime is not murder, my dear."

"Some kind of killing is murder anytime it's done."

"War is a time of moral ambiguities."

She wondered where he had picked up that smooth little bit

of philosophy. "There's nothing morally ambiguous about harboring a murderer like Fletcher. It's vile!"

"You sound almost like a Lincolnite, Miriam."

"I despise this war on all sides. I'm no Lincolnite and I'm no Secessionist."

"Really? Your condemnation seems pretty one-sided to me. Where'd you pick up this Union doctrine? From that pilot who helped lead you here? What did you say his name was?"

Miriam was caught. As Greeley had instructed, she had made no mention of his name to Fitz, making up a false one. But what was that name? Matheson! That was it. "Reuben Matheson," she said as quickly as possible, but not quickly enough.

He frowned skeptically. "Never heard of any such pilot."

"He'd never heard of you, either."

"Well, he or somebody else must have spewed plenty of Lincolnite nonsense your way, and you seem to have swallowed a lot of it. From the way you've been talking, I . . . confound it, Miriam, why do you keep looking at that coffeepot?"

Her mind filled with the memory of a funny, cordial old man, chattering on and boiling coffee he was proud to possess and prouder to share. "Because I think I know where Fletcher got it," she said. "And I suspect I know how."

She rose, tears flooding, and went to her bed. Fitz sat with a startled, puzzled look on his face. He dug a pipe from his pocket and filled it with exaggerated motions, packing the bowl tight and drawing too hard as he lit it. His lack of care made it a very unsatisfying smoke, which fit in quite nicely with the way everything else in his life seemed to be going this evening.

Cecilia awakened abruptly in the darkest part of the night, and tears came.

She had just solved the mystery of that nagging, teasing disquiet that had come upon her beneath the house after Fletcher rode away, and it made her so nauseous she feared she would be sick right there in her bed.

She rose, taking deep breaths, trying not to cry aloud. The

loft seemed constricting all of a sudden, and she descended into the dark and sleeping house below.

"Cecilia?"

She turned with a start. Her mother was there, unseen in the darkness. Her figure emerged from the black into the dim light of stars and moon coming in through the nearest window.

"You couldn't sleep, Cecilia? I couldn't, either."

It was an invitation for her to speak, something Cecilia had not done with her mother for a long time now. Cecilia had been too resentful to want to talk to her. Her mother had committed the unpardonable sin of marrying Vaughn Fitz, and sometimes Cecilia thought she hated her for it. She had withheld communication as a way of punishing.

This time, though, she did reply. Her mother needed to know what she knew.

She whispered, "Mama, Greeley Brown is dead."

Miriam looked at her in silence, came a step closer. "What?"

"Greeley Brown is dead."

"How could you know?"

"I saw his rifle. Fletcher had it. I watched from under the house. He told Uncle Vaughn he had taken it from a Union pilot he had killed." Cecilia's voice cracked. "I know it was Greeley Brown's rifle. I remembered it, just now. Greeley Brown is dead! Fletcher has killed him!"

She put her arms around her mother and wept. Miriam embraced her daughter and struggled not to weep, too. "Maybe it was someone else's rifle," she said. "You don't know much about rifles, Cecilia."

"It was his . . . it was his. . . ."

Miriam closed her eyes tightly.

Off in his bed in the next room, Vaughn Fitz snored, alone, and oblivious to all.

Chapter 29

The first edition of *The Knoxville Sage & Torch* came off the press in July, and instantly stirred controversy. The news spread: Horatio Eaton, the troublesome, ink-slinging abolitionist, who had published the reviled *Reason's Torch* and continually advocated the abolishment of slavery, was back in Knoxville and publishing again! When he left in '61, few had mourned his departure nor hoped he would find cause to return. However great the differences had been between Unionists and Secessionists in those early days, on one thing they had mostly agreed: The abolitionist Horatio Eaton was far too radical.

Now Eaton was at it again. He was listed as editor and co-publisher with one A. D. Hanover. The use of initials in the latter name fooled few; savvy readers realized at once that this was Amy Deacon Hanover, and less savvy ones soon had it pointed out to them in a sarcastic editorial by Brownlow in the *Whig*. Brownlow sniffingly derided the *Sage & Torch* as a "newspaper bound to publish hopelessly airy nonsense generated by the windy minds of its two bumbling publishers, whose only regret in life is that they weren't themselves born as swarthy Negroes, thereby to better understand the suffering of that downtrodden race."

Most Knoxvillians greeted the new publication with groans as soon as they saw Eaton's name on the editorial masthead, but they also snatched up the tiny paper—the first edition was a single sheet, printed on two sides—to see what Eaton was going to advocate this time. Lincoln had already signed the Emancipation Proclamation, so the old abolitionist couldn't harp on that anymore.

Eaton surprised most, showing that he was a dog capable of more than one bark. His theme was the problem of refugees and contrabands, how best to deal with the crisis while war went on, and possible longer-term policies for "restoration" once the war was done. He decried certain inept separatist ideas that had already been broached: a designated region in the West, a reservation, as it were, for freedmen; and various plans to send freedmen back to their "native soil" of Africa, which of course was a land few living blacks had ever seen and of which they were no more "natives" than were American whites. All in all, however, the Eaton of the *Sage & Torch* was less preachy and idealistic than the Eaton of his former publication, and he seemed as concerned about the welfare of white refugees, particularly homeless Unionists, as about the black contrabands most would expect him to focus upon.

This was due to the mostly background influence of Amy Hanover. Though she contributed no written material to the first edition of the *Sage & Torch* beyond a brief discussion of the book she was writing about the persecution and displacement of Tennessee and Carolina mountain Unionists, she shaped Eaton's work through her suggestions and editing, and kept him from launching off into extreme progressivist diatribe, as he was wont to do on his own. One important fact Amy had learned in her days in Nashville: One gains nothing for his cause by attacking and estranging those he should be seeking to persuade. Her own husband had failed to follow that dictum in one of his own editorials, and generated such ire that it got him killed.

Amy paid less attention to the new journal than she would have in normal circumstances. In mid-June, while the first edition was forming, she gave birth to a son. Fine, strong, stout, and with full control of ample lungs and a much-used voice box apparently inherited from his late, stentorian maternal grandfather, Adam B. Hanover had his mother's features and hair, and his late father's eyes. When the old black midwife had laid the newly born wet bundle in Amy's arms, Amy looked into the pinched face and wept. Most of the tears sprang from happiness, a few from the grief of a mother who could never enjoy the experience of presenting her firstborn to his father.

Horatio Eaton had demonstrated his typical social awkwardness when he first saw the baby. He held little Adam in his thin arms in a tense, uncomfortable posture, his face full of terror. After mumblingly declaring the child a "fine, fine, fine, lad of a boy," he quickly placed him back in Amy's arms.

"So, you've got you an Adam, Junior, there, right, Amy?"

"Not a Junior," Amy said. "My husband's middle name was William. My son's is Benjamin."

Eaton puzzled over it a moment, then said, "Ah . . . after Benjamin Scarlett, maybe?"

Amy nodded, and felt a wave of sadness. She had looked forward to presenting her son to Ben, but Ben was gone now, for many weeks, and she'd heard nothing from him at all. She prayed for him every night, and eagerly scanned every envelope of every piece of mail she received. But nothing. No word from Ben.

Childbirth slowed Amy down only a few days, then she began drifting back into work again, the bulk of that being more interviews with the refugees who were arriving now at even greater pace than before.

Amy, always a close watcher of war developments, began mentally dividing the news she received into two grand categories. There was news of the war at large, the regular war, and news of the narrower irregular war being waged, as if behind a veil, in western North Carolina and East Tennessee. Often the two varieties of news seemed to have little to do with one another. The mountain war had a life and impetus all its own.

News of the regular war taking place close at hand was pretty much the same as it had been in East Tennessee since the beginning of the year. Knoxville remained under Federal control, with no serious rebel threat to change that. But there had been skirmishes galore all around. In January there was skirmishing at Dandridge, Mossy Creek, Tazewell, Strawberry Plains, Newport, and in the immediate vicinity of Knoxville itself. In February the Federals conducted reconnaissance from nearby Maryville on to Sevierville, with scouting thrusts going as far as White and Putnam counties in Middle Tennessee. At New Market, Federal soldiers created outrage among some of the local supporters of the Confederacy when they took over a church in the town and destroyed part of it, and at Dandridge they used tombstones pulled from a graveyard to make fireplaces in their huts. They parked wagons right atop the graves, as well.

As winter had given way to spring, skirmishing increased. Fights broke out at or near Panther Springs, Strawberry Plains, Bull's Gap, Bean's Station, Cheek's Crossroads, Greeneville, and Rheatown. The country east of Knoxville was contested territory, Federals moving through and dominating one day, Confederates the next. The people had little and struggled to keep what they possessed, often in vain, because each gang of soldiers passing through took what it could find. Fence rails became firewood. Livestock became food.

As summer came and the weather grew hotter, the hell of hidden war in the mountains did the same. Amy particularly sought out those refugees who came to Knoxville from Carter and Johnson counties, and gathered more stories of atrocities and murders. Various names of perpetrators kept recurring, particularly Parker, Teener . . . Fletcher. The refugees talked of burning cabins, of men hauled into the woods and shot, of others who vanished without explanation and were never found. They talked as well of those who were found, and how many of these, particularly in Carter County, bore the mark of Fletcher's Cross on their faces.

There were occasional stories of Unionist reprisal. Daniel Ellis, whose own house had been robbed by rebels since Amy's last conversation with him, had begun some retaliatory bushwhacking against the rebels, and was beginning to steal mules and horses from those who supported them, and sell these to the Federal government. In early summer Ellis had also led a raid into Johnson County in response to the theft of goods from mountain Unionists by rebels out of that county.

Amy began to hear other less specific, more mysterious tales of retaliation against rebels, as well, focusing mostly on men who rode with Fletcher.

Starting in mid-July some of Fletcher's men began turning up dead in the mountains. Dead in or near their own camps, usually; though he had a main camp as yet unfound, Fletcher's frequent pattern was for his men to divide into small groups of two or three and camp scattered through the mountains. Twice now such small parties, two men to a camp, had been found dead. Someone in the Carter County hills, no one knew whom, apparently had taken it upon himself to seek out and punish Fletcher's ruffians. The Unionists weren't complaining, but they were puzzled. At one of the campsites where Fletcher men had been killed, tracks were found. One set clearly belonged to a man, but the other tracks were of someone lighter and smaller, like a woman.

It seemed odd to most to think of a woman and man working together on such a grim business as vengeance. But many women had suffered greatly because of Fletcher and his band. Perhaps one of them had decided to help do something about it.

Amy listened to the tales, wrote extensive notes, and shaped them into outline form. She produced draft versions of proposed chapters, editing, revising, and expanding as she went along and new facts came her way.

The more she worked, however, the less pleased she was with the idea of producing the final book in Knoxville. It was one thing to relate facts and stories told to her by others. It was another thing to see the facts and stories firsthand.

The mountains were calling to Amy Deacon Hanover, and she was doing her best to resist the call. She had a child now, and part of the responsibility for Horatio Eaton's newspaper. It was not a good time to think of leaving Knoxville, especially to head into the dark country of the mountain war. Impossible, really. Nonsensical. Irrational.

But still the mountains called, and still she listened.

From the night she told her mother that she'd recognized Greeley Brown's rifle in the hands of Fletcher, Cecilia Fry had not spoken a word to another living being except her beloved cat, and now even that outlet was closed. The cat was gone. Just vanished, as cats would, and had not returned.

She had not called to it, even though she'd wanted to. To do so would have let Vaughn Fitz hear her speak, which she would not allow. She might be forced to do many things she did not choose, including living in the home of a man she despised more every day—but she would not be forced to speak.

So now Cecilia lived in a world that was almost utterly imploded, encased in silence, cocooned. It was a small world, and lonely, but it was hers.

Vaughn Fitz's land included an orchard up near the head of the hollow. Poor trees that made poor apples, but these days even bad fruit was good. Cecilia moved among the gnarled and leaning trees, picking apples from the ground, examining them, discarding some, keeping others. She would explore the apples within her reach on the branches themselves in a second sweep of the grove. Occasionally, when a new ripe apple thumped to the earth from one of the branches, she sought it out at once, knowing it would be ripe but not yet infested with the vermin of the soil. Few of these choice apples went into the sack she carried, which held fruit her mother would make into jelly and apple butter. These best apples almost all went into Cecilia's mouth, a reward she chose to give herself simply because there happened to be no one at hand to tell her not to.

Shortly before dusk, and having just found the finest and most pure-skinned apple of the day, Cecilia retired, with her sack nearly full, to a huge stone at the corner of the orchard. The lower portion of the stone and part of its upper reaches were covered with ivy, none of it poisonous, but a shelf at its center was clean and level, and one of Cecilia's favorite spots for sitting and watching the world around her. It was also inarguably the best spot to be at dusk on a day when the sunset promised to be beautiful and one had just been handed the finest apple of the day by a tree too weary to hold it any longer. Cecilia clambered onto the rock, taking care not to scuff or bruise her special apple in the process, then settled herself to watch the sun go down and to eat her treat.

The apple crunched nicely between her teeth, spilling flavorful sweet juice across her tongue. She chewed and swallowed, observed the world around her, enjoyed the breeze and the approach of sunset . . . for now, little was to be disliked in Cecilia Fry's private world. She did miss her cat. And little James. Sometimes she missed what it was like to hold him. If James were here, she would talk to him.

She took another bite of apple and looked to her left. The sweetness of the bite faded a bit as she noted her uncle Vaughn striding across the field and down toward the house. He'd been in one of the far fields, where corn had been planted in the spring. Most of the crop had been picked green by heaven only knew whom—hungry neighbors, bushwhackers, outliers of many varieties. In the mountains during war, what a man sowed he didn't necessarily reap. Often someone else enjoyed the latter benefit.

Cecilia chewed the bite slowly and glowered across the distance at her uncle. She despised him as much, maybe more, than ever. He was not a kind man, snapping often at her mother, and sometimes at her, though he seemed pleased to ignore her most of the time. That pleased her, too. He had given up trying to make her talk to him months ago.

Cecilia found many things to dislike about Vaughn Fitz, but chief among them was that he continued to harbor Cap Fletcher and his band . . . a diminishing band, to some measure, Cecilia had heard. Only two nights ago Uncle Vaughn had talked in a low voice to her mother about the corpses of Fletcher's men beginning to turn up lately. Shot through the head, the body. No ceremony or ritual, no marking of the faces like Fletcher himself did . . . just efficient infliction of death on those who had inflicted much death on their own.

Good, Miriam had said. *I hope whoever it is kills them all.* And Vaughn Fitz had put his finger to his lips and winced, looking around as if he feared Fletcher himself was listening at the window.

Coward! Fool! Cecilia held Fitz in great contempt. But her greatest hatred of all was reserved for Cap Fletcher himself. She hated him because she knew the kinds of things he did. She hadn't forgotten that hanging skeleton she'd found in the woods that snowy day. That one hadn't been a Fletcher victim, having been there too long for that, but that was, even so, the kind of evil thing Fletcher did to people. And worst of all, had done to Greeley Brown, the man Cecilia liked better than any man she'd known, besides her father.

Cecilia took another bite of her apple and watched Vaughn Fitz cross down to the house. He hadn't looked toward her. Good. She didn't like it when he looked at her, with that hateful, ugly face of his. She withheld the sound of her voice from him, to her own satisfaction. She wished there was a magical way she could make herself invisible to those whom she chose. Then she could withhold from him the very sight of her, and that would be satisfying indeed.

She had swallowed the last bite of the apple and was rising to her feet to see how far she could toss the core when she saw another figure at the edge of the same field Vaughn Fitz had crossed. The dusk had thickened, the sunlight going red and orange, not very bright, so it was difficult to tell much about this man, other than that he was, indeed, a man. Squinting, she could make out his hat, his beard, his general form. Lean, of average height . . . familiar, maybe. Dropping the apple, she reached up and pressed her hands against her temples, something she had always fancied made her see a little better. Leaning forward, studying him, she was shocked to notice that he now seemed to be studying her in return—in fact, had perhaps just lowered an object from his eye. She saw him put it into a pocket.

A spyglass?

This she didn't like at all, so she took a step back and was going to leap off the rock, when suddenly she *knew*. Gasping, putting her hand to her mouth in surprise, she stared at him over the distance and wondered if there was such a thing as ghosts, because if she had to attach a name to the figure she seemed to be seeing, that name would be Greeley Brown.

He seemed to be seeing her, too, because he lifted an arm and waved at her. She saw him turn his head twice and look toward the house, as if concerned about being seen from there. Cautiously, unsure she should, Cecilia lifted her own arm and waved back.

The figure knelt, then stood again, holding a flat, dark something—a flat stone, it appeared to Cecilia. He waved it above his head so she could see it, then knelt and seemed perhaps to be marking it. He lifted it one more time for her see, then placed it back where it was. Lifting his arm a final time, he turned and vanished into the woods.

Just then her mother's voice came calling from the house: "Cecilia! Time to come home!"

For a few moments Cecilia stood indecisive. She wanted to race through the orchard, into the field, and up to the place where the Greeley Brown figure—she wasn't yet ready to tell herself that it actually *was* the authentic Greeley Brown, for she had thought of him too long as dead and gone—but her mother's call had come at the wrong time.

"Cecilia!"

She looked at the place she'd seen him. Nothing there now. It was as if she might have imagined him. But she hadn't. He had been real. And she was almost sure he had been Greeley Brown.

"Cecilia, come home *now*! If I have to come up there and fetch you myself, you'll wish I hadn't!"

She surrendered to the inevitable, leaped off the boulder, shouldered her bag of apples, and headed down the hollow toward the house, casting glance after glance at the edge of the tree line across the field.

While Vaughn Fitz and her mother slept together in their cold and loveless bed in their equally cold and loveless bedroom, Cecilia lay awake in her own bed in the loft, counting the minutes until she felt certain she could move undetected.

When she could wait no longer, she sat up and listened to the house. She heard Fitz's snoring. Her mother never snored; just now Cecilia wished that she did, so she could have some way to gauge whether she was sleeping. Often her mother lay in that room beside her husband, silent but awake long into the night. Cecilia wondered what her mother thought about at those times. Maybe she thought about how perhaps it hadn't been worth it after all to rush into marriage to a man who had nothing to offer her but a roof and safe domestic harbor where she could hide from the thing she had done, which made her fearful now of the outer world, its courts and laws and prisons.

Impatience at last got the best of Cecilia. She would take the chance that her mother was really asleep. Moving cautiously and as quietly as she could, she dressed herself and went down to the lower level of the house, over to the fireplace. On the mantel lay Vaughn Fitz's much protected block of matches. Cecilia took it down and slipped it into the pocket of her dress, hoping that Fitz didn't keep count of the matches. There would be at least one less when she returned the block to the mantelpiece.

She left the house with no one to stop her. Once outside, she felt a thrill of liberation, and darted across the yard, the road, through the narrow grove of chestnut trees, and on to the meadow across which Vaughn Fitz had strode earlier in the day. The night was cloudy, so she slowed from a run to a walk, not wanting to fall over anything unseen.

The field seemed more vast at night than in the day, and a trifle eerie. The notion that maybe she had seen a ghost rather than a man seemed suddenly plausible, and frightening. She paused, thought about returning, but went on.

As she neared the place she'd seen the figure, she stopped to listen and, as best she could, to look. A night of fear returned to her mind, when a gravedigger had broken into her room and forced himself upon her in the most repellent of manners. What if the man she'd seen wasn't Greeley Brown? What if he was like that gravedigger, and placed that marked stone, or whatever it was, to lure her here so he could hurt her?

She wished she'd thought to bring that knife she had found beneath the house and kept hidden under her bed ever since.

When almost five minutes of listening and watching failed to reveal anything troubling. Cecilia made herself relax, then advanced. Where precisely had that man stood? It was difficult to tell in the dark; the entire perspective of the land was different by night. But she did recall that he placed the stone right past the edge of the woods, in the field. Moving slowly along the tree line, testing the ground with her toe, she sought for it that way, and not two minutes later nudged up against something hard and flat.

She knelt and fumbled with the matches, struck one, clumsily, and lost the match head. The second flared but blew out instantly in the wind—by the brief flash, however, she saw just enough to determine that she had indeed found the correct stone, and that there were faint white markings on it, made by a chunk of limestone used as chalk.

The third match held its fire longer, and she managed to read a part of what was there. The spelling was as poor as the weak and flickering light of the match, forcing her to interpret. Cecilia was displeased by this poor spelling; she was a naturally good speller herself, and felt there was no excuse for anyone to bungle up the language—one of the very few aspects of the young lady that might be considered haughty. She had no pride in her prettiness—she blamed her comeliness for attracting that foul gravedigger on that evil night, in fact—but she did take pride in her spelling.

The next match revealed the remainder of the rough text, and the match after that the thing she was most pleased to see: the initial and name "G. Brown."

He was alive! She must have been wrong about the rifle that Fletcher had showed off. It must have been someone else's.

Not wanting Fitz or any other undesirable party to see what was written on the stone, she turned it facedown.

She was crossing the field back to the cabin when she heard the sound of horsemen. Terror struck. Fletcher! Or some of his men—and either way she did not want to see them.

Cecilia dropped to her face in the field, hiding in the high August grass, as four riders galloped by, crossing in front of the house and heading for the hidden, high meadow on the other end of the hollow.

Fitz had ordered her never to go to that meadow. It was an unnecessary command. Cecilia wanted nothing to do with that field. Fletcher used that field.

She went back to the house, hoping the passing riders hadn't stirred Fitz awake. She was about to mount the porch when the door rattled. She dropped to the ground and rolled up against the foundation, holding her breath.

Fitz emerged from the house. He walked off the porch, into the yard, and looked up the road in the direction the riders had gone. Shaking his head, he mumbled something to himself, then returned to the house and went back inside. Cecilia winced as she heard him close the latch.

She was locked out.

• • •

Miriam, as usual, was the first to rise. Fletcher had been keeping the Fitz family almost continually supplied with coffee ever since that first "wedding gift," with only a couple of coffeeless gaps. Miriam often wondered how he managed to obtain so much of it. However he obtained it, and from whomever, she figured it was taken by force.

Fitz now required that she rise early, brew up a potful, and bring him a cup in bed. "If you refuse me all other wifely kindnesses, you can at least provide me that much favor," he had gruffly said.

Miriam did that, actually glad to have a reason to rise early and get out of his presence for a few minutes. This morning, however, she faced a problem. No matches. The usual block of them was gone from the mantel. She searched every place she could think of but could not find them. Well, it was surely Vaughn's fault; he was the one who controlled and watched the match block as if it were some kind of personal treasure. So he'd just have to do without his coffee until he rose and made it himself, or at least gave her the matches. She'd be hanged before she'd go asking for them.

That matter settled, she followed her usual practice and slipped onto the front porch for a time of quiet, usually while the coffee heated. She was joltingly surprised to find Cecilia on the porch, curled into a tight ball and huddled against the house. Surprise became fear when she realized that the last time she'd found Cecilia in that protective, fetal posture had been after the night of the gravedigger, the ordeal. . . .

But Cecilia seemed fine now. She sat up as Miriam came to her, and smiled.

"I was locked out, Mama."

She had spoken. For the first time since the night Cecilia told her Greeley Brown was dead, she'd spoken. Miriam was left hung between two emotional poles—shock that her daughter, somehow, had actually spent a night locked outside, and joy that she'd chosen to take down the wall of silence.

"Oh, Cecilia! What happened?"

"He's alive, Mama. I saw him yesterday. And he left a message for you, on a stone up by the woods yonder!"

"Who? What message?"

"Greeley Brown, Mama! I saw him yesterday, while I was picking apples." She softly told the tale of the distant figure with the spyglass, and Miriam was simultaneously happy merely to hear Cecilia's voice again and confused by the things Cecilia said. Was she hearing about something that had really happened, or had Cecilia dreamed vividly, and maybe walked onto the porch in her sleep?

"Cecilia, are you sure about this? Might you have just dreamed?"

"No, Mama! He's real! I saw the message he left last night, on the rock. I went up to the woods and found it, and read it."

Miriam's suspicion that she was hearing a fantasy became stronger. "You read it in the dark?"

"No . . . with these." She produced the block of matches.

"Oh, my! Vaughn will be furious with you, Cecilia!"

"Tell him you used them, Mama, to start the coffee fire."

"Say that again, Cecilia."

"What, Mama?"

"*That* . . . 'Mama.' Oh, it's so good to hear your voice calling me that again."

"Everything's going to be good again, Mama. Greeley Brown is alive, and he wants to see you."

"Wants to . . . Cecilia, you surely are dreaming all this, aren't you?"

"No! I'll show you, if I can. The stone is still there, still written on. He wants you to come meet him, early Friday morning, before dawn, near the big rock at the orchard."

"Cecilia, you're sure?"

"I'll show you the stone, Mama. You can see for yourself."

"Friday . . . he wants to see me?"

"Yes, Mama."

Miriam hugged her daughter, and Cecilia hugged her back. It was as if a cold veil had dropped from around Cecilia's shoulders and she was again the girl she'd been before her ordeal and withdrawal.

But when Fitz's voice came booming out of the house, demanding coffee, Miriam felt Cecilia tense again, felt the veil fall back into place. She knew that for now, Cecilia would speak no more, and it made her despise Vaughn Fitz. And herself for having married him. Had she known what she knew of him now, she would never have done it. The dreadful circumstance that had led her to accept him to begin with now seemed no more dreadful than the marriage itself.

She took the matches from Cecilia, and together mother and daughter slipped through the front door and into the house.

Chapter 30

He knew there was something wrong as soon as the cabin came in sight.

Greeley Brown stopped, watching. He knelt, cradling in the crook of his arm the Henry rifle that once had belonged to scouter Hank Heth, and he pulled a spyglass from his pocket. The spyglass, like the rifle, had been a gift from Sally Clung. She had gotten it from an old "man of the sea," as she put it, and from her manner as she said it, Greeley had wondered if once there had been a husband, or at least a lover, in the life of Sally Clung.

He had treasured both the spyglass and the rifle. He'd put both to good use, and wasn't finished yet.

He studied the cabin through the lenses and grew more concerned. Rising, he put the glass away and touched the butt of one of the two Colt revolvers holstered at his waist. Both of these weapons came courtesy of Fletcher's raiders. He'd killed four raiders so far, two each in two camps, and had taken a pistol and ammunition away from each one, along with food and other booty. Sally had been with him during the first attack; the second he had undertaken alone. By the time he was through with Fletcher and his raiders, he aimed to possess again the Henry rifle Fletcher had taken. He intended to take it from the dead fingers of Fletcher himself.

As he walked toward the cabin, his limp was only slight. He was recovered fully as he ever would be from the injuries he had received at the hand of Fletcher and his men. His cracked ribs now gave him no pain except an occasional slight twinge when he coughed. His ankle and knee gave no sign that any damage they had suffered was going to linger. Only two visible aspects of Greeley Brown bore witness to what he had suffered the day Fletcher hanged him from the sapling. One was the handkerchief bound around his neck, covering the ugly scar left by the hanging rope. The other was the even uglier scar on his cheek, only partially obscured by his whiskers. This was the permanent brand of Fletcher's Cross, the mocking cross mark that filled him with hatred every time he saw his reflection when he knelt at a spring or creek to drink.

At the beginning, what had most driven him to begin this lethal campaign against Fletcher and his raiders were the fierce words Sally Clung had chanted into his ear time and again while he was lingering between death and life and his mind was susceptible to influence. Now Sally and her words didn't much matter. What drove him now was the fury that rose in him every time he touched the scar on his face or saw it in reflection.

He reached the door, which was ajar. By now Greeley was sure of two things when he finally began walking again toward the cabin: Something was amiss, and no one was about. No one alive, at least. A glance through the opening revealed a cabin strewn with leaves, with chairs and table overturned, animal droppings throughout. This door had been ajar for a long time. Maybe months. Beasts had come and gone through it at will.

Greeley put his hand against the door and pushed it open a little farther. Steeling himself for what he expected to find, he stooped slightly and entered.

What remained of Mathen Ricker was still in its chair, near the fireplace. The chair, however, lay on its side, and thus the corpse did, too. Greeley felt a lump rise in his throat as he drew near. Not much remained of Mathen except bone, ragged and rotted clothing, and leathery skin. The meager flesh remaining on the head was pulled back tight against the skull. His white hair was all still there, though his eyes weren't. Birds, or maybe ants, had done away with them a long time back. The lower portion of his left leg was gone, too, probably carried away by some carnivore.

Greeley raised the chair and was surprised that Mathen rose with it. He realized the body was tied to the seat. Greeley felt a surge of hate, his most familiar emotion these days. They had tied him in his chair, just an old man! Tied him up as if he could have been any kind of threat to them, and then shot him!

When Mathen was seated upright again, Greeley stepped back and read the placard his killers had hung from his neck:

HARBORED LINCOLNITES

Greeley closed his eyes, suffering. The only Unionist Mathen had ever harbored was the man now standing before his corpse. Mathen had died, in short, because he'd been a friend to Greeley Brown, and word had somehow gotten out.

In earlier days Greeley would have been moved to tears by such a realization, but these days there seemed to be no tears left inside him. Only bitter anger.

He wondered who had done this to Mathen.

Greeley bent and looked into the dead and decayed face. Suddenly his own face twitched spasmodically and his eye flashed. Though the lines and creases of decay had initially made it hard to be sure, this closer look left no doubt about it: On the leathery husk of Mathen Ricker's face was the same mark that scarred the left jaw of Greeley himself, the mark of Fletcher's Cross.

At that moment, many miles and mountains way, within the enclosed compound that was the Confederate prisoner-of-war camp at Salisbury, North Carolina, another man named Brown was staring at another corpse. And like his brother in Mathen Ricker's old cabin in Carter County, East Tennessee, Thatcher Brown was finding himself unable to weep even as he gazed at the body of an old and dear friend.

Maybe it was the scurvy, the exhaustion, the endless boredom and rising hopelessness that had rendered him emotionless.

Thatcher didn't care to know. What did it matter? All that mattered was that Rockwell Griffin had at long last made the escape attempt that for him had always been going to happen tonight, or tomorrow, or the day after tomorrow. He'd made the attempt, and he had died.

It all seemed manifestly absurd to Thatcher. Why, there might even be something comic in it, had this tale been told of a stranger and not Griffin. As he had so often declared he would do, Griffin had taken the direct, brash approach to escape. An almost cliché approach, Thatcher perceived it: torn sheets tied into a rope and lowered from a window. Griffin had climbed out, begun to lower himself, and then had fallen. Straight down, onto his head. He was dead by the time the guards reached him.

"Well, Rock, you told me that one day I'd pull down a sheet and find your dead face under it," Thatcher said. "You were right, my friend. God help me. You were right."

He remembered also what he had told Griffin: When Griffin made his escape, he would be with him. Then at the last day, Thatcher had broken that promise. Some instinct, maybe some burst of cowardice he didn't want to admit . . . whatever it was, it had made him back away, and encourage Griffin to do the same. It isn't going to work, he had said. Let's don't try this, Rock. Let's wait until a better time, find a better way.

Griffin had been furious when Thatcher said that. He'd called him a yellowbelly and told him that if he wouldn't come along, he'd go alone. He'd made the attempt that night, and he had died. Angry at Thatcher when he left him, angry at him as he began his descent, probably still angry at him when he plunged and struck the ground. The emotional knot this unhappy final parting left snarled inside Thatcher was so Gordian that he doubted he'd ever untangle it.

"Well, Griffin, old fellow, you did accuse me of always trying to prove myself right. This time you went and proved it for me. You shouldn't have tried it, my friend. You should have listened to opinionated old Thatcher one more time. Now you've gone and left me alone here, and I don't much appreciate it."

He let the sheet fall back over Griffin's face and walked slowly away, toward the prison hospital. He had duties in that hospital now, assigned by the general superintendent of the prison, who had reasoned that a journalist would surely have organizational and record-keeping abilities. So far Thatcher had hated the work, though he'd gotten good at it, but today he was glad to have something to occupy him.

He stopped at the entrance of the hospital and looked around, then suddenly chuckled at the realization that he was looking for Griffin. Absurd. He was looking for a dead man. The chuckle grew, then faded, and he wondered how it was that a man who could not cry could still laugh.

He looked across the prison yard and thought: I've got to get out of here.

There were three in the camp, arguing about who would keep watch. As the sun edged down, he watched them from hiding, examining their faces through the spyglass until he was sure. These in fact were three of the ones who had been there at his hanging. Fletcher men. It was all he needed to see. He folded and put away the spyglass, and waited for them to settle their argument.

They did this, after much expending of time and profanity, through the drawing of straws. The unlucky loser settled back against a tree, rifle across his middle, while the others lay down on their blankets. They began to snore after five minutes or so, and before another five were past, the man on watch began to nod off, head drooping down toward his chest.

A single slash of the knife from behind the tree laid open his throat and ensured he would not awaken again. He slumped to the ground sideways, still holding his rifle. Greeley rose and stepped around the tree and across his body, kneeling to wipe the blade clean on the man's shirt. The others still snored.

He sheathed the knife and drew out one of his pistols. "Hey, there," he said.

The first one to wake looked at him stupidly, bleary-eyed, then came out of his blankets while groping for his rifle. The report of the pistol shot that instantly killed him awakened the other with a start. He erupted from the ground with a yell, reaching for the gun belt he had laid beside his head when he retired. Greeley waited until the man got his hand onto the butt of his holstered weapon before he fired again. The bullet entered the man's right side, knocking him down. He moved and moaned for no more than three seconds before he was dead.

Greeley holstered his pistol and examined the dead ones and their possessions, taking a small hide-out pistol from the pocket of the sentry, some food from their packs, and usable ammunition. The rest he left behind, and disappeared into the thick forest.

The next day, Cap Fletcher, alone for once, appeared at the door of the Fitz house in Limestone Cove. Miriam answered the door, feeling the fear and disgust she always knew in this man's presence. Fletcher was in an odd, distracted mood, not at all his usual cordial self toward her, and said flatly that he wished to speak to her husband in private. She was sent out of the house, and he and Vaughn retired to the rear and leaned across a table, conferring seriously, Fletcher occasionally rising to pace about, sometimes pounding the table with his fist.

Below the house, Cecilia was ensconced. She heard all that went on above, because Fletcher was talking very loudly today, and reported it to her mother in secret later on.

Fletcher had come to talk to Fitz because he was concerned. Angry. Worried. Within the last few weeks he had lost seven men—*seven!*—right in their camps. It was unimaginable. Three had died only the evening before, not two miles from this house. It was as if some ghost was doing the killing. Not that there were ghosts, mind you, Vaughn, but what kind of man could do so efficient a lethal job? How could he not be detected? His men always kept watch in their individual camps. Whoever was killing Fletcher's scattered band was either very lucky, or very skilled.

Vaughn Fitz had no answers. Cecilia heard him scuff about in his chair, yes-sirring and no-sirring, and agreeing with anything Fletcher threw at him, but saying nothing of consequence. No doubt he was wondering what any of this had to do with him.

Fletcher went on. He'd always favored dividing his men

into small, scattered groups for encampment purposes. That way they could not be caught as one large body. Now it seemed he would have to change his strategy and maintain a larger general encampment far more regularly. Which meant he and his men would more often be on Fitz's land. Fitz was not invited to reject this. It was simply presented to him. His land would no longer be the occasional hiding point it had been. Fletcher was effectively taking over the back meadow as his permanent encampment.

Below the house, listening, Cecilia imagined Fitz's big head bobbing obediently up and down, letting Fletcher dictate his intentions to him. There would be no resistance. Fitz was far too compliant a coward for that.

Fletcher talked on, pacing back and forth above Cecilia, dictating his thoughts and plans to Fitz like some factory procurer ordering up raw goods. With his camp made virtually permanent back in Fitz's meadow, it would be prudent to guard the head of the hollow. Two men would probably suffice for that. Fitz would be expected to help them any way he could. Water, food, and so on. The women should be kept close in around the house unless Fletcher called on them for some kind of errand. If they came near his camp without permission, however, Fletcher would not be responsible for their safety. The same was true for Fitz. And Fitz's own goings from this narrow valley should always be told in advance to the sentinels, otherwise he might be shot by accident coming back. And if there was any hint of betrayal on Fitz's part, any hint at all . . .

Cecilia had closed her eyes, vividly picturing Fletcher leaning across the table, finger shaking in Fitz's no doubt pallid face like a pistol.

Fitz sputtered, laughed cordially. Of course there would be no betrayal! Why, Captain Fletcher was welcome to ensconce his men in the back meadow any time he desired. Forevermore, if he wanted!

The conversation had gone on awhile longer, really more a fierce monologue by Fletcher than a dialogue. He had ranted and stomped, cursing whoever it was who was getting the best of his men. Seven men! Seven of them, killed right in camp! From a band of forty-five men besides himself, he was now reduced to thirty-eight. Fletcher swore and stomped and declared he'd find this killer, somehow, and make him regret the day he had ever turned a knife or gun against Fletcher's raiders! He'd regret the very day he had taken his first breath, once he was through with him! And if the fellow proved unfindable, and the killings somehow continued . . . well, he, Fletcher, would make *all* the people of the mountains regret it. If he couldn't punish the right one, he'd punish all, until someone in the know spoke up and put the culprit in his hands.

And then, with that declaration made, Fletcher abruptly changed. Cecilia had been able to detect it even from her sub-floor hiding place. His voice had changed, even his footfall. He had vented his anger, and suddenly he was cordial to Fitz, the obedient recipient of it all.

Cecilia heard joking, laughter, and the giving of a gift. Then Fletcher departed, mounting his horse outside and riding on to the back meadow, where his men awaited. Surely, Cecilia thought, they were a more somber band than the cocksure gang she had seen before, now that they'd been given seven reasons to realize they were not invulnerable. Before he rode off, Cecilia heard Fletcher say a kind and cheerful farewell to her mother, who had bided her time while exiled from the house by clearing weeds from the garden.

Cecilia waited a few minutes, then crawled out from beneath the house. She went to her mother and they moved off behind a tree, where Cecilia could talk without Fitz chancing to see her. There, Cecilia faithfully reported all she had heard, and watched her mother's face take on a burdened look. The hated Fletcher was going to be a greater part of their lives than ever.

When Cecilia and Miriam went back into the house, Fitz was locked in his bedroom. They heard him pacing around in there, mumbling.

On the back table they found the gift Fletcher had left for Fitz. A jug of whiskey.

Fitz drank some of the whiskey that night. Not too much, but enough to make him slightly drunk and very maudlin and brooding. Then he drank a little more, and brooding turned to abusiveness.

He stared at Cecilia, who peeled apples into a big wooden bowl on the other side of the room.

"Girl."

She looked up at him.

"Put that knife down and come here."

Cecilia did neither. She stared at him, silent.

"I told you to put that knife down and come here!"

She laid the paring knife aside and went to him, standing before him with arms limp at her sides.

"Why won't you ever talk to nobody, girl?"

There was, of course, no reply. On the other side of the room, Miriam looked worried, and said, "Vaughn—" He waved a hand impatiently at her, an excluding gesture.

"Answer me, Cecilia! You got a tongue in your head, don't you?"

Cecilia continued to stare.

"Damn you, girl, talk to me! What is it you want? You think standing around like some dumb beast is going to make folks feel sorry for you? Think that's going to make them get all touched over your little 'ordeal,' like your mama always wants to call it? That it?"

Cecilia's face and stony silence went unchanged.

"Answer me!"

"Vaughn, in the name of heaven—"

"Shut up, Miriam! It ain't you I want to hear! I want to hear this one say something! I know she can talk! It's damned rude of her to treat me like she does, like I ain't even worth being spoke to! I'm her father now, damn it! And a father wants to hear his girl's voice."

And to his surprise, and Miriam's, suddenly he did. Cecilia looked him in the eye and said, "You're not my father."

So stunning was it to hear her speak that Vaughn didn't react at once. A pall of silence fell in the room.

"Huh!" he grunted a few moments later. "Well, I married your mama, and I reckon that makes me your father."

"You're not my father. I hate you."

She had spoken it softly, but because it was said by a voice so long unheard, the words bore a great impact. Fitz literally flinched to hear them.

"Cecilia . . ." Miriam said, sounding more afraid than chiding.

Fitz rose. "You hate me, do you? Well, I don't see you hating the food I put in your mouth every day!"

He waited for her to reply. Cecilia merely stared at him. Silent again. She had said what she wanted and would say no more.

"I don't see you hating that roof over your head when it rains!"

He waited again. Nothing. He began to seethe.

"I don't see you hating that I gave you a home even though you're no more than a little bastard-birthing harlot!"

Miriam came to her feet. "Vaughn!"

He aimed a finger at her. The whiskey in him was making him burn. "I told you to shut up, woman! It's this little trollop I'm talking to now!" He stuck his ugly face down toward Cecilia. And grinned. His teeth were yellow and his breath smelled of whiskey. "Tell me, girl . . . did that gravedigger really bust in on you, or did you ask him in? Huh?"

Cecilia's expression did not alter at all. His smile mutated into a snarl. He swore and pulled back his fist.

Miriam was there at once. She grabbed his arm before he could swing it down. Cecilia had not moved nor changed her look. Her arms still hung limp and straight.

Miriam made him look at her. "You want to hit somebody, Vaughn, you hit them—but not *her*! You never hit her, you hear me? You have to hit somebody, then you hit yourself, or hit me, but never Cecilia!"

"However you want it, Miriam," he said. He jerked his arm from her grasp, balled his fist again, and hit Miriam hard on the left side of the face. She staggered back and collapsed.

He stood panting, looking at her as if he'd just seen her, then at his fist. "Oh, God . . . Miriam, I'm sorry. I'm sorry." He went to her, reaching out. In tears, holding the place his fist had struck her, she shook her head and scooted away. He fell to his knees, hands still out. "I'm sorry, Miriam. I shouldn't have done that . . . please, honey, forgive me!"

Miriam pulled her legs up against her body and turned her face away from him, crying, rejecting him, refusing even to look at him. He pleaded and wept. Miriam closed herself off. He could not break through.

He came to his feet, sobbing and slobbering, and turned to Cecilia. She stood where she'd been before, hands still at her sides, but now her fists were clenched and her eyes glared.

"Cecilia, I'm sorry. I'm sorry I lifted my hand to you. I'm sorry I said all that, and I'm sure sorry I hit your mama. Oh, forgive me, Lord. Forgive me."

He stumbled toward his bedroom, then halted, stumbled back again to get the whiskey jug. Weeping, blubbering, he went into his room and closed the door. The bed creaked loudly as he threw himself onto it.

Cecilia went to her mother and knelt beside, stroking her arm gently.

"Greeley Brown wants to see you Friday morning, Mama," she said. "You'll go see him, won't you?"

"Yes," Miriam said. "And I'm going to ask him to take us away from here."

"Are you going to tell him, Mama? You know . . . about what happened?"

"I don't know. No. No, there's no reason I should."

"But someday you'll have to tell him."

"Someday? What 'someday' do you mean, Cecilia?"

"If you married him, I mean."

Miriam shook her head. "Oh, Cecilia, I can't marry anyone now. I've already got a husband."

Cecilia listened to the bed creaking in the other room, and Fitz's voice mumbling his assorted angers, regrets, and sorrows to the ceiling.

"I wish you didn't have a husband."

"I know. I was wrong to marry him. It wasn't fair to any of us. Not even to him. He thought I was taking him as a husband, when all I was doing was using him as a refuge."

"We'll go away from here, Mama?"

"Yes. The moment he raised his fist to strike you, I knew we would go away."

"Will Greeley Brown take us?"

"I hope he will."

"Once we're gone from here, will we still need refuge? Will they still be looking for you?"

"Yes. I suppose they will."

"Then we'll have to find some other place to be safe."

"Yes."

"Where?"

"I don't know, Cecilia. Some things we will have to deal with as they arise. I can't see the future clearly right now. Maybe Greeley can help find us a place."

"You're going to have tell Greeley Brown what you did, Mama. He's going to want to know why you have to hide."

"Then . . . maybe I'll tell him. I don't know yet."

"He would understand, Mama. He isn't like Uncle Vaughn, or Fletcher. He's a good man. I could tell when I was with him that he's good."

"Cecilia, you really did see him? There really was a message on a stone? You're sure?"

"I'm sure. I saw him. I know it was him. I read the stone. He'll really be there, Friday morning."

"Then I'll be there, too. Somehow. I wonder why he wants to talk to me?"

Cecilia started suddenly, in realization. "Mama! Oh no . . . today when Uncle Vaughn and Fletcher were talking, Fletcher said he was going to put guards to watch the mouth of the hollow. That's near where the big rock is that you are supposed to meet Greeley Brown."

"Oh." This cast a new light on the anticipated rendezvous.

"If there are guards there, he won't be able to come."

Miriam mulled it over, concern mounting. She cursed Fletcher in her mind—was that human demon going to deprive her even of this?

"I suppose we'll just have to trust to Greeley Brown's ability to take care of himself," she said. "He's a strong man." She put on a smile and patted Cecilia's leg confidently. "Maybe it will be easier than we think. Maybe there won't be a guard there at all."

Chapter 31

But there was a guard there. In the dimmest light of the earliest moments of dawn, Miriam saw him. He was just inside a small grove of woods, where he had a good view of the road leading into the hollow, through the gap that was the only access besides the rugged slopes of the enclosing ridges themselves. As she watched the sentinel there, Miriam thought, grudgingly, how clever Fletcher was to have chosen this hollow as his place of encampment. It was remote, easily defended, and occupied only by a compliant Confederate sympathizer with a backbone as weak as if it had been soaked in vinegar for a month. It was odd, when she considered it: Many of the same factors that had drawn Fletcher here were also what had drawn her. They were alike in that way, she and Fletcher. Both of their situations called for remoteness, isolation, concealment.

The thought displeased her. She did not like to think of herself as like Fletcher in any way.

Yet there was one more similarity between them, one she pushed far from her mind.

A noise behind her made her gasp. She let out her breath

slowly, pressing her hand to her throat. "Cecilia!" she scolded in a whisper. "Why are you here? You shouldn't have followed me!"

"I had to, Mama," she said. "I couldn't just stay down there, with *him*, while you were up here. I want to see Greeley Brown. Maybe he'll take us away today, right now!"

"What if Vaughn wakes up and finds us both gone?"

"He won't wake up. He drank too much whiskey last night."

This, Miriam knew, was probably true. She had put herself through quite an ordeal late the night before, acting kind to her unwanted husband, smiling at him, stroking him, putting on the finest male-manipulating performance of a life that had included many of these. And all the while she had urged whiskey upon him, pouring glass after glass of it from what remained in the jug Fletcher had given him some days ago. She had filled him with it, promising him pleasures to come later in the night . . . but in the meantime, wouldn't he like another drink? Of course he would . . .

He had passed out sometime around two in the morning. Then Miriam called Cecilia down from her loft, and together they carried him to his bed to sleep it off—late into the morning, with any luck. After which time, Miriam was prepared to regale him with stories of what an astonishingly manly and virile fellow he had proven himself to be.

"Cecilia, you must go back anyway. It isn't safe. Fletcher does have a guard posted. See over there, in the trees? Don't lift your head very far—he might see you."

Cecilia looked, cautiously. "There's no one there, Mama."

"There is. I saw him. Look right over there, into that little stand of . . ." She trailed off, puzzled. Cecilia was right. There was no one there—but there *had* been, only moments before.

"I don't understand. Maybe he's moved. Or—Cecilia, what if he's seen us? He might be sneaking toward us!"

"Don't worry about him."

The voice caught them both by surprise. It came from behind them; they rose and turned as one.

Greeley Brown was there. He looked leaner than ever, almost gaunt in his leanness. His beard was longer, grayer, his eyes more intense. A cross-mark scar marred his left cheek, and around his neck was a kerchief. He carried a Henry rifle, a bit different than the one he'd borne when they were with him last, and two pistol butts stuck out from holsters on his belt, along with a long knife. Unseen to them was yet a fourth bit of armament, the hide-out gun he had taken from one of the three Fletcher men he'd killed in the camp the night after he found Mathen Ricker's drying remains.

The sudden way he had appeared, and his altered, powerful appearance, generated in the two females for a few moments a feeling akin to that of pious visitants receiving a vision of the Holy Virgin. Then he smiled, just a little, and the feeling became one of relief and happiness, mixed with confusion over that vanishing sentinel.

"Greeley! Oh, I'm so glad to see you!" Miriam exclaimed, moving toward him. Something in his manner brought her to a halt before she reached him, and suddenly it was clear that this was to be no emotional and affectionate reunion. Miriam suddenly felt small in his presence, and looked for something to say. "What happened to the guard, Greeley?"

"He's dead," Greeley replied flatly.

"Dead . . . oh. There might be another one, though. Cecilia heard Fletcher talking to Vaughn, you see, and he said he would post two guards. . . ." She faltered, wondering why she was so intimidated by him. This did not seem the same casual Greeley Brown she had chatted with one night in the dark in the backyard of the inn in Sevierville, or the one who had been so easygoing and pleasant all through their winter journey to this place.

"There was another one," Greeley replied. "You didn't see him. He was dead before you came here. A knife through the throat."

No one said anything for a couple of moments. Greeley looked at Cecilia, and his smile came again, flickering a little longer and more warmly than the one he'd given Miriam. "Hello, little lady. Are you willing to speak to me today?"

"Yes," Cecilia replied very softly. "Hello, Mr. Brown."

"Call me Greeley. I ain't never been a 'mister' to nobody." He seemed more his old self now, Miriam noticed. But he turned back to her, and the new, hardened Greeley Brown was suddenly there again. "Mrs. Fitz, I hope you don't mind I've come to see you."

"Oh, no, no . . . I'm glad you came. We both are. Please, Greeley, don't call me Mrs. Fitz. I'm Miriam, remember?"

"I think Mrs. Fitz is best. It's the truth, ain't it? You married him?"

"Yes."

He nodded. "I thought so. I'm going to ask you a few things more, and I want you to tell me the truth. Not the kind of stories I heard from you before. You understand me?"

"Yes." She wouldn't have dared lie to this ardent a man. She stared at him, dismayed, actually finding it hard to believe this really was Greeley Brown. Something fundamental to the man had transformed dramatically since she'd last seen him.

"Good. First off, when we was traveling together before, you already knew your sister was dead, didn't you? And don't try to tell me no tales. I've seen her tombstone, and I know she died months before you even commenced heading for Carter County."

Miriam stuck out her chin, determined to endure her intimidation with as much grace as possible. "Yes, I already knew."

"And you come knowing that Fitz was waiting for you and aiming to marry you as soon as you arrived. Am I right?"

"Yes."

"Well, I want to know why you told me the stories you did. There was times I truly thought that maybe you held me in the kind of regard a woman holds a man she might be smit by, or besotten of. You knew I felt that way, didn't you."

He had made the latter comment as a flat statement, not a question, but he seemed to want to hear her confirm it. She nodded. "Yes. I could tell how you felt."

"You played me along, didn't you! Played me for a man to be toyed with for your own benefit, just like that foolish old landlord in Sevierville. Is that why you made up the story about your sister? Did you think I wouldn't be as inclined to help you if you had just said straight out you were coming here to get married?"

"Yes . . . no . . . I don't know how to answer."

"How about honestly?"

"All right. Very well. Yes, I did use the story of an ailing sister to get sympathy and help from men—men who might have been much less inclined to give me help if I said I was simply heading for marriage to another man. You have to understand men from the perspective of a woman in need, Greeley. So many of the things men do for women they do on the fantasy that they have a chance to gain that woman's romantic affection. A married woman, or even an engaged woman, in their eyes is like a calf that's already penned. They might help her out, but not as full-heartedly as if there remains that one slight hope, that one chance, that maybe this woman will decide that *this* man is surely the man for me! I developed the story about my sick sister early on, long before I met you in Sevierville. So at that point I was pretty much saddled with it. I had to play the hand I had already dealt myself."

"It's all a game, in your eyes. Say what you got to say to get them to do what you want them to do."

"No! It wasn't like that, Greeley. Not at all—not with *you*. Oh, you don't know how I admired you! If I could have had any sense at all that there was any hope of . . . I don't know, a bonding or relationship between us, oh, I would have welcomed it!"

He clearly didn't believe her. "So why did you play me like a dupe? Why didn't you just confess you'd been making up tales, and tell me the honest truth about Fitz and this marriage business?"

"Because at the time I felt I had no choice. No choice at all, about anything I did from the time I left my own home until I came here. It was my situation, my circumstances. I had to have security. Immediate security, in a place where I could just . . . vanish. A place no one would look for me. Vaughn Fitz offered that, and his was the only offer I had at the time. I believed I had to play out the game I had started, to make sure I could get to him safely. That was all that mattered at that point: to get to him, and away from the situation I was in."

He studied her, solemn. "I always had the sense you were running from something. Something you never told. What was it?"

She hung her head. "Something I did. Something that was right . . . but something the law would not allow."

Greeley shifted his eyes to Cecilia, then back to Miriam. When he spoke next he was a little less intense, not so foreboding in manner. "You killed somebody. Is that it?"

She nodded.

"The man who hurt Cecilia?"

She lifted her face and looked at him squarely. "Yes."

His brows narrowed together; his jaw moved subtly, making the cross-mark scar on his face ripple very slightly. "You did the right thing, then. He earned it."

"The law doesn't agree with that sentiment. I had to run. I didn't even use my real name until I was far away from Livingston. I didn't use it, in fact, until I entered the Campbell boardinghouse, where we met."

"So you came here to wed your widower brother-in-law and hide yourself and Cecilia in these mountains."

"That's right. Yes. I didn't see that I had a choice. I had no means of supporting myself, no prospects for any kind of life for myself and my daughter, other than what Vaughn Fitz had already offered me twice through proposals of marriage. I had turned him down before. When he asked the third time, I said yes. The proposal had come right after I killed the gravedigger."

"Gravedigger?"

"Yes. It was a gravedigger who attacked Cecilia. The very gravedigger who put my husband beneath the ground. Ironic, isn't it?"

"When did you kill him?"

"Last year. After he hurt Cecilia, he vanished. No one could find him. But he started coming around again. An ugly, taunting, wicked man . . . Cecilia was terrified. Me, too. So when he came to our house one night, drunk, I shot him. I hid the body. In a cave, deep in a mountain. I dragged him in . . . there was a pit in there. I'd found it when I was just a girl, exploring with my brother. No one else knew about the cave. I pushed the body in, then went on the run."

"Does Vaughn Fitz know about the killing?"

"No. Oh, no. He was willing to stand for the situation involving Cecilia and little James—though he thinks of that as a 'scandal'—but I knew that if he was aware that his lovely new wife had *killed* a man . . . oh, my. He wouldn't have stood for that at all."

"So tell me, Mrs. Fitz—"

"Please, *please* don't call me that, Greeley! Please call me

by my name . . . I can't abide the *coldness* of hearing you talk
to me so formally."

"All right. I'll call you by your name. But can you see,
Miriam, how it is I'm a bit shy about getting friendly with you?
You kept me in the dark for day after day, mile after mile. You
had me guiding you here thinking you was on a mission of
good charity for a dying sister, when all along you was doing
nothing but running from the law, and to a man you were going
to marry just because you could hide behind him. When I left
on that last stampeder run, I'd sworn not to return to these
mountains. I come back only for your sake, and that 'dying'
sister you was going to take care of. And because I come back,
I almost got myself killed."

Miriam looked at his face. "The scar . . . Fletcher's Cross?"

"That's right. And this . . ." He ripped off the kerchief from
around his neck, revealing the ugly, burnlike marks left by a
rope, eliciting gasps from both Miriam and Cecilia. "This is the
scar left by Fletcher's noose."

"Oh, Greeley!"

Cecilia came closer, staring. "You were hanged?"

"That's right. By Fletcher and his men. One of the two sen-
tries I killed this morning, I recognized him as one of the ones
who beat me with his rifle butt while I was swinging."

"How did you survive?" Miriam asked.

"By the grace of God and the help of an old mountain
woman named Sally Clung, who come along at the right
moment and cut me down. From that day on she's tended me,
fed me, got me back to health. She's brought me weapons—
this rifle, this knife—and she's chanted in my ear since before I
could grasp the words, that I was saved from death for a purpose. She says I was saved to avenge myself, and all the Union
people of these mountains who've suffered so bad, against Cap
Fletcher and his raiders."

Miriam looked at the place where a sentinel who would
never stand again had stood only minutes before. "Have you
been fulfilling that purpose, Greeley?"

"I have. The two that died this morning, that makes nine
so far."

Cecilia, speaking in the voice that was always a surprise to hear, said, "Cap Fletcher has a camp in this valley. On my Uncle Vaughn's land."

"I know," Greeley replied. "I ferreted out that he'd been camping here that same night I saw you among the apple trees. 'Uncle Vaughn,' you call him. You don't call him Pa, or Pap?"

"He's not my father. He'll never be. I despise him."

Greeley frowned, taking that in. He looked at Miriam. "A bad man, your new husband?"

"A weak man. A man I shouldn't have married." She remembered him drawing his fist back to strike at Cecilia, the same fist that struck her instead. She touched the place. "Yes. A bad man."

Greeley frowned and looked closer, the rising light revealing that what he'd taken for a shadow was in fact a bruise. "He struck you?"

"Yes."

"Tell me, is he in cahoots with Fletcher? Letting him camp on his land of his own free will?"

"He goes along. I don't think he likes it, but he's afraid of Fletcher. He won't stand up to him. As far as I'm concerned, he's in cahoots with him, yes. Fletcher gives him things— coffee, whiskey. Payment of sorts, I suppose. Fletcher himself gave me a coffee kettle—a 'wedding gift.' I believe it was the same kettle that old Mr. Ricker used to boil that coffee for all of us the day we stopped at his house."

"Oh, Mama!" This from Cecilia, who had not noticed on her own that it was the same kettle, and whom her mother had declined to tell, sparing her the grim knowledge.

"It likely was," Greeley replied. "I went calling on Mathen some days ago, wanting him to know I was alive, for as I understand it, Fletcher has been bragging all among the Confederate sympathizers who help him that he hanged Greeley Brown. I figured Mathen had heard the story and been grieved by it."

"So he's alive?"

"No. Tied in a chair and shot to death, and this . . ." He touched his own facial mutilation. ". . . carved onto his face."

Miriam slumped, looking weak. "Fletcher."

"Yep. I never saw a man so keen on murdering. He's the

worst by far that's come into these hills. Worse than Bozen, Parker, Teener, any of them."

"I hate him," Cecilia said.

"So do I, honey," Greeley replied. "I aim to fulfill that duty that Sally Clung whispered in my ear. I'm going to kill that man. And as many of his raiders as I can get along the way while I'm looking for him." He looked squarely at Miriam. "And I'll tell you this, Miriam: If Vaughn Fitz has been giving aid to Fletcher, as far as I'm concerned he's one and the same as one of Fletcher's raiders himself. And if I have to, I'll kill him just as quick as I've killed the other nine so far."

Miriam did not know what to reply to that. She had no love for Vaughn Fitz, but the notion of agreeing to what Greeley had said seemed barbaric. Then she realized he was not asking for her agreement or approval. He was simply laying out the truth before her. She saw how right she'd been in what she said once before about Greeley Brown: This man was authentic. What he was he laid out in the open, without falsehood or deceit. A far different kind of personality, she thought with some chagrin, than she herself was.

She decided that at this moment perhaps the best she could do for herself, and for Cecilia, was be just as forthright as Greeley himself. "Greeley, I want to leave this place. I want you to guide Cecilia and me again, like before. Take us out of these mountains."

"You're abandoning your husband?"

"He's my husband in name only. He tried to hit Cecilia, Greeley. He did hit me. He gives support to a murderer. I'll not stay with him."

Cecilia looked up at Greeley with eyes that touched his heart—a much harder heart than had beat in his chest before Fletcher put his noose around his neck, but a heart still readily accessible to the influence of this marvelous child. "Will you guide us, Greeley?"

He reached out to touch her shoulder, then wondered if he should. She had been so hurt by men. She might reject even his touch. But she did not flinch back, and he caressed her shoulder gently, only for a moment.

"I'll guide you."

Miriam asked, "Greeley, is that why you came here? To guide us away?"

He shook his head. "No. I came to find out the truth about you, Miriam. And to make sure that Cecilia was doing well. Mostly I came hunting Fletcher. I'd tracked him, you see, and he led me right here."

It struck Miriam at that point that she had lost Greeley Brown. There had been opportunity before, a chance to have gotten to know this man, and to come to love him. It would have been easy. But in her fear, her desire for quick refuge, she had bypassed him and gone to Vaughn Fitz instead. She had made her decision, a bad one. And now, sadly, it appeared that Greeley Brown had made his.

Chapter 32

She looked sickly, Greeley thought. Not just old and wrinkled up anymore, but pallid. And it ain't like Sally to sit about like this.

He squatted on his haunches, facing the old woman, who sat on a log section outside her cabin, grinning at him, displaying the five teeth remaining in her head. "How you feeling, Sally?"

"A little puny, to tell you the truth. Been puny for a couple of days now."

"Just how old are you, anyway? You been up in these mountains as long as I can remember, and even when I was a boy folks called you 'Old Sally.' "

"If I knowed how old I was, I'd tell you, Greeley. But I lost count about the age of sixty, and that was many a year back."

"Tell me something: Do the mountains really talk to you, like folks say?"

"The mountains will talk to anybody who knows how to listen."

He smiled as he thought about that. He knew what she meant.

"The mountains, they're a sad and weary place now," she said, the grin declining. "Too much warring and wickedness."

"Sad and weary," he repeated. "Sort of the way you seem today, Sally."

She did not dispute him.

He reached over and took her hand. "Sally, I'll be leaving the mountains for a while. Just a little while, that's all. Got to guide some folks out."

"Stampeders?"

"No. A woman and her daughter. They need to get away. The woman's husband has become cruel to her, and he's been giving aid to Fletcher. Letting him camp his men on his land."

"His main camp?"

"So it appears. Apparently Fletcher used it every now and then up until his men started turning up dead in their smaller camps. Now he's there most all the time."

"I've looked for Fletcher's camp. Ain't never found it."

"I have. And I'll deal with it later, when I'm through with this little piloting run. We'll be leaving tomorrow, Lord willing and nothing interfering. I'll be back, I don't know, soon as I can."

"Where you taking them?"

"I ain't sure. I suppose I'll see if they've got kin or friends they can go to, and take them there. The woman is on the run, because of something she did in Middle Tennessee."

"Something bad?"

"Something the law won't stand for, but no, under the circumstances, nothing I'd call bad. She killed a man who deserved it."

"There's another man deserves killing."

"I know. I'll be back for him."

"It was why you was saved from death, Greeley."

"So you've told me."

"It's the truth."

He grinned, just a little. "Who told it to you? The mountain?"

"Yes," she said.

He was going to chuckle, but realized she was utterly serious.

Vaughn Fitz awakened with the first hint of dawn. His back hurt and an undefined sense of disquiet was stirring inside him. He looked at the ceiling and slowly began to wonder why he was in such an odd and uncomfortable position, arms raised above his head, wrists crossed and sore. He moved his arms and found he couldn't. Something restrained them.

"What the—"

He tugged; the entire bed creaked and shook.

Craning his neck, he saw that his wrists were tied together, very tightly, and lashed to the headboard. Eyes bugging wide, he looked down and realized his feet were bound, too.

Oh, no, he thought, it's surely Fletcher. He's decided to rid himself of me, have this valley, and Miriam, for himself, and he's bound me up while I slept and is surely going to kill me. . . .

Involuntarily, he let out a moan.

The bedroom door opened and Miriam entered. She was clad in some of his own extra clothing, and looked scared. Standing just inside the door, she stared at him silently, reminding him just then of her own defiantly silent daughter.

"Miriam, what the devil is going on here? Why am I tied up? Where's Fletcher?"

"I don't know where Fletcher is. Probably back in the rear meadow. You're tied up because we had to do it."

"He made you?"

"Fletcher? No, Vaughn, Fletcher has nothing to do with this. It's Cecilia and me. We're leaving you. We tied you so you wouldn't try to stop us."

"*Leaving* me! What do you mean, leaving?"

She didn't look scared now. Just defiant and coldly angry. "Leaving means leaving. We're going away. You shouldn't have hit me, Vaughn. You shouldn't have tried to hit Cecilia. And most of all you shouldn't have tied yourself in with a murdering ruffian like Cap Fletcher."

Vaughn Fitz swore and spat and pulled at his ropes. They would not yield, and the headboard, made of heavy iron, would not either.

"I'd hoped you wouldn't wake up until we were gone," Miriam went on. "But maybe it's best this way. At least you know what is happening. Whenever I'm settled, elsewhere, I'll be in contact with you through a lawyer, and we can arrange a divorce."

"Miriam, let me go! Let's talk about this, please!"

"There's nothing to talk about. And there's no point in pulling on those ropes—I made sure they were tight enough that you wouldn't be able to get out of them. They may be too tight, really, and I hope no harm will come to your hands from that. They're certainly no tighter than the nooses that go around the necks of innocent people hanged by that murderer you harbor on your land."

His face reddened; he began to blubber. "Miriam, oh please, Miriam, don't go! Don't! I don't want you to! You're my wife!"

"I'm not. I never have been. Not really. I married you because you were the only sure form of refuge available to me at a time I needed it. I owe you an apology for that, Vaughn. I used you, and it was wrong. But that doesn't change what I have to do today."

"Miriam, I don't care what's wrong, I'm willing to do whatever needs doing to fix it! I'll never raise a hand against you or Cecilia again!"

"No, that you won't. Because we won't be here. Good-bye, Vaughn."

"You can't leave me here like this!"

"You'll not be tied up that long. Your friend Fletcher is bound to pay you another call soon. If you haven't worked your way loose by then, he'll cut you free."

She left the room, closing the door behind her.

"Miriam, come back!"

He heard the front door open, close. His mind scrambled for some way to stop her from leaving. "Wait, Miriam—you can't go out by the road! Fletcher has guards at the head of the hollow! Miriam, can you hear me?"

The bedroom door breezed open, silently, and Cecilia entered. Like her mother, she wore some of Fitz's own garb in place of her usual dress.

"Cecilia! Hello, girl! Oh, I'm glad to see you. See how I'm all trussed up here? Heh heh! I'm in quite a fix, ain't I! But you can help me, if you will. You can cut me free. Come on, Cecilia. Please?"

She approached the bed and stood beside it, looking down on him.

"Ain't you going to talk to me today? You did the other evening. I didn't much like what you said to me, but I'll overlook it if you'll get a knife and cut me free. Why, I'll reward you! That's it! I'll get you money . . . or a new cat. I know your old cat run off. I'll get you a new one . . . I'll get you *two* cats. Can you find a knife?"

She broke her silence. "I've got a knife." Bringing her hand from around her back, she displayed the rusted knife she had found beneath the floor of the house.

"Why, so you do! That's good. Looks rusty, but I'd say it would cut."

Outside, Miriam's voice called, not too loudly: "Cecilia? Where are you?"

"It would cut," she said.

"If you'll cut my bonds now—"

"I hate you," she said.

"I know, and you know what? I don't blame you. I ain't been a nice man to you, and I don't blame you a bit for not liking me. But that'll all be different after you cut me free." He licked his lips and flicked his eyes toward the front wall. "Hurry, please, before your mama comes back in!"

"Cecilia?" Miriam was beginning to sound worried.

"She should never have married you," Cecilia said to Fitz. "Now she can't marry nobody else, because she's already married to you."

"I'll set her free, if that's what she wants. I'll do whatever needs doing, if you'll just cut these ropes. Cut me free, heh heh, and I'll cut *her* free!"

"I could cut her free myself, right now." Cecilia raised the knife and held it above him. Fitz stared at it, disbelieving.

"Cecilia, no! No!"

The blade trembled in her hand. Her face began to tremor and tighten, her eyes to redden. Fitz looked from the knife to her face and back again, eyes flicking, waiting for the terrible plunge, the painful piercing. But beneath it all he wondered also what Cecilia saw as she stared at him. In her eyes, was he merely Vaughn Fitz, uncle turned undesired stepfather, or was he to her every wicked thing a man could be? When she saw his face, did she also see that of the gravedigger who had forced his way into her room on the night that had changed her life forever?

"Cecilia, please, don't kill me!" He was pitiful as he begged.

The front door opened. "Cecilia?" Miriam sounded frantic.

"Miriam, she's in here!" he shouted.

Miriam pushed open the bedroom door, entered, and saw at once what was happening.

"Cecilia . . . no, Cecilia. Don't do that . . . give me the knife."

"I could set you free, Mama. If he was dead, you could marry Greeley Brown."

"Miriam, take that knife from her hand. Please!"

"Cecilia, you cannot do this. It would be murder to kill him."

"But you killed, Mama. You killed the gravedigger."

Fitz said, "She did *what?*"

"It was different, Cecilia. That was justice. The only justice he would have ever received for what he did to you. He was going to escape. I stopped him, the only way I could. But that's not the same as us in this room today. If you murdered Vaughn, there would be no justice in it. We may not like him, Cecilia, but he hasn't done anything to deserve that kind of punishment. He's different than the gravedigger, don't you see?"

Cecilia began to cry. She kept the blade where it was, still trembling in the air above Fitz's chest.

"Put down the knife, Cecilia," Miriam said, stepping slowly toward her. "Let me take it from you, then you and I will go meet Greeley."

"But you can't marry Greeley, Mama, as long as *he* is alive!"

"Cecilia, Greeley Brown will never marry me. Even if Vaughn was dead, or we were divorced, he'd still never marry me. I've made too many mistakes, told him too many lies. I'm not the woman he thought he knew. And I think . . . I think that he isn't even the same man he was. He's different now. Didn't you detect it, hearing him talk about the killings he's done? Something has changed inside him, because of what he went through. He and I will never marry one another. It just couldn't be."

Cecilia lowered the knife. Her arms went limp at her sides

and she stood as she had the night Vaughn Fitz knocked her mother to the floor, though this time with a knife gripped in her right hand.

"Let's go, Cecilia. Greeley will be waiting for us."

"Miriam . . ."

She refused to look at him.

"Miriam, please don't leave me like this!"

"I wouldn't be begging for more favors from me, Vaughn. I just now saved your life. I think that's sufficient to fulfill any duty I have toward you. Good-bye. Give your beloved Fletcher my best regards." Miriam couldn't resist adding one more thing: "Tell him to keep an eye over his shoulder. Tell him there's a ghost stalking him. The ghost of a man he hanged."

"Ghost? What are you talking about, Miriam? Please, let me go. I won't stop you from leaving! Miriam, did you really kill that gravedigger? Come on, now, let me go!"

She closed the bedroom door. Fitz heard her and Cecilia leaving the house.

"Wait! Come back!"

He heard them running across the yard, away from the house.

"Miriam!"

No one replied. They were gone.

They knew better than to try to leave the valley by the road, because of Fletcher's guards at the hollow's mouth. Four guards now, in that two had by their deaths proven insufficient.

Miriam thought about the "ghost" comment she had made to be passed on to Fletcher. She regretted it a little, hoping that if ever it really did get back to Fletcher, he wouldn't be able to figure out that the hanged man she had referred to was Greeley Brown. Yet she was also glad she'd said it, because surely it would cause a moment of worry in Fletcher's mind. Nine men, killed by someone unidentified and unseen in their camp or at their sentry post . . . surely those events already had a ghostly, terrifying aura about them to Fletcher.

Miriam and Cecilia crossed the fields, entered the woods at about the same area Greeley had marked that flat stone, and were just out of sight of the road when Fletcher and his entire band—what remained of it—came pounding down the road on horseback, leaving their hidden encampment and heading toward the hollow's head. Miriam put her arm around Cecilia and drew her close while they passed, and though they were far off the road and well-hidden, she felt a nervous prickle until the last horseman had gone by. The sky, gray and cloudy today, rumbled with distant thunder while the dust of the riders settled. It sounded appropriately ominous.

Fletcher was riding today. It could only mean more cabins raided, robbed, burned. Maybe more men killed. More cross marks burned into Fletcher's McClellan saddle and carved onto the faces of unfortunate victims.

It also meant that Vaughn Fitz was going to have a long day on that bed, unless he could figure out how to wriggle free without taking all the hide off his hands and feet doing it.

Miriam was glad to be leaving this place. She wished she had never come to begin with.

With Cecilia she passed through the woods and to the ridge that faced the front of Fitz's house. It was steep, but could be climbed; there was only one portion of it that was truly sheer, but the face of it was rugged, with many handholds and footholds. They would be able to manage it, perhaps at the price of a few scuffed knuckles and abrasions, but that was a low cost to pay for leaving this terrible valley where murderers hid.

Once atop the ridge, they would pass westward along it until they reached a point designated by Greeley at their last meeting. There they would either find him waiting for them or they would wait for him. Either way, in the end they would come together and begin the long trek away from here.

Miriam had already decided where she would go. Besides Cecilia, she had only one living relative that she knew of within five hundred miles. That was a cousin, a widow about ten years Miriam's senior, who as of eight or nine years back was living in the old town of Jonesborough in Washington County, Tennessee. Miriam would go to her—if she was still in that town—explain her situation as best she could and as far as she could, and hope for the best. Maybe her cousin would take her in for a while, at least help her in some manner. If not . . . she would worry about that later. The only thing that really mattered now was getting away from Vaughn Fitz, Cap Fletcher, and his band of raiders.

She and Cecilia reached the base of the ridge, paused to rest and ready themselves, then began the ascent, toward the gray sky and freedom.

Some hours after Miriam and Cecilia achieved their rendezvous with Greeley Brown, who was already waiting for them when they reached the ridgetop, an event occurred a few miles away that would end up having a substantial impact on the lives of all three of them, and several others as well.

The event was another mountain killing, performed by Cap Fletcher and his raiders. All in all it was typical of his style: A known Unionist, accused by rebel neighbors of carrying food, weapons, and news to hiding-out dodgers of the Confederate draft, was caught near his home, abused, and killed with the usual ceremony, the customary mark put on the face. Though Fletcher often hung the corpses of his victims by the heels in front of their burning dwellings, this time he altered his style slightly and hanged the dead man up by his right hand, which Fletcher thought was amusing in that it was the only hand the fellow had. His left hand was missing, and in its place was a hook.

The murdered man's name was Joe Waters, a harmless small-time subsistence farmer known around Carter County as Stumpy. Unmarried all his life, Stumpy Waters was congenial and well-liked, known for his kindness, slight simplemindedness, and a fondness for drinking mountain-brewed whiskey. He had lived most of his early years in the Telford community a few miles from Jonesborough, and reportedly had moved to Carter County only because he won a tiny tract of mountain land in that county in a card game with a man who was more flush in property than in cash. Some who saw Stumpy's miserable little scrap of property wondered if the man who lost that card game might not have done so on purpose, just to get rid of a piece of useless real estate. Still, Stumpy got by on his place, living in a log hut, hunting his meat, raising his vegetables in a small garden patch.

When Stumpy Waters's corpse was found hanging by the

hand in front of his burning cabin, his homely face marked by Fletcher's Cross, the story spread rapidly because it was so appalling. That anyone would kill Stumpy Waters was atrocious—he was liked by people on both sides of the conflict, and had been known to give aid to anyone he knew regardless of their political viewpoint.

Before long the story of the death of Stumpy Waters spread beyond the mountains, carried by refugees and stampeders. It remained unrecorded for a long time, thriving instead in the word-of-mouth undercurrent, somehow always missing being recorded by any journalist. Thus, floating free without the solidifying effect of becoming written, the story did what all such stories will do, and mutated steadily, taking on distortions on one end, losing facts on the other. Stumpy Waters's name became Stump Walters, Stump Williams, Will Stump, then Bill Stemp, Bill Sparks, and finally eroded away entirely, until the one-armed man who died in Carter County became entirely anonymous.

Somewhere early along this progression, someone had mentioned that Stumpy Waters had come from a community near Jonesborough. This fact as well became distorted, and before long the death itself was reported to have occurred at or near Jonesborough rather than in Carter County. Thus, in mere weeks, the totally true story of Stump Walters's murder in Carter County at the hands of Cap Fletcher became a almost utterly false mishmash.

In this distorted condition, the story finally reached Knoxville. Though the natural recipient of such a tale would have been Amy Hanover, this one somehow missed her and went instead to the ear of Parson Brownlow. Brownlow jotted it down in his notes for use sometime when he needed a handy reference to a rebel-inflicted mountain atrocity over which to express outrage in a *Whig* editorial.

It was November before the story finally found its way into print, just a sentence or two in the *Whig*. Over at the offices of the *Sage & Torch*, it was Horatio Eaton, rather than Amy, who first happened to pick up that edition. He read the editorial without much interest until he reached those particular sentences. His eyes widened and he laid the paper across his lap.

"Oh, my! Oh, my goodness!" He read through that portion

again, just to be sure. When he laid the paper across his lap again, he took off his spectacles and rubbed his eyes. Poor Ben Scarlett. What a tragedy, him ending his life in so sad a way!

Steeling himself for the delivery of the bad news, Eaton stood and walked toward Amy's office, newspaper in hand.

She took it surprisingly well, which Eaton attributed to shock more than anything else. She left the office at once, returning home with little Adam, and Eaton didn't see her again until the next morning, when she walked into the office with Adam on her hip and a determined expression on her face. He knew she had made a decision, and suspected he knew what that decision was.

"It does sound like it's Ben who has been killed," she told him then. "But it isn't certain. And you understand, Horatio, that I must know. I'm not willing to believe Ben has been killed until I have the proof before me, not just some vague lines from Brownlow."

"I understand."

"I believe the time has come for me to make that move I've been talking about so long."

"Jonesborough?"

"Yes. We can continue our work there, do better work, really. And I can search for the truth about what has become of Ben. Do you object to uprooting so abruptly?"

He smiled. "I've already begun packing the type cases and breaking down the press."

She smiled back. Dear, odd old Horatio! He had anticipated her decision. She went to him and gave him a gentle hug.

"Well, let's get to work. We've got a lot to do."

Part VI

★ ★ ★ ★ ★ ★ ★

THE GATHERING

Chapter 33

***The Confederate prison camp at Salisbury,
North Carolina, mid-December, 1864***

It had become truly terrible in October.

New prisoners had arrived by the thousands, almost all at once, poured into a camp able to deal with only a few hundred. They came in with few clothes, a dearth of shoes, a lack of coats and blankets, and health already in decline. There was little shelter available to most of these, especially at the beginning, and when the Confederacy at last issued tents, only about half enough to accommodate the crowd were given. The one redeeming aspect of the Salisbury prison—the open, breeze-swept yard—now became a hellish place of misery, crowded with men so desperate for shelter that many dug pits in the earth, like beasts.

Thatcher Brown, thinner than ever, weak and scurvied, moved down a line of even thinner, sicker men, writing the admission date and various medical conditions into the designated spots on a printed form. Some of the men begged him for food, medicine, water, but he ignored them for the most part, unable to help them and, after so many weeks of seeing so much suffering, unwilling to invest as much emotion on their behalf as he had at the beginning. To do so now would drain him. There was simply too much misery, too many men. So he did his assigned task as if cut off from it all, grateful to have work that at least kept him in the relatively better conditions of the prison hospital and fed better than most of those among whom he moved.

He reached the last pallet in the row, went to the young skeleton of a man lying on it. He looked closely, and wrote across the designated line, below the name: DECEASED, Dec. 18, 1864.

Another one for the "dead cart." Another one to be dumped in a trench outside, piled like cordwood with his fellows, covered with dirt and forgotten, except by some grieving family off in—he consulted the paper—Pennsylvania.

Thatcher leaned against the wall, weary. It required much effort even to walk about these days, and he was better-fed and better-housed than most here. He hated the Confederacy for allowing men to be penned in worse condition than animals. He hated the Federal government for its unwillingness to exchange prisoners, a policy based on the practical but inhumane consideration that it made little sense to give relatively healthy soldiers back to the Confederacy in exchange for emaciated skeletons.

"Mr. Brown."

Thatcher lifted his head and looked into the earnest, always intense face of Dr. J. Elton Best, prison surgeon. As always when he met Best, Thatcher was suddenly filled with new strength. He felt blood rush into his face.

Dr. Best, born and raised at Carter's Station, Tennessee, and brother of one Evan Best, a Unionist guided safely to the Federal lines by Greeley Brown back in 1862, represented the one living bit of hope that existed for Thatcher Brown in this horrific place. Thatcher's path crossed with that of Dr. Best only once in a while, but when it did, it was always by Best's design, and always the occasion for a new piece of information in the secret little conspiracy being worked out between the doctor and himself.

"Good morning, sir."

"You look bad today, Mr. Brown."

"I feel bad, sir."

"Step out here a moment. I have some information for you."

Greeley straightened. Heart thumping hard, he walked with the doctor to a private spot near the hospital ward.

"Let's take a look at your notes there, just in case anyone should be watching us."

Thatcher held up the pad of paper, and Best, brow knitted, pretended to study it. He put his head close to Thatcher's and spoke in a low voice. The dead cart, a big two-wheeled conveyance in which corpses were hauled out of the prison for burial, stood nearby, stained and ugly.

"I've talked to Mr. Able, in the village. The arrangements have been made."

Thatcher's heart thumped even faster. "When, sir?"

"At any point, theoretically, but for reasons I'll explain, I want you to wait until after Christmas."

"The clothing, food . . ."

"Already in place, in a haversack. Inside the shed you'll find a wide, flat stone, covering most of the floor. Lift it and the pit is below. When you get inside, put the stone back in place and be ready to stay there for up to a week. There's enough food, nonperishable, to sustain you, and some written instruction giving you information about where to go next."

A couple of gray-clad soldiers passed. Thatcher pointed to one of the entries on the pad and said, loud enough for them to hear, ". . . and this one, it appears, is going to be ready for dismissal soon, as best I can judge. You'll want to check him over yourself, of course."

The soldiers passed out of earshot. Thatcher watched them from the corner of his eye until they were gone.

"Is there a weapon in the pit?"

"No. I'm sorry, but that far I cannot go, Mr. Brown. I'm doing this, you realize, because of our brothers. I don't see eye-to-eye with my brother where this war is concerned, but I'm deeply appreciative of your brother giving him safe guidance out of a dangerous situation. By helping you out of this place, I'm evening the balance. My way of saying thank you."

Thatcher smiled. "I like the way you say thank you, sir. Greeley will appreciate it, too. I intend to find him when I get out of here."

"You must understand that the odds of success are remote.

Even if you get out of the prison itself, you'll probably be found and captured before you reach Federal territory."

"I know, sir. And should that happen, you have my assurance that no one here will ever know of your involvement."

"I'm counting on that, Mr. Brown. You don't know how badly it would go for me if it were known I conspired to help a prisoner escape."

"I think I do know, sir. Believe me, I'll die before I betray you."

"Indeed you might."

That comment, delivered in a cold, solemn tone, made Thatcher feel weak again.

"How do you suggest I make the actual break?" Thatcher asked.

"I'm going to Captain Fuqua this afternoon and having a pass arranged for you, giving you the right to pass the inner gate as a medicine courier. You'll have it in hand tomorrow, the next day at the latest. I encourage you to use it properly for a couple of weeks, to build confidence, and to let the sentinels become accustomed to seeing you go in and out. Now, the Christmas business. I'm arranging to have a Confederate uniform obtained for you, but I won't have it until the twenty-third or twenty-fourth. I'm going to leave it hidden in a box in the corner of the medicine supply house, marked with my name and something to indicate it should not be disturbed. The day after Christmas, I'll have you sent out with a medicine box, ostensibly to bring some supplies in. You'll exchange that medicine box for the one with my name on it, and go to a little outbuilding standing near the supply house. There's a gap beneath its foundation, and you'll crawl through there and hide beneath the hut until dark. Change into the uniform there. Exit the hut just before midnight, and keep out of view. There'll be a changing of the guard at midnight, and you should be able to lose yourself among the guards and get outside the outer gate. Make your way to Mr. Able's shed at once and hide as I've instructed you. Don't give in to the temptation to make an immediate run. They'll be looking for you, and they won't expect you to remain close to the prison. After a few days the search will be called off and you should be able to leave unmolested. Keep that uniform with you—it may prove the best tool you'll have to get you through the countryside without rousing suspicion. You do know where Able's shed is, don't you?"

The doctor had given clear directions to that shed at their last conspiratorial meeting. "Yes. I could find it with my eyes closed."

"Very well. And if you do find your brother, sir, give him my thanks for what he did for Evan. I've heard what conditions are like for the Union men back in my home area. He probably saved Evan's life by piloting him out of that situation."

"Just as you are probably saving mine now."

Christmas Day, Jonesborough, Tennessee

She saw it, peeking at her around the corner of the building, one alley down. Cecilia Fry, living here under the assumed name of Cecilia Goode, grinned and tilted her head and advanced slowly, like a cat stalking prey.

In this case the prey *was* a cat, a pretty white one that seemed to be a stray. It was about half tame and had allowed her to catch and feed it two days before, but now seemed a little skittish again. Cecilia advanced, calling softly, hand extended as if it held something. The cat eyed her with feline suspicion, but didn't run. Cecilia reached the edge of the alley, almost within touching distance . . . and across the street something thumped rhythmically, and the cat bolted down the alley and out of sight.

Cecilia stood, sighing, and looked with a frown to see what had foiled the capture. What she saw made her forget the cat.

It was that woman again, that pretty, dark-haired lady who had arrived in Jonesborough only a few days before and moved into a rented house only two buildings down from the little hotel and rooming house where she and Miriam now resided. The woman had her baby with her, wrapped in a blanket, and was struggling to hold the baby while trying to tack up a paper on a porch post at a store. Her hammering was what had spooked the cat.

Cecilia watched, intrigued. She had wondered who this woman was from the first time she'd seen her, and the baby held even more interest for her. It stirred in her the maternal feelings she had felt toward her own little James. It made her miss him.

There was a mystery about this newcomer woman that made her all the more fascinating to Cecilia. She had arrived in town with a funny-looking, bespectacled little man whom Cecilia had assumed was her husband—though it seemed odd that such an attractive woman would be married to so homely a fellow—but the funny man hadn't moved into the house the woman had rented, as a husband would have done. Instead he'd taken a room in the same hotel as Cecilia and her mother. Cecilia knew nothing about him except that his last name was Eaton, and that her second cousin, Egypt Munsey, proprietress of the Munsey Hotel and a woman Cecilia and Miriam viewed as a savior almost equal to Greeley Brown, thought him a "truly odd character." Miriam had confided jokingly to Cecilia that Egypt Munsey ought to be good at identifying odd characters, being so odd a one herself.

Cecilia watched as the pretty woman managed to get the broadside tacked up without dropping the baby. On impulse, she started across the street. Before coming to Jonesborough, Cecilia would scarcely have dared approach a stranger to speak to him or her, but she had changed. Living in this town had been very good for her. She was not afraid here, as she'd been during her long flight across Tennessee with her mother and the late James. She was not full of bitterness, as she'd been in the home of Vaughn Fitz, whom she still refused to recognize even to herself as her stepfather. Here, life was good. Egypt Munsey was benevolent. She had welcomed her cousin Miriam, whom she hardly knew, and given her not only a home, but work in the hotel. Egypt had greeted Miriam's arrival as a godsend. Her arthritis was growing worse with the years; she had considered closing down the hotel. Miriam's arrival made it possible to go on.

Cecilia moved across the street toward the woman, who was just then turning to step off the porch and move on down the street toward the courthouse. The woman started slightly, then smiled, when she saw Cecilia almost upon her. Cecilia, like the felines she loved so dearly, moved silently on her feet.

"Hello!" the woman said brightly. "Merry Christmas to you!"

"Merry Christmas," Cecilia replied in her soft voice. "You have a pretty baby."

"Thank you," the woman said. "His name is Adam."

"I saw you were having trouble doing what you are doing, and holding him. Do you mind if I—"

"Not at all." And Cecilia felt a warmth rise in her as, for the first time since she had last held her own infant James, a small human filled her arms. She smiled at the handsome little face, and felt stirrings in breasts that once fed a child of her own but had since gone dry. It would be a long time, though, before her body lost the memory of its maternal function, a long time before the presence, feel, and smell of a baby ceased to rouse the feeling that always accompanied the letting down of her mother's milk.

"He's beautiful," Cecilia said.

"Thank you."

Cecilia stepped onto the porch and looked at the broadside hanging on the post.

ANNOUNCEMENT:

Mrs. Amy D. Hanover, Main Street, is seeking information about a man possibly living in the Jonesborough area. Anyone with information regarding Mr. Benjamin Scarlett is requested to convey the same to Mrs. Hanover at her residence. Mr. Scarlett stands about five feet eight inches in height, has dark hair and beard, slightly graying, brown eyes, a lean frame, and is missing a left hand, generally wearing a hook in its place. Information will be kept confidential.

Cecilia said, "You are Mrs. Hanover?"

"I am. And you are . . ."

"Cecilia. Cecilia Goode."

"I'm pleased to meet you, Cecilia. You live here in town?"

"I live in the Munsey Hotel. My mother's cousin owns it, and my mother—her name is Miriam—is running it for her now."

"I know the hotel. My own house is just down from it. And my business associate, Mr. Horatio Eaton, has taken a room there."

"I've seen him."

Amy grinned. "Not a sight you are likely to forget. He's an odd little man, isn't he?"

Cecilia laughed, instantly liking this woman.

Amy added: "But don't tell him I said that. He's a good man, a good friend. I hope you'll get to know him."

"I thought he was your husband when I saw him the first time. He was walking with you."

"No, no, Mr. Eaton is certainly not my husband." She laughed. Her smile declined slightly as she added, "My husband is dead."

"Oh. I'm sorry. My father is dead, too."

"The war?"

"No. He was sick. Did your husband die in the war?"

Any thought back to the day Adam Hanover had died on the street in Nashville. "In a way, yes," she said.

Cecilia glanced at the stack of broadsides in Amy's hand. "Who is Benjamin Scarlett?"

"A friend. A missing friend. I think he might have come to Jonesborough, or somewhere close. I'm afraid something bad has happened to him, and I'm trying to find out about that."

"Something bad?"

"I'm afraid he might have been killed. But I'm not willing to believe it until I know."

"He has only one hand?"

"Yes. Have you seen anyone like that in town?"

"No, except for a soldier who had no right arm. But I've only been in Jonesborough a few months."

"Where did you come from?"

Cecilia glanced away. "Just somewhere. The mountains."

"In East Tennessee?"

"Yes."

Amy, with her vested interest in what went on in wartime in the East Tennessee mountains, and particularly in those people who were driven out of them, wanted to ask more, but sensed it was a delicate topic. She filed the information away, however, thinking that perhaps later the opportunity might come.

Cecilia looked at her, shifting Adam in her arms. "I can hold your baby while you hang the papers, if you want me to."

"That would be delightful, Cecilia. Thank you."

They moved down the street, Amy pausing at the next available porch post to hang another broadside. "You know, once Mr. Scarlett himself helped me hang up broadsides on the street. A long time ago, or so it seems."

"In Jonesborough?"

"No. Knoxville. It's where I'm from."

"I've never been there."

"It's a fine city. Maybe you can visit it when the war is through."

"I don't want to visit anywhere. I like it here. I want to stay here forever."

Amy smiled. "I like it, too. I'm thinking of making it my home, and starting a newspaper, with Mr. Eaton. That's my business, newspapers. And writing in general. I'm working on a book right now."

"A made-up book?"

Amy sensed a possible inroad for that potential future interview. "No. True stories. About people who have lived in the East Tennessee mountains, but who were driven out by the rebels because they supported the Union."

Cecilia seemed to withdraw. "Oh." Her mother had given her firm instructions not to say much about their past circumstances, and Cecilia wondered if she had already made a mistake, even telling Amy Hanover that she had lived in the East Tennessee mountains. By her mother's instruction, the past was to be closed. There was no rape, no little James, no killing of the gravedigger, no flight to the mountains, no Carter County residency, no Vaughn Fitz. The story now was that Miriam's husband had been William Goode, of Johnson County, dead of a heart ailment for about two years. They had given this tale even to Egypt Munsey, who knew no better than to accept it. Until Miriam had showed up at her door, Egypt had known nothing at all of her cousin's circumstances anytime past early girlhood, beyond that Miriam had gotten married somewhere along the way.

Amy sensed that Cecilia did not wish to discuss the mountains. It was not hard to understand. She had heard enough tales to know just how terrible the mountain war could be. Who could say what Cecilia had seen or experienced? And who should say, if Cecilia did not wish to discuss it?

They went on down the street, hanging broadsides and talking of inconsequential matters.

Cecilia told her mother and Egypt Munsey about Amy Hanover that night, and her plans to start a newspaper with Horatio Eaton, the funny man in their hotel. By design, however, she did not mention Amy's book and its subject, which was so uncomfortably close to home for herself and her mother.

"A newspaper!" the thin-framed Egypt Munsey said, sitting in her favorite well-stuffed chair near the fireplace in the small hotel lobby and sitting room. She somehow managed to look regal despite her old dress and her bent, arthritic fingers. She seemed a decade older than her actual forty-seven years of age. "Well, I do declare. That should be interesting. This town hasn't had a newspaper since Mr. Slack's *Daily Telegraph* closed down. I didn't much care for that newspaper. All rebel bilge. It's no surprise it didn't survive here. You know, that name is beginning to ring a bell for me. Eaton . . . Eaton. There was an abolitionist publisher in Knoxville by that name. My goodness! Do you think we've got the very man?"

"What would you think if we did?" Miriam asked, having no idea where her cousin stood on the slavery issue. Miriam herself didn't much care for slavery, but as with most of the large issues of the day, she didn't involve herself deeply in the debate. Her life had given her plenty to deal with without taking up social cudgels.

"I would find it a most intriguing experience," Egypt replied cryptically. "I have some very strong views on this matter of freeing the coloreds. If our Mr. Eaton proves to be who I suspect, he and I have some interesting conversations ahead of us, to be sure!"

Chapter 34

The following evening, Horatio Eaton had a most interesting supper at the table of Egypt Munsey. Though she did not generally serve meals to her guests in the manner of a full-fledged boardinghouse, Eaton received a special invitation. He quickly discovered why, as shortly into the meal Egypt Munsey commenced a forthright grilling of him in her deep, almost masculine voice.

He had just filled his mouth with potatoes when the first question struck. "Mr. Eaton, I must ask you: Are you the same Horatio Eaton who was a publisher in Knoxville?"

Eaton stopped chewing for a moment, eyes shifting from side to side like those of a man suddenly suspecting a trap. He'd been pummeled so many times over the years for his point of view that he had become quite wary of inquiries. "I did publish a journal in Knoxville some years ago, yes, and then continued it in the North. And recently, with your new neighbor Mrs. Hanover, I undertook a new venture in Knoxville."

"This former journal of yours . . . might it have been that publication called *Reason's Torch*, which sought to persuade our society to turn loose its coloreds?"

Eaton got the bite down with a labored gulp. "Uh, it was an abolitionist publication, yes indeed."

"I see, I see. So you, sir, are the very man who has gained such titles as the Great Radical, the Darky Lover, and others which I would not repeat as a decent woman?"

"I've been called many things, ma'am, and it's fair to say that most have been intended to insult. My point of view, you see, has always been on the minority side."

"Umm-hmmm. I see." She paused and sipped her coffee, which wasn't really coffee at all, but a beverage brewed from toasted grain. She frowned at the cup. "Cold."

At that moment a very elderly black woman entered the room, bearing a plate of corn bread, which she sat down near Egypt. When she turned to go, Egypt's voice burst out, nearly in a shout: "Hehaheggamanga!"

Horatio Eaton was so startled he almost dropped his fork.

Miriam and Cecilia glanced at one another and smiled. This was a routine they knew well, but Horatio Eaton was experiencing it for the first time. On their first occasion of it, they had been just as staggered as he.

The old woman, whose name was Nelly, turned slowly. "What's that, Miz Egypt?"

"I say, heat up my cup a bit, would you?"

"Yes indeed, ma'am." She took the cup and slowly trailed out of the room.

Egypt Munsey returned her attention to Eaton, who was looking like he wished he'd taken his supper elsewhere. "Well, sir! So it's your opinion that this nation is best off without the old institution of slavery. Am I correct?"

"I object to slavery on moral grounds, ma'am. If it has had good economic benefits in some ways, that still leaves the moral issue unresolved. And of course, you must consider the negative effect slavery has on the availability of paid labor opportunities for poor whites in the South."

"Sir, I didn't ask for a dissertation. You may save that for your publications!"

Old Nelly walked back in with the cup now steaming in her hand. She sat it in front of Egypt and again turned away.

"Habahabahabahaba!"

"What you say, Miz Egypt?"

"I say, please see if anyone else needs more."

"None for me," Miriam said. Cecilia waved her off as well. Both were on the verge of laughter.

"No, thank you," the increasingly unnerved Eaton said.

The old woman nodded and left once more.

"Well, Mr. Eaton," Egypt said, brows lowering over her eyes. "You and I, sir, could have quite a few interesting discussions on this slavery matter."

Eaton took another bite of potatoes, listlessly, waiting for another of the verbal assaults his views had brought upon him all his adult life, His hand trembled as he lifted the fork, and as the unburdened fork touched his plate again, it rattled rhythmically against it for a second.

"But before we do, I wish to do one thing. I've wanted to do this since the first time I read your work and realized just what kind of notion it was you were putting forth." With effort, the arthritic woman rose, straightened slowly, and came around the table toward him. His eyes, magnified anyway by his glasses, truly looked big now. He quailed down in his chair as if expecting a blow.

Egypt instead smiled and stuck out her misshapen hand toward him, leaving him gaping.

"Mr. Eaton, I do wish to congratulate you, sir, for your progressive and sane viewpoint, and the excellent task you have done in advocating for the coloreds through the years. Lord knows they've had few enough voices speaking for them."

"You are a . . . you mean, you *agree* with me?"

"I have for years, sir. I'm an abolitionist by pure moral instinct. And I've enjoyed many an hour reading and reasoning along with your *Torch*. You, Mr. Eaton, are a scholar and a *hero*! No less! Why, your arguments are so persuasive that only sheer stubbornness can account for anyone not accepting them."

Eaton shook her hand, loosely, too awed to speak.

Nelly reentered the room, bearing more potatoes in a bowl.

"Halabamamba! Halabalabula!"

"What's that, ma'am?"

"I say, Nelly, come here and shake hands with a man you'll be honored to know. It turns out our Mr. Eaton here is the very man who published *Reason's Torch*!"

Nelly's mouth opened into a grin. She shuffled over and

pumped his hand vigorously. "Oh, God bless you, sir. God bless you for speaking so well for all us Negroes."

"Uh . . . thank you. Yes."

"Nelly used to read the *Torch* as faithfully as I did, sir. I've seen it move her to tears many a time."

"Nelly reads?"

"Yes, sir. I taught her."

"You taught a slave to read?"

"She's never been my slave, Mr. Eaton. Why, how could I hold a slave? Nelly's been freed ever since my father, who bought her, had a change of heart in his advancing years. Nelly's been with me ever since, but not as a slave. I've paid her for what she does, and given her every benefit I could."

Eaton's countenance was much brighter now, and the shaking was past. "Well! I do say! How marvelous!"

"Mongamongamongamonga!"

"Yes, ma'am?"

"I say, bring in that vinegar pie as soon as we've finished our main course here. We'll celebrate our honored guest with some sweetening." To Eaton she added, "Made with sorghum instead of sugar, and too little sorghum at that, but Nelly can make a vinegar pie like none other."

She went back around to her chair and settled down, bones popping as she did so, face wincing in obvious pain, but no complaint being voiced.

"Mrs. Munsey, may I ask—"

"Miss Munsey, sir. I never married. Far too homely for any man."

It was one of those comments allowing for no socially appropriate response, so Eaton fumbled a moment, then said, "Well, then, Miss Munsey, may I ask you something?"

"Certainly."

"Why do you make those odd noises, or tongues, or whatever they are, at Nelly?"

"Oh!" She laughed. "I'm sorry. I've done it so many years I forget that not everyone knows what that's all about. Miriam was as surprised as you when she first heard it. Tell him, Miriam."

"Nelly is nearly deaf," Miriam explained. "She never understands anything the first time it's said, so Egypt has ceased bothering to say anything the first time."

"It's easier that way," Egypt continued. "It's all noise to Nelly the first time she hears it, anyway. She can't make out a thing until she knows to give you her full attention."

"Oh . . . well, all right. Very artful. Yes. Very artful procedure."

"Well, sir, tell us about your new newspaper."

Eaton began discoursing about the publication and its focus, well established through the few editions already published in Knoxville. Enjoying the rare privilege of an agreeable audience, he bubbled on at a fast pace. Egypt in turn informed Eaton that Jonesborough itself had some long-standing connections to abolitionism. In the town, the oldest in the state, one Elihu Embree had published two journals, *The Emancipator* and *The Manumission Intelligencer*, almost fifty years before—the first periodicals in the nation devoted entirely to advocating abolition of slavery.

Conversation lasted well past the meal and the vinegar pie, which indeed was tasty. At length the discussion of abolition in the abstract gave way to more specific talk about Eaton's current publication plans, about Amy Hanover and her fascinating personal history, and the reasons she had come to Jonesborough.

Thus, inevitably, the matter of Ben Scarlett arose, and this piqued Egypt's attention at once.

"Hold on, sir—describe that fellow again?"

"Well, he's a lean man, dark-haired, looks like he's well into his forties, although he's actually younger. His most distinctive feature is that he has only one hand. The left one is gone—amputated because of mortification a couple of years ago, I believe. Mrs. Hanover suspects that he might be living somewhere around Jonesborough—if he's living at all. There was a story in Brownlow's paper in Knoxville that described the killing by a bushwhacker of someone who seemed to match Ben's description in some detail."

"A one-handed man . . . hook in place of the left hand, maybe?"

"Why, yes—you haven't seen such a fellow, have you?"

"Indeed I have. But it's been weeks, maybe months back."

Eaton came to his feet, suddenly excited. "He was dark-haired? Bearded?"

"Dark-haired, yes, but with quite a bit of gray creeping in."

"My goodness. Oh, my! I believe you've surely seen our man!"

"Mr. Eaton, I doubt this would be the kind of fellow anyone would be looking for." She leaned forward and spoke in a confidential tone. "This man was very, very drunk."

"That's him! That's Mr. Scarlett! Oh, Miss Munsey, please excuse me—I must go fetch Mrs. Hanover at once. She'll want to talk to you about this."

"What? Tonight?"

"Well, yes, if you would . . . you don't know how important this fellow is to her."

"She has some abiding affection for a drunkard, does she?" Egypt quirked her brows and looked a bit haughty. "I'm not sure that says too much in my book in Mrs. Hanover's favor! This fellow was as dissipated a man as ever I saw. Why, I had to run him off my very doorstep! He came trying to sell that hook of his for money. To buy more whiskey, no doubt. Disgusting! Disgusting fellow!"

"That's Ben Scarlett, indeed! Please pardon me, ladies—I'll be directly back, with Mrs. Hanover."

Egypt shook her head and said, "Now, wait a moment, sir . . . I don't know that I'm looking for further company this evening—"

He was out the door on the run before she could finish her sentence. Egypt Munsey sighed and shook her head. "Oh, well. I guess I'll be having further company anyway." Looking at the others, she said, "Odd fellow, that Eaton. It's often that way with men of intellect. I expect we'll find Mrs. Hanover is odd, as well."

"She's very nice," Cecilia contributed. "And she has a dear baby."

"And I suppose she'll bring the baby with her. Watch and see if there aren't wet stains on my furniture or my rug before the evening is through." She cocked her head slightly over her shoulder. "Hamamamamamama!"

"Yes, ma'am?"

"You'd best brew some more of that ersatz coffee, Nelly. We've got more visiting ahead."

Egypt Munsey's prediction of stained furnishings came true not ten minutes after Amy arrived with Adam swinging from her arm. Eaton was as wide-eyed as ever, and Amy scarcely concealed her own equivalent excitement. Introductions were rushed through, then Amy peppered Egypt with questions while Cecilia played with Adam on the floor, and winced when he abruptly soaked through his gown and diaper and left a big ring on the rug. Egypt Munsey saw it from the corner of her eye, looked sad, but voiced no complaint. Cecilia swept the baby off to clean him up and find something to try to soak up the urine in the rug.

"Miss Munsey, the more exactly you can recall the time you saw this man, the more helpful it would be," Amy said. "There is a story, you see, that he might have been killed. Or someone was killed, at least, who sounds much like him by description."

"So Mr. Eaton told me," Egypt replied, eyeing the wet spot on the rug and beginning to sound weary. She was a woman who generally went to bed quite early. "But I can't recall anything exactly. It was just sometime earlier in the year. Late summer, perhaps."

"He didn't give a name?"

"No."

"Did he seem polite? Ben is almost always polite, even when he's been drinking."

"I didn't notice his manners. All I noticed was that he was drunk, and smelled as bad as those wounded soldiers I've seen them haul on the trains. I can't abide drunkenness nor uncleanliness. I sent him directly away."

Amy sank back in her chair. "It must have been Ben. I'm sure of it."

"But that doesn't help us much," Eaton said. "Brownlow's editorial didn't state when this murder of a one-handed man occurred. It very well could have happened since Miss Munsey saw him."

"I know. But at least we have further reason to believe that Ben did come to Jonesborough. He'd said he would come here."

"Yes, and that he'd find you after you moved the newspaper east."

"Maybe he'll come into town and see one of the flyers I hung."

"Perhaps."

Cecilia came back in with a newly dried and changed baby, and a rag, with which she went to work on the stain under the unhappy eye of Egypt Munsey. Amy noted the older woman's expression.

"I'm sorry about the accident, ma'am."

"So goes life when children are around," Egypt replied.

Amy pondered a few moments. "Miss Munsey, some years ago Ben Scarlett lived in Jonesborough, or somewhere near. He worked for a family . . . oh, what was the name? He told me several times, but I can't recall. But I do know the family operated a niter mine somewhere in the area."

"Why, that might have been the Mainard family," Egypt said. "Good Union people. They employed quite a few Union men in the mines, and saved them from conscription that way."

"Mainard . . . yes, I think that's right! Is the family still around?"

"No, no. The eldest Mainard is dead, and his wife. All the rest of the family has scattered away because of the war. One of them was a preacher, I believe. I don't know what became of him, but I know he's no longer around."

"Yes, there was a preacher, and he was the one who helped out Ben. But if they are all gone now . . . that means Ben couldn't have found them when he came looking. He'd wanted to see if they would take him in and help him like before."

"Why did this Mr. Scarlett leave Knoxville to begin with? If he was your employee, and had room and board and pay—"

"It was because of the drinking," Amy said quickly. "I had a rule that he was not to drink, and when he fell into the habit again, he left because he was ashamed and knew I'd have to let him go, anyway."

"I do despise a drunkard," Egypt muttered. "No worse types for trying to destroying themselves."

"Mr. Scarlett is a good man at heart," Eaton said. "He's simply become a slave to whiskey. He's broken the bond a few times, but somehow it always manages to wrap itself around him again."

"I see no excuse for any man to drink to excess," Egypt proclaimed. "Slave to whiskey, my eye!"

"It does happen, ma'am. There are more kinds of slavery than the sort you and I oppose."

"A drunk is a drunk. That's that." Egypt propped an elbow on the armrest of her chair and laid her head against her hand.

Amy stood. "Miss Munsey, I see that you are tired. I'm sorry to have intruded into your evening this way. But it is very important to me to find out what has become of my friend. If you should remember anything else he said, or exactly when you saw him, or if you see him again, please do let me know."

"I will. But if he comes to my porch again, I'll run him right off. I won't take drunks into this hotel."

"Good evening, Miss Munsey. And thank you again."

Miriam and Cecilia, the latter still carrying Adam, followed Amy and Eaton onto the porch, while inside, Nelly helped Egypt Munsey make her slow way toward her bedroom.

I don't feel I properly met you in all the rush in there," Miriam said, putting her hand out to Amy. "I'm Miriam Goode, Cecilia's mother."

"Yes. So please to meet you. I've grown quickly fond of your beautiful girl, too. She's got quite a touch with Adam." Amy smiled and added, "Cecilia, you are so skilled with babies that I could almost imagine you were a mother yourself!"

Miriam glanced down quickly; Cecilia's smile was quick and small, and she looked past Amy at once.

Amy, still thinking mostly about this possible clue toward Ben Scarlett, didn't notice. Nor did Eaton, who was looking across the yard, squinting, and shivering without his coat.

Cecilia handed Adam to Amy. "Thank you, Cecilia. By the way, might you be interested in watching Adam for me sometimes? For pay, of course. He's a good baby, but having to tend to him all day makes it hard for me to devote enough time to my book."

Cecilia smiled and glanced at her mother. "Could I?"

Miriam smiled. "Of course. Thank you, Mrs. Hanover. What a kind and unexpected offer."

"Believe me, I'd be the one to most benefit. And as I said, I would pay for Cecilia's time."

"That would be more helpful than you can know. My cousin doesn't make much money with this hotel—often it has been taken over for days at a time by officers when different armies have passed through, and sometimes she's compensated for that, sometimes not. She can't afford to pay me much to run it for her. Mostly Cecilia and I stay here for boarding and meals."

"These are hard times for everyone. But I've been blessed through circumstances in my life to have some degree of money, enough to allow me to be comfortable and do what I need to do. And occasionally I'm able to help others in their own situations. I'll be so pleased to have Cecilia be little Adam's shepherd when she can."

Eaton, having endured all he could of the cold, quickly bid the others good evening and reentered the hotel.

"Did I hear you say you were writing a book, Mrs. Hanover?"

"Please, call me Amy. Yes, I am. For several months now I've been interviewing Unionist refugees from the mountains, people who have been run from their homes, had fathers and sons murdered by rebel bushwhackers, had their cabins burned. Mostly Carter and Johnson counties. It's atrocious, what is happening in those mountains." She paused. "But I suppose you know that. Cecilia told me you came here from Johnson County."

Miriam was making a valiant effort to maintain a placid expression. "Yes."

"If I might make the request . . . if there is anything from your experience you could share with me for my book, I'd be pleased to—"

Miriam's tone was suddenly quite firm and crisp. "No, no. I'd prefer not to talk about myself. Thank you. But no. I'd have nothing to tell you."

"I feel maybe I've unintentionally insulted you, somehow, Mrs. Goode. I apologize."

"No, you've not insulted me. It's just as I said: I prefer not to talk about myself. And do call me Miriam."

"Certainly. Good night, Miriam. And Cecilia, might you be free tomorrow to help me with Adam?"

"I think so. Mama?"

"Surely, dear. I can't think of a better use you could put your time to."

"Tomorrow, then. Good night."

"Good night, Amy."

They watched her walk across the yard and to the street, then down toward her rented house.

"I like her," Cecilia said.

"Yes. But be careful what you say around her, Cecilia. Let nothing slip. If she's been talking to people from the mountain counties, she'll know about Fletcher and all of that. We mustn't let anything out that we shouldn't. Our past must remain hidden, utterly hidden. Do you understand?"

"Yes, Mama. I won't say a word I shouldn't. I promise."

"Good."

They went back inside. The wind howled around the eaves of the hotel, and light snow began to drift down, unseen beyond closed shutters and drawn curtains.

Chapter 35

He hoped desperately that he would not cough. The notion was strong in his head that to make any sound at all would somehow betray him, make the incoming guards at the outer prison gate say, *Hey there, wait a minute, you! Come here and show your face! Who are you?*

He coughed anyway. Like virtually every prisoner in this overcrowded, hellish camp, Thatcher Brown coughed from morning until night, and often awakened himself hacking even in his sleep. But he was well, compared to most. Of the thousands there, he doubted there were more than a few hundred who were truly healthy. And those were mostly the "fresh fish," newcomers not yet ruined by the terrible conditions, the filth and waste and bad food. Before long they would be like the others, scavenging ground that looked like hogs had rooted through it, looking for edible scraps, eating bugs and rotted plants and anything else that looked like maybe it would stay in a man's stomach if he could manage to get it down his throat. They would become sick and old before their years, and many would wind up as naked passengers on the dead cart, while prisoners fortunate—or perhaps unfortunate—enough to survive scrounged for their clothing and shoes.

But no more for Thatcher Brown. Not if all went as well as it had so far. Dr. Best had been as good as his word, and Thatcher was even now drifting over as casually as possible to the body of uniformed guards clumping up to exit the outer wall of the camp while a new shift came in to replace them.

The uniform Best had left for him was far too large for his emaciated frame, but he wasn't particularly worried that this would betray him. Many of the true Confederate soldiers were equally ill-fitted, and besides, he'd found a gray blanket in the medicine supply house and thrown it across him like a cloak, in the common manner of many of the guards.

He tried to appear casual, and was grateful for the cold, because it gave him a good reason, besides his true one, for pulling his cap low and huddling the blanket up around the lower portion of his face. He moved into the rear of the band of guards, drawing only one glance, and that one didn't linger.

Some of the guards muttered greetings or idle comments to one another as they passed. "Cold night," one said to Thatcher. "Uh-huh," he grunted back, unwilling to risk actually saying anything. His native North Carolinian accent had died long ago under the influence of the scores of other dialects he'd encountered in his years of traveling as a journalist. If anything, Thatcher Brown's speech was not the "Yank talk" that the guards on that railroad car had attributed to him, but a plain, midwestern speaking style.

He began to feel light-headed as he passed out of the gate. He fancied he could feel the blood coursing through every vein, hear his own heart pounding in his thin chest. For the first time since his capture at Vicksburg, he was walking on soil without a rebel guard watching over him! Before him in the night lay the open land of freedom . . . but not truly freedom, he reminded himself. Being outside the walls was a fine thing, but he was still in the heart of Confederate country, and many a prisoner had escaped for a hundred miles or more and still been recaptured.

The body of guards began to disperse. Thatcher slowed his pace, held back, let them get well away from him, and then slowly meandered toward one of the outbuildings standing beyond the prison walls. He slid into a shadowed area, coughed despite himself, and waited until the way seemed clear. Stepping forward, he almost tripped on one of the too-long cuffs of his trousers, and paused to roll the cuff up again before proceeding on.

He expected at any moment to be assailed from some unseen quarter, to hear men running toward him, the command to halt. None of this happened. He walked on, the prison wall receding behind him. No one was about. He kept in the shadows, trying now to remember the directions that Best had drilled into his head long before. He had recited them to himself daily ever since, but now his mind was buzzing, not working efficiently, and he strained to remember. But he did remember.

He entered a street, dark and still as the midnight hour that had just chimed on a distant clock. He looked for the landmarks Best had told him about—a certain tree, a certain house with three gables in front, and a church within view down the way. There . . . he saw them, and walked on.

A man appeared on the street, coming the other way. Panic rose, but he kept it controlled. Just a civilian, chasing down a dog that had gotten out of its pen. The man said his hello, complained for a moment about the troublesome dog, and Thatcher grunted as before in response.

He reached a new avenue where the trees grew thick along one side. Another landmark. He entered the trees and felt safer. Proceeding, he saw it at last: a tall, narrow white house, and beyond it, a shed. Praying no one would notice, praying no dogs would bark, he headed toward it, and found the door open. Going inside, he knelt and found a flat, round stone covering most of the floor. He was already winded from exertion and tension, and lifting the stone was difficult. But again he succeeded. A dark pit yawned beneath him. He slid into it, then lowered the stone in place above him.

Sinking to the floor, he panted for a long time, and noticed he was sweating despite the cold temperature. A few minutes later he felt about and located the items Best had promised would be awaiting him there.

It all seemed unreal and dreamlike. Hard to accept.

He sank onto the damp, cold floor of the pit and rested. Slowly he began to chuckle, then to laugh, spastically. Then tears mixed with the laughter and he wept, and coughed, and wept some more.

He had done it. He'd escaped the Salisbury prison, and vowed to himself, and to the memory of Rockwell Griffin, that he would not go back again, no matter what.

11:30 P.M., December 30, 1864; Jonesborough, Tennessee

A lonely, furtive figure moved in the shadows of the back portions of the town, three stolen eggs in one pocket and half a stolen pie in his one real hand.

Ben Scarlett couldn't figure why anyone would have thrown out such a fine, big portion of a delicious apple pie. He'd tasted it already and found nothing wrong with it. But there must be something amiss, something that made it unpalatable to the average eater—a child sneezing on it, a dog licking it, a mouse leaving some droppings atop it. . . . Best not to know. It looked all right and tasted better, and Ben wasn't a choosy man these days.

He had already asked God to forgive him for the stolen eggs. It was wrong to steal, especially wrong when the thief was a man who claimed to have repented his sinful ways and promised not to return to them—but what was a hungry man to do? Even a backslider had to eat. Just to be safe, he said another prayer, asking again for forgiveness. He was good at such prayers, said them all the time. He hadn't gotten drunk a single time in the past year that he hadn't prayed for forgiveness after every swallow. Sometimes, when the bottle was empty and he was good and soused, he'd read the Bible, just to make up for things a little further.

He hoped the Lord realized it was all Skunk Linden's fault. If Skunk hadn't have left that bottle on his doorstep in Knoxville, he'd never have fallen so far from grace.

It was the fault of the Mainard family, too, he reminded the Creator. If old man Mainard hadn't gone and died, and the other Mainards scattered off to heaven only knew where because of the war, most likely he'd be sober as a deacon these days, working hard, earning money, living like a good Christian citizen, keeping clean, going to church. But don't hold the Mainards too much to this account, Lord, he prayed. They didn't realize that in leaving Jonesborough, they were betraying poor Ben Scarlett's chance at a new life. Perhaps he should term it *another* new life. He'd had two or three new lives already, and they hadn't seemed to last.

Ben didn't come into Jonesborough very often, and almost never by day. Small-town folks didn't like vagrants such as he wandering their streets in broad daylight, and besides, it was hard to steal during the day. And stealing was how Ben maintained his living these days. That and the occasional odd job for a farmer here and there, or anybody else that might give him a coin or a few bills in exchange for one thing or another. Once, a gang of rowdy rebel soldiers on furlough had paid him an authentic greenback just to goose a passing Negro woman with his hook. He'd felt bad about that, not being a disrespectful or carnal man—but that was a real greenback, and he'd wanted it awfully bad. And it had been funny to watch her jump and claw at her rump when the hook hit her. And surely it wasn't as bad to do it to a colored woman as it would have been if she were white. Besides, he'd asked the Lord to forgive him, later on. The greenback had gone to buy some homemade blackberry wine, the best libation he'd been able to find right at that time.

He was living in a squat old cabin east of town, a place dating back at least to the Revolutionary War, and with half the roof rotted away. Being inside wasn't much different than being outside, especially when it rained or snowed, but there was a fireplace, and he was able to stay warm enough to live. He had no idea who owned the land his cabin sat on, and hoped he never would. Whoever it was probably had no idea he was squatting on their property, and if they did find out, he'd likely be cast out. So far so good, however.

He walked lightly, trying not to make noise and draw the attention of any light sleepers on the other side of the closed shutters and heat-enclosing house walls beside which he traveled, and also trying to avoid making those eggs in his pocket bump together too hard and break.

The wind gusted and blew chimney smoke down from rooftop level and into the alley where he was. A bit of the smoke bore the last remnant scent of a chicken that had been spit-roasted on someone's fire earlier in the evening. Ben paused, sniffing it, and was mentally taken back to Knoxville and the office of the *Sage*, and a day Nanny had roasted a chicken and for once done a good job of it. He smiled at the memory. That had been a good evening, a jovial supper, Amy—though still at that time fresh in her grief over her slain husband—had laughed much and told funny stories from her school days. Nanny had not seemed as sullen as usual that night, and even contributed a funny tale or two of her own. The food had been good, the company pleasant, the feeling of life rich and promising. Those kinds of times . . . those were the good times.

Ben lost his smile. The good times. Probably he'd never know them again. He'd let liquor claim him once more, despite every vow he'd made never to touch the stuff again. He knew it was possible to get off the stuff—he'd done it several times already. The problem was, he went back to it as many times as he left it. He wasn't sure now that it could ever be any way but that.

The worst part was that unless he did get off the whiskey again, he could see Amy Hanover no more. That much he had vowed, and this vow he wouldn't break, like he did most vows. He wanted Amy to think of him as she'd last known him—hardworking, sober, well-behaved, honest. Not like he was now, stealing down an alley with stolen eggs in his pocket and somebody's thrown-out pie in his hand.

At the end of the alley he stopped and looked up and down the dark, silent street. He glanced in the direction of the Odd Fellows Hall, up on a hill at the edge of town, and examined the high steeple of the Presbyterian Church, the nearby court-house, the mill on up the other direction, and all the scattering of various houses and places of commerce in between. Nice town, this one. He might have lived here under much better conditions had he behaved himself, and had he avoided that fateful fight with Cat Kingsley. He could have gone on living and working around Amy, and moved with her when she brought her newspaper east. If ever she really was going to do that. He'd kept his eyes and ears open for news of her coming to this area, but had detected no such news.

It's just as well, in a way, he thought. If she came, I'd just have to hide from her, probably have to move off somewhere else just to make sure she didn't run across me and see me in my shame.

He sighed and walked over to the porch of a dark store, hid in its night shadow, and leaned against a post. A melancholy mood was creeping over him, taking away even his happiness at having found an entire half pie. He began to nibble at it, hardly enjoying its taste, which mingled the tartness of dried apples with the sweetness of sorghum, the standard rural substitute for sugar in these wartime days.

Suddenly it came to him, as clear as the whisper of an angel in his ear. He was going to die. He paused right in the middle of a bite and knew it was true. He was going to die, no question about it, and very soon. He'd already outlived most of those he knew who were slaves to liquor. Now he was drinking as hard as ever, watching himself age and weaken by the day . . . and it would be his turn next. He'd be dead, all because of whiskey. Dead without seeing Amy again, and her baby. Several months old now, assuming everything had gone well and Nanny's curse had been lifted in time. Several months old, and he hadn't seen the child. Didn't even know if it was a boy or girl.

He wondered if Amy still thought about him. With a new child to occupy her, and her writing, probably not. She was probably forgetting old Ben Scarlett by now.

He took the bite, chewed without tasting, swallowed without enjoying, and wanted no more. He stood holding the greasy pie slab, leaning on the post, thinking more soberly than he had in months, despite the fact that he had drunk quite a bit of whiskey during the afternoon.

He was going to die. Old Scratch and his pet demon of whiskey were going to win the battle for Ben Scarlett, with his full cooperation. He would die . . . but he didn't want to. He wanted to live.

He'd been down this same mental road before, he recalled. Back in Nashville, when he'd gone looking for the woman he was once going to marry, he'd worked through all the same realizations. And he put the liquor aside afterward.

Maybe he could do it again. Give it one more try. The only alternative was to stay as he was, and die.

Well, maybe I ought to die, he thought. Me and my backsliding, my vow-breaking, my false repentances. I ain't worth being allowed to live. If I do get off the liquor, I'd just fall back into the whiskey barrel next time somebody like Skunk comes along waving temptation at me.

Hopelessness fell over him like a shroud dropping from above. He leaned harder against the porch post, and felt the eggs crush in his pocket against the wood. He swore, stood straight to try to clean out the pocket, then swore again and let it be. Leaning against the post once more, his arm brushed a piece of paper tacked there. He glanced at it, and straightened once more, his face reflecting a burst of awe, like he'd just actually seen that angel that had been whispering death in his ear.

He dropped the remnants of the pie from suddenly nerveless fingers and reached up to tear the broadside down. It was dark, almost impossible to read, but he was sure, astonishingly, that he had made out the name of Amy Hanover on it.

He held the paper close to his eyes, but the clouds had moved above him, blocking the meager light, and now he couldn't quite read it. Swearing to himself, he squinted. It was hopeless.

Ben had left his matches in his cabin, and here in a sleeping town, had no access to a lighted place. He walked right into the middle of the street, broadside in hand, looking around desperately, drawing the barks of several dogs. He didn't even care just now if someone saw him. He had to find a lighted place and read this thing, whatever it was.

His eye caught a glimmer of light coming from the back room of a house, spilling out beneath a closed shutter. Some insomniac was up reading or pacing around, maybe, or some young mother was up nursing a fitful child. Whoever it was, Ben Scarlett appreciated them, and their light. He trotted toward the light glimmer, creeping silently once he got close, and edged to the window, positioning the paper so the faint glow struck it. In an awkward posture he read the broadside. Then he read it again, through a sheen of rising tears.

She was here. Lord above, she was *here*! And asking about him, trying to find him.

She hadn't forgotten him any more than he'd forgotten her. She was looking for him. She remembered him. She cared about him.

He slipped away from the window and out of town, moving now in a world that seemed very different than it had earlier that same evening. He was different too, his thoughts and motives. No voices whispered death in his ear now. She had come! She was *advertising* for him! He'd never felt so flattered in his life.

With broken eggs in his coat pocket and the stains of purloined pie on his fingers, he traveled alone beneath the night sky, feeling younger, almost fleet. He reached his little half-roofed cabin and entered, digging out his matches, lighting a candle stub that flickered in the cold wind but didn't go out. He dug in his bag and pulled out the bottle of whiskey he'd drunk from earlier in the day. He'd saved the rest for tomorrow.

He unstoppered it and walked to the door. Hesitating only a moment or two, he turned the bottle over and let the contents gurgle onto the ground.

He lifted his eyes heavenward. "I ain't going to die. I can't die now. I got to get back to being the right kind of fellow again. No more whiskey, Lord. If you'll help me, this time I'll really put it away, like I have before, and try not to go back. I know you've heard this many a time from me . . . but please, Lord, hear it one more time. Or a hundred more times, if it comes to that. I got to get better again. She's come to find me. I got to get better."

Chapter 36

Thatcher Brown stretched out on the clean, white sheet, stretching his back over the prickly but soft hay beneath it, and told himself he would never say an unkind word about, or to, another person of color for the rest of his days.

He had found along his difficult and covert journey west from Salisbury that there were few things he could rely on. Directions had often proved inaccurate, warnings of danger and assurances of safety both frequently turned out to be off the mark, and the terrain he had traveled had not always proven to be what he was told. But one thing had proven constant all along: the faithfulness and cordiality of the slaves he met along the way. More than any others, they'd given him shelter and food, and he learned to trust their directions and admonitions above any received from whites. He had been told by others who escaped both from Libby and Salisbury, only to be recaptured and returned, that an escaping Yankee could almost invariably rely upon slaves for aid.

Nothing Thatcher encountered so far had given the lie to that counsel. He had spent several nights in slave huts, or in barn lofts, as he was now, fed by slaves, given clothing, guidance, shoes—and always pummeled with questions. Had

Lincoln truly freed the slaves? When would freedom actually come? Was it true that the war would end soon?

Thatcher had almost as little knowledge of these matters as those who asked the questions. Cut off in the prison camp, he had not had much access to newspapers, and what information came through to the prisoners was often slanted and distorted by the rebel guards. Only those citizens of Salisbury who secretly favored the Union, but who had convinced the rebel authorities that they were staunch Confederates, had given information the prisoners felt they could truly believe.

At first Thatcher answered the inquiries honestly, which was to say, he didn't provide many answers at all. As he progressed across North Carolina toward the mountains, however, he gradually began altering his approach, and telling the eager slaves what they wanted to hear—that the war indeed was all but done, slavery was ending and would soon be outlawed by Congress itself, and that the Lincoln government was ready to step in and do all that was necessary to take care of its black citizens. Thatcher did not really know how much of this was true, and his conscience bothered him for not being fully honest . . . but tickling the ears of his benefactors made them give him even greater care, and he knew it would also make them more prone to help the next Yankee escapee who came their way. So he told his tales and didn't worry much about it.

He was finding this business of being a fugitive quite tiring. Mentally as well as physically. Within one day he might go from deep, hopeless despair and a feeling of assurance that he would be captured just over the next hill, to a thrilling sense that the race was in fact already run, and never again would a rebel lay hands on him. From that peak he would spiral down to hopelessness again, and so it went, up and down, mile after mile.

He'd decided that the important part of that pattern had nothing to do with the fluctuating feelings, only with the mileage. As long as he kept going, there was hope no matter how he felt, and the farther he went, the less the likelihood of capture.

He heard noise in the barn below him and sat up fearfully. Though his benefactors of the moment had assured him that the master of the plantation was gone and he would not be discovered, every noise raised doubt.

But this time doubt was groundless. Three black faces peered back at him when he looked over the edge of the loft. And there was food—bread, sweet potatoes, pork meat. Thatcher's stomach rumbled, and he smiled the three right up the loft ladder and in moments was feasting better than at any time since his escape began.

They talked to him while he ate, asking what it was like to live in the North and how long it would be before they could go there themselves. They were full of curiosity about what would be done for freedmen, what their legal rights would be, and who would make sure they were enforced. Thatcher answered honestly when he knew the proper response, and improvised when he didn't. Mostly he ate, and thought about the next stop, and the one beyond that . . . and ultimately the blue mountains he would reach. Once he struck the mountains, travel would be much different. More rugged and difficult.

And once in the mountains, he would begin asking all who helped him where he might find the famous stampeder pilot named Greeley Brown.

The interview was going on in the next room, but the door was ajar and Cecilia could hear it all. What she heard repelled her, also fascinated her, made her want to cover her ears, and to move closer to the door so she could be sure not to miss a word.

The young man whom Amy Hanover was interviewing was named Bale Worley. A stranger to Cecilia. But the words he spoke touched on matters that were a deep part of her, relevant to a past that her mother declared gone and buried but which at this moment seemed very alive as Cecilia listened.

"There's not so many rebels bushwhacking and such right now, least, not in Carter County. When General Gillem and his Yanks come in late last year, it gave a fright to plenty of them, and I hear that most are up about Bristol these days. But there's one still there, covering Carter and Johnson County both, and I'm betting, ma'am, that you've heard aplenty about him from other folk you've talked to about such things."

"Cap Fletcher?" Amy said, and in the room on the other side of the half-closed door, Cecilia squeezed her eyes shut and cringed at the mere sound of the name. Adam, playing at her feet in his long child's dress, sitting on a quilt spread across the floor, giggled and sucked on a toy rocking horse.

"That's him. Devil Cap Fletcher, lots of folks call him now. Devil Cap. And he is a devil. Lord only knows how many he's killed. Over two counties I know of close to thirty he's murdered, and I don't know near all he's done. And houses he's burned—lands! Did you know that over the last fall and the first part of the winter alone, there's been more than a hundred houses of Union folk burned in Carter and Johnson alone? Fletcher didn't do them all, but he did his share, believe me."

"Does he still mutilate the faces of his victims?"

"Yep. Fletcher's Cross. Like the Mark of the Beast in the Bible. Just as wicked a thing, I swear, as the very Mark of the Beast. But let me tell you something, ma'am—the worm is turning. The worm is turning."

"Meaning what?"

"Meaning that Fletcher has followed the usual way of the wicked, and has had his own evil ways turned back on him. Have you heard about the ghost in the mountains?"

"Ghost? You mean a literal, true ghost?"

"I don't. Because I believe I know the truth behind the tale. But a lot who'd tell you this same story would say it was a real ghost. The ghost of a man Fletcher hung, they say. That ghost has come back to torment his killer, and to murder off Fletcher's raiders, one by one. And last of all, they say, the ghost will kill Fletcher himself."

"But you said you don't believe it's a ghost. Correct?"

"Yep. It is a man Fletcher hung, that much is true, but it ain't no ghost. It's a living man."

"Greeley Brown, the stampeder pilot?"

In the next room Cecilia gave a little jump at mention of the name. Not a day passed that she didn't think of Greeley, whom she had not seen since he piloted her and her mother here to Jonesborough. He hadn't lingered, but turned straight back to the mountains and the bloody work he'd undertaken there. But he had told Cecilia before he left that he would return someday, just to see that she was well. Lately she had taken to looking out her window quite often, hoping against hope to see his lean form striding up the street toward the hotel.

Amy's interviewee seemed quite let down to have had his grand revelation stolen away from him. "How'd you know about Greeley Brown being the ghost, ma'am?"

"I've had a couple of others mention it to me."

"Well, they're right." He quickly began to regain steam. "It is Greeley Brown. What happened was that Fletcher, right about a year ago, caught up with Mr. Brown in the mountains near Limestone Cove, and beat him good, put his mark on his face, and strung him to a sapling."

"Yes, and Mr. Brown managed to get himself down," Amy said, giving the version she had heard before.

Now her informant grew quite happy, for he had found something to contradict her upon. "Nope. He didn't get himself down. If folks are telling you that, they're wrong. I know the *truth* of the matter."

"Well? Go on."

"He didn't get himself down, but was got down by another person. And I know who."

A pause. Cecilia, overwhelmed by all this talk of people and matters that had seemed distant and unreal here in the refuge of Jonesborough, was trembling on the sofa in the next room. Adam was chewing now on the end of his dress, soaking the fabric.

"Who?" Amy asked, seeing the fellow desired prompting.

"Old Sally Clung. Or so I've heard it from a man who says Greeley Brown himself told him that."

"Sally Clung . . ." Amy had heard the name mentioned in some interview before, but not in any particularly relevant way, so she couldn't quite place the memory of who this woman was.

"She's an old mountain hermit woman lives up in some hid cabin. She's known to sneak about, follow people in the hills, creep right down to houses and such and listen at people talking. Been caught at it quite a few times. But she's harmless, and helps out the Union scouters and so on. It was her who cut Greeley Brown down, then nursed him for weeks and weeks until he was healed up and ready to go hunting Fletcher. Likely she'd been following Fletcher's raiders and so was there when they caught Mr. Brown. They say Sally has a fierce hatred of Cap Fletcher, and she's been known to follow folks for miles. I knowed a couple of hunters who told me she once traced along behind them for nigh on twenty miles, them catching sight of her every now and then, but her always staying off from them, just watching. They never knowed why she done it, but with her, you never know anyhow. She has her own reasons for what she does, I reckon."

Amy wrote it down, fascinated. An old mountain woman rescuing a stampeder pilot from the noose, nursing him back to health, him undertaking a campaign of vengeance against the man who had tried to kill him . . . this was the raw material of legendry.

Cecilia sat rigidly on the other side of the door, listening to the scratch of Amy's pen. How much more she could tell Amy Hanover! And how purging it might feel to do it! But her mother had forbidden it. There was irony here: The same young woman who had opted for silence for so long now wished to speak, and couldn't.

"How many of Fletcher's men has Greeley Brown killed?" she asked.

"Don't know for certain. Maybe twenty. Maybe a few more."

"It's astonishing. It's like a one-man war," Amy said.

"Yep. But Fletcher himself has escaped it so far. And as glad as people has been to see his raiders having their ranks thinned and Fletcher himself get so flustered about, there's been a bad side to it all. Fletcher's turned even meaner since it all commenced. He can't catch Greeley Brown to punish him, so he punishes other folks in his place. That's why he's continuing to linger in Carter County after so many other rebels have took to fleeing. It's a personal grudge for him now, you see."

Amy frowned. "I wonder how Greeley Brown feels about what he's doing, considering that it's making Fletcher 'meaner,' as you said."

"I don't know that, ma'am. But I can tell you this: I've not met a Unionist in them hills yet who would have Greeley Brown doing other than what he's doing. Fletcher was a killer before Mr. Brown started his vengeance, and he'd have been a killer even if Mr. Brown had died in that noose and never been able to start his avenging at all. They say he's something of a madman, and if that's the case, it might be he'd have turned meaner anyhow."

"What do you mean when you say Fletcher is meaner than before?"

"He makes more of a show of his killing. Cutting crosses on both sides of the face instead of just one, sometimes. He made one wife shoot her own husband, or so I hear. Threatened her child if she didn't, and the husband died telling her it was all right, go ahead and shoot me, honey. Things to break your heart. They don't break Fletcher's heart, though. Just harden it more. Why, let me tell you another tale to show you what I mean. This is a story that comes straight from the rebels, and they've heard it straight from Fletcher himself, or from his men. They brag on their wickedness, them Fletcherites. Anyhow, here's the tale: There was this man name of Vaughn Fitz living at Limestone Cove . . ."

In the other room, Cecilia's hand came to her mouth, cupped over it, remained. She stared unblinkingly across the room.

". . . and Fitz had a wife that Fletcher had took a shine to, or so go the whispers. Some real pretty woman. Don't know her name or nothing. But anyhow, this woman decides to leave Fitz, and tied him up tight in his bed one night while he slept, and left him that way, so he couldn't chase her down, you see. Fletcher found the fellow still tied to the bed two days later when he come to pay call, so he could see that woman, I suppose, and it made Fletcher boiling mad that this Fitz had treated his wife so that she run off. So instead of cutting this fellow loose, he just pulls out his big bowie knife, carves his cross on the fellow's chest, then stabs him through the heart. Killed him deader than the twelfth century."

Cecilia rose, stomach lurching, ran to the fireplace and heaved. Adam watched her, uncomprehending, cheerful, still scratching at the rocking horse.

The talk continued in the next room, but Cecilia wanted to hear no more of it. Vaughn Fitz . . . dead! Murdered by Fletcher! She didn't know how she felt, or how she should feel. Before she and Miriam fled, she'd been ready to kill Fitz herself. Her mother, thankfully, had stopped her. Here in this better world and brighter town, where she felt safe from the grim past, Cecilia was glad she did not have to look back and see a man's death on her account.

But in a way, it seemed to her, she had killed Fitz, or had helped her mother do so. By tying him in that bed, they'd left him at Fletcher's mercy, and by running away, Miriam had taken from Fletcher his only motivation for letting Fitz live at all. It would have been much simpler for Fletcher to have killed Fitz to begin with. Fitz had not been friends with anyone, never socialized at all. Fletcher could have killed him at any point, had the full run of the isolated hollow. Why hadn't he? Cecilia could only surmise it was for the sake of her mother. Fletcher might be cruel, but he wasn't going to openly murder the husband of a woman whose admiration he craved.

The door that had been ajar now opened fully, and Amy entered the room, having just ushered her informant out of the house through the outer door in the other chamber. When she saw Cecilia on hands and knees, head almost in the fireplace, and from the smell and sizzle of the fire realized that she had just been sick, Amy rushed to her and knelt beside her.

"Cecilia, what's wrong? Are you sick? Why are you crying?"

Cecilia turned to Amy, put her arms around her neck, and sobbed onto her shoulder. "I want to talk to you," she said. "My mother has told me not to . . . but I have to. I have to tell you some things, but you can't put them in your book. They're secret things. You have to promise not to tell anyone."

"I do promise, Cecilia. But are you sure these are things you really want to talk about?"

"Yes, yes! I have to! I can't bear not to! You won't put them in your book, will you?"

"No, Cecilia. I already told you. I promise. I'll just listen, that's all. You tell me whatever you want, and I'll just listen."

She did listen, for almost three hours straight.

Door latched, shutters closed, fire built up to drive away the chill that blew in on windy drafts that seemed to penetrate the solid walls, Amy sat with Adam sleeping on her lap and listened to Cecilia Goode—whom Amy now learned was in fact named Cecilia Fry—tell a story that rended the heart. She told of a happy, normal girlhood, broken by the death of a good father, then shattered to pieces by the ordeal of rape that made Cecilia cut herself off from the world in a shroud of self-imposed silence she had worn for two long years. She told of a baby, born out of violence but purified by the unconditional mother's love Cecilia found inside herself. The story became uglier then, a tale of a gravedigger killed by Miriam Fry because all other attempts at punishment had failed. Then came desperate flight across a war-torn state, a baby gradually sickening and weakening, then dying in a boardinghouse in Sevierville—where Cecilia and her mother met a man named Greeley Brown, whom Amy had never seen but had now come to feel as if she knew well.

Cecilia told about their entrance into the mountains, their parting from Greeley Brown, and her mother's undesired marriage to the abusive Vaughn Fitz. She told of Fletcher and his hold on Fitz, and how at last that hold, and the abuse Fitz had doled out to the Fry women, had led them to flee again, once more in the care of Greeley Brown. And now they were here, in Jonesborough, living with an eccentric but good cousin who knew nothing of their lives before. No one knew at all . . . except now Amy Hanover.

When the telling was done, Cecilia looked at Amy with the stain of tears on her face. "You won't tell, will you? Not anyone?"

Amy was uncertain for a moment. Cecilia's mother had killed a man, killed him outside the parameters of what was legal. In the eyes of the law, it was murder.

Then she looked at Adam, sleeping in her lap, and thought how she as a mother would react if anyone had hurt him as deeply as Miriam Fry had seen her daughter hurt. In those circumstances, she knew she could kill just as easily.

"I won't tell anyone," she said. "As far as I'm concerned, you're still Cecilia Goode, from Johnson County, and your business is your own. And your mother's business, too."

Cecilia nodded, and stared at the floor.

"Are you glad you told, Cecilia?"

"Yes. It's better now. Inside me, it's better, because I told."

"There's something I want to tell you, too," Amy said. "It has to do with Greeley Brown. You said that after he left you here in Jonesborough, he said he'd return. When he does, I want you to let me know. I need to speak with him."

"For your book?"

"Yes, but not only that. I received a letter from Mr. Brown, you see, a year ago. I don't know how he knew of me. I don't even know what the letter really said. It was damaged on its way to me, and I only saw a small portion of it. All I know is that it had to do with someone named Sam, who wanted Mr. Brown to get information to me."

"What information?"

"I don't know. That was the portion that was missing."

"Who was Sam?"

"I'm not sure about that, either, but I think it might be a young man named Sam Colter, who asked me once if I would marry him. I told him no."

Cecilia wiped her tears away, growing interested now in Amy's story. "You think maybe he was trying to ask you again?"

"I don't know. Maybe. But if he was, why was he doing it through Greeley Brown? And where is Sam now? I have no idea what became of him after the last time I saw him."

"Was he nice? Handsome?"

"Nice, yes. Handsome . . . no. But it's the nice part that matters most, don't you think?"

"Yes. Oh, yes. My father was nice. Not at all like Uncle Vaughn is . . . was. He's dead now. I heard the man telling you about it."

"Yes. I'm sorry. I suppose that's what I should say to you. I know you didn't like him, but I still feel like I have to say I'm sorry."

"I know. I'm sorry, too. I'm sorry anybody has to be killed by such a bad man as Fletcher. I hate him."

"So do I. The more I hear, the more I hate him."

"I hope Greeley Brown kills him. Do you?"

Amy felt precisely the same, but was too much a product of civilized society's protocol to vent that feeling as blatantly as Cecilia had. "I'll say it this way: If I heard that Cap Fletcher was dead, I'd not mourn a moment."

"Greeley Brown will kill him. I'm sure he will. Because he's purely good, and Fletcher is purely bad. And the good always destroys the bad in the end . . . doesn't it?"

It was a question Amy honestly could not answer. She had seen too much good, and too many good people, destroyed by the evil of war to be sure anymore that the good always prevailed.

Even Cecilia's declaration that Greeley Brown was "purely good" was something Amy wasn't sure she could agree with if pressed. Good he was in comparison to Fletcher, assuredly; good and righteous was his campaign to free the mountains of Fletcher's threat . . . but "purely good"? Was anything or any man purely good, when much of what drove him was hatred? Maybe, in some circumstances . . . but Amy wasn't sure. She was much less sure of many things in life these days.

"Cecilia, when Greeley Brown comes back, please be sure I know. I want him to tell me what he wrote in that letter."

"I will. And I hope what he wrote was that this Sam wants you to marry him, and that he's coming to take you away, like some king to his castle."

Amy laughed. "Oh, I don't know about kings and castles, Cecilia. I've never been one for fairy tales."

"I love fairy tales. In fairy tales, it's always the good people who live, and the bad ones who die."

Chapter 37

Sally Clung rose to greet Greeley Brown as he quietly entered her cabin, but he noticed how slowly she did so, and how sallow was her look. She seemed thinner than when he'd seen her last, and the cavities of her eyes had a vague, hollow look.

"Greeley!" she said, putting out a withered hand for him to hold. "I'm glad to see you. You're looking good and strong."

"No, I ain't," he said, smiling, trying to hide his concern over her obvious physical decline. "I got a scar on my face, a rope mark on my neck, and I'm weathered like an old log."

"But you are strong."

"I am strong, yes." He paused. "What about you?"

"I'm not strong. Not no more. I'm getting old, Greeley. My time is short."

"Hey now, I don't want to hear that kind of talk. You'll never be old, Sally."

"Where you been living, Greeley?"

"In a tree, lately. Big old hollow sycamore. I was in a cave awhile before that, but come to suspect some of Fletcher's men had found me. So I moved."

"Always moving. Always having to run."

"It goes with what I've been doing."

"I've got news for you, Greeley. I learned it from Mark Hubbard. He's still scouting, hiding out about Turkey Town. But he come to see me some days back. Brought me food."

"I didn't know Mark knew where you live."

"He's one of the few. He's been good to me many a time, and I been good to him. I've carried him many a victual while he was on the scout."

"You range a long way, Sally."

"Not no more. Not no more."

"What's the news?"

Her next words struck like a hammer. "Fletcher's dead."

"What?"

"He's dead, Greeley. Or so Mark Hubbard says."

"Dead . . . how?"

"Shot to death. A shotgun blast to the head. Killed by some Union men in Johnson County."

"You're sure?"

"No. But Mark says it's true. He talked to a man who seen the corpse. A lot of the face was shot off, but he said it surely appeared to be Fletcher. And since then, not a cabin has burned, and not a soul has died with Fletcher's Cross on his face."

Greeley almost unconsciously reached up and touched the scar on his cheek. "Dead. I can't believe it. So it's over, then."

"It's over. Far as Fletcher is concerned."

"What about his raiders, or what's left of them?"

"Scattered. Gone off into Virginia, I hear. Help me sit down, Greeley. I'm stiff today."

He helped ease her back into her chair. Her breathing had a wheezing quality. Greeley went to the hearth and poked up the fire with the green hickory stick poker he had whittled out for Sally during his recuperation a year before. As the fire blazed up and warmed the cabin, he sat on the floor and stared into the flames.

"It's going to take some getting used to for you, ain't it?"

"It is," he replied.

"I can die happy now, knowing the plague is gone from the mountains."

"Kind of funny, Sally. You always said it was my destiny to kill him. The mountain told you wrong."

Sally didn't reply. He twisted to look at her and was afraid for a moment when he saw that her head had drooped toward her chest. He rose and lunged toward her, then heard her snore. She had simply fallen asleep in that rapid manner of the aged.

He sat down at the fire again, thinking how odd it was that sometimes momentous changes came in such an odd way, as fast and unheralded as old Sally's suddenly falling asleep in her chair. Fletcher was dead. Over in Wilmington, on the coast, the Federals now held Fort Fisher and had closed down the last rebel port. Sherman's army was even now moving through North Carolina in a sweeping invasion, having already scoured Georgia and burned Atlanta. Lincoln was due to be inaugurated for his second term, with Tennessee's own Andrew Johnson as his vice-president, and the political talk these days had less to do with waging war than with handling all the reconstruction that would follow it. And here in the mountains, where Federal soldiers had finally penetrated, it seemed the rebels were truly on the run, and the Union people prevailing.

And Fletcher was dead. The last and worst of the rebel marauders was gone.

It was actually anticlimactic for Greeley. His vision of himself as a Union avenger, with a very focused purpose, suddenly didn't seem to fit anymore.

He remained where he was a long time, letting himself accommodate to this startling development. Strange, how uncomfortably it fit his mind. But as an hour passed and another began, he began to feel a slowly rising relief. Fletcher was gone. No more did he have to pursue and kill. Greeley Brown could turn away from being the ghostly pursuer of a madman and become himself again . . . if that were possible. He wasn't sure it was. He wasn't the same man he'd been when the war started. He'd been carefree, free-ranging, jovial, not prone to take life seriously. A friend to everyone, even many who had gone on to favor the Confederacy he hated.

It struck him that the Greeley Brown whom Old Sally had cut down from Fletcher's hanging rope might not be exactly the same man whom Fletcher had put into it.

The old Greeley Brown had been quick to forgive and forget. He wasn't sure he had that capability any longer.

He'd have to learn all over again to forgive. And as he

thought about that, it came to him that he knew where, and with whom, he'd like to make the first effort.

He remained unmoving for almost another hour, thinking about Miriam. He had heard of the death of Vaughn Fitz. She was a free woman now, though possibly she didn't even know it herself. She was free, he was free, and the war was winding down. The deception she had foisted on him, the danger she had placed him in by luring him back into the mountains under false pretenses—it didn't seem to matter so much now.

There would be a life beyond this war. If he could forgive Miriam, and if she would accept him, maybe that life wouldn't have to be lonely any longer for Greeley Brown.

Greeley stayed at Sally's house for four more days. He'd moved away from this place shortly after starting his vengeance campaign against Fletcher, fearing she would suffer the same kind of reprisal that Mathen Ricker had, should he remain and possibly be detected. Now, with Fletcher dead, he figured that wasn't a matter to worry about any longer. But he knew he couldn't remain here forever. This was not his cabin or his life.

The first day in particular he worried much about her, and wondered how to persuade her that the time might have come for her to consider leaving this isolated life of hers and moving where there were people around to watch over her. Otherwise she would surely die alone up here.

The second day, however, Sally rallied remarkably. He attributed this initially to his mere presence, cheering her up, but on the third day it grew evident that she was truly improving in health. By the fourth day she seemed as strong and lively as he'd ever known her. The relief this brought was great. He could leave here now without feeling he was abandoning her to a lonely and potentially suffering fate.

Sally told him another piece of news from Mark Hubbard: There were still men in the mountains wanting to stampede to the Federals, including many members of the Confederate Home Guard who saw that their cause was lost and who wanted to switch their allegiances before the war ended, to avoid whatever reprisals might come otherwise. Plenty of Confederate deserters in the mountain country had the same ambition, and there were even yet Unionist men, who had remained in the mountains through the entire war for the sake of their families, who now believed they could best help their families by enlisting and helping the Federal army bring this long-standing war to an end. Such men could use Greeley Brown's piloting skills.

Greeley liked that idea. He had been an avenger long enough. The idea of conducting one more piloting run was quite appealing. And after that, he could go to Jonesborough, find Miriam and Cecilia . . . and who could say what might happen? The possibility of walking out of this war and into a ready-made family was marvelously enticing. He'd ached for years to have a family of his own again.

Greeley left Sally's remote cabin feeling like a man unburdened. He would hide no longer. He'd live in caves and trees never again. The "ghost" who pursued Fletcher was coming back to life again, and reentering the world of men.

Greeley Brown would avenge no more, and hide no longer.

The story of Fletcher's death reached Amy Hanover via another refugee interview, and she immediately shared it with Cecilia.

"Was it Greeley Brown?" Cecilia asked.

"I don't know," Amy replied. "Fletcher died in Johnson County, as I hear it. It could have been Mr. Brown who killed him, I suppose. It hardly matters. What matters is that he is dead."

"Yes."

Amy asked a question she'd been holding back for many days, feeling it intrusive. This time she couldn't resist. "Have you told your mother about Vaughn Fitz?"

"Yes," Cecilia replied. "I told her I overheard it while you were interviewing. She doesn't know that you know about him being her husband."

"Of course not. And she'll never know that I know, unless she tells me herself. How did she react?"

"She seemed . . . shocked. She didn't love him, but still . . . I didn't tell her that he was still tied on his bed when Fletcher killed him. That would make her feel like it was partly her fault. It was Mama who tied him there. I hope she never hears how he died."

"You're wise beyond your years, Cecilia. And she'll never learn how he died from me. I've chosen for Miriam's sake not to include the story in my book."

Cecilia smiled and looked relieved.

Amy went on. "Cecilia, this news about Fletcher could be significant in terms of Mr. Brown. If he has been devoting himself to hunting Fletcher, he's now free of that burden. Maybe now he'll come see you, like he promised."

"I hope so."

"So do I."

The first edition of the Jonesborough–based version of the *Sage & Torch* came off the press a day later. Amy looked it over and was forced to admit to herself that it wasn't a particularly impressive bit of work. Paper, hard to come by even in Knoxville, was even less available here, and the single little ten-by-twelve, two-sided sheet seemed awfully meager. But there was sufficient advertising lined along the bottom of the front page and down the right two columns of the second to offset the cost, even if not to make much profit.

Eaton seemed discouraged. "Don't worry, Horatio," Amy told him. "We will grow here. When the war is over, times will improve. There will be much local news, not just all the war material."

"Yes, but my ambition is to focus on the refugees and contrabands. I've never wanted to be just a local newspaperman, printing up deaths and births and resolutions from town aldermen. By the time I fit in the advertising, the war news, and a couple of local items, there was hardly any room left to write about the things that really concern me."

"Patience, Horatio. All in good time. Besides, when the war is over and our society here starts rebuilding itself, you'll find that the refugee and freedmen issues will become one and the same with local concerns. We'll adjust, adapt, and do what we have to do to make this newspaper successful, but also keep focus on the broad matters that concern us both. Don't lose heart. I'm expecting to receive more information soon about this new Thirteenth Amendment that's coming now to the states, and you can use it in the next edition. We'll advocate for it with full vigor. And we should be able to give a good full account of Lincoln's peace conference with those Confederate leaders."

"His *failed* peace conference. The South still insists on autonomy."

"Yes, but at least they talked to one another. I have a good feeling, Horatio. We'll be past this war soon, and then we can really concentrate on making this nation what it should be, and advocating for the freedmen to have their rightful place in it. Keep the faith, Horatio!" She slapped him on the shoulder in an almost masculine gesture and gave him a wry smile.

He smiled back. "Don't worry. I'll be keeping the faith until the day I die."

Having devoted herself to cheering up Eaton, Amy went home that night and descended into despondency herself.

Part of the problem was Adam, who was croupy and fitful and kept her rising through the night. When she was able to stay in bed, she was unable to sleep.

Giving up the fight, she got up, lit a candle, and sat down at her desk to work on her book. But her heart wasn't in it. She put down her pen with a sigh and opened the drawer of her desk. From a little leather folder she removed the stained and torn letter fragment she had received in Knoxville and read its few legible lines for the thousandth time.

Sam Colter. Surely that was who Greeley Brown was writing about. She had become even more sure of that recently, having heard from one of her refugee informants that at the beginning of the war, Sam had actually helped Greeley in his piloting work. So there was an undeniable connection between the two.

Amy stared at the letter fragment, but didn't really see it. She was remembering Sam as she'd first known him . . . just a lanky, shy mountain boy from North Carolina, trying to become a townsman and merchant. Amy had come to like him very much, but at that time she was full of enthusiasm for the causes that drove her and sure that wartime was no time for anyone to marry—a viewpoint she had quickly changed after meeting Adam Hanover in Nashville.

She wondered what would have happened had she accepted Sam's proposal. Her life would have been much less adventurous, to be sure. There would have been no marriage to Adam Hanover, no little Adam Benjamin Hanover fussing at her from his crib this very night. No journalism and advocacy in Nashville and Knoxville, and now here. Quite possibly no book in the works about the terrors of Unionist life in the mountains.

She would have missed certain joys that had blessed her life, and many pains. But equally so, she surely would have experienced different joys, living as Sam Colter's wife, and there would have been pains that she could not now know about.

It was all a great, futile exercise in what-if. A waste of time. She tucked the letter back into the desk and tried to forget about it. If Greeley Brown ever did show up in Jonesborough, she could find out what the letter had to say.

She already had a suspicion, and it wasn't happy. If Sam Colter had a message to give her, surely he could have sent it himself, not gone through Greeley Brown and that poor stranger who had died on the railroad tracks.

The full letter probably would have told her that Sam was dead. Probably a victim of the war.

She closed the desk drawer, thinking that maybe she wasn't all that eager to have the mystery solved after all. As long as she didn't know the facts, she could still hope that Sam was alive and well somewhere.

Amy rose and went back to her bed, very sleepy all at once. Adam wasn't fussing now; his breathing was steady and smooth, no croupy undertone.

Amy closed her eyes and let her thoughts drift freely. Within a few minutes she was asleep.

A dog barking outside awakened her early. She opened her eyes in a room still dark. The dog sounded quite upset, its bark loud even though the windows and shutters were closed against the lingering cold. She guessed the time at about four o'clock.

"Stupid beast!" she murmured. "It's going to wake up Adam."

She figured it would hush in a minute or so, but the barking went on, frantic and stirring her further and further awake. Adam made a threatening gurgle over in his crib. He'd be awake in moments if that dog didn't shut up.

She went to the window, pulled back the curtain, flipped the latch, and slid up the lower frame. Cold air sliced in through the vented shutters. She unlatched, pushed one of them open, and looked out to command the dog to be quiet. But she noticed it was at the outhouse, yapping at the closed door.

Why would it do that? Another dog couldn't have entered an outhouse and closed the door behind it. Only a human could do that.

Amy closed the shutter and latched it back, firmly, then closed the window and latched it, too. Smoothing the curtains back into place, she went over and checked on Adam, as if the mere presence of a prowler outside might somehow have harmed him. It was an irrational notion and she knew it, but this was motherly instinct at work, not rationality. Amy had noticed that since giving birth, she'd become a much less practical-minded, rational person.

Adam was fine, of course. She went to the wardrobe and opened it, removing the cap-and-ball rifle she kept hidden there. She had purchased it shortly after Ben Scarlett fled Knoxville. Oddly, she had never felt the need for such protection when he was nearby, even if only down the street in his room above the *Sage* office. Ben had seemed a protective presence. Horatio Eaton had occupied Ben's old room after he left, but he wasn't the kind to generate feelings of protection. Amy figured a ten-year-old girl could probably defeat Horatio at fisticuffs, if she were riled up enough, and the notion of Horatio using firearms was downright scary. The poor little man would no doubt shoot himself just trying to load up.

Amy loaded the rifle, laid it across the foot of her bed, then crawled in herself, where she sat up with the covers pulled up around her chin, wondering what she should do. A few moments later she got up, lifted Adam from his crib, and put him in bed beside her, taking care not to rouse him. Then it was back to sitting, huddling under the covers, and worrying.

She frowned at her sleeping baby. In a whisper she said, "Adam, what's wrong with me? I've helped slaves escape on the Underground Railroad. I've smuggled counterfeit currency through rebel lines in hostile territory, and gotten shot doing it. I've worked in Federal army hospitals with wounded men screaming and bleeding all around me. And now I'm huddling here because somebody might be in my outhouse. Most likely it's just a rat that's crawled in through a hole."

The dog was still barking outside.

"Must be a really big rat," she whispered to the unhearing child.

A notion arose that she might just take the rifle, go on out there, and confront whomever was in that shed, if anyone. The notion didn't live long. She wasn't about to roust out some stranger in a outhouse all alone in the pit of night.

"You've got no courage at all, Amy Deacon Hanover!" she chided herself. "What's changed about you?"

A glance at Adam was all it took to answer that question.

The dog quit barking at last, and Amy settled down to sleep, her hand lightly resting on her sleeping baby. Dawn came less than an hour after she finally went to sleep. Even the muted light coming in through the shuttered, curtained windows was enough to make her feel much more bold than she had when all was dark.

Adam was still sleeping, so she gently took him back to his crib, threw on a housecoat and slippers, and with the rifle in hand, headed out of her house and around to the outhouse.

The door was still closed. Amy crept close, listening . . . and jumped back, almost dropping the rifle in alarm.

Someone was snoring in there. Sitting in an outhouse— there was certainly no room to lie down, and who would want to?—and sleeping! Of all the brash, intrusive behavior! She swallowed, working up her anger so it would make her brave, reached for the latch . . .

And stopped, trembling, eyes widening, because she suddenly recognized that snore.

She did not yank the door as first intended, but lifted the latch gently and slowly opened it.

Light streaming in on Ben Scarlett, who was seated beneath a blanket on the outhouse seat, made him wince and twitch in his sleep, then jerk slightly and open his eyes. He blinked, squinting, and smiled when he saw Amy.

"Well, hello, Miss Amy!" he said in a hoarse but cheerful voice. "Why, this takes me back to Cumberland Gap and the time I was living in an outhouse full-time, and you came out and saw me there. I hope you don't mind me putting up for the night in your poop shed—whoops! Pardon my language—but I got here sort of late in the evening and didn't want to rouse you at that hour. How are you, Miss Amy? Did you ever have that baby?"

"Ben!" she said. She put the rifle aside, leaning it against a tree. "Oh, Ben!"

She swept into the outhouse and had her arms around him before he could even stand.

Chapter 38

For Amy, the day was the most grand and wonderful since the birth of her son. She spent it engaged in rich conversation with an old friend she feared had come to his end at the hands of a bushwhacker.

There was much joy between them, particularly when Ben met little Adam for the first time and discovered the child's middle name. That brought tears, and a choked voice, and Ben Scarlett rendered weak with emotion for a full minute.

"That's the finest thing anybody's ever done for me, Miss Amy. To have a child named for me . . . oh, Miss Amy, what an honor it is. What an honor."

Ben told her his story, slowly and in detail. It was a sad tale, right up to its happy ending in the present moment. From Knoxville he had made his way across the countryside, usually on foot, usually traveling in woods and along the edges of fields, and on back trails rather than open roads. It had been a hard and fearful journey. Ben told of being chased by a pack of hungry dogs, of walking into the middle of a skirmish between two detachments of soldiers, and of finding the body of a dead boy, shot to death beside a creek, only a day before the countryside filled with rumors that a bushwhacker had come through the area vowing to even the score with a rebel sympathizer who had betrayed him somehow, by killing a member of his family. The son had paid the price.

He told about being given food by a kindly woman at New Market who was living in a hovel outside of town, having been driven out of her fine town home by neighbors who resented the political stance taken by her preacher husband. The husband was not with her now, being forced to live on the run farther east in the state. He'd been dragged from his pulpit one Sunday evening, beaten, and told that if he didn't leave New Market, it would go all the worse for him.

"There's typical rebel cruelty for you," Amy commented.

"Not this time," Ben corrected. "The folks who beat that preacher were Unionists. It was the preacher who was the rebel."

"Oh."

"I've learned a bit since I been with you last, Miss Amy. Like how maybe there's more than one side to this war business, especially now that the Union folk are feeling stronger. Some of them are starting to treat the rebels just as cruel as the rebels treated them."

Amy did not reply to that. It did not accommodate itself comfortably into her image of reality.

Ben had been in Greeneville, sleeping in the loft of a woodshed, drunk on whiskey he had stolen from a house he'd broken into, on the very night that Confederate General John Hunt Morgan was ambushed at a local mansion and shot to death in the yard, clad in trousers and a pajama shirt. Who shot Morgan—a private and Confederate soldier turned Federal named Andrew Campbell, originally from Dublin, Ireland—was not in dispute, but as early as the day after the death, people were arguing about who had betrayed the famed rebel raider's presence in the big three-story house to Union forces stationed nearby. Ben had not stayed around to find out the answer, but set off across country again, heading for Jonesborough.

Once there, he tried to find the Mainard family, which had befriended him long ago, only to discover all were either dead or gone elsewhere. Ben had traveled all the way across East Tennessee for nothing. He was alone and friendless in Jonesborough, hooked again on whiskey, and feeling too tired and unworthy of life even to care.

"I'm fortunate that I ain't killed myself, living like I have since I left Knoxville," he told her. "I've been spending most of my time in a cabin with half the roof gone, living on stolen food and wild winter greens and stew made from rat meat, doing anything I can to earn or steal a dollar here and there, and staying drunk every moment I could. I should have died, Miss Amy. Should have died a score of times in my life, and yet I'm living still. I don't know why the Lord allows me to stay. And it ain't just that I'm alive . . . I'm still able to think clear, in spite of all I've done to myself. So many folks who drink like I have get their minds clouded up by liquor . . . but me, I can still think. It's a mercy that's been given to me that I don't deserve."

"Maybe there's important work you've got still to do," she said.

"Me? Ah, I doubt that. I can't figure a thing I could ever do for nobody that would be important."

"How did you find me, Ben?"

"From that paper you hung up, asking for me." He told her about that nocturnal visit to town at the end of the prior year.

"But Ben, why did you wait so long to show yourself? That's been months back!"

"Why, I couldn't show myself to you as I was then. All drunk and sorry . . . oh, no. I couldn't have done that."

"So what did you do?"

"I went back to my little cabin, and I poured out my whiskey, and I prayed and told the Lord I was ready to sweat it out again, like I've done before. For three days I did sweat it out, and then I got myself right back into town and bought more whiskey from a darky man I know who sells for a man with a still up in the hills. I got drunk again, quit it again, sweated it out a week and a half, next time, and went back for more. But I only drunk three swallows of what I bought, and somehow I was able after that to dump out the rest, and from that moment on I ain't touched any. It was fearsome hard, but I believe I've shook the devil off my back again. And I'm proud that this time I done it all by myself. You didn't have to see me go through it, like you did in Nashville."

"And you won't drink again?"

"Let me tell you something that I've figured out, sitting there alone in that cabin freezing my skinny white . . . I mean,

freezing half to death. I've figured out that life don't come to a
man all at once, but a moment at a time. That's all a man is
ever given to live at any time: just one moment. I pondered on
that and wondered why it was set up that way, and the best I
can see it, it's for the sake of folks like me, who can't handle a
lifetime worth a hoot, but who can sometimes do what they
ought for a moment or two. You see, it's sort of like that trip I
made from Knoxville here to Jonesborough. I didn't make it all
in one big step, but a bunch of little ones. One step, another
one, another one, and so on. It's the same way with living. If
you want to make that journey go right, you don't go trying to
live your lifetime all at once. You live it like it comes to you: a
day at a time, an hour at a time, a minute at a time. You asked
me if I'm not going to drink for the rest of my life, and all I can
say is, I don't know. A lifetime is a mighty big bite to try to
chew all at once. But I do know this: I ain't going to drink in
this present hour. And when the hour has passed and another
comes, I'll forget this one and deal with that one. But I'll be
danged if I'll try to deal with it before it gets to me."

Amy mulled it and said, "I believe you've become a very
capable philosopher, Ben Scarlett."

"Even a fool can learn a bit of something, I reckon."

"Ben, I want to ask you a question you may not want to
answer."

"What's that?"

"When you left Knoxville, you told Horatio you had gotten
into some trouble. Horatio said it appeared you'd been not only
drinking, but fighting. Then after you left, we learned that Cat
Kingsley had been found, dead. Stabbed in an apparent fight.
Ben, I have to ask you—"

"Don't ask me," he said. "Don't. Because I don't know the
answer. Ain't no lie there. I truly don't know. I did fight with
Cat, yes. I went to the contraband camp to try to find Nanny
and persuade her to take that hex off your child. I found her on
my way home, and she said she'd already lifted it. But Cat was
there. Drunk. He attacked me, and I struggled with him. I do
remember that I got a knife into my hand somewhere along the
way . . . but I don't ever remember cutting him with it. The last
thing I recollect is him hitting me with a rock." He pointed at
his forehead. "See there? Still a trace of scar from where it

knocked the skin off. But Miss Amy, I swear to you, I don't believe I killed him. The more I've studied on it, the more times I've run that day through my head, I swear to God I don't believe I did it."

"Then who?"

"I believe maybe it was Nanny. She was there. She was fighting him, trying to keep him from killing me."

"Nanny. Yes. The police mentioned her as one of the suspected ones. They never mentioned you, Ben."

"That's because they never knew I fit with him. You see, I figured all this stuff out better after I left. At the beginning it was all confused, and I was scared to death. I just wanted to run, as far as I could. But later on, thinking back, I knew there was no way the police could figure I done it unless they knew I was there. And they didn't . . . unless Nanny told them, because nobody else saw me and Cat but Nanny."

"Nanny didn't tell them anything. They never found her. She was gone already when Cat's body was discovered."

"Then I fled for nothing . . . no, no. There was still reason to go. The whiskey. That was reason enough. I couldn't have beared having you see me fall back down so low again. I couldn't have beared having you fire me."

"I wouldn't have wanted to do it."

"But you would have. You'd have had to."

"Maybe. I don't know what I would have done."

"Well, I'm glad you didn't see me like I was right then. It would have shamed me."

"Well, I'm seeing you now, and that's what counts. I was afraid you were dead, Ben."

"What, from drinking?"

"No. There was a story in Brownlow's newspaper—no names given, not many facts. Just something about a man with one hand missing, and wearing a hook in its place, being killed near Jonesborough by bushwhackers. It sounded for all the world like you. That's what made me decide to go ahead and leave Knoxville, and move my publishing work here."

"You mean to say you come here just to look for me?"

"Not just that, no. You already know I'd been talking for months about moving here. But it was you who prompted me to do it when I did. It distressed me very badly, Ben, thinking you might have been killed. So the first thing I did when I got here was begin asking about you, and hanging those broadsides."

"It was provident I come into town and found one, then."

"I'm so glad you did. But I wish you hadn't waited to show yourself to me. I would have helped you through the hard times while you got off whiskey. It wouldn't have bothered me."

"Would have bothered me, though. So tell me, how's the newspaper doing?"

"Not terribly good. Not terribly bad. Horatio is discouraged, but when the war's over, things will improve."

"You think the war will end soon?"

"I think so. I hope so."

"Me, too."

Conversation waned a moment. Ben cleared his throat. "Miss Amy . . . you reckon that your newspaper will get going well enough that Mr. Eaton might need him a pressman?"

"I believe so. In fact, I'm inclined to think he could use one now. Horatio is awfully clumsy handling type."

"Me, I can handle type like a juggler handles pins, with just one hand and a hook."

"I know." She reached across and patted his hand. "Welcome back, Ben. You're going to like this town. And there are several people you'll be meeting. Good people. And you can put up at the hotel, like Horatio is."

"I got no money."

"You have a job again, remember? I'll advance you. Ben, I'm so glad you're back. Things will be good again."

"I believe they will."

Without design, they had become a small society of companions: Amy Hanover, Horatio Eaton, Miriam, Cecilia, Egypt, and deaf old Nelly. In days that followed, Ben Scarlett was drawn in as well.

There was one more room at the hotel, used for storage, but Egypt Munsey had Horatio shove the crates and so on to one side, and placed a cot in there, and as far as Ben was concerned, he was in king's quarters. There was a roof above his head, walls that actually kept out the wind, a window to look out of, and a table to which he was welcomed each day.

The only thing that didn't go well for Ben was his pressman's work. He was long out of practice, and his latest round of drinking had given him a slight tremor of the extremities that made it hard to deal with type. Horatio Eaton didn't complain about his inadequate new help. He knew it would make no difference. Ben was and always would be far more than a mere employee to Amy. A bond existed between the pair that defied any breaking and any clear definition. The experiences Ben and Amy had shared were a glue that would never give way. Besides, he liked Ben himself, though he couldn't say just why.

Ben's best service wound up going to Egypt Munsey, who used him as a general handyman around the hotel when he wasn't busy working for Amy and Eaton. Egypt griped about everything Ben did, finding fault with all his work, yet it was clear she was developing a deep affection for him. Amy found it amusing, and not surprising. Ben had that way about him. Despite all his flaws and weaknesses, he was a man it was hard for anyone not to like once they got to know him.

Of all the members of the little informal society of friends, the slowest to warm to Ben was Cecilia. She was initially quite wary of him, Amy noticed. She wondered why. Did Ben resemble the gravedigger who had hurt her years before, or perhaps Vaughn Fitz, or even Fletcher? A few days later, when Cecilia had gotten over her apprehensions about Ben, she admitted it was nothing more than the hook that had bothered her.

Once the apprehensions were out of the way, Cecilia and Ben became quite good friends. They toasted Lincoln's inauguration together with cups of milk—and Ben barely managed to get his down. He'd developed a distaste for milk years ago, his preferences always being for much harder beverages. After his cup was drained, Cecilia laughed at him as he grinned back at her, his beard and moustache all milk-soaked. The hand tremors had made Ben into quite a sloppy drinker. Egypt Munsey complained about it a lot when Ben took supper at her table, saying he shook out as much beverage as he imbibed. But she always had Nelly refill his glass promptly once it was empty.

Chapter 39

The old man had but one eye. The second one, blue and filmy, reminded Thatcher of those he had seen staring skyward from the faces of the dead men in the cart at Salisbury, on their way to a pit for mass burial. The other eye, however, glared and glittered with more than enough light to compensate for the blind one. At the moment it was studying him quite closely while he ate some sort of unidentifiable gruel the old man had served him in a wooden bowl. The old man's name was Jimmy Pigg, and it had already crossed Thatcher's mind, when he first entered the foul and cluttered little cabin on this to-him-nameless ridge, that no surname could have been more fitting.

"Yes indeedy, I do see Greeley's look about you. Hell-for-certain, I believe you *are* his brother!"

"And he's alive, and well, as far as you know?"

"He's alive. And well enough, considering what he's been through. I seen him last week. First time in many a month. Greeley Brown's been a hidden kind of fellow ever since Fletcher got to him."

Thatcher had begun hearing of Fletcher and his atrocities shortly after crossing from North Carolina into Tennessee. But he had heard nothing about Fletcher having done anything to his brother. "What do you mean?"

"Fletcher hung him, son! You ain't heard?"

"Hung him? But he's still alive?"

"Oh, yes. Hell-for-certain alive. He was cut from the rope by Old Sally Clung and nursed back to health. And then he took to ghosting after Fletcher, trailing his men, killing them in their camps. Fletcher tried every way to stop it, keeping his men ganged together most of the time, but even then old Greeley kept at it, killing them sometimes within spitting distance of the others. He killed three when they'd gone off in the woods to squat."

"How do you know all this?"

"Greeley told me, his own self! Everybody knows it now. For a long time folks weren't sure who was killing Fletcher's boys. Some declared it a ghost. It could have been a ghost, for all I knowed. I seen plenty of them in these hills, ghosts of men who hunted these mountains years before, and ghosts of Injuns."

Thatcher was so intrigued with this news of his brother that he put down his spoon despite his hunger. "I had no idea. None at all. All I'd ever heard about Greeley was that he was piloting Union men to the lines."

"He's doing that very thing again, now that Fletcher's dead."

"He's dead? Did Greeley kill him?"

"Nope. He was done in over in Johnson County. God bless whoever done it."

"And now Greeley's piloting again . . ."

"That's right. One last run. He's been moving through these mountains, mostly letting folks know he's alive, and telling them the truth about these stories of a ghost on Fletcher's tail. Ha! Ain't no ghost could have done a better job than old Greeley of giving hell-for-certain to Fletcher!"

Thatcher ate more of the gruel. "I want to find him," he said.

"You'll have to move fast, then, son. He's taking his stampeders out any time now. Bunch of Union men, along with some Home Guards and rebel deserters who are getting right repentant here lately, seeing the writing on the wall. A few niggers, too." The old man leaned over and spat on the dirt floor. "I don't favor him guiding them Home Guards. The reb deserters I can forgive, and I got naught against niggers, but I despise the Home Guards. I wish he'd just shoot them. Greeley'll have a hell-for-certain time of it, just keeping the Union men from killing them Home Guard devils."

"Can you get me to Greeley before he goes?"

"Well . . . I believe so. Why, yes sir! We'll get to him, and if he's gone on, we'll follow. I know which ways they'll be going, and I could track them even if I didn't. I'm a good tracker, son. I could track a skeeter through a swamp."

"When do we go?"

"In the morning. You'd best eat hearty, son, and sleep some good sleep tonight. You'll have to strain to keep up with Jimmy Pigg in the mountains."

Thatcher finished off the bowl and scooted it to Pigg for a refill. As he watched the old fellow, who looked ancient, stooped, slow, dip a new bowlful from the kettle at his fireplace, he had his doubts about having to strain to keep up with him. If anything, Pigg would surely slow him down. But he'd have to put up with it if he wanted to find Greeley. He hadn't been in these mountains since he was a child, and knew how easily a man could become lost.

He couldn't have been more wrong about Pigg. Once in the mountains, the old fellow moved like fluid, up hills and down, speed never varying. Thatcher had walked many a mile since his escape, and his legs were strong, but his general constitution was still weakened by months of prison life, and he feared several times that he would fail to keep up with the old man.

Pigg stopped only when Thatcher fell too far behind, and seemed quite irritable with him when he caught up. By afternoon Thatcher was begging for rest stops, but few were granted. Pigg berated him the entire duration of such stops, asking him if he wanted to find his brother or not. Thatcher assured him that he did, though as the day waned and approaching exhaustion made his head light and legs heavy, he wasn't quite so sure anymore.

As they neared the area on Buffalo Creek where Greeley was to commence his stampeder run, Thatcher found new strength born of anticipation. He was about to reunite with a brother he hadn't seen since boyhood, yet who, through his trials with the Confederacy, he'd come to feel a new closeness to, knowing that Greeley had undergone trials of his own, from the same source. He actually began to crowd Pigg, who was finally slowing down a little, wearing down.

Disappointment came at the end of the trek. They reached the designated place as darkness was beginning to fall, and found not a soul present. Pigg swore, knelt and examined the earth. There were tracks aplenty, fresh, showing that the stampeders had already assembled there, and already gone on.

Thatcher flopped down on his rump, panting and dejected. Pigg spat and cussed, stomped around a bit over in the clearing, then came back to him and sat down beside him.

"Well, son, them stops of yours have surely ruint us. We've missed them, hell-for-certain."

"What now? Do we sleep here?"

"Sleep? I reckon not. You want to find them, don't you?"

"Yes, but how? They've gone on."

"How do you think? We go on, too."

"Tonight?"

"I swear, son, I don't believe you *do* want to find that brother of yourn. Of course we go on tonight."

"Can I rest, just awhile?"

"Just awhile. And after that we're plunging into them woods, and we ain't stopping until we reach them. You up to it?"

"No."

"Too bad. You'll have to do it anyway."

"I know."

Thatcher stretched out, basking in the coldness of the ground against his hot, weary back, and fell asleep for about fifteen minutes. Then Pigg shook him awake and they went on.

Greeley Brown settled back against an oak tree and scuffed his rump about until he was nestled comfortably, then turned his attention to the jerked meat and bread that comprised his supper. It was the first food he'd eaten since midday, when he had one hunk of the jerky and a few crumbs of bread. As usual, he ate slowly, knowing he would be wanting more when he was finished.

He looked around at the men with him. There were fifty or so of them, including six black men, four rebel deserters, and three former Home Guard members who sat off by themselves, receiving periodic verbal abuse from the Unionists around them. Among those Unionists were five who were already enlisted men. These had been furloughed to visit their homes during an earlier Federal thrust into the mountains, and were cut off from returning to their posts.

The bruised eye and scabbed lip of one of the former Home Guards gave evidence of abuse received earlier that was more than verbal. Greeley had been forced to break up a row in the afternoon, brought about when the burlier of the enlisted men thought he heard one of the Home Guardsmen mutter some disparaging comment beneath his breath. Or so he claimed. Greeley suspected the attacker had lighted into his victim without provocation. He broke up the fight a little less slowly than he might have in other circumstances. He too had no love for anyone who'd ridden with the Home Guard.

There was money in his pocket again, stampeder fees. Less now than earlier in the day, however. At the Nolichucky River he and his men had encountered several starved-looking women, bearing baskets, who had come on rumor that some wagoner had brought in corn and smoked meat for sale at a point farther down the river. When Greeley inquired, he discovered that most of the women had no money to pay for provisions even if they did find the wagoner. How did they intend to persuade him to provision them for nothing? he'd asked. The reply was shrugs and a few tears, vainly fought against. He parted forthwith with over half of the money in his pocket, knowing that those women no doubt had children at home, if they had a home left at all. Conditions in the mountains had never been good, even in peacetime, but now they were downright primitive, with entire families living in caverns, or tented up in group camps in fields where burned-out cabins sat.

Greeley took another bite and noticed the Home Guard fellows were staring at him. He shot a harsh glance their way, making them turn their heads quickly. By heaven, he might guide them, might keep them from being beaten fully to a pulp by his other stampeders, but he'd be hanged before he let them stare at him.

He understood why they were prone to stare, though. He was a legend to them, the ghost who stalked Fletcher and killed a score of his men, yet without ever being caught or seen. The scar of Fletcher's Cross on his cheek was a fearsome badge; even more so the permanent rope burn around his neck. When they looked at Greeley Brown, they were looking at a scarred, weathered figure of a slaughterer of their own kind, a persecutor and executioner who seemingly couldn't be killed himself, nor stopped from killing rebels.

But Greeley had stopped now. He was determined to kill no more. Better things and brighter awaited at the end of this run. The best and brightest of all would be in Jonesborough.

They had built a few fires, despite a certain risk. Greeley suspected from sign he encountered that there might be some rebel bushwhackers straggling about in the region, but if so, they were probably few in number and wouldn't be likely to attack so large a band as this one. The five uniformed Federal soldiers made the band look a little more imposing yet.

After the eating was done and the weary conversations concluded, the stampeders lay down to sleep around their fires. Greeley had volunteered for first guard, still a mite concerned about the possibility of rebel irregulars following them. He sat with his back toward the fire to keep his eyes adjusted to darkness and scanned the cold forest. Ears were more important than eyes in such a setting, so mostly he listened. He heard nothing threatening, only the snores of the stampeders behind him and the occasional starting and low outcry of one of the Home Guardsmen who seemed sure he was going to be knifed in his sleep and sat up at every noise.

Greeley was fighting the urge to doze off himself when something unusual caught his ear. He cocked his head, listening, then rose silently, checked his rifle, and headed into the woods.

Someone was out there, moving in toward the camp, and he aimed to give them the opportunity to meet him a bit sooner than they might be anticipating.

• • •

"There they is," Pigg said, pointing at the flickering light of low-burning campfires making firefly glimmers beyond the trees. "Good thing for us they didn't travel on through the night, like Greeley's been prone to do sometimes. I hell-for-certain don't believe I'd have had enough wind to follow them much farther."

Thatcher made a noise. It was the best he could do; speech was out of the question. His lungs burned even though the air was cold, his skin was drenched with sweat, his heart hammering so fiercely that it actually hurt and, he feared, was about to give out on him. Thatcher sank to his knees, gasping, staring at the semidistant fires. He let his haversack slip off his shoulders. Though there was little in it, just the Confederate uniform he had used to get out of the prison and had worn occasionally along the way in rebel-infested territory, posing as a furloughed soldier, the sack felt to him like it was full of lead ore.

When he had caught sufficient wind, he asked, "How do we go in there without stirring them?"

"I don't quite know, son. We might be best to wait it out until morning, and go in when they can see us. I'd hate to be shot by some jumpy guard."

Thatcher was thinking that getting shot didn't seem as terrible a prospect as it normally would. A shot man could lay down and die, and death would surely be more endurable than this painful exhaustion.

"I'll lie down and sleep right here," he said. "You just say the word."

"Let's go in a mite closer," Pigg said. "It's more level up that way. Better sleeping ground."

Thatcher came to his feet with effort, picked up the haversack, and followed Pigg on another hundred yards. The fires glowed more brightly, looking awfully inviting. Thatcher thought almost lustfully about how delicious it would be to curl up near one of those fires and sleep until sometime in the next season.

He spread his blankets as soon as Pigg selected their camping place, and lay down with knees curled up near his chest. He had just enough energy left to feel the slightest thrill at the thought of his brother being encamped mere yards away.

Tomorrow he'd see Greeley again. The brother who had always been his boyhood defender and supporter against a mentally unstable mother who held him responsible for her widowed state. The brother who had grown up to become a hero to the mountain Unionists, the brother about whom he intended to write when he put this entire adventure of his into book form . . .

Thatcher's thoughts faded. He slept, profoundly.

Waking up was difficult, despite the nagging alarm screaming at him in the back of his mind, telling him that he was in danger and that he'd best come around and deal with it at once. He tried to move but found his body pinned, immobile. It was almost impossible to breathe. Something sharp was poking at his throat. Thatcher opened his eyes and saw the dark form of a figure above him. A man, sitting on Thatcher's chest and squeezing the very air out of him, was probing a knife uncomfortably hard against his neck.

"Whaauugh . . . hey . . ."

"Give me a good reason, friend, why I shouldn't slice your throat like a summer melon?"

"I can think of one, Greeley," said a voice from nearby. Pigg's voice. He had heard the approach of the man with the knife, and slipped from his blankets into the woods. "It's me, Greeley. Jimmy Pigg. And that fellow you got pinned down there, he's come a hell-for-certain long way to find you, all the way from the reb prison camp in Salisbury. Greeley Brown, I'd like you to meet my friend, and your brother, Mr. Thatcher Brown."

They were strangers to one another at the beginning, and the necessity of completing the stampeder journey provided little opportunity for them to become more than that. Greeley went through the rest of the journey as a man dazed, unable to comprehend that the emaciated, wind-burned, bearded wisp of a man now traveling at his side was his own brother.

Conversation was sparse, strained. If Thatcher hadn't been so sick with weariness that would not seem to go away even

after sleep, he would have despaired at the anticlimactic nature
of it all.

They passed through Shelton Laurel, Shell's Cove—where
they found signs of rebel presence, and proceeded carefully—
and spent a cold night in a stand of pines. Greeley and Thatcher,
moving off from the others, talked at some length that night,
softly . . . and the distance of years and divergent lives between
them was significantly lessened by the time they took to their
blankets and slept.

They came at last to Strawberry Plains, where Greeley
parted with his stampeders and was left only with his brother.
A friend now. No longer an unseen, mysterious stranger, but a
man he knew.

He was also a man who was ill. The stress of prison life,
escape, and hard winter travel caught up with Thatcher at last
and he grew too weak to go on. Greeley took him to the Franklin
House Hotel, and there they took a room under assumed names
to assure no one would bother them. Greeley was a famous,
notorious figure now, prone to attract the adoring attention of the
Unionist press and Federal military, as well as the potentially
deadly attention of bitter, defeated Confederates to whom his
name was anathema.

Thatcher got the bed; Greeley slept on blankets piled on the
floor and tended to his brother. The illness was debilitating, but
not serious, and soon Thatcher began to improve. He and
Greeley talked for hours at a time, sharing their biographies
with one another.

Thatcher grew stronger. On the day news came that Gen-
erals Lee and Grant had met at the courthouse in Appomattox,
Virginia, Greeley went out, managed to locate a bottle of
whiskey, and they drank together to the ending of war.

Somewhere along the way, and almost unnoticed by both,
something had transformed, something had grown. They had
entered the Franklin House as near strangers struggling to
know one another, but when they left to begin the northeast-
ward journey toward Jonesborough, they were far more than
that. They were brothers.

Part VII

SCARLETT'S LAMENT

Chapter 40

On the afternoon of Wednesday, May 10, 1865, the same day an ex-president named Jefferson Davis was captured by Union cavalrymen in a town in Georgia, destined for two often humiliating years of imprisonment, and as a nation still reeled from the shock of a different president's death a month before at the hands of an actor-turned-assassin, a wedding occurred in the high-steepled Presbyterian Church on the main thoroughfare in Jonesborough, Tennessee. Attendance was high and predominated by those locals who had gone through the war supporting the Union, because the groom was a man who had become an almost mystical Union hero: Greeley Brown, stampeder pilot and angel of vengeance on the back of Devil Cap Fletcher.

Miriam had not instantly accepted Greeley's proposal, which had come as abruptly and unexpectedly as his unannounced arrival in Jonesborough. Her hesitation had not come from doubt, but utter surprise. When she had last seen him in this town, he'd given no evidence of anything but cold feelings toward her, and his promise to return later had been made not to her, but to Cecilia. All he had promised even then was a visit.

Quite a visit the actual return wound up to be! Greeley, thought just as scarred and battered as before, and with the same intensity in his gaze, came back to Jonesborough a changed man. He hadn't come alone, but brought another lean and battered fellow with him, one sharing a strong family resemblance and the same surname—a friendly, thoroughly engaging traveling journalist and former Confederate prisoner of war named Thatcher Brown.

Greeley had not seemed surprised by Miriam's hesitance in replying to his proposal, which he had delivered in classic fashion, upon one knee, her hand clasped in his. In fact, he'd expected it, and used it as an occasion for explanation of the change that had come upon him.

"When last I was with you, Miriam, I was a bitter man, and a driven man, full of one purpose, and that being the killing of Cap Fletcher and as many of his men as I could get. And I was angry at you, I admit it, because you had told me false tales about why you were coming to the mountains in the first place. I felt like you'd made a fool of me and put me in danger . . . and indeed there was danger, considering what happened to me.

"But things are different now. The war is done, except for what little leftover fighting you'll see here and there. The rebs west of the Mississippi will be surrendering before long. It's a time to forget the things that happened during the war, and go on. And I want to forget anything that ever happened to make me think harsh about you—and if I've done ary to make you feel harsh toward me, I ask you to forgive it, and accept my proposal. I've admired you nigh from the first time I laid an eye on you at the boardinghouse there in Sevierville, Miriam. I know Mr. Fitz is dead now, and you're free, and I'd like to make you my wife, and take Cecilia as my daughter."

She accepted, gratefully. Egypt Munsey helped her plan the wedding, which was scheduled as quickly as possible. There was an urgency in life now that the survivors of the war had seen how easily life could be shortened. There were lost years to be made up for, delayed joys to be swiftly claimed.

Amy very atypically wept as the bride and groom emerged from the big ground-level door of the church, and Cecilia wept beside her. Amy put her arm around Cecilia's waist; the girl had grown since coming to Jonesborough and was now almost Amy's height.

"You are happy, aren't you, Cecilia?"

"Yes, Cecilia replied. "I am. I love Greeley. I've loved him almost since I've known him. That's why I'm crying. But why are you crying, ma'am? You're happy, aren't you?"

"Yes, I'm very happy. Especially happy for you, because I believe Mr. Brown will be so fine a father for you."

There was another, unhappy reason for her tears, though, that she did not share with Cecilia. She and Greeley had sat down together for a long-awaited talk the night after his arrival, and at last the mystery of the tattered letter had been resolved.

The news was what she had expected. Sam Colter was dead, dead since shortly after Burnside's invasion of Knoxville in '63. She listened as Greeley described what had become of Sam since she parted from him, his brief career as a conscripted rebel soldier, his desertion to the North Carolina mountains, his involvement in bushwhacking, from which he had finally turned away in disgust, only to find that the deeds of the past were not dead, and that even if bushwhacked dead men could not kill, their sons could.

Greeley had told her how Sam had talked about her at the very end of his life, and regretted that he would never have another opportunity to make to her the marriage proposal she had once rejected.

She regretted it, too, and so she stood beside Cecilia in the yard of the Presbyterian church and cried for Sam Colter and what might have been.

A week later, after Greeley and Miriam returned from a week's honeymoon in nearby Telford—not much of a journey to make nor much of a place to go, but they had enjoyed it all the same—Greeley sat across the desk from Amy and firmly shook his head.

"I don't want no charity from nobody," he said. "I'll make a way for myself and my family on my own."

"Mr. Brown, this is not charity. This is a business proposition.

I'm purchasing business property for myself, with more room than will be necessary for my needs. There's a barn on the property. I propose allowing you to use it, rent-deferrred, initially, and develop this wagon-making business you've been talking about. I am in a position to offer you a small loan to allow you to get the supplies you'll need to get started. Then, as your business grows, we can work out back payment and terms for the future. Eventually, I'm sure, you'll want to buy land of your own and get away from the need to rent."

"I don't know. I ain't comfortable with it."

"I can't force you to accept the offer, but it does stand. I hope you'll accept it."

He looked away from her, sullen but thinking.

"I have another thing I'd like you to consider . . . possibly, if you'd allow Ben Scarlett to help you, at least initially . . ."

"I thought he worked for you."

"He does. But Ben has had a problem through the years with drinking, and I'm afraid his last round of it has left him with a trembling in his hands that's making him not too efficient at working with type. Horatio has been getting very exasperated with it, and I believe Ben has, too, but neither one will say anything about it. I think if he could work at something where the motions and so on aren't so small and delicate and fine—"

"Mrs. Hanover, I'm asking you: Are you offering to set me up in business just so you can find a better line of work for Ben Scarlett?"

"Please, call me Amy. There's more to it than that. Sure, I want to see Ben in the most appropriate line of work for him, but I also want to see you get well-placed. You were Sam's partner, and you've done so much for the Union. You deserve to see better times now that the war is through. And there's Miriam, whom I think so highly of, and Cecilia. Particularly Cecilia. She's a dear young lady. She's had a hard time in life."

He squinted a little, looked at her with head slightly cocked. "How much do you know about Cecilia's life?"

A pause. "Confidentially, Mr. Brown, I know more than her mother realizes. I know enough."

"You don't look down on her in no way?"

"Look down on her? Heavens, sir, no! I admire her. She

knows how to endure, to survive." Amy smiled. "She reminds me a little of myself."

Greeley scratched his beard. Amy studied the scar on his face, the mark around his neck. This was a man who would literally bear the scars of war all his life.

"I'll accept your offer," he said.

"Good."

"You want me to sign something?"

"No. I want only one thing."

"What's that?"

"I've told you about my book. I'd like to interview you, at length, about what has gone on in the mountains in your experience. All that you are willing to tell, that is. I realize there may be some things best left unstated."

"I ain't much for talking about myself. I ain't looking for anybody's praise."

"I'm not asking you to do it for that reason. It's for the sake of the loyal mountain people. Their stories can't be forgotten. And not just for abstract reasons, either. There've been many people in the mountains who have suffered loss because of this war. I have no doubt that someday there will be congressional investigation of what has happened there in the course of the war. The more we can document, the better. It could result in some compensation for them, down the road."

"Well . . . if you think of it that way, I reckon I could go along. How close are you to finishing the book up?"

"What you tell me will be the final piece of it. I really thought I'd be finished long before now. My work on it has outlasted the war itself! There's just so much to tell."

"Well, I'll cooperate with you all I can."

"Thank you. Oh, and Horatio also wants to write about you for the newspaper."

"Now, that I don't know about. That's getting into that business of looking for praise. I just want to live my life in private from now on, and be left alone."

"I believe you'd be left alone best if you go ahead and tell the public what it wants to know. You saw all those strangers who came to your wedding, and all the people who've stopped to gawk at you on the street. You're an object of curiosity, and the more mysterious and withdrawn you are about it, the more the curiosity will grow. Go ahead and do the interview with Horatio. Tell him what you want said and don't tell him anything beyond that. You'll get the public curiosity satisfied, and after that you'll have a lot more peace."

"You're kind of a bossy woman for somebody so young."

"I'm not young anymore. I don't feel it. I feel old and tired and ugly."

Greeley smiled mischeviously. "Thatcher thinks you're anything but ugly."

Amy was caught by surprise, and said nothing. Greeley's grin widened. "You're blushing, ma'am."

"Sir, I don't know what it is you want me to say."

"I don't want nothing. Thatcher, that might be a different story. He finds you a fascinating kind of woman, coming from the background you do, living the life you have. It's sort of similar to his own, in some ways."

"Well, you tell your brother that—that . . . don't tell him anything. I have no message for him." She pondered a few seconds. "He's right, though. Our backgrounds are somewhat similar. Journalism, surreptitious kinds of work . . ."

"And he's planning to write a book, too, just like you're doing."

"Really? Well, that's an excellent idea. His experience as a traveling journalist and prisoner of war would make some fascinating reading."

"Thatcher's already talked the newspaper trade up and down with Mr. Eaton. I believe he aims to give Mr. Eaton a hand with his publishing while he's still in Jonesborough. Maybe you and Thatcher could sit down together and talk the writing trade sometime before long, while he's still here."

"Is that your idea, or his?"

"His." Greeley grinned anew. "You're blushing again, ma'am. And maybe grinning a bit."

Cecilia called from the next room, something about Adam. Amy thought it well-timed. She stood. "Good day, Mr. Brown . . . Greeley."

"Good day to you, Amy."

• • •

Greeley was living at the hotel now, sharing a single room with Miriam and Cecilia, and was getting awfully tired of it. So was Miriam. There was no privacy at all, with Cecilia there, and Cecilia was obviously uncomfortable living in the same room with a man she loved and now regarded as her father, but who was still a man and partial stranger all the same. But Greeley had no means to rent a house at the moment. His notion was to frame in a couple of rooms at the rear of the barn where he would be making wagons, and make a temporary home of that. It would be rough, but Miriam and Cecilia both seemed to find the idea appealing. Certainly he would have no problem living in he rear of a barn, Greeley thought, accustomed as he was to life in hollow trees, caves, and the crudest mountain huts.

He and Thatcher sat rocking on the small covered porch at the hotel's rear. Inside, Egypt Munsey was loudly fussing at Nelly over something Ben Scarlett had done. The brothers listened, privately amused. Greeley reached into his pocket and pulled out two cigars, offering one to Thatcher, who accepted.

Thatcher provided the match. They puffed the cigars into full light, then sat back and rocked.

"You had your interview with Horatio today, did you, Greeley?"

"Yep. He asked a durn sight of questions. Nervous little fellow, ain't he?"

"Yes. I like him, though. He reminds me of a couple of editors I worked with in New York."

New York. Greeley tried to imagine the place, a city that big. He couldn't.

"I like him, too," Greeley said. "But I still don't like the notion of being writ up in the paper for everybody to read about."

"Why?"

"I don't know. It just don't feel right. It don't feel safe. Dang it, Thatcher, I've had a reb reward on my head for years. I got used to lying low for that reason alone. Then when I commenced punishing the Fletcherites, I had all the more cause to hide out. Now to turn about and lay myself out in the newspaper . . . makes me feel like I would have if I'd walked into that church to get married, and looked down and seen I was stark naked."

Thatcher laughed. "Now, that would have been a sight!" He coughed, hacking out of control a few moments. He apologized and blamed the cigar, but Greeley knew the cough was one of the lingering, but fading, remnants of Thatcher's prison experience. When he had control of his voice again, Thatcher continued, "You must realize the war has ended, Greeley. There's no rebel government left to pay any reward on your head. By the way, did Fletcher ever try to collect that reward when he thought he'd killed you?"

"Not as I know of. That tells you something about him, too. He was too much a criminal even to pay call on his own government. When it comes right down to it, Fletcher was no true rebel. Just a sorry murderer, out to avenge wrongs that was done to his family. And they was wrongs, true wrongs, if what I was told was true. I don't justify them, if they happened. Some say Fletcher made a lot of it up. But even if his family was abused like the rebs say, you can't justify the way Fletcher hurt innocent folks because of it."

"No. But Fletcher's dead now. He'll not hurt anybody else."

"Thank the Lord for that."

"Amen." Thatcher pulled on his cigar. "Has Amy Hanover interviewed you yet?"

"Some. There's still more to come."

"Do me a favor, Greeley. See if you can get her interested in interviewing me."

"What would she interview you for? You weren't in the mountains during the war."

"No, but I was a traveling journalist. A prisoner of war. A really fascinating fellow all around. She really ought to write about me."

"I thought you was planning to write about yourself."

"Well, I am. But—"

"But you're just looking for some reason to get her to set down and talk to you for a while. You're besot, Thatcher. Just as besot as a schoolboy in love with the new schoolmarm."

"Can you blame me for wanting to talk to her? Do you know a woman so pretty?"

"Yep. I married one."

"Besides her."

"Cecilia's mighty pretty."

"She's a child, Greeley! Amy Hanover is . . . ideal. Not only pretty, but wise, confident in herself. The more I hear about the things she has done, the more in awe of her I am. To think of a woman so young, having such an air of authority. She has the power to make things happen."

"She's inherited money. If she's got power, that's what it comes down to. Her father had a bit of money, and as I understand it, even though they fell out with one another, he never dropped her from his will. And her uncle, he was a merchant, not a rich man, but what he had come to her. Then she married into a right well-off family in Nashville, and her husband got killed, and there she was with another inheritance. That gal has never really made money on her own."

"Don't talk badly about her, Greeley. I have good instincts about people, and I like her."

"I ain't talking her down. Just stating the truth."

"You wait until that book of hers is published. She'll make money then. That story will capture the attention of a nation."

"I hope you're right. I want folks to know what happened in the hills. But get back to Amy for a minute. If you're so keen to talk to her, why not just go and do it yourself, instead of asking me to arrange it for you?"

"I have tried. She won't talk to me, Greeley. Nothing beyond the most shallow conversation. I don't even think she notices me."

Greeley remembered that final blush on Amy's face, and the poorly hidden little smile. "I believe she does."

"What do you mean by that?"

Greeley puffed his cigar and looked at Thatcher from the side of his eye.

"I asked you what you meant by that!"

Greeley rose. "If you'll pardon me, Thatcher, I need to make a visit to yonder privy." He walked off the porch and across the yard, trailing smoke behind him.

A week later Greeley sat up in bed, reading the last lines of Horatio Eaton's extended story about him and his wartime career. Miriam, leaning back beside him against the headboard, had an identical copy spread across her lap. A faster reader than her new husband, she had already finished it. Cecilia was sound asleep on a cot in the corner of the room.

Greeley put down the paper and stared at the place his feet made the covers hump at the bottom of the bed.

"What do you think of it?" Miriam asked.

"Don't like it."

"Why? Isn't it accurate?"

"No. It is. That's what I don't like."

"What do you mean?"

"I mean, it tells so durn much about me. About us. Where we live, your name—"

"Just my first name. And it uses the 'Goode' last name and says I'm from Johnson County. No one would ever know I was Miriam Fry from Livingston, Tennessee."

"They might when they notice that 'Miriam Goode Brown' has a daughter named Cecilia, just like Miriam Fry, of Livingston, Tennessee."

Miriam frowned and did not reply. Greeley glanced toward her and realized he had worried her. So he quickly went on. "That ain't what concerns me, though, honey. I don't believe that anybody is ever going to come looking for Miriam Fry. You hid the body in a pit inside a cave no one even knows about. No one even knows he's dead . . . I'm sure of it. I'm more concerned about somebody coming looking for me."

"Why? There's no more reward. No more Fletcher. And his men have scattered. They have nothing to gain from hurting you now."

"I know. It's just a feeling I have. I worry too much, I suppose."

"You do." She reached over, took the paper from his hand, tossed it onto the floor, then kissed him.

He noticed how she avoided the cross-mark scar when she kissed him. She always did. He didn't blame her for that, but still it bothered him. Reminded him.

"Let's get some sleep, Greeley. We have a lot to do tomorrow."

He nodded. Turning, he kissed her lips. Dousing the lights, they settled down together, embracing in the darkness, letting sleep creep in upon them.

• • •

Horatio Eaton's telling of the Greeley Brown story caught the attention not only of the public, but of other press organs. It began appearing in attributed reprint in newspapers across the region, then the country. Letters began arriving, most of them from the North and usually addressed merely: MR. GREELEY BROWN, JONESBOROUGH, TENNESSEE. Almost all were laudatory. A few were from former stampeders Greeley had guided northward early in the war. Some were from their families, telling him that the men he had guided to the lines had never come home again, having died in battle or in prison camps. Three had died aboard the overloaded steamer *Sultana*, which had exploded on the Mississippi River near the end of April, killing hundreds of men recently freed from rebel prison camps and finally on their way home.

A few came from bitter rebels, full of venom. When Miriam saw that these bothered Greeley, she intervened and made an offer. From now on she would open and preread all letters that came to him, weeding out those whose reading would serve him no purpose. Greeley agreed. He had suffered rebel abuse for an entire war, and had no desire to hear more of it now.

The letters arrived, a minimum of five or six a day, sometimes ten or more. Always the same . . . Mr. Greeley Brown, Jonesborough, Tennessee.

One day a letter arrived with a different addressee. Miriam stared at her own name on the envelope, written in a rough masculine hand. She opened it and pulled out a piece of paper with one line scrawled upon it:

MIRIAM, TELL YOUR NEW HUSBIND TO BEWEAR OF GHOSTS.

She read it several times. Unnerved, she went to the nearest fireplace, struck a match to it, and watched it curl and blacken into ash.

Chapter 41

Three more nearly identical letters arrived, and both Greeley and Cecilia had detected and commented upon a change in Miriam's manner before she decided she could not keep it to herself any longer. She went to Greeley as he worked framing in the rooms in the rear of the barn that would become both home and place of commerce for the Brown family. She was ashen-faced, with the latest letter in her hand. She had no others to show him—she'd burned them all—but she described them and the way she had kept them from him.

"Greeley, I'm afraid. I read those letters and I think . . . *Fletcher.*"

He held the letter in his hand, staring at it. He was grimed with sawdust and sticky with sweat. "Why?"

"Because of the ghost part. You know what people said about Fletcher being punished by the ghost of a man he had hanged."

He nodded. "Why, of course I know about that. So does everybody else, since they've read Eaton's story. It talked all about that."

"But why are the letters addressed to me, instead of you?"

"Well, most likely because it's me they're trying to get to."

"But I don't understand."

"The way to get to a man is through his wife. You get her all tore up over something, he'll be tore up worse. You make her afraid, you make him furious. Don't you see what's happening here, Miriam? There's some rebel out there who don't like me, and who's decided to get square with me by trying to scare you. He's heard this Fletcher-chased-by-a-ghost tale, and decided to turn it on me by making you afraid that somebody's after me in the same way I was after Fletcher. Just some sour-faced old follower of Jeff Davis, mad because he lost his precious war. That's all it is."

"But how can you be sure?"

"Fletcher's dead, honey. Dead. He was killed in Johnson County, and we don't have to think about him no more."

"Are you sure?"

"Sally Clung herself told me about it. I ain't never known her to be wrong about nothing like that."

"Greeley, I'm sorry if I've been too upset by this. I'm not accustomed to thinking of people out there, somewhere, having the kind of anger that would make them want to torment someone like this."

"There's plenty of them. Half a nation of them. And it will be a long time before they go away."

"Nothing bad is going to happen, is it, Greeley?"

"War's over, Miriam. Nothing bad is going to happen. And next time one of these comes, you just give it to me. You'll recognize the writing on the envelope?"

"Yes. I think so. I've read enough of them now."

"You get an envelope writ like that, don't even open it. Just give it to me."

She smiled and kissed him. She had been wrong about him, it seemed. Threatening letters obviously didn't bother him like she thought they did.

"Miriam."

"Yes?"

"I want to ask you something . . . don't make anything of it." He looked around, came closer, and spoke very softly. "Are you sure beyond any doubt that the gravedigger you killed was dead?"

She knew that he was. She knew how many times he'd been

stabbed, how pierced his heart had been, how long he'd lain with eyes glassy and staring. She knew how far he had fallen into the blackest of cavern pits, and how hard he'd struck far below. Yet even so, hearing the question chilled her. "Yes. I know he was dead."

"No doubt?"

"No doubt."

"Did he have kin?"

"I . . . don't know. I think, maybe. But somewhere else. He lived alone." A tremor ran through her. "Oh, Greeley, are you thinking that—"

"No, no. Not really. Just a foolish thought that crossed my mind."

She nodded and walked away, slowly. He watched her.

When she was gone, he looked again at the letter in his hand and frowned deeply. Wadding it, he tossed it into a pile of scrap wood, due to be burned. It was just a piece of paper. Rebel nonsense. Nothing to waste more time thinking about.

He did think about it, though. All the rest of the day.

Miriam woke in the night and found Greeley not in his place. She sat up, looking for him in the room. He was not there.

Slipping to the door, she entered the hall and crept lightly along it, not wanting to disturb. At the stairs she paused and looked down into the small lobby. There was no light burning, but moonlight spilled through a window.

Greeley was there, sitting in a chair, staring at the dark hearth. Not reading or moving. Just sitting, staring. Thinking about something.

She was about to go down to him. But she paused before her foot touched the top stair. Did she really want to know what had him wakeful?

She hesitated, then quietly turned and went back to her own bed.

Ben Scarlett joined Greeley at the barn the next day. "Miss Amy said you could use some help, sir. I'm glad to offer a hand." He grinned. "Just one, of course. It's all you left me."

Greeley gave him a curious look. "You have hard feelings because I took your hand off all them years ago, Mr. Scarlett?"

"Oh, no. If not for you I'd have died on that mountain. If you and your stampeders hadn't found me, I wouldn't be here today."

"How do you fare, having just a hook for a left hand?"

"I do pretty well. A man's just got to learn to be careful how he swings his arm around. And it's mighty handy for scratching in close places."

Greeley grunted and smiled. Ben thought he seemed distracted.

They worked for two hours. Ben tried to make conversation, a failed effort, so finally he settled for singing. His selections were old tunes, bright and quick ones, matching his mood.

Greeley's mood was quite different. He was somber and withdrawn, and if Ben hadn't been distracted by his own good humor, he might have wondered if Greeley had something against him.

Greeley paused in the midst of labor. "Mr. Scarlett, would the mail have been distributed by now?"

Ben removed a pocket watch, an old one Egypt Munsey had given him, telling him that now he would have no excuse to be late for supper. It was a battered timepiece, but Ben had shined it up and was quite proud of it. He squinted at the face.

"I believe they'll have it out in half an hour or so, if they go as usual."

"I'm going to take a rest and walk to the post office. I'm in the mood to stretch my legs."

"Anything you'd want me to do while you're gone?"

"Yep. Take a rest yourself. And have a cigar." He tossed a fresh smoke to Ben, who failed to catch it because a hammer filled his real hand, and hooks aren't much for catching cigars on the fly. Ben knelt, put the hammer aside, and quickly retrieved the cigar.

"Thank you much, Mr. Greeley!"

Greeley was already out the door and did not respond.

Greeley stood outside the post office, holding the newly arrived envelope, staring at the writing upon it. The same writing that had been on the letter Miriam had shown him, as best he could tell. He had come to the post office when he had based on impulse, the sense that today he should get his hands on the mail before Miriam did. He saw now that the feeling was surely precognizant.

He left the post office and ducked into the nearest alley. Tearing open the envelope, he steeled himself for the inevitable, and pulled the letter out.

Opening it, he read, then shook his head and, with a very solemn expression on his face, stared at the brick side wall of the building before him. He said aloud, "Greeley Brown, you are indeed the greatest of fools."

The letter was from Greeneville, a man writing in response to an advertisement Miriam had placed, at Egypt's direction, for a used hotel counter to replace the overly battered old front desk in Egypt's establishment. It was going to be embarrassing to have Miriam see he'd opened it.

Greeley stuck the letter into his pocket and headed back down the street. His step was much lighter now, and halfway back to the hotel, where he would drop off the letter with full confession to his wife of his misguided intuition about the day's deliveries. He'd been worried about nothing. He'd even misjudged the handwriting on the envelope.

Good to know, in a way. Better than worrying about something and finding out there was really something there to worry about. He'd share that thought with Miriam. Maybe it would make her worry a little less, too.

Ben was back the next day, and found a much happier and more talkative Greeley Brown awaiting him than had been there the day before. They worked through a most pleasant morning, which seemed to rush by. Conversation covered many topics, but wandered around to the war. Greeley began to tell about the things he'd seen families go through, and as he went on with the seemingly endless litany of suffering, Ben's happy mood declined.

After their lunch, the sky clouded over, the wind whipped up, and Ben grew depressed. Rain would fall by late afternoon. Ben felt like it was already falling inside himself.

Conversation was largely absent during the afternoon. Ben sang again, old, slow, hymns, funeral requiems, tragic mountain love ballads. Greeley complimented his music several times, to which Ben would sigh, say thank you, and move on to some new dirge even more doleful.

He came inevitably to the song he'd begun composing the prior year but never completed. He sang it out as far as the words went, then cut off.

Greeley had stopped working while Ben sang that one. He had a solemn but entranced look about him.

"Ain't you going to finish that one?"

"There ain't no finish," Ben replied. "That's one I made up myself, and it's as far as I got."

"You made that up?"

"Yeah. I used to do that when I was a boy, making up tunes and words, or putting words to old melodies. I quit all that when I started drinking and my voice got bad. Last year I picked up on it again, just a little, and tried to write that there song. I just ain't found the finish for it yet."

"What do you call it?"

"Ain't got a title."

"That's a mighty mournful song. All full of lamentation. Hey, there's you a name for it. The Lament. No . . . Scarlett's Lament. That way people will know you're the one made it up."

"Scarlett's Lament it is, then."

"What made you think to write such a sad song? Because you caught it, Ben. You caught the very mournful heart of the mountain war in them words and that tune."

"It was Miss Amy and her talking to the refugees that made me start in on it. She'd tell me some of the tales she picked up, and sometimes I'd hear the people she talked to, talking to her in her office. That's when the song begun to come to me."

"Ben, should something happen to me and you outlive me, I want you to finish up that song and sing it at my funeral."

"At your *funeral*? What, you planning to die on us?"

"No, no. I'm just saying *if*. Would you do that for me, if I should die?"

"All right. *If* you do, I will. But you won't."

Greeley chuckled. "Fair enough."

"I don't like to hear folks talking of dying," Ben said. "That's what the Injuns would call bad medicine."

"A man never knows how long he's going to live, Ben. The Lord can call you away anytime."

"That's true, but I see no reason to go planting the notion in his head by talking about it out loud."

They were all but finished with the framing in of the living quarters by the next afternoon. Ben and Greeley were enwrapped in conversation about how best to finish out a corner when Ben noticed Horatio Eaton striding toward the building.

"Look there—it's Eaton. Looks worked up."

Greeley said, "He always looks worked up."

"That's true."

But when Eaton reached them, they saw that he was downright pale and looked more than usually distraught. "Hello, Ben, Greeley. How are you doing today?"

"Fine. You?"

"Well enough, well enough . . . oh, gentlemen, there's some distressing news."

They put down their tools. "What's wrong?"

"A man has been killed."

"What? Here?"

"No, no. In Carter County."

"Someone you know?"

"No, no. I don't even know the man's name."

Ben and Greeley glanced at one another, passing between them the mutual silent question as to why Eaton should be so distressed by the death of a stranger in another county. "I don't understand," Greeley said.

"He's been killed, sir! The war's over, and he's been killed anyway!"

"There's going to be a lot of that for a long time to come. There's been plenty of grudges stirred in this old war," Greeley said. "I doubt this man is the first killed since the papers was signed."

"No, you just don't see. It's not just that he was killed, it was how. And what was done after."

"What do you mean?"

"This man . . . he was found hanging up before his cabin, upside down. The cabin was on fire. And his face had a cross mark cut into the flesh."

"It's bosh and nonsense!" Egypt Munsey was declaring with the usual utmost confidence. "There's not the slightest bit of evidence in what has happened that this Fletcher fellow is alive. Anyone can kill someone else. And anyone can make efforts to make it appear that some other person is responsible. That's precisely what has happened here. Mongamongamonga-monga!"

"What is it, ma'am?"

"I say, give Mr. Eaton another slice of pie. A big one. Mr. Eaton, you're dangerously thin. A thin person is in mortal danger of his life should he develop a bad tooth. Did you know that? It's a fact of science. And *you*, Ben: Benjamin Scarlett, strong and able, get your elbows off the table!"

"Yes, ma'am." Ben sat up straight and complied.

"And I must say, Ben, that I've been sitting here disgusted at whatever sediment that is crusting the end of your hook. Have you been cleaning your nostrils with that thing?"

"No! No!" He examined the hook with a frown. "I don't know *what* that is." He swiped it on his trousers beneath the table, out of view, and looked chagrined.

Greeley had been staring at his piece of pie, so far only one bite taken. "You're almost certainly right, Miss Munsey," he said. "The odds are that somebody is imitating Fletcher's way of killing, either to try to rouse notions that Fletcher is still living, or for some kind of . . . of . . ." He struggled for the right word.

Miriam said, "Symbolic?"

"Yeah . . . for some kind of symbolic reason. Like saying Fletcher's fight ain't over just because he's dead. Something like that."

Eaton was typically all atremble. "The entire thing just distresses me all to death."

Egypt was in the most outspoken form she had yet exhibited for any of them, except Nelly, who had been with her for years and seen every type of display from the old eccentric. "Mr. Eaton, I'm not surprised you're distressed. As much as I admire you, sir, you seem the kind of man who would be 'distressed all to death' if someone yelled boo behind you. Get some backbone, sir! And a bit of common sense to go with that keen intellect!"

Greeley, paying little attention to anything but his own private train of thought, said, "I can tell you this: If I'd known any sign, no matter how weak and unlikely, was going to show up that Fletcher might still be living, I'd have never agreed to talk to you for your newspaper, Mr. Eaton."

"Oh, oh . . . it's my fault. I'm sorry. I'm so sorry."

"It's nobody's fault," Miriam said. "It just an odd event . . . and like Miss Egypt said, it's almost certainly someone imitating Fletcher, not Fletcher himself."

"You think the same about them letters?" Ben asked. At the beginning of this little gathering of this circle of friends, pulled together this night specifically to discuss the issue at hand, Greeley and Miriam had told the others about the odd letters they had received and now called "ghost letters."

"Them letters are still a puzzlement. But they most likely got nothing to do with this man killed in Carter County. I'd be surprised if they did."

"What's the postmark say?"

Greeley didn't seem eager to answer. "Elizabethton," he said.

"Carter County, then," Thatcher threw in.

"If you ask me, this is all jabber about nothing," Egypt said. "I'm tired of it. Ready for bed."

That was the unsubtle signal for the gathering to ungather. They rose, talking among themselves a moment more, saying their good nights, then scattering to their various places.

The circle was rendered temporarily smaller the next day, by a design that had been in place for several days. Amy, now within pages of the ending of her book, had decided to return to Knoxville, there to confer with selected printers and binders about the possibility of hiring out the actual book production work. She was not happy any longer with the notion of trying to print the book on her own press. The work was quality; it merited quality handling.

Cecilia went along—a pleasure trip for her, but a practical benefit for Amy, in that she now had Cecilia to mind little Adam while she talked business. And Thatcher Brown, too, made the journey. Self-invited. He had dropped many a hint before Amy, all but asking for an invitation, and when none came, he had grown bold and declared he was going along, on his own time and own money. He came up with a good pretext: He was working on a book himself, after all, and in case he decided to go the self-publication route, as Amy was, he could benefit from gaining the same information Amy would be obtaining. Might as well sit in.

Greeley noticed with interest that Amy Hanover didn't seem to mind the intrusion much at all. This pleased him. He and Miriam had already put their heads together and decided that Thatcher and Amy were destined for one another, even if they—or Amy, at least—didn't know it yet.

The travelers set out. It was a cloudy, windy day, but with no immediate threat of rain. Ben and Greeley, having seen off the departees, headed for the barn to do the final bit of work and to decide what kind of furniture the unorthodox but cozy new dwelling area would require.

Another "ghost letter" came that day. Miriam picked it up and recognized the handwriting at once.

The envelope felt odd this time. More stuffed than usual, and with something that didn't quite feel like paper, or at least just paper.

Miriam wasn't about to open it alone. She went to the barn and straight to Greeley, and handed it to him without a word or a smile.

He held it lightly, feeling the odd texture of whatever was in it. Frowning, also unspeaking, he tore open the envelope and peered in.

Miriam saw his face go pale before her eyes.

He tore the envelope further. A slip of paper fluttered out amid the material that had given the envelope the odd feel.

Hair. Gray, long hair. Flecks of what might be blackened

blood upon it. Greeley picked up the hair in his hand, which began to tremble. Miriam looked at his face and saw tears forming in his eyes, and that scared her more than anything yet.

"Greeley, what does it mean?"

"It's Sally's. Sally Clung."

"That's Sally Clung's hair?"

"Yes!"

"How can you know? Gray hair is gray hair. It could be—"

"It *is* hers! I know from the smell. That's Sally's smell."

Miriam did not seek to argue with that. She had already detected that Greeley's sense of smell was, like that of many mountaineers, far more developed and far more used than the identical sense in a townsman. Greeley, like the old long hunters, followed not only his eyes and ears in the wilds, but his nose as well.

Miriam, shaking, knelt and picked up the slip of paper that had fallen out of the envelope.

Greeley, staring at the gray hairs in his hand, trembling, tears pouring down, asked, "What does it say?"

Miriam looked at it. "It says: 'She harbored Lincolnites.' "

Greeley let the hair fall from his fingers to the floor.

Ben Scarlett walked up, stared down at the silver-gray pile of hair.

"Fletcher's back?" he asked.

"Fletcher's back," Greeley replied. "And he's gotten Old Sally. Damn his black soul! Damn him to hell! He's murdered her, just like he murdered Mathen Ricker! Murdered her because she helped *me*."

Chapter 42

She looked at the man seated in the rocker, staring out the dark window, and wondered if she knew him. Greeley seemed cut off, unapproachable, lost in a world of rage and grief. The rocker made a steady back-and-forth creaking sound. His hands clenched the ends of the rocker's armrests. The knuckles were white.

It was late, almost midnight, and Greeley usually went to bed no later than ten. Miriam steeled her nerve and approached him.

"Greeley?"

He did not answer nor look at her. He kept rocking, back and forth, back and forth.

"Greeley, don't you think you should come to bed?"

"He's toying with me, Miriam. Trying to torment me like I tormented him."

"Greeley, you don't know it's Fletcher. It's probably somebody else. A friend of his, or one of his raiders. They're trying to get to you."

"It's Fletcher, Miriam. I know it is. I feel it."

"And if it is, what do you intend to do? You have a family now. A new home. The war is past."

"No. It's not past. It won't be past for me as long as Fletcher is alive."

"He isn't alive. He's dead."

"He is alive, and he's murdered Sally Clung."

"Then contact the law in Carter County and report it. Let them deal with it. Let the army go in and find Fletcher. He's their responsibility, not yours."

"He's mine, Miriam. This is personal now. He's murdered Sally."

"So what do you intend to do?"

"I don't know yet."

"Greeley, come to bed."

"I ain't sleepy. I need to think."

"You can't think clearly unless you sleep. Don't let him—whoever he is—get to you like this. This person—and I'm not willing to believe it's Fletcher—is playing with your mind and your feelings. He's trying to make you like this. Don't let him succeed."

"This is just the beginning. Fletcher isn't going to quit. I know enough of how his mind works to know that." Greeley looked at his wife for the first time since she had come to his side. "Miriam, he's addressed all the letters to you. He's sent them for me, when it comes down to it, but he's addressed them all in your name. It's a message. A threat."

"What do you mean?"

"You told yourself that you believed Fletcher admired you. You know that as soon as you left your husband, Fletcher murdered him. It was for your sake he let Fitz go on living even up to that point. He's read Eaton's story in one of the papers. He's figured out that I married you . . . me, the man he hates more than anyone . . . and it's eating him alive. The woman he admired, married to the man he hates. By sending them letters in your name, he's letting me know it ain't just me he's got in mind for whatever the devil he does have in mind. He's thinking about you, too. And most likely Cecilia."

Miriam shivered. She tried not to let it show, but it did. She was glad that at the moment Cecilia was still off with Amy Hanover, Thatcher, and little Adam in Knoxville.

"I got to go after him, Miriam."

"No, Greeley! Not that. It's what he wants you to do."

"It's also what I have to do."

"Well, tell me how you intend to find him! He could be any-where in those mountains. Or maybe no longer there at all."

His eyes veered back to the dark window again. "I have a feeling he'll let me know where I can find him."

"Greeley, don't go after him. You think Fletcher would play fair? He'll lure you out, but it wouldn't be just you against him. He'd have his men ambush you. . . ."

"If he has any men left willing to follow him, now that his cause is lost."

"Greeley, come to bed. Don't be trying to make decisions right now. Get some rest."

"I'll come to bed a little later. I don't want to just now."

She didn't argue more. As she closed her eyes, he was still in the chair; she fell asleep to the rhythmic creak of the rocker. Sometime in the night the rocking ceased, but when the dark-ened window out which Greeley had stared filled with light again, he was still in the chair, head drooped to the side and eyes closed, fingers twitching slightly on the armrests.

The next letter came two miserable, long days later, addressed to Greeley himself. He received it from the hand of the post-master and tore it open in a rush. Reading the message within, he drew in a deep, nostril-flaring breath, crumpled the paper and thrust it into his pocket, and left the post office at a trot.

Ben was at the barn, looking about for further work to do. Greeley had been a poor supervisor the last couple of days, not really seeming to care what was or was not done on the reno-vations. He came up to Ben quickly, took the saw from his hand and cast it aside, and said, "Listen to me, Ben: There's something you have to do. I've got somewhere to go. I need you to keep an eye on Miriam for me. Keep her around the hotel. If she asks you where I've gone, tell her I had to head up toward the Long Island. Business. I'll be back as soon as I can."

"Business? The wagon business, you mean?"

"Just business. Personal business."

"Greeley, this ain't nothing to do with them letters, or Fletcher, is it?"

"Ben, I've asked you to watch over my wife for me. I don't have more to say about it than that. Will you do it?"

"Well, surely. But what do I say if she asks me what you're doing?"

"Say I'm tying up some loose ends."

"All right. Are you sure what you're up to is—"

"No more questions, Ben. Understand me?"

Ben nodded.

"I'm going back to the hotel now," Greeley said. "I'm going to quietly gather up my weapons and a few other things and slip them out the window of my room. I don't want to advertise my going. And I don't want you to go back to the hotel for at least another hour. You understand? 'Cause Miriam's sure to ask you where I am, and I want to be long gone before that happens. I don't want anybody trying to follow me."

"It *is* Fletcher you're going after!"

"Mind your own affairs, Ben. I'm minding mine. The only way I can."

Ben nodded solemnly. "You're doing what you feel you have to, I reckon."

"Keep an eye on Miriam."

"What do you think is going to happen to her?"

"Nothing. I'd just feel better knowing there was somebody watching, just in case. And I'm glad that Cecilia's still off with Amy and the others. That works out well."

"Take care of yourself, Greeley."

"I will. And I'll be back. With some things settled, once and for all."

The storm began to build in the form of clouds and an oppressive, heavy atmosphere about the time he reached Boone's Creek. Dusk was falling and he was a few miles short of Long Island on the Holston River when lightning began to sear. His horse was weary and skittish, but he pushed it on mercilessly. He did not have much farther to go now.

Darkness was almost completely upon him when he saw the old mill. Fire had been set here sometime during the war, and only half of the building remained. The wheel was still there, but damaged by the blaze.

Fletcher was here. He could feel him, smell him. Greeley dismounted, sliding the Henry from its saddle boot. He tied the exhausted horse and walked down toward the mill. Every step was taken in caution.

The sky let loose, gushing down hard, drenching rain. It slammed against the brim of his hat, bending it downward, making water cascade off it, front and back. Greeley didn't mind the rain. Like the darkness, it masked him. Through the deluge he headed for the ruined mill, eyes moving, ears working hard to hear above the slam of the rain and the gushing of the river nearby.

He entered through an empty doorway and backed up against a wall to let his eyes adjust to the darker interior. He struggled to breathe silently, listening.

Nothing. If Fletcher was here, he was holding utterly silent. Greeley heard nothing but rain hitting what remained of the roof and coursing down from the ragged edge of the burned-out area to splatter on the mill floor. And a sound he couldn't quite figure, like a broadside or old sheet of newspaper moving and rustling in the breeze back inside the sheltered, dry portion of the mill.

He'd better be here, curse his soul! Greeley thought. I've not come this far to be deprived of ending this thing, one way or the other. Him or me.

Greeley stayed where he was a full five minutes, hearing nothing to indicate another human presence. Lightning flared suddenly, striking just on the other side of the river, and for a second the interior of the mill was lighted in brilliant white. The cannonlike thunder boom was simultaneous with the electric burst, so close was he.

In the momentary flash, Greeley saw something that chilled him. His breath failed him.

"Fletcher?" he said aloud. "Fletcher, where are you?"

No reply came. Another flash of lightning struck, farther away, but giving enough light to let him see again what had taken his breath before.

Nothing to it, really. Just a piece of paper pinned to a wall, flapping in the wind. Words on it.

Greeley advanced to it and tore it down. Moving back into a dry and dark area where the wind did not reach, he knelt, spreading the paper on the floor before him. Trembling, he pulled a match case from his pocket and struck fire to the little candle built onto its side.

By the flame he read mocking words in big, blocky letters, and knew that he'd been a fool to come here. He should have known better, should have realized that Fletcher would put his own malevolent twist into the scenario he had set up.

Greeley tilted back his head and yelled at the top of his voice, but the sound was utterly lost in another boom of thunder.

Rising, he ran back to where his weary horse stood shaking in the driving rain. He booted the rifle, leaped astride the saddle, and rode the horse as hard as it would go. Rode it for a mile, then another, rode it until it would run no more. Pulling his knife from its sheath, he reached back and jabbed it into the horse, driving it on. He pushed the horse until it collapsed and could rise no more. Greeley rose from where he'd been pitched, retrieved his rifle from the saddle and ran on through the rain. A mile, then two. Almost expended by that point, he slowed to a trot and looked for a barn or stable.

He found a stable a half mile onward, and from it stole a horse and saddle. The storm continued at full power. A boy of about fifteen appeared in the big doorway of the barn, holding a shotgun and nervously ordering Greeley to desist from stealing his grandfather's horse. Greeley's reply was to butt him in the head with the Henry rifle and leave him senseless on the ground.

Greeley mounted the horse and ran it into the storm. He put a mile behind him before he slowed, against the strongest impulse to keep running the horse. But he had calmed enough to realize that he would come out better in the long run to not push this horse to exhaustion or possible death, as he had his original mount.

The storm dwindled away, though he heard thunder continue for a long time, farther west. The rain didn't cease, not fully. He rode through the night, wishing he could shrink the miles and the hours that remained between himself and home, yet dreading what he was sure to find when he reached the end.

• • •

He arrived just before dawn. The hotel had been unoccupied the last several days by anyone but the share of its permanent and semipermanent residents who hadn't gone off with Amy to Knoxville—Egypt, Nelly, Ben, Eaton, Miriam, and Greeley himself.

The lobby was dark, but the door wasn't fully shut. Greeley, drenched to the bone, so tired he could hardly stand, yet driven with a fearsome wild energy, strode in, stopped. He sensed human presence, silent. Striking a match, he lit the nearest lamp and set the bowl back in place.

Egypt Munsey was seated on the couch. Lying on the couch with her head on Egypt's lap was Nelly. Egypt's gnarled hand was stroking the old servant's black-gray hair. Greeley might have thought Nelly asleep, but her eyes were half open, staring, and not blinking at all.

Egypt seemed dazed. "It was her tired old heart, I guess. She couldn't bear the fright. Poor Mr. Eaton had it so much worse."

Only then did Greeley notice the figure occupying the over-stuffed chair where Egypt usually rested her arthritic frame. It was Eaton, blood on his chest. He was dead, evidently stabbed. Fletcher's Cross marred the fair skin of the left side of his face.

"How long ago?"

"Oh, about dark, I believe. Yes, that was right. I was thinking about going to bed when he came in. It gets dark so much later this time of year, you know. You can go to bed just after sunset."

"Where's Miriam?"

"He took her. She didn't want to go. He made her."

"Ben?"

"He took him, too. He told me to tell you not to follow. He said he'd be sending Mr. Scarlett back tomorrow to tell you where to come. And he said . . . he said . . ." She frowned, struggling to remember.

Greeley wanted to shout at her, but knew not to. It was not her fault. She was just a terrified woman who had seen a good man murdered in her own dwelling, and watched her old servant die from a heart stopped by pure fright.

"Oh, yes. I remember now. He said for me to tell you not to involve the law or the army. If you did, he said Miriam would wish you hadn't. The way he said it, I believe he was hinting he might hurt her, Mr. Brown. He seemed such a bad man. He stabbed Mr. Eaton. See?" She sounded very old and lifeless now, Greeley noticed. A very different, far more muted woman than the forthright curmudgeon he had grown accustomed to.

"Yes. You didn't tell the law or the army, did you, Miss Munsey?"

"No. I've been right here since he left, just saying my good-bye to poor Nelly. It was so unjust of that man. He frightened Nelly to death. I've never seen anyone frightened to death before." She frowned at him abruptly; a little of her usual border-line rudeness came into her manner. "Where were you, anyway? Why weren't you around to try to stop all this?"

"It was Fletcher, Miss Munsey. He sent me a letter, telling me to come to an old abandoned mill on the Holston. Miles away. He said he'd be there, and that we'd settle our grudges for good. But he wasn't there. When I got there, all I found was a paper, telling me what he was really doing, where he really was. I was a fool not to have known something like that would happen. A fool."

"He carved poor Mr. Eaton's face. It was terrible. Why would he do it?"

"So I would know it was really him."

"He has Miriam. And Ben. Will you go after them now?"

"No. God knows I want to, but I can't. I don't know where they would have gone, and the rain has fallen all night. They couldn't be tracked. You said he was going to send back Ben, with a message?"

"Yes. That's what he said."

"Then I'll wait. It's all I can do. Wait and try to rest." He paused. "We can't let it be known about Horatio and Nelly being dead. Not yet. That would bring the law into it, and we can't do that. I'll have to bury them, temporarily. Later, when I have Miriam back, we can do it again, properly. With services and so on. But now the only important thing is getting Miriam back. I'm glad Cecilia wasn't here. He might have taken her, too." This thought gave rise to another. "Miss Munsey, when did Amy say they'd be returning from Knoxville?"

The woman tried to remember, but only frowned and shook her head.

Greeley's weary brain had trouble pulling out the information, too, but finally he decided that Amy and her traveling companions were not to return until Friday. Two days away yet. That was good. Probably Ben would be back before then, and he himself could go after Miriam before the others returned. It would be easier that way. He didn't want them getting involved.

He knew Fletcher would want it that way, too. This was between the two of them. No one else.

Chapter 43

The absurdity was the worst of it. The sheer, galling absurdity. He glanced at the clock and shifted in his chair again.

Here he was, sitting on his rump, cleaning his weapons over and over, looking at the clock every ten seconds. Out there somewhere his wife was in the clutches of a madman. And he was in here, sitting. In the dirt floor of the woodshed behind the hotel, two bodies lay buried in temporary graves three feet deep. And he was sitting. Absurd.

Back in her room, Egypt Munsey lay on her bed, looking pale and weak and old. Greeley believed she was going to die from the sheer trauma of what she'd witnessed. A woman, so full of life and vinegar two days before, now was old, pitiful, maybe dying. Absurd.

He looked at the clock again. He couldn't even tell the hands had moved. He fidgeted. Stood. Paced. Sat down again. Fidgeted. Looked again at the clock.

Greeley, with four hours of insubstantial, unsatisfying sleep behind him, was alone in the hotel lobby. The front door was locked, all shutters closed and curtains drawn but one, opened just enough to let him keep watch outside for the return of Ben

Scarlett. No customers would be welcome at this hotel today. He would answer the door for no one but Ben.

That is, if Ben ever returned. Why believe that Fletcher would really send him back? That pledge might have been no more than a ploy to make him sit and wait, giving Fletcher time to take Miriam that much farther away.

It was absurd. So absurd it made Greeley's stomach burn.

Yet he could do no more than he was. He could not pursue without a trail, and there was no way to know which way Fletcher had gone with Miriam. All he could do was sit here and hope that Fletcher had told the truth when he promised to send Ben Scarlett back with news of where he could find him.

There was at least some ground for hope that Ben really would return. It all depended upon Fletcher's ultimate motives.

If his goal was to possess Miriam as his own, then Greeley knew he had little going for him. Fletcher would surely kill Ben and haul Miriam off as far away as he could, never letting her out of his sight, never leaving any kind of authentic clue as to where he had gone.

But if, as Greeley believed, Fletcher's deepest motivation was to attain, not Miriam, but revenge, then quite likely he would send Ben Scarlett back, with truthful information about his next whereabouts. He would want Greeley to find him. He would want him to come. Because then Fletcher could kill him, right before the eyes of his own wife.

Greeley glanced at the clock. Cleaned his pistol. Waited.

Thought about how absurd it all was.

The front door rattled at four-thirty in the afternoon. Greeley jerked in his chair and opened his eyes. He'd fallen asleep.

The door rattled again. Ben's voice came through. "Miss Munsey! Greeley! Somebody! It's Ben Scarlett!"

Greeley opened the door. Ben all but fell inside.

Greeley grabbed him by the shoulders.

"Is she well?"

"When last I saw her, yes."

"Fletcher?"

"Yes, yes. He says he's Fletcher. I believe him. He hates you, Greeley. He aims to kill you."

"Tell me where to find him. I'll give him his chance."

Ben told. Greeley nodded grimly. One thing he had to admire about Fletcher. The man had a showman's sense of staging, and a dramatist's sense of irony.

"Where's Miss Munsey?" Ben asked.

"In her bed," Greeley replied, sweeping up his very clean weapons. "I think she's dying. Eaton is dead. Nelly, too. But you know that already."

"Nelly? I didn't know about Nelly. How?"

"Her heart. Fright. She and Eaton are buried inside the woodshed. Don't tell the law, don't tell anyone that they are dead. If Fletcher suspects the law or the military knows anything about what he's done, he'll kill Miriam."

"I won't tell. Greeley, Amy and the others will be home tomorrow. What do I tell them?"

"The truth. But tell them that if they interfere, it could be Miriam who pays the price. Or me. Tell them to stay here. I'll be back, with Miriam, after I kill Fletcher."

"You'll have to kill him," Ben said. "It's the only way. He hates you, and I swear, I believe he's insane."

"He is insane. And I will kill him."

He was gone, riding away with a small armory of weapons on his person and his saddle, and with a spare horse trailing behind him.

Ben went to Egypt's room and peeked in. She was still, lying on her back, but breathing. Asleep.

He went to the kitchen and ate what food he could find. He tasted none of it. Then he went back to the lobby, sat in Egypt Munsey's big chair, and cried out loud for ten minutes.

The thoughts of Greeley Brown flowed of their own accord as he traveled toward the mountains. He hated Fletcher for what he had done and most of all for what he was doing. Yet, ironically, there seemed to be, if not an appropriateness, at least an inevitability to what was happening here. It now seemed to Greeley that matters could have never really fallen out otherwise. From the moment Sally Clung had cut him down from Fletcher's noose, this final confrontation had surely been as fated as the end of time.

He rode with surprisingly little sense of hurry. The course was set now. He knew where he was going, and that Fletcher would await him.

Once and for all, it would be settled. The mountain war was finally going to end. In death, in life, Greeley could not say. But it would end.

Greeley prayed as he rode. Readying himself for either of the two fates he was sure awaited him. He thought back on his plan of early '64 to flee the mountain war, trail off to Kentucky or some other haven. It seemed a foolish notion now. At the time he couldn't see that fate had already laid her hand on him. He could not have fled the mountain war any more than a panther could flee her blackness. It was part of him, and he of it. And for him its closure would require more than names signed on papers in distant towns and cities.

He and Fletcher could only end this war as they had fought it for that bloody year: man-to-man.

He rode on, his pace as steady and relentless as concern for the horses would allow. He reached the mountains, tried to listen to them as Sally Clung had. He thought he heard them speak, though he wasn't sure. He thought he heard them tell him to come on, come on, come on and find the end of war.

He rode on.

Late afternoon. Greeley entered the hollow by the road, making no particular effort to hide. He did not believe that Fletcher would kill him by mere sniping. If that had been his goal, he could have found opportunity much more simply than this. He rode past the apple trees and down a trail well-beaten by the coming and going of Fletcher's raiders in the days not long ago when they had encamped in secret in the hidden meadow at the back of this hollow.

The house was a burned-out shell, walls gone, nothing standing but a few charred timbers and the occasionally gapped foundation wall behind which Cecilia had so often played. He paused when the remains of the house came into sight, and felt his heart jolt in his chest when he saw that she was there. Alone.

Miriam stood in the midst of what had been the house of Vaughn Fitz. Pacing back and forth, never setting foot beyond the line marked by the charred foundation walls.

Fletcher had told her to stay there. It was the only thing Greeley could figure.

Nearby he saw a tent pitched, standing in what had been the front yard of the house. No one appeared to be about it.

He dismounted and slipped the Henry from its saddle boot. His eyes scanned the valley. No sign of Fletcher. He wondered if he might be in the tent. Possibly. Yet he doubted it.

He was out *there* somewhere. Watching.

Greeley advanced on foot toward the burned-out house, leading his horses. She saw him, lunged in his direction, but did not pass beyond the wall of the foundation.

He knew then that Fletcher had a rifle, and had told her that if she stepped beyond the foundation, she would be shot. Or perhaps Greeley would.

Either way, it meant Fletcher was within rifle range. Greeley flicked his eyes about, looking at likely locations, finding nothing to tell him where Fletcher hid.

He was tense, half expecting to be shot, or see her shot, at any moment. He wished she would drop, hide behind the foundation wall. Fletcher couldn't shoot her then.

A cold hand closed around the back of Greeley's neck when he thought: Maybe Fletcher is already behind that wall himself, lying down, ready to kill her just as I reach her. That would suit his cruel ways, something like that. Or maybe he intends to rise from behind that wall and shoot me.

Greeley stopped. He and Miriam looked at one another, silent. She looked very afraid. Her eyes were locked straight ahead.

"Miriam."

"Yes, Greeley."

"Are you well? Have you been hurt?"

"No."

"Where is Fletcher?"

"I don't know." She glanced about. "Out there."

"Watching me? And you?"

"Yes."

"Miriam, is he behind that wall?"

"No."

He was unsure whether to believe her. If Fletcher was there, he of course would have told her to deny it.

Greeley took his chance. He advanced, leading the horses. He saw her trembling, afraid and yet eager for him to reach her. He tied the horses to a charred sapling in what had been the side yard. He lifted his leg, stepped over the wall, reached her, felt her touch and saw her tears. . . .

The crack of the rifle sounded farther away than it was. Greeley grabbed Miriam, heaved her to the earth behind the foundation wall, covering her with his body. The lead horse fell where it was tied, shot through the neck. The other horse kicked and tried to bolt, but its leads were linked to the saddle of the fallen horse and it could go nowhere. A second shot made it spasm, blood spraying out one of its ears. It fell, twitching, kicking, dying.

Greeley could have sworn at himself for having left the horses exposed.

"Well, Mr. Brown!" The voice rang out from somewhere on the other side of the road. "Pleased to see you back with your wife again! Quite a lady, that Miriam! I've thought highly of her for quite some time! And oh, what fine company she made for me on the way here! My oh my!"

Greeley asked, "Miriam, did he—"

"No," she said. "No. He didn't touch me. He's saying that to make you mad. All of this, Greeley, it's all for revenge."

"Aren't you going to speak to me, Mr. Brown? Aren't you going to thank me for seeing that no harm came to your wife all the way here?"

Miriam went on: "He talked of you almost the entire time. Bitter talk, sometimes little more than hateful babble. It was like, to him, that you've become the entire embodiment of the Union, and the kind of men who hurt his family a long time ago."

"Brown! Answer me!"

"I hear you, Fletcher!"

"Ah! I thought so! Well, now let's have a bit of a talk. I'm sorry about that little bespectacled man I had to kill back at that hotel. The fool tried to attack me. So I killed him, and left my mark so you'd be sure to know it was me who'd come to call."

"What do you want from me, Fletcher?"

"Revenge, Mr. Brown. Revenge! But I'm leaving you the choice of how I take it."

The light was beginning to fade. It would be dark within the hour. "What are you talking about?"

"I'm making you a proposition. If you want, you can leave this valley right now. With your wife. Just walk out and go home. I'll not hurt you."

"Or?"

"Or, you can come out and meet me, man-to-man, knife-to-knife, and we can settle our score right here."

"Tell me why I should take the second choice? It don't sound very appealing."

"Because if you leave this valley, Brown, I'll haunt you. I'll be in every shadow, behind every tree, creeping along each alley you pass. I'll let you know what kind of hell you've given me for the past year!"

Miriam said, "Greeley, don't go out there. He'll shoot you down before you ever reach him."

"No. He'll shoot us down, me and you both, if we try to leave. If I go . . . there's a chance he'll fight me fair. A chance I could survive."

"No, Greeley! You haven't been his prisoner! You didn't travel all the way from Jonesborough to here with him. You didn't hear the kind of things he said. He'll never fight you fairly. He doesn't intend to give you a chance to live. There's no honor in him."

Greeley pondered.

"What's your choice, Mr. Brown?" Fletcher's voice sounded mocking.

Greeley drew one of his pistols and handed it to Miriam. "Here. If it should go bad, and he comes back instead of me, you shoot him with this. Shoot him three, four times. Empty it if you have to. Make sure he's dead."

"Greeley, no! You can't go out there. He won't knife-fight you. He'll shoot you!"

"But he won't get the chance to shoot you. That's the point. I go out there now, maybe I can end this business, and win. We try to leave together, he'll kill both of us. And if not, he'll do just what he said, and we'll live with wondering when, and where, and how. There would be danger to Cecilia. To anyone around us. I came here ready to end this, Miriam. That's what I'm going to do."

Fletcher's voice rang through the thickening dark. "What's your choice, Greeley Brown?"

Greeley grasped his wife and kissed her, deeply. He stroked her hair. "I'll be back," he whispered. "I will."

He lifted his head. "I'm coming, Fletcher. We'll end this here, tonight."

"I'm waiting!" Fletcher shouted back. "Waiting out here in the dark for you. Like a ghost."

"Don't go, Greeley."

"It's the only way." He looked at her. "I love you, Miriam. Whatever happens . . . I love you."

He was gone before she could reply.

Even as Greeley Brown had still been moving through the mountains toward Vaughn Fitz's remote hollow, matters had not been sitting still in Jonesborough.

Amy Hanover and her fellow travelers had returned and learned of the tragedies that had come in their absence. Shock was great, but short-lived. Thatcher Brown declared that something must be done; they couldn't sit idle while Greeley and Miriam were in danger. And if they didn't dare involve legal or military authorities, whatever was done would have to be done by themselves. Amy Hanover agreed, and almost instantly life became a confusing flurry of activity for Ben Scarlett. He was glad of it. He had never known a more tense, miserable, helpless time than the gap between Greeley's departure and the travelers' return. He'd been able to think of little but whiskey. But he'd done no more than think. Hadn't touched a drop. He was proud of himself.

He was walking now through the rear door of Egypt Munsey's hotel, which brought him into the dining room. The front doors and windows were still locked and shuttered. With him was a tall, broadly built, auburn-haired man named Judah Lemmons, a newcomer to Jonesborough who had come from Turkey Town in Carter County and had been one of Amy's most helpful informants toward her now-nearly-finished book.

The atmosphere was odd, Ben thought, sort of like the sorrowfulness of a funeral parlor mixed with the hurry of a factory that's behind on its manufacturing schedule and trying to make it up.

To his companion, Ben said, "Well now, Judah, here we are, and—"

Amy swept into the room, cutting Ben off. With her hand outthrust, she approached Judah Lemmons. "Hello, Mr. Lemmons. Thank you for coming. Did Ben explain the situation to you?"

"Yes, yes he did."

"You'll be willing to guide us?"

"Yes, I will. I despised Fletcher. Lost two good friends to him. I had a near run-in with five of his raiders once myself. It makes me sick to find out he ain't dead after all. I'm glad to do anything that would help—"

"You have horses available for us, Mr. Lemmons?"

"Yes. I been doing some trading out of Knoxville, and I've got saddles, too. I can provide mounts for all of us, and a couple of extra besides."

"That's helpful beyond measure," Amy said. This was true. The war had almost depleted the northeastern end of the state of horses. Only since the end of the war had good mounts begun showing up in pastures and stables again.

"I hope we haul in Fletcher's corpse on one of them horses," Lemmons went on. "I'd love to end his life my own self, like he ended the lives of so many good folks I've knowed."

"My main concern is to get Miriam and Greeley Brown back safely. But if Fletcher is eliminated in the process, I'll have no complaint. Mr. Lemmons, you are vital to what we're doing. Without your guidance, and your horses, we would have little chance to find them."

"Well, I'm happy I can—"

But she was already gone.

Ben grinned weakly at Lemmons. "She's in a big way just

now. Been that way since she got back and found what had happened."

Fitful crying drew Ben's eyes. Through the door into the next room he saw Cecilia seated, stiffly, in a straight-backed chair, Adam on her knee. He had been stung on the leg earlier in the morning and was still upset about it. Cecilia was trying to comfort him, but her manner was of a person stunned. Ben knew she was trying to accommodate the incredible realization that her mother was miles away, prisoner of a murderer, and that her beloved stepfather had gone after her and into a scenario whose key design was to destroy him.

Ben could see the disbelief still lingering in Cecilia's eyes. That had been the most difficult part of it all: simply making them believe him. He could easily see how it must have sounded from their point of view. Hello, Miss Amy! Welcome home! By the way, Fletcher's still alive, and he's come and kidnapped Miriam and murdered Mr. Eaton and now Greeley's gone off after them, most likely to walk into a trap and get himself killed. Oh, and Nelly died, too. Scared to death. She and Mr. Eaton are buried in the woodshed. Miss Egypt is still all dazed from it all. Can I help you carry your bag?

He hadn't presented it that way, of course, yet surely it must have seemed hardly different than that to them.

But now they did know, and did believe, and Amy was in typical leader fashion crafting her response. Her mind had sailed into the problem just as quickly as it had ceased spinning. She and Thatcher sat down together and talked intently, and the plan had come into place.

Such as it was. All they had decided to do was go after Greeley. They had the advantage, through Ben, of knowing precisely where Fletcher had told Greeley to meet him. But of their number, only Cecilia had personal familiarity with Vaughn Fitz's valley, and she would not be going. She would remain here to care for Adam and poor Egypt, who seemed to have been inflicted with the effects of two more decades of life, all within a span of days.

Amy was the one who thought of Judah Lemmons. He was right there in Jonesborough already, he knew Carter County as well as any man alive, and he was tough, trailwise, and full of bitterness toward the rebels. Thatcher agreed that Lemmons sounded like just the guide for this journey. She sent Ben scurrying at once to tell him what had happened here and to recruit him as a guide. Lemmons, Ben found, was immediately ready to agree.

The plan seemed to be falling into place. Four of them would go: Lemmons, Thatcher, Ben, and Amy. Ben liked that arrangement . . . all but the last of it.

"Well," he said to Lemmons, "I'm going to go give a try to talking Miss Amy out of going. This ain't no woman's job. Especially one with a baby who needs her."

"Reckon not," Lemmons replied, but without force. He could have told Ben many a tale of mountain women who had faced and endured the greatest of terrors during the mountain war, many of these with whole housefuls of babies and children.

Ben strode up to Amy, who was counting out ammunition for her cap-and-ball rifle.

"Amy, I want to talk to you about—"

"Ben! I need something. Trousers. A shirt. Some of yours. Go get them for me."

"Huh?"

"I'm not going into the mountains in skirts, Ben. Get me a pair of your trousers and a shirt!"

"Well, I don't think you ought to go into the mountains at all, Miss Amy. This ain't a woman's task. You need to stay here with Cecilia and Adam."

"What? Of course I'm going! Now go get me that clothing!"

"But it ain't right for—"

"Now, Ben! And don't try any more to talk me out of this. I will go. If there's anyone who ought not, it's you. Do you even own a weapon?"

"No, but Mr. Lemmons is loaning me a pistol."

"A pistol is far inferior to a rifle in mountain conditions. Could you even hold a pistol steady enough to shoot it?"

"Well, yes, if I had to."

"Ben, I don't think you should go."

"The devil! I seen with my own eyes what Fletcher done here! I'll not sit back on my rump while others go after him! I want to be part of this, and I *will*!"

Thatcher was nearby, overhearing. "He is the only one of u

here who has seen Fletcher in person," he said. "Might prove useful if we have to identify him."

"All right. Ben's in," Amy said. "And so am I. And I swear, I'll shoot anyone who suggests otherwise!"

"You'll hear nothing from me," Thatcher said, raising his hands. Ben wondered if, during their Knoxville journey, Thatcher had been given opportunity to learn that Amy Hanover could sometimes not only bark, but bite.

They finished their preparations. When they were through, Ben thought them a pitiful little army, in a way. An absurd little army, really.

Kind of funny, he thought. I made it through a whole war and never become a soldier. Now the war's done, and I'm off to invade the mountains with two other fellows and a woman. Funny how things work out sometimes. Funny, and frightening, too.

For the first time it struck him just how dangerous this might turn out to be, and for a moment the old, self-serving side of Ben Scarlett asserted itself and he wished that maybe he hadn't been so insistent that he go along. A man never knew. He might ride off and never ride back again.

Chapter 44

In the mountains of Carter County

It was dusk, the light dim and growing dimmer, but sufficient to reveal what had caught their attention. Lemmons handed the folding spyglass over to Thatcher, who peered through it, nodded, and handed the glass over to Amy in turn. They were all crouched, side by side, on a ridge looking down into the hollow. There, amidst of the burned rubble of what had been the house of Vaughn Fitz, two figures moved.

Ben Scarlett, least important of this little band and last in line to receive a peep through the spyglass, asked, "Is it them?"

"Yes," Thatcher replied. "It's Greeley and Miriam. But it's Miriam doing most of the moving about. Greeley's lying down. She's got him positioned fairly close to the foundation wall, so the wall protects him."

"Is he hurt?"

Amy handed Ben the spyglass. "Look for yourself."

But Ben, with a hook for a hand, was clumsy with the glass and could not get it focused. "I can't see nothing."

"I believe he is hurt," Thatcher said. "And I think she's tending him, and trying to keep him lying where no one could get a shot at him."

"She's got a weapon herself—that I can see even without the glass," Ben said.

"That's right, and from her manner, I believe she's fearful of somebody still out there in the valley."

"Fletcher."

"So I'd figure."

"How can we approach her without spooking her?" Ben asked.

"I ain't sure we can," Lemmons replied. The others gave him full attention. In the hurried course of their journey here, he had proven a very capable guide. The others were no woodsmen; only Thatcher had any recent experience of wilderness travel, but that had been as a prisoner receiving aid along the way from slaves and Unionists. Lemmons was the man in authority where travel and strategy were concerned. "It'll be dark before we can get down there to her. I suggest we wait until morning and go in by light."

"No," Thatcher said. "That's my brother down there. I believe he's injured. I'll not sit up here and wait, only to find out in the morning that he's died."

"Well, in that case, we can only take our chances, and try to alert her as to who we are before she shoots us. Or before Fletcher does, if he's out there."

"She's acting like he's out there," Ben said. "See how she keeps low, and keeps peeping out that way?"

"Well, if we're going, then let's go now," Lemmons said. "We'll walk in from the head of the hollow, horses on our right side, in case Fletcher or somebody is out there sniping. The horses will help block us from gunfire . . . unless it comes from the woman."

Thatcher was the first to rise. "Let's go. I want to get to Greeley."

"I'll lead the way," Lemmons said. "Remember, keep your horse between yourself and the woods there. And Thatcher, you be ready to give a holler to her when I tell you to. Tell her who we are, so she won't shoot before she knows."

They rose. Amy looked at Ben. "You look scared, Ben."

"I am scared."

"If you want to stay behind, wait for us to return . . ."

"Well, I guess I could watch the horses."

"We're taking the horses with us. Remember?"

"Oh. Yeah. Well, I guess then I'll have to go, too." He forced out a smile and chuckle, trying to make the whole business seem lighthearted. The chuckle was jerky and false, the smile ghastly.

They went back to the horses and began the trek down into the hollow, following Lemmons.

It worked out quite well, no shots coming from the woods, nor from Miriam. They strode down within shouting range and Lemmons directed Thatcher to call out to her. She was now invisible to them down there in the darkness.

"Miriam! Greeley! It's Thatcher! And Amy Hanover, and others, come to help! Don't shoot!"

The only reply they heard from her was a sobbing cry of relief.

They found her and Greeley, however, in a desperate situation. Miriam was frantic, full of distress. And Greeley was hurt, only half conscious, fever already rising in him. He'd been shot. Amy, with experience in dealing with wounded men deriving from her hospital volunteerism in Nashville, went to work at once on his wound, using bandaging and cleansing materials she'd brought among her own provisions, in case of just such a situation. But it was dark; the best she could do was wash the crusting blood away from the ugly hole.

"It was Fletcher," Miriam told them. "He challenged Greeley to come out and fight him, with knives, and to settle everything for good. Otherwise, he said, we could ride out and he would let us go in peace, but he'd 'haunt' Greeley like Greeley did him and his men, and kill him later. Greeley didn't believe Fletcher would really let us leave the valley, thought it was a trick. So he went out to fight him."

"I'd have made the same choice," Lemmons said. "Fletcher ain't to be trusted, ever."

"Greeley shouldn't have trusted him even as far as that challenge," Miriam said. "Fletcher shot him. But Greeley was able to get out one of his pistols, and he shot at Fletcher. He came back here, bleeding, and said he was sure he'd hit Fletcher, though he didn't know if it was mortal or not. It wasn't . . . Fletcher shot at us a few minutes later. Three shots. All of them high and wild. That was all."

"Nothing after that?" Lemmons asked. "No yells or movement or nothing?"

"No. Just silence."

"I'll be!" Lemmons bit his whiskered lower lip a moment and gazed thoughtfully out into the dark. "You know what that surely does mean, don't you?"

"What?" Ben asked. He'd walked into the conversation a moment before, having been out giving the horses some of the feed grain they had brought with them on the back of one of the two riderless mounts.

"I think I know," Thatcher said. "It means Fletcher was probably badly hurt when he fired those last three shots. Probably desperate shots. Probably shots fired by a man who was dying himself even when he fired them."

"That's right. And I'm betting that the old murderer is lying dead out there in them trees right now. You ain't heard no peep at all from that direction since them three shots, ma'am?"

"I heard nothing at all until you arrived."

"By gum, I'm going out there," Lemmons said. "I'll bet you I can find that corpse of his in less than ten minutes."

"In the dark?" Thatcher said. "Why risk it? Wait until daylight."

"There ain't no risk. That bastard's dead. If he wasn't, he'd have been down here long ago to finish off your brother, Mr. Brown there. He'd have known he was shot and helpless. And I don't believe he'd have been afraid of Miriam enough to keep him away. No, he's dead. I know it."

"I think Thatcher's right," Ben said. "You ought to wait until morning."

"I'll see you in fifteen minutes. Not a bit later," Lemmons said. "It's going to be sweet, dragging in the corpse of that murdering bushwhacker. By gum, I think I'll take it home with me. Get me an undertaker to preserve him in something. I'll sell tickets for folks to see . . ." His tone became that of a sideshow barker. ". . . the corpse of Devil Cap Fletcher, killed by Greeley Brown, the very man who wiped out a score of his raiders during the last year of the war!"

Thatcher and Ben glanced at one another, not quite so sure about this man any longer.

"Back in fifteen minutes, me and Fletcher both," he said, and went over the wall and into the darkness beyond.

Ben shook his head and wandered to the rear of the foundation. He sat down on the wall, near a pile of charred roof timbers that had fallen in but not fully burned up. His foot moved a round stone. He reached down, picked it up, and began tossing it idly in his hand, up and down.

Ten minutes passed, then fifteen. Lemmons did not return. Ben tossed the stone more rapidly. Thirty minutes went by. An hour. Still no Lemmons.

Ben prayed, silently. For Greeley to go on living. For him to recover. He was asking for a miracle and knew it.

He consulted his pocket watch, holding it right to his eye before he could make it out. An hour and fifteen minutes. Lemmons still was gone.

Ben began to worry. He also began to ponder, without full consciousness of it, that this stone was awfully light in weight, considering its size. It didn't quite feel like a stone, either. He stopped tossing it and held it close to his face in the darkness. There was just enough light to let him make out its contours.

What looked back at him was a skull. Charred and black, the color of rock but the texture of bone. Eye sockets empty of all but dirt and ash looked into his own widening eyes. Ben yelped beneath his breath and tossed the skull away, off into the charred tree grove behind the house. Rising, he swiftly paced back and forth, wiping his hand on his shirt.

He'd just made acquaintance with all that remained on earth of Vaughn Fitz. He figured it prudent not to mention the meeting to Miriam. She was seated beside Greeley, who was now growing raving and delirious, while Amy and Thatcher worked to restrain him from thrashing about. Miriam had enough weighing on her without having to hear the gruesome news that her former husband was still upon the scene, in a way.

Greeley moaned and yelled. Ben kept pacing, wiping his hand, and wondering what had become of Lemmons.

An hour before dawn Greeley became quiet. He still

breathed, but was not conscious. Miriam wept silently beside him, and Ben felt that death would surely descend soon. Lemmons still had not returned.

Amy came to Ben's side. "Sing something, Ben. Something soft and pretty. I remember in the hospitals how sickly men would regain their color sometimes when someone sang to them. I've seen badly hurt men smile and get stronger while they listened to someone sing. Sing for Greeley."

Ben cleared his throat. The sad but beautiful tones of "Scarlett's Lament" drifted out from the burned-out house and into the darkness beyond. Miriam stroked Greeley's hair. He did not move nor open his eyes.

Ben sang all of the song he had completed, paused, then kept going. He rather surprised himself. He'd done it! He'd finished out the song without half trying. It was almost like the sadness of the moment, the grim setting, the sense of death about to descend, had completed it for him.

When he was finished, Ben lowered his head and wiped at his eyes.

"Sing it again, Ben," Amy said.

It astonished them all. Greeley Brown was still breathing. His face was as gray as that of a dead man, his consciousness fully absent, but his chest continued to move up and down, jerkily.

By the light of dawn Amy tended the wound again, cleaning it better, putting on fresh bandaging. But it was evident that more significant treatment was required if Greeley was to survive much longer. The wound was miscolored, swollen, ugly.

The sky was miscolored, too, and uglier by the moment. Clouds were building. A storm would strike the mountains today.

Thatcher pointed at the small tent standing in the yard of the former house. "Fletcher's?" he asked Miriam.

"Yes. He pitched it after we got here. He made me stay here, though, inside the walls of the foundation. He wanted Greeley to find me here. He said he'd kill me if I stepped outside the wall." She shook her head. "You know, I haven't stepped outside it yet. I still have the feeling that if I do, I'll die on the spot, like he promised."

"I don't think so now," Thatcher said. "I believe Lemmons is right. Fletcher's dead now. The wound Greeley gave him must have done him in." He frowned. "Where is Lemmons, anyway?"

"I think he's run out on us," Ben said. "I hate to say it, but it appears to be true."

Thatcher shook his head. "No, no. He wouldn't have done that. I'll bet he's gone on to find help."

"Without telling nobody?"

Thatcher pondered, frowning. "Well, I can't explain it. But I do know this: We're going to require some help if Greeley's to have any chance of living. Ben, let's you and me get that tent up, and move it over here and cover Greeley with it. There's going to be rain. Then I'm going to go out and find somebody who can help us."

"I'll come with you."

"No. You'll stay here. Guard Greeley and the women."

Ben was glad Amy didn't hear that last comment. Nothing would have angered her more than the presumption that she required a tremoring, one-handed fellow, armed with a pistol he didn't even know how to shoot, to be safe. But Ben didn't argue. He was a follower, not a leader, and would do whatever the others thought best.

He and Thatcher got the tent moved and over Greeley within half an hour. Miriam crawled inside with her husband, seated with him, talking quietly and lovingly into his ear, telling him to hang on, hang on, there would be help soon.

"I'm going for help," Thatcher announced to Amy. "I'll bring in a wagon from someplace, and we'll get Greeley out of here and to someplace where there's medical care available."

"I'm coming with you," she said.

"I think it would be best if you stayed with Greeley."

"I'm coming with you," she replied. "There's still too much bushwhacking and so on going on in these hills to risk having you try to find help alone. People would respond more quickly to a woman than to a man. And with two of us, should something happen to one of us, there would be the other to continue on. We do have to find help for Greeley, and fast. Otherwise he'll be too far gone and there'll be no chance he can pull through."

"I think you should stay," Thatcher argued. "You're the one with some medical experience. Your father was a physician. You've worked in military hospitals."

"Yes, and I've got enough experience to tell you that I've done all I can for Greeley. He needs a physician. That bullet has to come out, and I don't have the skills to remove it. You worked in the hospital at the Salisbury prison, you said. Did you deal with bullet wounds?"

"Very seldom. We mostly saw communicable sicknesses and exposure-related illnesses there."

"Then neither one of us can help Greeley by remaining here. I wish Lemmons hadn't vanished! He could find help more quickly than anyone."

"I still think that possibly that's what he's gone to do. All right, we'll leave," Thatcher said, pretending his agreement had bearing even though Amy had already made up her mind. "We'll leave Ben and Miriam to keep watch over Greeley, and go at once, on the two best horses." He frowned again. "The horses! There's another mystery. Why would Lemmons leave at all and not take a horse?"

"Maybe something happened to him," Ben said. "He went looking for Fletcher's corpse. Maybe he found Fletcher, and Fletcher wasn't a corpse at all."

That comment brought silence for a moment. Thatcher shook his head. "No, no. We'd have heard shots if there had been a fight. And certainly we'd have been visited by Fletcher by now if he were still alive. He'd have already dealt with Greeley before we even got here."

"I suppose you're right. But I wonder what's become of Lemmons," Ben replied thoughtfully.

"No time to talk more," Amy said. "Thatcher, let's go."

"I'll be praying for you," Ben said.

"Do that. And keep watch over Miriam and Greeley. When that storm hits, make sure the tent is keeping Greeley dry," Thatcher instructed. "At Salisbury I saw how badly exposure to the weather could hurt injured and sick men."

"I'll do all I can to keep him comfortable."

They saddled the best horses, mounted, and rode off. Ben waved as they departed, then lifted his eyes to squint at the cloud-filled sky. Thunder rumbled, way off in the west.

The same day, late afternoon

Miriam was near exhaustion, but would not let herself sleep.
Ben understood why. She feared that if she slept, she would
awaken to find her husband's spirit had slipped away in the
meantime. She would not take her eyes off Greeley's face. Ben
had tried to make her eat, but she wouldn't do that, either.

Ben was back in the tent again, with her and Greeley. He'd
come in and out a dozen times over the hours since Amy and
Thatcher had left, just to see if Greeley was better or worse.
Each time, Greeley seemed just as he'd been before.

Ben had spoken only a little to Miriam, knowing she was in
no mood to talk. But he'd been thinking out there, while the
hours rolled past, and felt he had something he must say.

"Miriam, I'm sorry I wasn't able to protect you when
Fletcher broke in on us," he told her. "If I'd done better, maybe
none of this would have happened. Greeley told me to watch
over you. I thought I was. I just never expected a madman to
show up to take you away."

Miriam turned her weary face to him. "You did the best you
could. No one was prepared."

"I can't figure yet how brash a man has to be to do what
Fletcher done. Coming in and kidnapping two grown folk right
on the edge of a town! Stabbing a man to death in the lobby of
a hotel! You know, he'd have killed me, too, if he hadn't
needed somebody to be alive to deliver the message back to
Greeley about where to find him." He reflected a few moments.
"Smart man, in his own way, that Fletcher was. Sending
Greeley off chasing a wild goose, then hauling me halfway
here before sending me back again. It gave him all kinds of
time to get where he wanted without Greeley having any
opportunity at all of pursuing. Smart man."

"Wicked man. I hope he's dead."

"I'd say he is. If Greeley shot him, he's likely dead and
gone."

Ben exited the tent, still wondering about Lemmons. Something surely had happened to him. He peered toward the grove
of woods toward which Lemmons had moved last night. No
sign of him. Ben squinted harder—and realized, abruptly, that

he was beginning to need glasses, and that brought a frown—and suddenly whispered, "Hey, now! What's that?"

Out among the trees, which were whipping hard now that the storm was moving in, he'd seen something shift and flap. Something blue, seemingly fabric. Blue like the shirt Lemmons had been wearing.

He was coming back! Ben smiled, lifted his hand, waved, anticipated seeing Lemmons breaking out of the trees at any second.

He didn't appear. The trees moved again. Once more Ben saw the blue bit of fabric. Flapping, he noticed, like a banner.

"Huh!" He wished he had that spyglass with him.

He went back to the tent and stuck his head through the flap. "Miriam, I'm running over to the woods. I think I see Mr. Lemmons, that fellow who guided us, but I ain't sure. I'll be right back."

She didn't answer him. Ben had never seen anyone look so sad, empty.

Ben checked his pistol, just glancing at it to reassure himself it was there. He stepped across the foundation wall and walked across what had been a front yard, out to the road, across it, and into the trees beyond. Entering them, he immediately saw the blue, flapping thing. It was a shirt, not on anyone, but hung in a tree. Blown up there by the wind, maybe, and caught upon a branch. He squinted at it and walked toward it. Oh, Lord, he thought. That's blood on that shirt, sure as the world.

He went to it, stood looking up at it. A blue shirt. Lemmons's shirt, he was sure. It was caked with blood, as if someone had used it to dab bleeding wounds.

Ben swallowed, feeling queasy. He turned, and his eyes widened.

Lemmons was seated beneath a maple tree. Shirt off. He was bloody and dead. Knife wounds in the chest, it appeared. Ben pieced it together. Lemmons had found Fletcher, but Fletcher was not dead. Wounded, maybe, but not dead. He had stabbed Lemmons. Lemmons, stunned and dying, had staggered over to this maple, sat down beneath it, and torn off his own shirt to try to staunch the flow of blood with it. It hadn't worked. He had died. The sodden shirt had dried through the rest of the night, and been picked up by the wind as the storm built, flung up into that tree to wave like a flag.

Ben heard the first rattle of raindrops in the overarching leaves above him. Lightning fired down a few miles away.

He wondered where Fletcher was and if he was still alive. He pulled out the pistol, looked around wildly.

Miriam . . . she and Greeley were alone.

Ben turned and ran back out of the woods, onto the road. He jerked to a halt.

Cap Fletcher, his left arm crudely bandaged and bloody, stood beside the tent, a shotgun in his hand. Miriam was beside him.

The rain began to fall very hard. Ben advanced, pistol rising, but his hand tremoring badly. Swallowing, struggling to breathe despite choking fear, he kept his eye on Fletcher, leveling the pistol at him as best he could.

Fletcher looked pallid as a dead man. His face twisted. A grin? Ben couldn't put a name on the expression. Praying for courage even as he cursed himself for having left Miriam and Greeley alone, even for a few minutes, he swallowed hard and prepared to order Fletcher to drop the shotgun.

Before he could even part his dried lips, Fletcher raised the shotgun at Ben and fired.

Ben's pistol hit the ground only a second or so before he did.

Ben sat up, the rain hammering him. Fletcher still had that odd, grimacing half grin. Ben gaped at him, then down at his right forearm. A chunk of it was torn away, like a dog had bitten out a chew of his flesh. Blood streamed. Ben stared helplessly at it, feeling faint, then up at Fletcher again.

Miriam was like a statue. She was too scared to cry. The storm built. Lighting seared and the rain fell harder. It slapped hard against the ground, making the dust of the road behind Ben into mud.

"Hello, Bill Scarlett. Didn't expect to see me, did you!"

"My name's Ben."

"I don't care what your name is. All I care about is that I'm about to kill Mr. Greeley Brown. Then I'll kill his woman here, and then I'll kill you. Or maybe I'll kill you first."

"You killed Mr. Lemmons. I found him back in the woods."

"He was a fool. What'd he come back there in them woods for, in the dark?"

"He thought you was dead. He wanted to find your corpse, and save it, and put it out to show to the public." Ben looked at his arm again. "I'm bleeding. You shouldn't have shot my good arm. You might have shot off the only hand I got left."

"You'd have had you a matching set then, wouldn't you! Come here! Get up off them knees and come here! I don't like yelling through this rain."

Ben came to his feet, holding his numb, bleeding arm against his side. He advanced toward the house.

"Step on over inside here."

Ben complied. Miriam looked at him, but he wasn't sure she saw him. She seemed many miles away, like her spirit had already left her.

Ben hoped Greeley would go ahead and die before Fletcher could do anything else to him. He hoped that when Miriam died, Fletcher would do it quickly. And he hoped that when Fletcher killed him, it wouldn't hurt too much, and that when he got to heaven, his mother would come out with Jesus and all the angels to meet him.

"I got a bone to pick with you, Mr. Stump-arm. Why'd you bring all them folks here, when I told you clear that it was to be only Greeley Brown who was to come?"

"Because all them folks are friends and loved ones to Greeley and Miriam both. They weren't going to sit back and let you kill them without at least trying to do something about it. Besides, at the beginning, Greeley was the only one I told."

"I'm going to let you watch me kill him. And her, too. No, no I won't. Hell, I'll kill you first. You betrayed me."

"Why'd you wait so long to come out and do this, Fletcher? We been here all day, and you made no peep, nor showed yourself."

"I was right busy today, digging a bullet out of my arm starting about sunup, just as quick as I could see to do it. You ever gouged a knife into your own wound, Stumpy, and not even letting yourself give a yell? It ain't easy. It took the strength out of me for hours. I was in no shape to come in earlier, when I was still fresh wounded. After me and Greeley shot each other, I followed him back this way. Fired two or three shots after him, but missed. I was passed out then for I don't know how long. When I come around, there was you and all them others here. Too many to come in after. I was surprised as hell when that big one come out there in the woods, by himself. He shouldn't have done it. What was his name?"

"Lemmons."

"Well, they can write that on his gravestone, if they ever find him."

"Let Miriam go, Mr. Fletcher. She ain't hurt you."

"Oh, she did!" He turned his face to her. "I believe you know I've held you in regard from the first time I seen you, don't you, woman! I brung you gifts, treated you polite, let that turd of a husband of yours live as long as you were here. But you run off and married another man. Greeley Brown, no less! That, I don't appreciate, Miriam. No, ma'am."

Fletcher made that odd wincing smile again. Ben realized his wound was hurting him, that maybe Fletcher was worse off than he appeared. Any man who could dig a bullet out of his own body and not yell would probably be tough enough to stand up even if he was half dead.

"I heard somebody singing last night," Fletcher said. "Real pretty singing. Was that you, Stumpy?"

"Yes."

"I liked that song. Couldn't hear it good, where I was, though. You sing it for me now. You do it good enough, maybe I'll not kill Miriam after all. Maybe I'll just take her with me."

"I don't know I want to sing."

"Then I'll kill her before your eyes."

"No, no. I'll sing for you. That same song?"

"That's right. What do you call that song?"

"Ain't got no name. Greeley, he just called it 'Scarlett's Lament.' "

"Why? You made that up?"

"Yes."

"I'll be damned." He grinned, but the grin became another look of pain. "Sing it! Now!"

And so Ben sang. The melody was minor, the words styled like those of the old ballads Ben had heard all his young life, sung by his mother and her mother, too. In the midst of the driving storm, the melody and words of "Scarlett's Lament" sounded, voiced for the pleasure of a madman who was about to bring down death, and who might be awaiting it to fall on him, as well.

> *"As I went out walking one evening in autumn,*
> *When summer was fading, a-dying away,*
> > *Across the wide meadow,*
> > *Down from the high mountain,*
> *I heard a maid weep while the sun sank away . . ."*

Fletcher smiled, nodded. "That's it. That's the song. I like that. It's pretty."

> *"I stood and I listened while stood she a-weeping,*
> *a woman of sorrows, of suffering and woe,*
> > *I longed, as I heard her,*
> > *To find her, to see her,*
> *I followed her crying, to her did I go."*

"That's good singing. Pretty singing," Fletcher said.

> *"Oh, why are you weeping, I asked of the lady,*
> *For where comes your sorrow? For whom do you cry?*
> > *I cry for the thousands,*
> > *The people of shadows,*
> *The thousands who suffer, the thousands who die.*
>
> *I cry for the husband whose chair now is empty,*
> *I cry for the boy-child beneath the cold sod,*
> > *I weep for the lost ones,*
> > *Who left us in silence,*
> *Who died in the darkness, seen only by God."*

"That's pretty, pretty singing," Fletcher said. "Sad but pretty. Sing it out, Scarlett."

He did sing. The words rose from inside him, his last words, he felt sure, and thus sung from the deepest part of him. Ben Scarlett's lament, Ben Scarlett's cry. Ben Scarlett's final contribution to a world to which it now seemed he had given far too little, but which he loved dearly and would truly hate to leave.

The song went on, verse by verse, a litany of the loss and tragedy that had been the war in these mountains, war waged by men such as Cap Fletcher and Greeley Brown, war so terrible and sweeping and morally confusing that a man hardly was able to have a clear thought or feeling about it sometimes, beyond the unquestionable knowledge that somehow, surely, such things should never have been.

He reached the final verses, which had come to him as he sang the same song the night before:

> *"She fell then to silence, and so did I ask her:*
> *Who are you, my lady? And what is your name?*
> *My name, it is Mercy,*
> *My name, it is Kindness,*
> *By War am I wounded, by War am I slain.*
>
> *And then, in the darkness, no more could I see her,*
> *Though hard did I seek her, my eyes now were blind.*
> *I wandered and called her,*
> *I called out for Mercy,*
> *I called out for Kindness, but naught I did find.*
>
> *But often, at evening, as I roam in the mountains,*
> *I wait for her voice, I wait for her song,*
> *I search now for Mercy,*
> *I search now for Kindness,*
> *For the one I heard weeping, in the mountains, alone."*

Then he was done. He looked at Fletcher, who stared back at him, solemn. The rain declined, just a little.

"That was pretty singing, sir," he said. "I salute you for it. It's a good song for us here. A good one for people who are all soon to die."

"You too, Fletcher? Will you yourself be the last one shot here today?"

"Yes. I will be the last one." He pulled a pistol from his belt, tossed aside the shotgun. "First her, then you, then Greeley Brown. Then me."

He turned to Miriam. He lifted the pistol, pointed it at her head, clicked back the hammer.

Ben advanced. He was still bleeding from his arm, his head light. Suddenly it was hard to see Fletcher.

"No!" he yelled. "No!" Then he put out his left arm, swinging the hook, lunging at Fletcher.

His hook caught Fletcher's ear as he turned toward Ben. The pistol blasted, deafening, almost in Ben's face. Ben pulled back his arm for another swing, but Fletcher kicked him down. Suddenly he was atop Ben, pulling back the hammer, aiming the pistol at Ben's face . . .

Ben saw Miriam behind Fletcher. She had the shotgun he'd thrown aside. Ben heard her scream, heard the blast of the shotgun, simultaneous with that of Fletcher's pistol. His throat filled with heat, pain. He tried to yell, but no sound came . . .

Chapter 45

. . . and suddenly, the world was transformed.

The pain in Ben's throat vanished, and also in his wounded arm. The lightness that had been in his head became a lightness of his entire person, and he felt himself rising, as if up through Fletcher himself, and as soon as he gained his perspective, he found it, unexpectedly, to be as if from above. He seemed to be flying, moving in the sky itself, right in the midst of the storm, but unaffected by it.

He looked down and saw himself lying in the rain, on his back, bearded face turned up. His wounded arm was ugly, so also the red stains now on his throat, and the burned, chewed place in his neck where Fletcher's bullet had struck.

"I'll be," he said, though there was no sound to it. "Look at me, lying there! I look pitiful! Plain old pitiful!"

He looked away from himself and to the broader scene. There was Miriam, weeping, dropping the shotgun, bringing her hands to her face, covering it. And Fletcher—he was there too, staggering off to the side, having dropped his pistol. He was clutching his hands to his throat.

Ben laughed. Apparently Miriam's shotgun blast had missed. Point-blank, aimed right at his head, and she'd missed!

That's a woman for you, he thought. Most of them don't shoot no better than I do.

And yet, something was wrong with Fletcher. He staggered away, stooped, and though Ben could now only see, but not hear, the world below him, he sensed that Fletcher was gagging and gasping.

Ben realized what had happened. In that last moment before he himself was shot, he'd managed to get his hook into Fletcher's throat and tear it out.

The perspective changed again, grew farther away, broader. Ben was able to perceive events over a wide area. . . . He saw riders, approaching from a distance. A small band of blue-clad soldiers, heading for the hollow, and he knew that Amy and Thatcher were with them. They had found a detachment of Federals, obviously, probably sent into the mountains to roust out bushwhackers. . . .

And now Ben knew all was going to be well. Amy and Thatcher and those soldiers would be there at the burned-out house in moments. They'd take care of Miriam, and Greeley.

He understood why he was allowed to see them. He knew now it was all right to go on.

And then it all changed again. The sights of the present faded away for him, and he seemed to see the mountains in their entirety, and without the limiting perspective of time. Everywhere his mental eye probed into the mountains he saw the phantoms of men, of bronze-colored ones hunting and living and warring, of tribes moving in and out. He saw the ghosts of men in buckskins, trailing across the high passes and through the deep hollows, and then, more vividly yet, he saw armies marching, in blue and gray, through the hills. He moved in close and saw the places where bodies lay hidden or hanged, where men knelt across logs and stumps, dead and long forgotten, bullets in their brains and their souls departed. He saw the cabins that burned, heard the shrieks of children and the death groans of wounded men. He heard the crack of rifles where innocents died at Shelton Laurel and Limestone Cove. He saw and sensed and heard the entire horror of the mountain war, funneled to him, terrible. . . .

But above there was none of it. Light and a tunnel, a way out. He knew there would be no war at the end of that tunnel, and no end to the peace and light.

The sounds of war clamoring in his ears faded, becoming a dull roar similar to that a diver experiences upon his first plunge beneath the surface. He knew he could rise through that tunnel and put all earthly trouble behind him forever, if only he chose.

"Jesus, I think I'll come on and join you, if it's all right with you," he said.

But then, in the roaring that was noise without being noise, he heard something else, weak and distant. The voice of Amy Deacon Hanover, thin and far away. . . .

"Come back to me, Ben. Come back to me."

He paused, existing in a world that seemed halfway between the realm of flesh and the realm of spirit. Paused, and listened.

"Come back to me. Don't go, Ben. Come back to me."

He knew it was up to him. His choice.

"Come back to me. . . ."

He did.

Ben Scarlett lay in a cabin at the foot of the mountains, breathing through a broken piece of pipe stem stuck into a hole cut into his neck. Amy Deacon's work, recalled from having seen the same thing done by surgeons in Nashville to men whose throats were blocked and their breath cut off.

She had cut the hole in Ben's windpipe herself, snapped off and inserted the pipe stem, then waited for, prayed for, the hiss of air that would tell her he was breathing again. Fletcher's bullet had passed through his throat, tearing out his larynx, flooding his throat with blood.

She had knelt and whispered into his ear, "Come back to me." Over and over. Praying and whispering, waiting for him to return because she couldn't bear to lose him.

He had breathed, he had moved. He was breathing and moving still, and the physician that had been fetched up from Elizabethton said he would probably go on living. He'd never speak again—maybe make a whisper or two—but he might live. His throat would be scarred and ugly . . . but this fellow was on the homely side anyway, the surgeon noted. He was fortunate that someone with the skill of Amy Hanover had gotten to him when she did and opened up a breathing passage. He'd have been gone a minute or so later.

It seemed a miracle, but no more so than the fact that Greeley Brown still lived, too. The surgeon had cut the bullet out of him and told them to expect him to die at any time. They were still waiting for that to happen. It didn't appear that it was going to. Greeley, stubborn as always, was still clinging to life.

Fletcher hadn't been so fortunate. He had died not ten yards from the burned-out house, drowning in his own blood, which had filled his lungs from his torn-out throat. Quite a surprise, and quite a catch, members of the Federal detachment had said. It was widely believed that Fletcher was dead. It was quite likely that Ben Scarlett was looking at a Federal reward, if he pulled through. Miriam Brown was ready to swear that he was the one who actually killed Fletcher. With that hook, of all things.

When the ailing were sufficiently well, they were moved back to Egypt Munsey's hotel with the aid of the Federal army. There, Greeley Brown and Ben Scarlett received the deepest of attention from Amy, Miriam, Cecilia. Even Egypt, when she was able, because she, too, did not die. She worked through the shock and despair of what she'd witnessed, and became again the cantankerous woman they had known.

Every night for the first three months, though, she cried for Nelly.

Ben was strong enough to attend the funeral service held for Horatio Eaton and Nelly. Greeley, far more gravely wounded, was not. He would be abed for weeks, and the physician who attended him warned Miriam repeatedly that her husband might be a weaker man than before because of what he'd been through.

Miriam didn't care, nor did Cecilia. Greeley would live. They, and he, would be a family. And now there was no more Fletcher to threaten their situation. No more war to be fought.

Thatcher Brown, who had come to Jonesborough on the assumption that he would stay only temporarily, then return to his employing newspaper in New York, never left at all. He took over Horatio Eaton's role at the newspaper and served informally as editor when Amy completed her book at last. The dramatic story of what had happened to Fletcher provided the culmination of the sorrowful, true tale—and the words of "Scarlett's Lament," written down by Ben as soon as his shotgun-wounded arm was well enough to let him grip a pen, were published on the first page after the frontispiece.

Ben would never sing the song again. Nor would he speak. The voice Amy Hanover had come to love so much would be heard no more. Fletcher's last gunshot had rendered Ben voiceless, capable of no more than the softest of whispers. Amy could converse with him only by keeping her ear turned close to his face, reading his lips from the corner of her eye.

She hated Fletcher for this theft of Ben's voice almost as much as for his murder of Horatio Eaton. It was obscene, in Amy's perception, that the same voice that had so beautifully bemoaned the tragedies of war in "Scarlett's Lament," should now be silenced.

Ben told her, in his silent voice, not to hold anger about what had happened. "Sometimes there's good in silence," he said.

Amy didn't understand what he meant. But Cecilia, to whom he had said the same thing, understood full well. She had known silence well in her own life. It was not always a bad companion to have.

Amy's book was published near the end of September, to instant, widespread success. At the last moment Amy had changed her plans for simple, imprintless self-publication, and formed her own small publishing house, hiring out the printing and binding under her own imprint, naming herself publisher, Thatcher Brown editor. She also quickly contracted with him for the right to publish his own book, already in progress. It would tell the full story of his journalistic adventure, his capture, prison life, escape, and final reuniting with his brother. He told her he'd already written the dedication, and showed it to her: "To Rockwell Griffin, who died for his love for freedom. To Greeley Brown, a brother lost, and rediscovered. And lastly, and most of all, to Amy Deacon Hanover, who is to me all that is grand and good and courageous, and to whom I offer my life and my love."

He asked her if she objected to the dedication, or to the sentiment it contained.

She did not object. And Thatcher Brown knew on the spot that he would never go back to New York at all.

In mid-October, as Amy's book stirred the national waters more deeply than she could have dared to dream, and the press in Knoxville that kept it in print ran almost endlessly to keep pace with demand, Amy received a visit she did not expect. She was not surprised that her visitor was able to find her—fame deriving from the book was putting Amy's name in the national mind and Jonesborough, Tennessee, onto the nation's literary map—but she was surprised that this visitor *chose* to find her.

She arrived without being heralded, pulling up before Amy's house in a rough, old wagon, pulled by a broken-down horse team and driven by a strong-looking, weathered black man.

Amy was planting a tree in her yard when the wagon pulled up. She sat, wiped her hands on her apron, and advanced, hardly believing whom she saw approaching her in turn.

"Nanny?"

"Hello, Miss Amy." Nanny sounded frightened. And she looked like she had aged more than the passing time could account for. "I hope you don't mind, ma'am, that I've come to see you."

"Mind? Oh, Nanny, I'm glad you came! Please, come in the house. And your . . . friend, there, tell him to join us."

"He's my husband, Miss Amy. He told me he'd just sit there on the wagon and wait for me. It won't take me long to tell you what needs telling."

"Well . . . very well. Whatever you wish."

"First off, ma'am, I want to know how the baby was."

Amy wasn't sure how to interpret the question for a moment, but she remembered the old business of Nanny's curse, and made sense of it. "The baby was fine, Nanny. A boy, healthy and strong. He's hardly been sick a day since he was born. He'll be two years old next June."

Nanny looked pleased. "I'm glad. I didn't mean it when I said the child should die, ma'am. I was just mad, that's all."

"It's been forgiven and forgotten long ago. And if I recall, Nanny, you weren't the only one who said terrible things that day. I want your forgiveness, too. Some of what I said was . . . deplorable."

"It didn't hurt me. Words, they don't cut flesh."

"But they can cut souls."

"I reckon."

"Was there something else you wanted to tell me, Nanny?"

"Yes, ma'am. I wanted you to know that, no matter what it looked like, I wasn't whoring with Cat Kingsley. I was trying to get me a baby, just like I told you. Because I'd left my own baby behind, you know."

"I believe you. I'm sorry I didn't believe you then. But those pills . . ."

"Cat give them to me. He didn't want me to have no baby. I wasn't going to eat them pills, though. I swear it."

Amy nodded. It was easy to believe now what had seemed so hard to accept that awful night Ben had been shot and she and Nanny had fought.

"After I left Knoxville, Miss Amy, I went looking for my baby, the one I'd left in North Carolina."

"You went back?"

"Yes, ma'am. And there was no more plantation there. It had been burned to the ground. None of the slaves were left. They were all gone. Joel with them."

"I'm sorry."

"I know. But I'm going to find him."

"How? Do you have any clues?"

"No. No. But somehow, I'll find him. I'll search all my life if I have to. My husband, his name is Tom. He says he'll help me. I'm going to learn to read and write, so I can write letters and things to see where they might have took Joel."

"Stay here, Nanny. We'll find a place for you. I'll teach you to read and write."

"Thank you, ma'am, but no. Tom, he wants to go to Nashville. I reckon we will."

"Good luck, Nanny. If ever you need help, you can find me here."

"You going to stay in this town, Miss Amy?"

"Yes. I'm happy here. I've got a fine circle of friends around me."

"Have you got yourself a husband, Miss Amy?"

Amy smiled. "Not just yet. Maybe soon. We'll see."

"What's his name?"

"Thatcher. Thatcher Brown. He's a good man. You'd like him."

"I hope you and him is real happy, ma'am."

"Nanny, would you like to see my son?"

"Well, yes, ma'am, if he ain't sleeping."

"If he is, we'll wake him. Go tell your husband to come in, too, if he wants."

Nanny went to the wagon, came back alone. "Tom says he'll just sit, thank you, ma'am."

They went inside. Cecilia was dozing in a chair; Adam lay on a blanket stretched across the rug. Nanny approached him, knelt beside him.

"He's a beautiful child, Miss Amy. Just a beautiful child."

"Thank you, Nanny."

"I'm glad nothing bad happened to him 'cause of what I said."

"Words are words, Nanny. It's like you said. They can't cut flesh. I don't believe there's any such thing as curses."

"Mr. Ben Scarlett, he believed."

"Ben's here with me. In this town. He works now for another friend of mine who is a wagon maker. Greeley Brown is his name. I wrote about him in a book."

"I seen that book, Miss Amy. They say everybody's reading it. I know Greeley Brown, too. He was a help to me once."

"You know him? Then let's go see him while you're here! And Ben, too."

"No, ma'am, thank you. Tom and me will be going on. I just wanted to see you, and see that baby boy. Don't wake him up. Let him sleep."

They went back out. Tom still waited patiently at the wagon, smoking a pipe made from a corncob and a reed.

"You sure you don't want to see Ben, at least?" Amy asked.

"No, ma'am. I doubt he'd want to see me. I'd just remind him of troubled times. Is he . . . all right?"

"He was hurt recently by a bushwhacker who I guess didn't think the war was over. But he's recovered . . . mostly. His voice is gone."

"But what about earlier . . . in Knoxville? Did he get all right? I heard he had a fight with somebody."

Amy understood. Nanny was trying to find out the aftermath of the fight that had left Cat Kingsley dead. She'd been there, but didn't want to say it. Amy realized that the last time Nanny had seen Ben, he was lying unconscious near the contraband camp.

"Ben recovered, yes. But he had an idea in his head that he'd killed Cat Kingsley." It was as close as Amy would come to asking Nanny to set the record straight, if she could. She wouldn't ask her straight out to admit to killing a man.

"You tell him, Miss Amy, that he didn't kill Cat. It was somebody else done that. It wasn't Mr. Ben."

Amy smiled. "I'll let him know."

"Where is Mr. Ben now? Working at that wagon shop?"

"Either there, or down in the church whose steeple you see rising yonder."

"In church?"

"When Ben was hurt by that bushwhacker, he almost died. Something . . . odd happened to him. An experience. Spiritual, I suppose you could say. But he came out of it believing that he has a special purpose in life that he's missed so far. His 'calling.' That's the way he puts it. He spends a lot of time now at the church, praying, trying to find what that calling is supposed to be."

"You tell Mr. Ben for me, ma'am, that I appreciate him for all the times he was good to me. Me and him, we didn't always get on good, but I believe he's a good man."

"He is. I'll tell him you said so."

"Good-bye, Miss Amy. I'd best be going on."

"Do you need anything, Nanny? Money? Food?"

"No, ma'am. We'll be fine on our own now. You just keep me in your prayers, ma'am, praying that someday I'll find my Joel again."

Amy felt a burning in her throat and behind her eyes. Just then it seemed all the tragedy of slavery and family division and human suffering and human remorse seemed embodied in the small frame of the black woman before her. Nanny was a woman who had desired freedom. Maybe desired it too much for her own good. She had made a choice, cast aside a child, in her quest for independence, and in so doing, had cast a new, invisible chain around herself: abiding, incurable regret.

Amy watched as Nanny climbed back onto the wagon. Tom snapped the leads, threw off the brake. The wagon rumbled off, laden with old, battered furniture, bags of personal goods. Nanny twisted and looked at Amy as they departed, and just before they went out of sight, raised her hand for a final wave.

Amy waved in turn, and as Nanny rode out of sight, Amy knew she would never see her again.

She heard Adam fussing inside the house, Cecilia trying to hush him. Turning, she went in, took up her child, and hugged him close, for a long time.

On a sunny day a week later, a preacher named Lucas Mainard, who once had been a friend and benefactor to Ben Scarlett in an earlier Jonesborough sojourn, came riding into town with ambitions and dreams for doing good. He met up with his old one-handed friend and they talked—as best Ben could talk to anyone, having no voice—and then he and Mainard together talked to Amy Hanover, who now enjoyed the benefits of a heightened wealth due to the phenomenal sales of her book, and who wished to do good with what she had gained. She had told Ben several times it did not seem suiting, profiting personally off the tales of suffering in the mountains. The money should go to some special purpose, to do good for others.

Ben left Jonesborough with Mainard at the first of 1866 and returned to Knoxville. He had found his calling, and Amy had found the work in which she wished to invest the profits of her book.

Near the end of February, Amy arrived in Knoxville in company with her fiancé, Thatcher Brown. She strode through the streets of the reviving city, showing him the places where she had roamed and played as a child, and the spot she had first met Ben Scarlett one day while she was hanging broadsides

announcing a Secessionist political rally sponsored by her late
father.

At last their slow, meandering walk took them to the place
where the house of Amy's father, the house in which she had
grown up, once stood. It was long gone, leveled by fire, but
now a new building stood in its place, one Amy's own dollars
had financed.

"It's beautiful, Amy," Thatcher said, slipping his arm
around her. "I'm proud of you. And proud of Ben, too! To
think that the old fellow has it in him to help out men who were
like he was!"

"It's his calling, like he's so fond of saying," Amy said. "He
told me months ago that he'd often wondered why he'd been
spared death, and even mental damage, from the hard way he
lived so much of his life. He told me how so many of the men
he once drank with are gone now, or just weak shells of themselves, hardly able to think a straight thought. Ben believes he
was spared for a reason. To do this." She waved up at the
big, white-painted, two-storied edifice, simple in design, yet
appealing. "The building isn't even completely finished off on
the inside yet, and there are already ten men staying here,
Thatcher. Drunks like Ben was, and others addicted to opium
or cocaine. The war created a whole new class of people
trapped by alcohol or other such things. Some of them, at least,
can find help here, with Ben and Reverend Mainard."

"They're getting good support?"

"So far, yes. The churches are coming together to help
finance them. And of course, anything I make through the
years from my book will go here, too."

"Look, there he is. Let's go up and see him."

Ben as he was now was a sight to bring tears to Amy's eyes.
There was a brightness in his eyes, a healthy color in his face.
His clothing, though plain, was clean and neat, his beard and
hair nicely trimmed, though he had let the beard grow long at
the chin, to hang down and hide the terrible scar left by
Fletcher's bullet when it pierced his throat and stole his voice
from him forever.

Ben had learned to make his whisper a little louder, Amy
detected when he first spoke. "What do you think of it, Miss
Amy?"

"It's beautiful, Ben. A glorious place. The building is so simple, though. Are you satisfied with it?"

"Yes, oh, yes. Come here, let me show you something."

He led them into the yard and down to the place where Amy's father had once planted a defiant sign, taking on proudly the name Parson Brownlow had attached, with mocking intent, to the big white house that had stood here. SECESSION HILL, the sign had read.

The sign remained, but it had been repaired, strengthened, and repainted only that day. The paint was still wet, still smelled strongly. "I came up with the name myself," Ben whispered, waving at the sign. "It seemed to fit, in a lot of different ways."

Amy read the sign and smiled. It said, in big, bold letters: RESTORATION HILL.

"Is it good, Miss Amy?"

She put her arm around him and hugged close the battered old former drunkard of the streets whom she would love the rest of her days. "Yes, Ben," she said. "It is good."

ABOUT THE AUTHOR

CAMERON JUDD is a former newspaper reporter and editor and the author of more than twenty published books. Noted for its historical accuracy and marked by a love of the land and the people who lived on it, his writing is authentic and entertaining. Cameron hails from near Greeneville, Tennessee.